MOON BOUND

MADDISON COLE

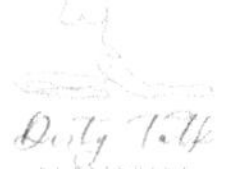
Dirty Talk
PUBLISHING

Dirty Talk
PUBLISHING

DEDICATION

To remembering our origins.

Gemma, Dani, Felicia and Orianne. You fantastic four were my original betas when the Exiled Heir was first released. With your support, much needed help and continual friendship, I dedicate this re-write to you.

Prologue

Lorcan

Moonlight bathes the landscape in an ethereal glow, and despite the fact that I'm in enemy territory, a peaceful stillness hangs in the air. I take a deep breath and take stock of my surroundings, but no sound reaches my highly sensitive ears. Not the flap of an owl's wings nor the scurry of a rat's tiny paws amongst the foliage. Pity. While crossing the shifter boundary line is suicide for any other vampire, as Vampire King... I can handle myself. It is as if the forest holds its breath, waiting for me to be discovered, but that is precisely my intention.

I weave between the trees, my gaze repeatedly drawn to the pristine, almost mirror-smooth, shimmering lake. So pure, yet so out of place, cast upon a land of depraved, savage beasts whose base needs overpower all rational thought. If I could transport the lake back to my castle, it would be a courtyard centerpiece, complete with shrubs and the glow of the moon, which I would find a way never to let fade.

areful not to crunch leaves beneath my glossy dress shoes, I circle the body of water in search of my prey. I know she's out there, lurking within the shadows. She may be a hunter by nature, but I'm a natural-born predator, hundreds of years older, ten times faster, and ruthless to the bone.

I drink blood from the vein, giving me strength that mere naturals can't comprehend. The expensive suit clinging to my frame tonight only adds to the power exuding from my very being. But she won't be afraid. Whether that makes her naïve or vain, I'm yet to decide.

A rustling to my right announces her arrival, and my lips slide over my fangs, a smile stretching across my face at the sight of the magnificent beast bursting from the forest. Her enormous frame, covered in speckled gray fur that ripples over her muscular body, sets her at a level height with me for a change. This is the only night her wolf can be set free, which also means it's my monthly chance to challenge her with my morals intact. Beating her in human form isn't a true win. I may be a living demon, but a King must have integrity, no matter the species.

The wolf circles me, her hazelnut eyes reflecting the light of the moon as her body moves across the grass. Taking her time to size me up. A snap of her teeth punctures the air as her gaze captures mine, and I grin. A black raven lands on an overhead branch in my peripheral vision, watching the scene intently, and my grin morphs into a rare chuckle that reverberates from deep within my chest. I turn my focus to the wolf in front of me, bracing myself on the muddy embankment as anticipation slithers down my spine for the attack I see coming long before she lunges. I did always enjoy toying with my food.

She snarls, lunging at me with a speed and ferocity that would make a lesser being cower. But I'm faster, more ruthless. Almost effortlessly, I evade her attack, and with a feral grin, I pivot, wrapping my arm around her muscular neck as she soars past me, and I use her momentum to bring us both crashing to the ground.

My once-immaculate suit and her sleek fur are now caked with mud, yet my smile grows impossibly wider as her muzzle snaps, and she fights against my hold with primal desperation, her powerful laws snapping in my face. The slick mud clinging to her coat allows her to slip from my hold, and she seizes the opportu-

nity. Her claw slashes across my bicep, but the wound knits together almost instantly. Not even a drop of blood marring my pale skin.

Still, I savor the fleeting pain, feasting on it just as I feast on the lifeblood that sings through my body from the bite of a vein. Except in this case, the agony feeds my soul, and I bask in the rare moment that allows me to mark this moment of my existence. A moment where I am able to feel... something. Anything.

Without looking back, the wolf darts into the forest's tree line for the shadows to envelope her once more. It's been too long since I gave in to the thrill of the hunt, and the notion pulls me after her now. Although a King shouldn't chase -- he only needs to wait for his target to come close enough and then unleash his attack -- this is different. Tonight, I'm different.

I could catch her in a heartbeat at full speed, but that would be too easy. I want to play this game. To ensure it lasts until sunrise. And with that in mind, I find myself using my acute eyesight to follow the fluffy, gray tail up ahead. We circle the lake through the woodlands before she turns sharply and leaps into the middle of a large weeping willow hanging over the water. Big mistake. Right behind, I tackle her bulk to the ground, dirtying her fur and my suit jacket even more. We roll dangerously close to the water's edge together, a mess of limbs and muscles battling for the upper hand.

I hook my legs around her middle, throwing my weight sideways, but the momentum takes me too far, and the wolf's weight lands over me, drool dripping from her bared teeth to my previously white shirt and pebble gray tie. Ironically, the same shade as her. Shoving my shoulder's further into the earth with massive paws, she glares at me with the hint of a canine's smile. My hands lock in her scruff, ready to throw her into the lake, when her snout drops to my neck, and the razor-sharp edges of her teeth graze my throat, her warm breath covering my skin. It would take her barely any effort to slice my carotid artery open and keep it exposed until the life drained from my body. Perhaps she should.

Many in my own ranks are preparing to challenge me for the crown. The wolf wars are on the rise, as are their camps. While our population dwindles, they thrive. It's only so long until strength no longer plays a part, but the simple fact of being purely outnumbered will see our ultimate defeat. It'll take a true, callous vampire to do what's necessary—one who can sacrifice in order to gain. Except, with the lack of females being born, it's not a risk I'm prepared to take, and eventually, that will be my biggest downfall.

A snarl is torn from the creature above. I vaguely realize I'm not even trying to fight anymore. My hands have loosened, and my body sags into the soil. With one snap of her teeth and carefully placed claw to the heart, I could simply no longer exist. Did I want that? I am not exactly sure. Suddenly, the rough pad of her tongue drags across my jaw and up my cheek, drawing a hearty laugh from me and temporarily clearing my thoughts. The sound leaving my throat is unfamiliar to my own sensitive ears. Her snout nuzzles me like one of her own, which I'd give anything to be right now. Fuck, I have armies of vampires that would have my head for just thinking it, but at least if I were a werewolf, I would have a chance. A real chance.

My hands travel, stroking the soft fur between her ears until she leaps off and dives into the water. A chilled spray covers me, but I enjoy the coolness of it. Rolling onto my knees, I use my hands to wash the mud from my jet-black hair and remove my filthy jacket. Dragging the tie looser, I toss it aside and strip out of my shirt. I've never grown accustomed to modern fashions, but being hundreds of miles from vampire territory, I have no inhibitions out here.

A cleaner version of the speckled wolf jumps onto the small island, shaking the remaining droplets from her body and soaking me through. I pull her to me, rubbing against me as if she is a living towel, but really, I just want the excuse to have her closer. I've waited too long, too caught up in another turf war with her people. If only they knew how often I've been on their land, fraternizing with one of their own.

We eventually resume our usual position, cuddled up against the thick willow trunk. The moon brightens the area from outside, spears of light piercing the dense foliage surrounding us. A breeze finds its way through the hanging vines, softly dancing through her marbled fur. I run my long fingers through the drying, velvety mane spread across my lap, marveling at the softness I'm still not accustomed to. The emotions I can't understand or ignore, no matter how hard I've tried. No matter how often I've reminded myself of my title or commitment to my people, I always end up right back here.

A purr vibrates from the divine creature while I continue my leisurely strokes up and down her spine. The contentedness I experience in her presence isn't strange or unnerving. Since our first off-chance meeting, it's been nothing but the most natural feeling in the world. My soul is at ease when she is nearby, the constant tightness in my chest finally loosening so I can breathe easier. She fills my mind with possibilities that can never be, but I am prepared to move the earth and moon to try. Glimpses of a future pass through my mind. Of her and I together, just like this, for the rest of our existence.

So many challenges are in our way. Obstacles that will refuse to move. Chances are we won't succeed. But I'll be damned if my own failures are for lack of trying.

Chapter One

Aspen

Crack.

I squeeze my eyes tight, breathing through the agonizing internal pain. Yet, every day, I return. Resuming this very position as my knees slot into the dips of earth molded around my torn jeans. And every day, I hear the crack. It coils within my ears as another broken fixture splinters through my heart. It shouldn't still hurt this much. The grief should have passed by now, but repeating those words to myself does nothing to ease the mourning my soul might never recover from.

Bending forward, intent on straightening the clusters of white dead nettles, I catch myself clinging onto the rounded slab of granite instead. My breathing is drawn out, weak. A state I can't allow myself to show in any other instance, but up on this hilltop, I have a moment of solace. No one would dare disturb me while I mourn the Alpha's mate. Or, more specifically, my mom.

We used to visit this hillside together—the picture-perfect family.

Images flash behind the safety of my eyelids, a smaller version of myself running across the grass, desperately trying to hold onto the kite string pulling me along. A flimsy linen summer dress whips around my thighs, a rope belt tied at the waist. Leather sandals cover my dainty feet, the straps cross-crossing up my legs to a bow at the back of each calf.

A beautiful woman chases me, her arms outstretched. Grabbing the string, she tugs the kite back into control against the strong wind with ease. Securing the string to my belt, a wide smile stretches across her face, and her brown eyes sparkle. Her hair is a unique shade of pebble gray to reflect her wolf, set in curls that swirl around her face. It was almost like the curls had a life force of their own, dancing to the aura she radiates, so full of vitality and life. Compassion and love. I lean into her side, my fingers brushing against her fur cloak as a figure approaches us.

"Papa!" I shout, and that's when my eyes snap open. Tears spill down my cheeks in thick valleys and my throat is clogged with emotion. No matter how many times the memory assaults me, I can never make it past there. It's too much, too fresh, even all these years later. A caw sounds in the distance, dragging me back to the present. I nod, aggressively wiping my cheeks on dirty sleeves.

Remnants of yesterday's storm whisp through my white hair, a bitter chill slipping into the worn-out hoodie that clings to my slim yet muscular frame. Blades of grass scratch at the tears in my black jeans, those slits long past fashionable. My clothing provides an exact visual representation of my life right now – tattered and holding on by barely a thread.

Once I regain the strength to sit up, I turn my attention back to the white nettles. They flourish here, a natural occurrence after I buried her at the top of this hill and the headstone was set. At least these plants are thriving, even if nothing else is. The archangel flower, a gift from Mother Nature herself, deters intruders with its fierce, toothed leaves. Yet, amidst these defensive features, delicate white flowers bloom, covered in fine hairs that feel surprisingly soft under my fingertips.

"Weeds," I sigh, smoothing the petals between my fingertips. "That's all we are." A raven spirals from the sky and perches on my shoulder as if summoned by my negativity. I smile and rest my cheek on the soft patch of his belly. Sawyer, as I named him, appeared the day my mother died and surprisingly is never far: as if the universe decided that being utterly alone was too severe a punishment for one being – outcast or not. Sawyer nuzzles his beak into my hair, making a mess of the white strands, and I stroke his head in return.

My eyes drift to the horizon before me, a crystal blue sea stretching as far as the eye can see. I can't see the waves crashing against the cliff beneath me from this angle, but I can hear each melodic crash of the water like a symphony playing just to ease the stress from my bones. Fresh sea air used to assault my nostrils with a sharp burn when I was younger, but now I'm accustomed to the scent, and instead, I find peace as it fills my lungs. I tip my head to the setting sun, admiring its perseverance in clearing all evidence of yesterday's heavy downpour whilst pushing a warm balm through the wind that refuses to quell, suddenly realizing I've sat up here far too long.

I fight the cold fingers caressing my heart and swallow despite the thick ache in the back of my throat. I can't stall anymore and ignore the impending return to a reality I hate. So, with a final glance at the nameless headstone, I kiss my fingers and place them on the stone slab before I grab my backpack. Securing it tightly on my back, my sneakers feel heavy as they take me back toward the forest before I'm fully ready to leave. If it were up to me, I never would. But I owe it to my mom not to waste away crying over what should have been, even if my existence isn't much to return to.

Once I hit the tree line, I break into a run. Not out of fear from those no doubt watching on, but through the need of exertion. Tension claws at my chest like a festering wound, and only through pushing myself to physical exhaustion will I be able to sleep tonight. Using the trunks and shrubs as my obstacle course, I relish the burn of my muscles. Savor the ache of labored panting only achievable by suppressing my supernatural abilities.

I know every inch of these woodlands, from the robins nesting in a cluster of cedars to the wildlife burrowed beneath each boulder. A stream bisects the forest, winding its way from the far-off mountain ranges – which we are forbidden to explore – to the sea on our side of the boundary line. Bracing myself against a trunk, my legs tense briefly before I launch myself high into the air, grabbing a branch to swing on. Once, twice, before launching my weight toward the next.

With a guttural howl, I land on a precarious branch in my worn-out sneakers living on borrowed time. But I don't hang around long enough for the branch to snap under my weight. Leaping through the trees, I catch sight of the modest hut nestled on the fringes of shifter territory – the place I call home

Home is a loose term, but it was mine. Complete with an old-style thatch roof that drips when it rains, paired with single-glazing windows that rattle in the slightest wind and topped with crumbling old brickwork. Vines have molded and weaved themselves into cracks around the exterior, like surgical stitches, almost as if nature itself is helping to keep the structure from collapsing. See? Home-sweet-home.

Admittedly, it's not all doom and gloom. After my banishment to the exile hut, I built my very own ensuite shower cubicle onto the side from thick branches, which have been stripped down and bounded together with an open pipe hanging above. If I heat the tank long enough, I can have up to seven minutes of pure, luxurious hot water all to myself. As if there was another option. It's fair to say that I'd been accustomed to fending for myself even before my mother died.

Leaping from the last branch, I touch down right in front of the stone steps. The wooden door is slightly open; there's no need for a lock since I have nothing worth stealing. Making my way around the clearing, I duck under a clothesline holding a few t-shirts and my only other pair of jeans. I reach my cherished vegetable patch, surrounded by a fence. It's my pride and joy, especially after I devised an anti-parasite spray to protect my sole food source. If only I could create a spray to fend off fellow shifters just as effectively.

Except...something smells off, and my mouth falls open, my body temporarily freezing as I approach the patch. *No.* The fertile soil has been upturned, half of my hard-earned crops in shambles, and the rest trodden on and squished into the earth. An entire month of food. Destroyed. Wasted. I shouldn't be shocked every time. It's common for the shifters to screw with what little happiness I manage to carve for myself. It's why I take a backpack of essentials everywhere I go, just in case I return one day to the whole hut up in flames. I scoff internally as if they'd actually wait for me to leave before sparking the light.

The pounding in my ears makes it hard to hear anything besides the blood coursing through my veins at a breakneck speed as I fight the urge to hunt down the scents mottling my once-perfect patch. Yet I can pick up the sound of a branch breaking in the woodland to my left, and I spin to greet my visitor face-on as I swallow past the desire to cause the same amount of damage that is constantly bestowed on me.

My vision tunneling, I peer closely into the forest beyond, past the darkness emanating from the dense foliage and the wide tree trunks jutting toward the sky to block out the setting sun's dying rays. I take a deep breath, weaving past the heavy scent of the boundary line indicating the edge of the shifter territory. The boundary is not visible by sight. Instead, it was denoted by the thick, cloying odor of old blood that the earth has digested and covered naturally with soil and weeds, time and time again. With every change of leadership, the Alpha redraws the boundary line with the blood from their very veins, thereby announcing their reign and denouncing the old. Supernatural beings of any other kind aren't allowed to cross it, which is how I know the animalistic scent filtering closer must be one of my own - a wolf.

A familiar and unwelcome scent finally through my nostrils as a female, also familiar and unwelcome, steps out from behind a mossy trunk with a smile pulling at the corner of her mouth, which doesn't reach her eyes.

Forcing my shoulders to relax, I speak past the pain of my clenched jaw, "What do you want, Aleena?" I ask.

Although, I already know the answer that would be hidden under whatever response came out of her mouth. Which is to fuck with me, piss me off, and see just how far they can push me. Realistically, the continuous taunting and disrespect that I've received and endured for almost eight years are boring and uninspired. However, I am fucking over it.

I narrow my eyes and observe her as she comes closer, an inch taller than me with chestnut brown hair that starkly contrasts mine and dressed in the pack's usual leathers and furs. I watch as she lifts a brow over her muddy brown eyes, the look somehow conveying her assumption that she is better than me. She isn't. We had been best friends once upon a time, her family living in the cabin next to ours. As girls, we would always sneak out to run through the woodlands and dive from the cliff into the sea. I like to think I've retained my fearless, reckless nature, whereas Aleena's soured into a callous bitch who'd sooner forget I existed than admit she once considered me a sister.

"Thought you might be hungry," she smirks. Raising her arms, she opens her fisted hands, and a string of crushed carrots and lettuce tumble onto the forest floor. Then to add insult to injury, she rubs her hands together and then proceeds to push the evidence into the mushy ground under her boot.

Like a worn, tattered rope, I feel the last vestiges of my patience start to tear, "famished," I agree, but not for food. No, my hunger was for revenge on those who have looked down on me. It was for everyone who comes to laugh at the one they call a reject. It's obvious to myself and the entire shifter camp I don't belong here. I spare a look behind me towards the boundary line. Nothing except my mother's gravestone is keeping me here. But if I don't visit her, no one will, and what will that prove? That her choices defined her memory? That she's the forgotten traitor, everybody says she is? I can't have that.

After reading my thoughts, a pesky ability she developed on her first shift, Aleena makes a noise in the back of her throat. Her cruel smile, stretching from ear to ear, agrees with everything I thought. My mom is destined to be forgotten and I, indeed, have nowhere else to go. Exiled from the Shifter camp and forced to live on the fringes is one thing; utterly lost in the big wide world is another.

With a flick of her shoulder-length hair, Aleena pivots on her heel and walks away, her chuckle trailing behind her. As she strides away, my gaze is drawn to a piece of lettuce stuck to the bottom of her boot and the final fibers of that rope tear. A growl is torn from within, vibrating from the base of my chest to the tips of my elongating fangs. Now, I'm not really that mad about lettuce. I may have been alone for years, but I consider myself of sane mind. It's what the lettuce represents; my limp, discarded life, squashed beneath the shifter's heels.

Curling my shoulders inward, my body is pulled forward on an invisible string, carnal instinct taking over. My inner beast has been forced into submission for so long, maybe it's time she was let loose. Permitted to prowl the forest, and hunt those who seek to harm her. As soon as the thought passes through my mind, there's no turning back. Aleena's brown hair is clamped tightly in my fist, and her head rammed into the closest tree trunk before she can turn to defend herself. There, I hold her still, forcing her to listen to my every thought.

I'm done. Done with a life I was never meant to lead. Done with being the most powerful being on this side of the boundary line and suppressing my base needs. I could have flourished, and taken my rightful position as the next alpha's mate. Yet instead, I've allowed myself to wither and die inside every night I've sat alone in an empty hut, shunning the parts of myself that ache to be released. No more will I let you taunt me, and no more will I hold back.

Aleena's high-pitched squeal pierces the air as I slam her head back into the bark, blood trickling from her temple into her right eye. My pupils zero in on it, my inner beast causing the sticky substance to appear yellow against a darkening backdrop. Nothing else is of relevance. My stomach cramps, my tongue thickening in a pool of salvia.

"You know what," I growl inaudibly. "I changed my mind. I'm fucking starving." As I drag my tongue along her salty skin, savor the taste of her sweat and fear prickling amongst the blood, Aleena and I shudder together for wholly different reasons. Because as I struggle with the urge to satisfy my base need, the same one that I've been taught to despise, to hide at all costs, she understands that I can rip out her throat with my teeth and relish her blood as it pours through my throat. That fear? Is delicious.

"Run," I breathe in a guttural voice laced with the power of my wolf and my hunger. Aleena's breath hitches as I release her hair, and it's my turn to smirk. For someone ballsy enough to enter my domain, root up my food source *and* hang around to gloat, she sure smells like terror now. She hesitates briefly before she shoves off the trunk and flees. My fangs extend with a sharp, throbbing pain, yearning to pierce the tender flesh of a neck and drink my fill. Yet I cling to the one promise I've made to myself: I am a wolf shifter. Any other cursed traits that haunt me must be ignored and, whenever possible, erased from my memory.

Hanging back, I allow Aleena to escape out of view. We're around thirty miles from the main shifter camp, with a few secluded residents scattered around the vicinity. A fair trek for Aleena to run on two legs since she can't call for her wolf on any night that isn't a full moon. I, on the other hand, have full control of when and where mine can rise.

My wolf pushes beneath my skin, her fur toying with the goosebumps lining my arms. The eyes in my head, typically a dark shade of blue, begin to burn as a golden hue takes over, coating the land in shades of yellow and heat signatures. I race towards the one heading southwest, the bumbling whimpers from Aleena's lips catching my sensitive ears.

Just as I'm ready to unleash my wolf and release the tight reins I've held for far too long, a dark presence surges within me, winding its way around my organs, vying for control. My steps falter as my wolf fights back, their collision leaving me breathless. Still, above the internal war I've yet to master, one thought pervades: I can't let Aleena escape or have the last laugh.

Let me take control, a voice sounds inside my head. *It will feel so good.* My fangs throb, my throat squeezing tight. A sharp stab in my gut precedes the grumbling of my stomach, the depths of a hunger I've never been able to quell. I know what this entity wants. I just don't know what would happen to me if I relented.

"I'm. A. Wolf. Shifter." I grunt out loud, forcing my feet to keep moving.

Aleena is increasing her distance, her fearful whimpers becoming a chuckle of mockery.

You'd have caught her by now if you'd let me assist. The voice laughs inside my ears and trickles away. I stagger to a halt by a trunk, bracing myself as I catch my breath. After a few moments, despite the dryness in my throat, my throat loosens, and I manage a full inhale, expanding my lungs to max capacity. Then, I'm gone.

My thin sneakers hit the ground at an untraceable speed as my body shoots forward-- no more than a blur. She can't see me, but Aleena senses the shift in the air, and I relish the moment that her heart picks up a beat, the rush of blood pumping through her veins raging. My shoe scuffs the back of her boot, her hair threading through the fingers of my outstretched hand. I almost taste the victory, the sweet flow of blood that will finally appease the dryness in my throat. This time, the growl drawn from me is a blend of both of my beasts, my claws lengthening to grab her slender neck. One quick snap to appease my wolf and aggravate the voice in my head. Just as I relish in the sensation of my claws grazing the skin of Aleena's throat, I suddenly crash into a solid bar that appears from nowhere.

"The fuck?!" I snarl, my ass barely hitting the ground before I'm back on my feet. Metal bars cast from iron surround me in a vertical cage as blood spills from my nose, leaking into my mouth, somehow dulling the thirst within. *Gross.*

Still maintaining the eyes of my wolf, two unknown heat signatures step into view as I'm failing to pry the bars open by hand. I falter at their sheer size, stepping back into the center of the cage. They watch me with careful intent. And then there's Aleena.

"What took you so long?! She nearly killed me!" Aleena shrieks. My heart drops. The two males pay her no attention, their eyes infused with wonder and curiosity like I'm a damn freak show. Whereas I am fully invested in Aleena's intention. She tricked me. Led me directly into a trap with a species I'd only read about. Vampires. There's no other explanation for their glinting, pointed canines and enormous size. Well over six feet, thick with muscle that has been squeezed into cotton t-shirts and baggy trousers. Certainly not wolves. Not my kind.

Are you sure about that? The voice in my head returns, and I blink rapidly, shaking the sound out of my head. But it's too late. Doubt sets in, and the truth I've been so desperate to ignore becomes so glaringly obvious that I don't know how I've managed to suppress it for so long.

I was never meant to belong in Shifter Camp. Never meant to run under the full moon with a pack. Never meant to feel affectionate cuddles around a blazing fire. I could handle the wolves abandoning me, but Aleena, acting on their behalf, determined that accepting that fate wasn't enough. They've betrayed me, and they will live to regret that decision.

Chapter Two

Jaxon

"Hmmm," Torsten tilts his head towards the cage. It's the most noise he's made since we, Torsten, Chase, and I, received orders to run an errand in Shifter territory. None of us wanted to spend our well-deserved night off this way, but being the commander of the Vampire army technically means I don't get to be 'off-duty.' These two assholes are my second-in-command and best friends.

"Why isn't she healing?" Chase also approaches the cage. I hang back to glower at the wolf shifter still lingering nearby. We'd found her tearing up a tiny vegetable patch just after sunset, and I knew immediately she couldn't have been the female we were sent to retrieve. At least, I hoped it wasn't. Flashing my fangs, she gets the message and scrambles back to whatever shifter cesspit she's crawled out of. That just leaves the female in the cage, which Chase promptly kicks.

"Chase! Fall back!" I bark. He obeys without question, moving aside for me to approach. I can't blame him when the being before us is, indeed, refusing to heal. The scent of her blood alone is intoxicating. I inhale deeply, savoring the mix neither myself nor any other vamp has ever encountered. A heady scent that could easily unhinge us if we're not careful. More than that, the female snarling back from behind the bars juts out her chin in a clear challenge. "Heal yourself before you drive my men crazy."

"Men," she scoffs under her breath. Disgust emanates from her lithe body, hidden within a baggy hoodie and torn jeans. Regardless, she roughly wipes her nose clean on her sleeve, and my eyes track the stained cuff as she folds her arms. "Well, get the fuck on with it then." My brows raise. I scrub my stubbled jaw in an effort to hide my impressed smirk.

"What is it you'd like us to *get on with*?" I reply, and a standoff commences. I take that moment to catalog her every feature, starting with the pure white hair, wild from her run, reaching her lower back, and golden eyes crinkling at the sides as they dim to a dark navy hue, attempting to glare a hole through my head.

"You're calling the shots. I'm the one in the cage. Hurry up and make your move." A laugh is torn from my throat, mirrored by the assholes hovering behind me. She's feisty, and she'll need to be if she's going to survive the next few days.

With a jerk of my head, Chase, and Torsten step forward to lift each side of the cage with ease and balance it upon their shoulders. I maintain eye contact, waiting for the moment she is knocked off balance and her bravado slips. Only then do I turn away with a satisfied smile.

"Name's Jaxon, by the way," I toss back before breaking into a sprint. Not half as quickly as I'd prefer to go, wanting to leave sifter territory far behind before the Alpha realized we've been on his land, but still fast enough that a mere human couldn't track us – should there be any around. The vampires carefully chose their location within the mountain ranges to avoid such interactions. Tossing several looks behind, I ensure Torsten and Chase move smoothly to avoid jostling the cage too much. It happens to contain our princess, after all.

My footsteps over the boundary line when a caw sounds from overhead. I peer at a lone raven, wings spread wide against a crescent moon, circling us like prey. Dismissing it, I order my men to follow the trail along the stream when it sounds again. A cry of warning before the raven dives, an arrow of sleek black feathers I prepare to backhand at the last moment. Speeding towards me beak-first, the raven throws its wings wide, unleashing a plume of black smoke. A pair of boots slam into my chest rather than talons, throwing me backwards into the cage with momentum from an invisible gust of wind.

Momentarily speechless, I right myself as Chase roars, 'the fuck' as he leaps over me, without hesitation, to combat the new threat. Because where there should have been a swatted-down Raven, instead, stands a male before us, jet-black hair sweeping over his eyes. His trench coat, also black, whips around military-grade fatigues and a heavy set of boots that have snapped my collarbone. I force myself to recline until fully healed, watching as he smoothly dodges each of Chase's wide swings. If I had to place a bet on an immortal vampire and a bloody bird before now, it would have been a no-brainer. Yet my faith begins to falter as the male extends feathers as sharp as spears from his fingers and slices Chase's arms, neck, and face to shreds.

I watch as my friend stumbles, retreating to the cage and tapping out with Torsten, who's unable to withhold his laughter.

"Let a true warrior handle this one, yeah?" Torsten jumps to his feet and races into combat with the raven shifter. In tune with the princess' erratic heartbeat, I peer behind me with words of comfort that don't leave my lips. The cage is empty, with the only sign that someone was once confined there being the bars bent out of place by finger-shaped indentations. I scramble onto my knees, calling on my vampire vision to produce heat signatures, and that's when I see the lithe figure crawling up behind Chase. Silently stealthy, if only her ragged pants didn't give her away. Peering over his shoulder, her fangs elongated as her eyes burst to life with a golden glow, set on the crimson rivets coating Chase's skin.

"On your six," I shout, rushing forward in a burst of speed. Linking my arms behind hers, I yank her back just in time. Chase spins at the sound of gnashing teeth beside his ear, pushing against her shoulders to keep her at bay.

"Watch it, Hellhound," he ducks his head, rubbing it on his shirt in an attempt to clear the blood away. Except, he manages to smudge it further, and the princess jolts forward an inch more. Fuck, she's strong. Stronger than anticipated and slippery enough to dislodge her arms from my grip.

"Bloodlust," Chase grunts, pushing his head as far back as possible.

"Feed her then," I command. This time, Chase doesn't follow my order.

"You must be joking. She'd rip my fucking throat out. Must be the first time she's smelt vampire blood." Using his boots against her stomach, Chase tosses her into the air, flinging her to the side. She lands on her feet, leaps into a crouch, snarls, and advances again—fur rippling along her arms in the same snowy shade as her hair. From the minimal information I've been provided, I know not to let her shift. Confronting the full range of her supernatural abilities and the intense hunger swirling in her eyes makes it far more challenging to confine her back into the cage. Who said this was to be an easy mission? Oh yeah, that was me.

Shoving Chase out of the way, I dive through the grass, placing myself directly in her path. Her golden eyes fill my vision as I become her new target. With her full weight propelling her forward, the princess growls and snaps like a frenzied animal slamming her fist into my ribs with a blow I didn't see coming. Bones splinter for the second time in the past few minutes, my reputation dwindling whilst I barely hold her back from tearing my jugular out. *Fuck.*

Time slows as I take a half second to quiet my thoughts and fully focus on the princess as she hovers over me, overcome, and blinded by bloodlust. Her threadbare clothes are even more tattered than before, and her eyes, glowing yellow, hold no visible shred of sanity as her now elongated canines drip with warm saliva that splatters against my face as she fights to get closer to my neck. Still, while her strength is impressive, I have to remind myself that she hasn't had the vigorous training I have.

As I exhale, time resumes its normal pace. In one swift motion, I tuck my knees up to my chest and hook my feet behind her legs while I twist my hips and use the leverage of my arms to push against her shoulders. With a powerful heave, I dislodge her, flipping us both over and straddling her middle, I use my feet to pin her thighs in place. Chase appears in time to hold her arms outstretched and pin them above her head. Raising my wrist to my lips, my fangs lengthen.

"Don't touch her!" a roar comes from an unrecognizable source. The raven is air-born again, trench coat flapping in the wind as he pulls back the string of a handmade bow and shoots a row of feather spears toward us. Taking advantage of my split second of inattentiveness, the princess receives the advantage she needs to buck me aside and disappear in a blur that not even I can track.

"Little help over here?!" Torst shouts, leaping and failing to grab for the shifter's coat. I roll my eyes.

"Kinda busy," I growl, pushing upright. "Besides, if you can't handle a fucking bird, I'm demoting you."

Leaving Torsten to sort it out, I turn towards the boundary line, presuming she'd run home. Yet the shifters I find there, all standing in a line to watch, make no move to intervene or aid the princess stalking towards me. She didn't flee but stayed to take on a vampire? She's either insane or incredibly confident. Or the third likely option, so overcome with bloodlust and anger, sanity and confidence didn't matter.

In a momentary lapse in judgment, as I try to make sense of her behavior, my limbs fall slack, costing me greatly. She runs at me, twisting beneath my attempt to grab her, and shoves her shoulder into my abdomen with as much power as she can manage. With a curse, I stumble back a few paces before righting myself to allow her to do it again...and again.

Each time may appear as a weakness, but I use every hit to log information-- to watch how she moves and understand how she strikes. After four hits, the next time she rushes forward, I dart aside and grab her throat from behind, ramming her petite body backward and flush against mine. Not wasting a second, I bite into my wrist and hold the dripping wound above her lips as I tilt her head back with the other hand.

Eyes flashing, she thrashes, seemingly more at war with herself, between attempting to shake the droplets away and the tiny pink tongue that pokes out to taste her bottom lip. A groan resonates from deep within her being. I give her a moment to adjust before slowly lowering my wrist to her responsive mouth. Almost in slow motion, I watch her as lips part eagerly, a half-second before they firmly affix to my skin in a tight seal, and she begins to suck, preventing the wound on my wrist from healing. Then, as the sensations of her ravenous mouth suckling at my wrist and her tongue sweeping against my skin almost reverently, despite her hunger, bring my every nerve ending to life, it's my turn to groan.

As she feeds, almost frantically, the world around us seems to vanish. My vision tunnels as I become uniquely aware of all five of my senses. Unique because, strangely, it is as if all my senses are honed into this very moment. I hear nothing but her low growls and gentle sucking from her lips. Scent nothing but the enticing aroma of the blood from her wounds mingles with her sweat, filling my nostrils. Feel nothing but the curve of her ass pushing against my crotch while her lips caress the now-sensitive skin inside my wrist. And despite the overwhelming desire to sink my teeth into the tender flesh of her neck, I taste nothing but my own blood as I unwittingly bite down on my tongue to prevent myself from pressing closer to her.

I fight against the sudden flush of warmth spreading through my body as the hatred that once permeated the air starts to wane and becomes... something I can't quite explain. But I do know that in this very moment, I'd give her the entirety of my life force to sate her hunger.

Her struggle eases, and the vibrant yellow hue of her eyes gradually recedes, giving way to the familiar deep blue. She swallows thickly with a bliss-filled sigh, and regretfully, I start to pull my wrist away. Except, she doesn't draw back. I doubt she even realizes where she is as those navy eyes flutter closed, and she merely stands there, completely relaxed, her head resting against my chest and my palm still beneath her chin.

I swallow past the sudden dryness in my throat. *She really is quite something.* I forget my ability to blink as the moonlight shines upon her delicate porcelain features, catching the way her pale lashes fan across her cheeks. Part of me was jealous of the Moonlight, at how it caressed her every feature and especially at the way it won't be pushed away when the princess realizes it was holding her in its embrace. Because despite being aware that there has never been anyone quite like her, laying my eyes on her was an entirely different matter. She was unique and unparalleled, possessing a vampire's ethereal paleness and a wolf's untamed fierceness.

Her eyes drift open and gaze at me with an emotion I can't quite name until she quickly elbows me in the ribs so hard, I hear a crack, and she shoots out of my grip. I huff out a wheeze and remain still so my rib bone can knit together again. I take it she isn't accustomed to saying, 'Thank you.' But at least my dick has taken the hint and stopped straining against my zipper.

"I said," a deep, graveled voice sounds beside my ear, "don't fucking touch her." A sword-like slice cuts across the front of my neck. My legs threaten to give out, but I don't let them, not before I toss myself backwards in the hopes of taking down my attacker too. Except there's no one, only plumes of black smoke that depart around me. My back hits the ground, a splatter of blood spurting from my throat. My head rolls aside to see my men in similar situations. Chase slashed at the wrists, and Torsten, with a feather, speared into his heart. A fucking feather. Then there's the raven flapping his wings to reappear as a male before the princess. Blood curdles in my ears, punctuated by the shallow thump of my heartbeat, but through it all, I manage to extend my supernatural hearing.

"This is your chance," the raven urges, his hands wrapping around her biceps. "Return to the hut, I'll meet you there and explain."

"Return to the hut…" the princess repeats back hollowly. She glances towards the boundary line, her movements sluggish as if in a daze. Or, since I know better, she's in a hungover-like state, akin to a food coma when a vamp gorges on too much blood. The raven shakes her, desperate for her to heed his warning.

"The vampires have overstepped. If they want you, there are rules. Supernatural laws even these blood-thirsty savages must abide by."

"Want me?" Her gaze slowly shifts towards the mountains. They can't be seen at this distance, but instinctually, she knows where they are. She's one of us. She deserves to know where she belongs. Pressing myself to heal quickly, I force my torso upright and push myself onto shaky legs.

"I've got you," Chase appears at my side. His wrists have just healed, the raised pink scars yet to settle back into his skin, so when he offers one to me, I take to lapping up the spilled blood like a bottom feeder. Desperate for scraps.

"No one hears about this," I mutter, leaning on Chase to make our way to Torsten. Yanking the spear from his heart, he gasps and shoots upright, choking out his words.

"You're damn right," Chase agrees. "Absolutely no one hears about this. The king would have our heads on spikes if he found out we've had our asses kicked by some feathery fucker."

"He still might if we don't complete our mission." I snarl at the thought of Lorcan sending us out here with little-to-know information.

Lorcan, the last remaining Elder, appears as youthful as the rest of us, despite his ancient status. His jet-black hair is always meticulously slicked back in a style that might be considered fashionable if it weren't for its austere nature. The bold geometry of his quiff highlights the sharp angles of his cheekbones. At first glance, his eyes seem as black as his hair, but up close, they are a deep shade of navy blue. Regardless, his penetrating gaze feels like it's drilling into my skull whenever he stares at me, making it impossible to discern his emotions. There's a reason he's been our king for so long; I can't imagine the weight of the decisions he's had to make throughout the years, and I don't envy him for it.

"Wait here," I nod, and with newfound strength, slink towards the raven, still trying to plead his case.

"I will only ever have your best interest at heart-" he's muttering to the princess. I grimace all over again.

"If I may interject," I slide in a step closer with an easier smirk than I feel. Losing isn't in my repertoire, and I feel like I've fucked up from all angles since I arrived here. Taking the princess' hand in mine, her navy-blue eyes swing to mine. My blood is in her system, and if anyone can make her see sense right now, it's me.

"I believe my men and I approached this situation from the wrong angle," I begin. The raven scoffs, glaring at me from the corner of my eye. I ignore him. His opinion is null and void. In fact, I shift, so he's hidden behind my back. "We were expecting to fight off an entire shifter camp for you, hence the cage for your protection. But the truth is, you want to know what's out there. As much as you want to know what's in here," I place my index finger in the center of her chest. "Is that right, Aspen?"

"I didn't give you my name," she takes an unsure step back. I allow her to retract her hand.

"You did not. Your father did." Aspen's façade falters. The mask she wears to act like she isn't affected by the world around her. She's as interested in her origins just as much as the vampires are curious about her. The infamous princess of two rival species. It's a wonder she wasn't surrounded by guards and was so easy to find, for that matter. Not that I'm complaining. "Join us at the castle. We have plenty to tell you and much more to teach you."

Seconds tick by while I wait for a response. Like a looming shadow, the unwanted male shifts back into a raven, flapping through a plume of smoke to nestle on Aspen's shoulder. She tilts her head into his wing, and whether she meant to or not, I clench my jaw against the urge to stab the bird right through the heart. She trusts this damn bird, so I'll either have to accept or kill him. I'll opt for the latter.

"Perhaps you should have started with that," Aspen finally announces. Striding for her discarded backpack, she swings it onto her shoulder and raises a brow at Chase and Torsten, lingering nearby. "Come on then, and try not to fall behind."

I've always been fast, but this is something else. Shooting across fields in mere seconds, the distance grows from those following behind. The raven only keeps up because he's clasped in my arms. Spotting a mass of boulders lining the stream, I skid behind them and throw Sawyer into the small clearing before me. He shifts in the air, landing in a crouch. Shoving his hair aside, a pair of bottomless onyx eyes stare through me—no irises or sclera – only blackness.

"You have thirty seconds to explain what the fucking fuck just... fucked?!" I whisper-scream, my breathing erratic but not from exertion. I lash out to kick his shin when he doesn't immediately reply.

"I'm your loyal protector. Raven shifters are rare; hence we're assigned as guardians to those the supernatural council deems...special."

A bitter laugh babbles from me while I fist my white hair. "And you couldn't find the time to tell me this before tonight?" Shuffling sounds before a large pair of hands encase mine. I peer up, becoming lost in the drowning sea of onyx.

"You're not supposed to know. I'm sworn to secre-" We're out of time. Thundering footsteps approach, and I shove Sawyer a step back. I don't miss the pinch of hurt in his brows as he shifts back. Flapping smokey wings to perch on my shoulder, I lean back on a boulder and inspect my nails.

"Tired, Princess?" a chuckle comes. I scowl at the blonde smirking down at me.

"Funnily enough, I don't appreciate being manhandled and mocked on the same night." I stand, shoving my shoulder into his arm as I barge past.

"Torsten doesn't mean to offend you," the male calling the shots - Jaxon - pitches in. "Referring to you as your formal title is a mark of respect." Without turning back, I wave him off, intent on ignoring the alarm bells ringing in my head. First, Sawyer refers to me as 'special.' Now I'm meant to accept becoming a princess. At least as the lonely outcast, sheltered from the real world by my crumbling hut, the only person I had to account for was myself. And Sawyer, apparently.

"Let's make one thing clear – you offered answers and training. Beyond that, I've made no promises to hang around. Show me what you went through all this trouble for, and then I'll be on my merry way." No other words are spoken, but I can sense the tension between the males at my back —the three I'm consciously trying to ignore. The daydreamer in me may have had moments of weakness in the past, hoping for a band of strong vampires to rescue me. But it's far too late. Through suffering and heartache, I've learned to rely on my instincts. The very ones screaming that I'm being used as a pawn in someone else's game – I just haven't yet deduced who's.

Somewhere along the way, Jaxon takes the lead, and considering I have no clue where I'm going, I fall to the back of the group, keeping pace with the three vampires in my view. All broad shoulders and biceps, clenched fists, and taut veins. Their arms pumping back and forth are laced with ink, intricate patterns I need the light to explore properly. Not that I'm going to. Torsten and the one I believe is Chase remain a step behind, showing their rank. Important enough to get sent for me, but a level beneath Jaxon for sure.

Eventually, after putting miles between myself and the life I once knew, we enter a dense forest—one which has been clearly and cleverly crafted into a maze. Every trunk is the same, trimmed white birches standing side by side, encased in autumn leaves. The three vampires carve a memorized path, leading me to where the tree line suddenly halts, as does my ability to breathe.

Laughter and music reach my sensitive ears on a faint breeze. Before us, a gigantic stone wall punctuated with an iron gate stands proud, but nothing could hide the silhouette of a castle looming a fair distance behind. Spiked shadows pierce the midnight sky, imposing turrets complete with jagged battlements. Enormous and daunting – exactly the type of residence I'd expect to house males this large and still adopt titles such as 'princess.'

Light from an unusually illuminated crescent moon bathes a watch tower overseeing the gate's activity. Shadowed guards patrol a surrounding balcony, their finer features lost against the luminous glow. All I can be sure of are the huge, muscled outlines and the crawling sense that they are all staring at me. I twist my head away, brushing my cheek against Sawyer's silken wing in a comforting act I've grown to rely on. Confirming the return of their own kind, a swift alarm tears through the night, and the iron gate begins to rise.

"After you," Jaxon gestures with an outstretched hand to 'graciously' allow me entry. Ignoring him, I swallow thickly and remain rooted to the spot. My heart has picked up a beat, and what's worse is that I'm finally surrounded by those who would notice. I've been taught to shun the vampires. To hold a deep and burning hatred for everything they stand for. Naturally, when my first shift didn't go as planned, it was already engrained in me to shun this side of myself. Now, I was standing in front of their castle, ready to face my...what exactly? My past? My history? My future? My*self?*

Exhaling through barely parted lips, Sawyer shifts to shake his head subtly, but I accept Jaxon's hand anyway.

This is my chance. To learn and understand. To find the answers, I've been convincing myself I didn't need. But as my sneakers land on the other side of the threshold to vampire territory, the truth became clearer than ever. It's not the answers I've been fearing but the thought of being rejected by both sides of my heritage.

The large hand gently closes when I attempt to retract mine, although I'm focused on the landscape sprawling before me. With the castle raised on a mound, an entire society lies at its feet. Rows of buildings separated by cobblestone streets hide curious shadows within. Signs hang above doorways, from the necessities like carpenters, blacksmiths, and mechanics, to tattoo studios and hairdressers.

The nervous flutters of my heart subside, leaving a gap for something much more toxic. Hope. I expected blood-thirsty monsters and caged humans hanging from the rafters, not a hidden oasis. Not a completely self-sufficient civilization. The tales I've been taught begin to unravel, and now I know I've made the right choice. I have to see what else the shifters are wrong about.

"There she is," a low whisper leaks from beneath a doorway. I turn to look at the woodworkers, and a pair of silhouettes in the window rush to duck out of view. Torsten stops at my other side, throwing a heavy arm over my shoulder with a knowing grin.

"We didn't want to overwhelm you. Take your time to explore. You won't be disturbed." I nod with understanding. Now I know what the alarm was for. Chase steps in behind me and lays his chin on top of my head.

"Or you permit everyone to come out of hiding, and we'll have ourselves one big orgy," he says playfully. Both Jaxon and Sawyer react – the vampires growling about speaking appropriately to a princess while the raven squawks and attempts to peck Chase's eyes out. At that moment, I get the overriding feeling that I'm more of a prop than a guest and shake the four of them off.

"Look, you mentioned my real father being here somewhere, and since you insist on keeping up the princess bullshit, I'm going to guess he's in there," I point to the castle. "It's been far too long since I've been a part of the whole pack-mentality thing, so I'm just going to see tonight through, and then I'll bounce." Without waiting around to see what all the furrowed brows are about, I shoot through wide alleyways toward the fortified structure.

The castle is more impressive up close. A mosaic of gray rocks form the exterior, every stained glass window open wide, allowing the night air to flood the interior. Thousands of occupants could be housed within the sturdy walls. Beyond the colossal structure, I spot the moon's shimmering reflection in an endless sea. The same one beyond the hill I would visit daily to mourn. A deep breath fills my lungs, allowing the salty scent and sounds of waves crashing over rocks to pervade my senses. I may have traveled to the other end of the country and felt the stretch from my mother's memory every step of the way, but the torment inside eases ever so slightly.

Sawyer lands on my shoulder, his claws digging into my flesh. He's concerned, and he has every right to be. A few hours ago, I was silently wishing for a different life. A better one. Could this be it? Rather than a passing visit, could I be accepted here for my true self? There's only one way to find out.

My heart thrashes inside my chest, my palms clammy as I reach out to press a hand to the aged wood of the front door. Intricate stone carvings surround the archway, each small figure clambering over the next in a bid to commit themselves to my memory. I want to remember every detail of this moment—this feeling of anticipation. Aspen, the rejected shifter, no longer exists. Aspen, the bloodthirsty wolf hybrid, is reborn tonight, and fuck anyone who doesn't accept her. Pressing my shoulders back, I steady myself for whatever is on the other side of the door before flexing and permitting myself entry.

An unexpected and invisible attack slams into me, pain searing through my skull. I turn away, crashing to my knees in the dirt. Holding my head in my hands in a meager attempt to force out the agony, a series of hands roam my body. Voices I can't make out vaguely call my name.

"Fuck, it burns!" Although muffled by the fangs shooting from my gums, the words burst from my lips. A blaze of agony invades my nostrils and throat, my inner wolf whimpering and rearing backward. I try to protect her, shield her from the assault. All the while, a thundering laugh booms inside my head.

Copper. Sweat. Wave after wave of arousal, the heady taste of lust hitting the back of my throat. Moans penetrate my ears, a true mixture of pain and pleasure, with the undercurrent of a hundred conversations, laughter, and even singing. I shudder, dragging in a ragged breath, but the agony continues, my skull splintering in two.

Finding myself airborne, I'm lifted into a pair of thick arms and crushed against a hard chest. My stomach rolls with each movement, a growl emanating from the emptiness of hunger so recently quelled.

"This was a terrible fucking idea," a deep voice snarls. Hands sink into my hair before being dragged away, and I can only lie there, too focused on my pain to argue. "I'm her guardian! I'm taking her far away from here and all of you!"

But that's not what you want, is it Aspen? The voice asks inside my mind. *The raven called you special. It's about time you found out why.* Cracking my eyelids, my head rolls aside. The door has been closed, the pain has begun to ebb, but not quickly enough. Weakness isn't a trait I'm comfortable being associated with.

A calloused hand cups my cheek, drawing me to gaze upon a pair of serene blue eyes. *Jaxon.* As bright as the sea on a glorious summer's day, I cast myself adrift in his gaze. A cool wash strokes my heated skin, my limbs becoming weightless as I float in his arms. He smells like the earth, and he feels like home.

"Aspen!" Sawyer calls, breaking my trance. Hunting for my feathery companion, I find a mass of vampires have flocked to aid Torsten and Chase in restraining him against the castle wall. I instantly throw myself out of Jaxon's hold, ungracefully hitting the ground, but I'm on my feet within seconds. Stumbling forward, I grab the t-shirt of the nearest male and toss him aside. Even in agony, the strength of my inner monsters prevails. The next, I grab by the hair, a braid similar to Jaxon's that I yank backward whilst driving my heel into his calf, a crack penetrating the air. And so, it continues until the vampires either step back with their hands raised or in a pile at my feet.

"Release him," I glare at Torsten. Chase stands between us, deciding the best way to tackle my anger is by telling me to 'calm down'—a bad choice. I move in a blur, breaking each of his ribs with my fists before slamming my knee into his balls just because I can. Torsten watches his friend topple aside and finally releases Sawyer, who'd stopped struggling in favor of gawking at me.

"For the second time tonight, I feel like the situation has gotten a little out of hand," Jaxon grunts. Whatever I thought I saw in his gaze earlier, concern or wonder, has dimmed. Instead, the commander of the army stands beside his injured men, radiating disappointment. "No one here will harm you, but your bird wasn't part of our mission."

"Consider your mission a failure," I scoff, hating to refer to myself that way. "Sawyer stays with me at all times, and it appears I'm unable to enter the castle. So, have your men stand down while we take our leave." I make it two steps before Jaxon and Torsten are in front of me, barring my exit.

"Why are you unable to enter the castle?" Jaxon asks patiently, despite the clench to his jaw. I can already see that he's not the type to handle losing well. Sawyer shifts back into his raven form, sitting on my shoulder as I narrow my eyes and bare my fangs. I wonder if I'm more irritated with myself for believing I could walk into a new life so easily or letting myself hope it was possible, but the vampires don't need to know that.

"Apparently, you missed the memo of what your little mission entailed, so let me break it down, *Jax*," I push a finger into his solid chest above his folded arms. "I'm Aspen fucking Winters. Born of vampire and werewolf. I can walk in sunlight, shift against the moon, and survive on a mixed diet of blood and food. I'm faster than you, heal quicker than you, and have *double* the heightened senses than you do. I can't just waltz into that cesspool," I gesture towards the huge wooden door. "The scents of blood, sex, and sweat, and the sounds within those encased walls, will all have my brain imploding before I make it over the threshold."

Using a finger gun, I hold it to my temple and act out a little gunshot-through-the-head scene, sound effects included. Jax doesn't react, his jaw remaining tight and stance wide. Torsten, on the other hand, has the good sense to rub his neck and look sheepish.

"Is that why you lived alone, so far from the shifter camp - because of your overactive senses?" Sawyer startles more than I do at Torsten's deduction, but I can't deny that my anger is dislodged as a new realization sets in. They have no clue about my banishment. Before any uninvited emotions surface, I shrug and continue to barge past. I'm halted by a hand wrapping around my wrist, surprised to find Chase responsible.

"Just wait out here," he says and speeds away, leaving me in front of an audience of healing vampires and the castle I'm longing to enter. I ignore their curious stares, some more impressed than pissed. Huffing, I pick a spot on the castle wall to lean against whilst Sawyer remains hyperalert from his perch on my shoulder.

The headache has finally subsided. I haven't felt a pain that intense since I was thirteen, and trust me, my teenage years were the worst. Inhaling an onslaught of strong scents causes a chronic sinus migraine my wolf can't fight off fast enough. Only lending myself to the other internal monster will do it, and that comes with its own consequences. Drinking from Jaxon is the only time I've managed to ingest blood without killing someone. Unlike the blood of humans kidnapped and presented to me as food sent me into a frenzy, Jaxon's soothed me. Sent me into a daze of bliss, much like that of a post-orgasm. Another use for the humans before their execution.

A flash of movement in my periphery announces Chase's return, two stuffed duffle bags hanging from each of his wrists. He stopped to change, swapping his t-shirt for a fitted vest barely holding together at the seams across his broad chest. Perhaps there were once sleeves, but his bulging biceps would have torn them clean off the black cotton. Instead, his tattoos are on full display, and I only realize I'm staring when Sawyer peeks me in the side of the head.

Chase's brow quirks, a smile pulling as his full lips. Damn it. Clearing my throat, I stand and face the horizon beyond the wall, staring at the forest instead of his temptation.

"I suppose you have a plan?" Jax asks gruffly. Chase throws them each a bag before slamming another into my gut. A sharp inhale sounds from the vamps still hanging around, but I merely reciprocate his smirk. It's about time they stopped treating me as fragile.

"I spoke to Lorcan," Chase nods, shouldering the last bag. "We can go somewhere else, but we'll be racing against the sunrise to get there."

"It's your call, Pri- uh, Aspen," Torsten inclines his head. Stony gray eyes lift to mine, uncertainty hidden within. Of the three, Torsten seems the most cautious of what he says and how he treats me. I assess him momentarily, knowing my mind is already made up. Nothing will stop me from seeing through this night, if only for the need for adventure.

Or to quench the thirst awakening inside of you, the voice in my head reminds me. Yeah, maybe that too.

Chapter Four

Torsten

We arrive at the woodland cabin with half an hour to spare. As soon as Chase mentioned where we were headed, it seemed to make sense. Too much sense for the one who only ever has three things on his mind-- training, fucking, and gorging. My worry is which of those things was at the forefront when he personally asked the king for use of his secret cabin.

Built three decades ago, the two-story lodge offers complete seclusion, well-hidden within the woodland. Built from oak-grain panels to act as camouflage, twisted columns secure a porch hanging over an unsuspecting front door. Large windows surround the upper level behind a wrap-around balcony to take in the views. Following the castle's coastline, a sandy beach and a vast ocean offer complete privacy for a midnight swim.

The retreat was commissioned for Lorcan's personal use. Most vamps don't know it exists or how our king sneaks here sometimes to be alone. He doesn't confide in many, but it's been obvious to those paying attention that the strains of his role have been affecting him more than they used to.

"We'd best get set up inside," I state, turning to Aspen. "Shall I take your bag from here?" I've refrained, watching her run with the duffle awkwardly bumping into her backpack, but it's been instilled in me to care for our women. That concept is striking tenfold now that I'm in the princess's presence.

"I'm sure you'd love that, huh?" Aspen scoffs, flipping her white hair over her shoulder. I frown in response. "I'm not a damsel in distress. I don't need babysitting." Following Jaxon to the porch, Chase chuckles and pats my back. Fuck me, I guess.

We're permitted entry after Jaxon punches the security code into a keypad hidden within a false panel. An advancement implemented by the 'Techies,' a group of vamps who are unnaturally good with technology, when they upgraded the windows. Despite Lorcan's wish to keep his cabin a secret, Jaxon convinced him that both the army and techies needed to be involved to ensure his safety.

"I'm taking the first shower!" Chase shouts, shooting through the cabin. Jaxon busies himself preparing a fire with the pre-cut wood. Aspen sits at the kitchen island, muttering to her bird with her back to us. So, I suppose I'll focus on what I do best—securing the perimeter.

An electronic pad sits on the wall just inside the front door, controlling the metal shutters that clamp down over every window upon being pressed and force the impending sunlight to stay where it belongs. I wasn't part of the construction team, but I remember hearing how they insisted to the King that the cabin didn't need any windows and then served time in the dungeons for questioning him so boldly. For whatever reason, Lorcan had a specific safe haven in mind and wouldn't be deterred. Windows, romantic backdrop, porch swing, and all.

Despite trusting the techies at what they do, I check each and every shutter for gaps between the metal and wood. Can't take any chances when we're about to be trapped in here for twelve hours with no chance of escaping a design flaw. Dropping my bag on the sofa, I fully inspect the cabin's interior. I may be second in command, but even Jaxon hasn't been permitted entry before. This is Lorcan's private space, which we've well and truly invaded.

Like the exterior, the wooden planks have been left exposed across the walls but shine through a glossy coat of white. The entire cabin is strangely bright. Whereas the castle drips with luxury and elegance, the décor here is cozy and intimate. The fireplace before Jaxon overlooks a spacious lounge area, blocked off by a curved teal sofa adorned in shaggy white and teal patterned cushions. A fur rug lies between the two, stark white and untouched. I can't tell what type, but from here, I would guess it's a snow leopard's pelt. I really hope, due to my present company, it's anything but wolf.

Through an archway at the opposite end of the room, the kitchen is modern and complete with a marbled breakfast bar. Furthering my exploration of the cups, wine glasses, and crockery through glass cabinets, my gaze drifts to where Aspen occupies one of two stools. Vampires can't consume real food, which begs the question - who did the king intend to bring here?

"Are you staring at my ass?" Aspen asks, not bothering to look back. My gaze clashes with the feathery fucker on the countertop, tipping his head back and forth. There's a crazed look in his eyes I'd happily wring the life out of if only to protect the princess. He's not one of us. He doesn't understand our ways or what's at stake. The silence stretches until Aspen looks back, quirking a brow.

"I'd rather not catch a stake to the heart for ogling the princess. And I don't mean by your familiar. The king wouldn't hesitate to kill me for even thinking about it."

"Is that so?" Aspen slides off her stool, seeming much more entertained suddenly. My death must be amusing because, to her, I'm just another peasant. A minion to be ordered around. "Seems we have quite the loyalist. Maybe we should place bets on how long it lasts. What do you think, Jax?" My friend and commander chuckles, stoking the fire he's long since lit.

Making her way to me, Aspen trails her fingers along the wooden slats of the staircase, causing a low thrumming sound to accompany her saunter. Stopping at the base of the stairs, she finds a light switch and flicks it several times, observing the lightbulbs in fascination. I watch her, intrigued, unsure why she would appear so amazed at a simple light switch. No doubt it pales compared to the splendor she would have grown up with. Aspen continues to run her index finger along the banister until reaching the third step.

"Whose cabin is this?" she asks, slowly spinning on the balls of her worn sneakers. The extra height only puts her at eye level with me, providing a view I wasn't prepared for. Large, rounded orbs of the deepest navy blue, framed by long lashes and a smattering of pale freckles. Aside from her vampire traits, Aspen bears no other resemblance to Lorcan. Thankfully. Gold flecks linger inside her irises, her wolf prowling just beneath the surface.

"It belongs to your father," I reply hollowly. The raven in the kitchen caws at the exact moment Aspen's features visibly shut down, blocking me out.

"Don't call him that." Lingering, Aspen searches my face and body, tugging her bottom lip between her teeth.

"Or what?" I ask, finding my voice. Maybe I just want to hold her attention a moment longer, or maybe, since she's decided to have it out for me, riling her the wrong way seemed like the best option.

Stretching out a lone finger, she drags her digit over the hole in my t-shirt where I was stabbed. "Or maybe that stake will come from a foe you didn't know you had." Hooking her finger in the hole, she tugs, tearing my shirt downwards before turning swiftly and climbing the wooden staircase. I suppose I've found the princess' new favorite hobby. Being a fucking cock tease.

"Just a friendly observation," Jaxon appears at my back. "I don't think she's a fan of diplomatic answers."

"You think," I growl, shoving him away when he remains too close. Grabbing my bag, I shoot up the stairs, my head a mess of how I've been raised and what I'd rather do. I'd envisioned the princess on my arm before the night was through, but at this rate, she might be better suited over my knee. I shake my head free of such thoughts, trying to remember what an honor being her security detail is. Our females are rare, precious commodities to be protected.

A rapid and unknown decline in pregnancies or female births has dwindled our numbers at a terrifying rate, and those who could conceive died in labor. Many of their mates walked straight into the midday sun for their souls to be reunited with loved ones, preferring to burn than live alone. Between this and a string of shifter wars over the last century, the vampires are all on edge.

For this reason, females at the castle are treated with the utmost care and respect, regardless of status. If a daughter is born successfully, the family is instantly boosted up through the ranks. All males begin training at a very young age to strengthen our armies, whereas the females are given classes in the arts; painting, singing, sewing, pottery, languages, gardening, and each one knows at least one instrument – forming our small orchestra. Something I highly doubt Aspen will conform to.

Peering into each room, except the one with steam billowing from beneath the door, Aspen finds the master bedroom. Floor-to-ceiling windows that would face out across the sea are covered by metal shutters, casting the room in a shadow dark as a moonless night. Not that Aspen nor I need light to see the gigantic bed inside, filling the majority of the space. A wooden wardrobe and white dressing table complete with a stool and dainty, rounded mirror are the only other furnishings, a door across the other side hinting at an ensuite bathroom.

"Look, I get it," I say, thrusting my boot forward when Aspen tries to slam the door closed. "You're used to being spoilt, getting your way-" her bitter laugh interrupts me. The raven swoops through the gap overhead, landing on the dressing table to watch our interaction. One that is evidently not going in my favor as I push my way inside. "What I'm trying to say is you've been waiting for the vampires to extend you an invitation to spend some time in our territory. I get how that could...inflate one's ego." The laughter grows, accompanied by the twittering of the bird.

"Seems you know all about overinflated egos," Aspen abandons her struggle to shut me out, throws her middle finger up, and heads for the bathroom. I'm not overly shocked by her display; we have feisty females in vampire territory. But we also have a princess of our own, and she'd never be permitted to act in such a way.

"I'll have you know, I'm quite the catch back at the castle," I blurt for some unknown reason.

Aspen throws another sarcastic smirk over her shoulder. "Then maybe you should have stayed behind."

I growl, tension racing through my shoulders with the need to prove myself. To show her I'm not the stuck-up asshole she's instantly pegged me for. Although, the reason why I even care for her opinion eludes me. She's a mission. One which has been extended until she's adjusted to our scents, but still just another task to be completed.

Aspen disappears into the bathroom, and I just stand there like a fool. Fully aware, the raven watches every indecisive pull of my features as I battle with what to do. Perhaps I should tell her the *real* reason we were sent to retrieve her tonight. Would that make me valiant for being honest or the reckless dick who scared her away? Ultimately, the decision is already made for me. We're following Lorcan's orders, and that's what I will continue to do. Aspen wasn't wrong when she called me a loyalist; I'll serve my king until my immortal life ends.

Some while later, Aspen emerges from the bathroom in only a towel. Her eyebrows shoot upright in surprise, then pinch in annoyance at finding me here. Apparently, she had no such qualms about the raven seeing her practically naked, her skin pebbled with droplets and white hair dripping onto the carpet. Every creamy, flawless inch on display calls to my animalistic side. Her breasts are fuller than the baggy hoodie suggested, squashed against the towel while her tiny waist remains cinched. I could wrap my hands around her middle with ease.

"Dude," Aspen groans, sensing the hunger shift in the air. "It's been a long night. I'm tired and quickly becoming grumpy, so I'm going to turn in," she inclines her gaze to the bed. "Maybe you should go find where you're going to hang upside down or whatever shit you do."

"Ha ha," I say dryly, rolling my eyes. Now she's mentioned it, sleeping by sunrise is a vampire's natural routine, and I have run the length of this country tonight retrieving a smart-mouthed sovereign. The same one who seems in a rush to brush me off. *Fuck it.* "Funnily enough, I've found where I'm going to sleep. Right here."

Dropping down on the edge of the king-size mattress, I kick off my boots and stuff the duffle bag under the bed, wanting to keep the blood bags I can smell inside close by for when I wake. Pulling my torn t-shirt over my head, I chuck it onto a brown leather armchair I hadn't noticed in the corner of the room. Next, I remove my trousers and socks, throw them on the growing pile, and opt to leave my boxers on this time. Call it a one-time courtesy because I sleep naked. Period.

"You look really comfortable and all, but…" Aspen drawls before a sudden thud hits my back. She lands horizontally, having booted me with her bare feet. I spin, knocking away her following kicks with ease. The real test is not peering down where her towel falls to cover her. I have too much honor for that. Aspen jumps upright on the mattress, one hand holding her towel in place whilst punching me square in the jaw with the other. "Seriously, get the fuck out. I'd kill you and your mom before I gave up the chance to sleep in a bed like this." I tackle her down, not wanting to hit her back, so I resort to almost tickling her. What the actual fuck has gotten into me?

"Jokes on you. My mother is already dead," I quip back and then pause. My brows pinch, the raven ducking his head beneath his wing as the tension in the air sours. In a rush of speed, I drag the cover over Aspen and roll her up like a sausage. "And only your stubborn ass said you had to leave. So, relax," I hold her squirming body still, "and go to fucking sleep. Your beauty is lethal, but I reckon you'll be even hotter with your mouth shut." At this point, it's probably best that my mother is deceased because if she heard me talking to royalty in such a way, she'd have my tongue.

Dropping onto the empty space beside her, my hand smooths over the bedsheet. I can't imagine Lorcan's sheets at the castle are this luxurious, and as for the padded cover at my back – vampires don't feel the cold. Everything about this cabin confuses me, but despite my curiosity, a fog starts to descend, and my limbs grow heavy. Tonight has been a wilder ride than I anticipated, but with the princess safe and snuggled, my fucks have extended as far as giving into the sleep beckoning me. To be sure, dreams of a lithe fanged shifter with stark white hair await me on the other side.

"Torsten?" her voice sounds small. I turn over in an instant. "Would you care to join me?" My jaw slackens. All the fight has fled her features and even the raven caws in curiosity. After a beat, I rush to unravel her from the cover and fan it over the both of us. She shimmies in closer, batting her lashes at me within the shadows. "I think...you might be right."

"Oh yeah?" I ask croakily. The way she's staring intently has me all wrapped up in knots, struggling to keep my breathing even. Her white hair splays across the pillow, and I have the sudden urge to see her writhing and panting beneath me whilst my cock is buried inside her.

"I am lethal," she agrees, instantly striking her shin into my balls.

I choke, sure that I will cough up blood as I roll away, tail surely hanging between my legs. I should have seen that one coming, but as I cup my crotch, I find my dick harder than ever. *What the fuck is wrong with me?*

I'm second in command in the vampire army; I'm well-versed in withholding emotion. Maintaining a stoic persona comes with the territory, but no female has ever infuriated me and turned me on so quickly. Sex is a base need—a task that goes hand-in-hand with feeding. However, I bet this spritely minx would ignite a fierce passion within me. She already captivates me, from the firmness of her muscles to the indent in her waist, her wild hair to her fierce eyes.

As I settle back down, I can't help but admit that I want to explore what other traits she bares that will tease me to insanity. Whatever they were, I'm sure they would provide plenty of fuel to fan the fire of my dreams. My eyelids drift closed again, and this time, I fall asleep within seconds.

"Can you believe that guy?" Sawyer barely shifted before throwing his fist into the nearest tree. I pick up a stone and chuck it at his head, my irritation still simmering after storming out of the master bedroom, passing the shower that was somehow still running and waltzing right on by the sleeping vampire on the sofa. Dressed in the clothes provided in the duffle bag – a black tank, baggy cargos belted tight at the waist – I knock the heavy combat boots on my feet against a boulder.

"Stop deflecting," I growl, dropping onto that same boulder with a sigh. Morning has broken, but I couldn't sleep even if I wanted to. A lively sea calls for me, offering to wash away my stress between each crashing wave. If I didn't know that the reason for my damn anxiety wouldn't be waiting for me on the sandy beach when I emerged, I might have dived in already.

"I'm deflecting?! You've just accepted an invite from three vampires you don't know to hang around for who knows what and haven't even bothered to ask why. It's a blessing you couldn't enter their castle. There would have been no coming back for you after that." Sawyer knocks my head with his fingers, most likely forgetting he can't get away with that shit out of bird form. Hopping off the boulder, the last thread of my sanity snaps.

"Well, maybe, my mind was already spinning about a raven," I shove at his chest, "who's been stalking me for eight years," another shove, "turning into an actual person and telling me he's my guardian." This time, he catches my wrists and spins me. My back slams into his front, his arms banding around me tightly. Sawyer's an incredible fighter, stronger than the usual shifter, but none of that's the reason I'm not currently bursting free of his hold. Heated breath fans my neck, his lips grazing my ear lobe.

"You can't use your bravado to hide from me. I *know* you, Aspen," he whispers, forcing me to stare at the sea's horizon. I huff, wondering if he meant that as a promise and a threat. "You're too dominant to sit around waiting for answers. Why aren't you asking the right questions?"

"Such as?" I query back in a bid to keep him talking. The fucking raven I've nuzzled and confided my every worry in. The creature who has apparently been protecting me from foes I didn't realize I had.

Loosening his hold, Sawyer turns me around to stare into his purely obsidian eyes. "Oh, I don't know, maybe why the vampires have suddenly taken an interest in you? They intended to kidnap you in a fucking cage.

Three of the most elite fighters dressed for battle. They've known of your existence since your mother died, and only now are they prepared to go to war to claim ownership over you?"

I exhale slowly through my nose. True, I'm avoiding conflict with the vampires for now, playing a long game, and it seems I have a few questions of my own to deal with first.

"How do you know when they learned of my existence?" I ask slowly. My heart has kicked up a beat, my gut clenching.

"I, um...I was the one who informed King Lorcan, as instructed by the Council. My first assignment as your official guardian was to deliver a note to the royal chamber. Your mother kept you a secret and for good reason." Sawyer has the good sense to look sheepish beneath his sweep of black hair, but it does nothing to quell the tornado of betrayal building within.

"All this time...." I struggle to keep my wolf calm, "you've had all the answers I've been searching for."

"I have rules to abide by, I need you to understand. But when the vamps appeared, I couldn't let you be taken. Not after the lengths your mother went through to protect you. The lengths I've gone through to continue to protect you. It's all for nothing now," his jaw clenches, and his eyes flash as his voice darkens. "You've dived, headfirst, into a viper's nest of lies and deceit." Sawyer steps away from me with a bitter smile and a shake of his head.

A tug pulls at my chest, the disappointment in his posture undeniable.

My jaw tightens, "Because the shifters were so much better? You weren't there the day I first shifted. You didn't see what I did, how they treated me. You weren't there," I repeat, shoving him again. "Why weren't you there?" My voice cracks, my vision clouds with tears I refuse to shed, and my fists rain down on Sawyer's torso. He doesn't even flinch, taking the attack of my anger as if it were merely feathers brushing his chest.

"I want to show you something," Sawyer says gently once the fight drains from me, and I drop my forehead against his chest. Easing me back a step, Sawyer shrugs from his trench coat, dropping it behind him. I stand motionless as he peels the black t-shirt over his head, revealing his body. My jaw drops.

The trench coat did well to conceal the huge bulk of muscles. But the true work of art was the tattoos seemingly embedded into his very skin that stretch from wrists to wide shoulders, over his solid torso to beyond where I can see. At first glance, I presumed them to be tribal markings, but on closer inspection, they're branches. I lift my hand to trace the black markings on his chest but think better of it and quickly let it fall to my side. But what the hands cannot touch, the eyes can caress and fuck if I will stop them from feeling their fill.

The sun's rays dance across his chiseled chest, its warm hues painting every contour of his muscles, bringing the tones of his skin and ink to life. My mouth grows dry as I follow the path of the sunlight until it stops to rest at the waistband of his pants, right at the deeply engrained V of his lower abdomen. My eyes must caress a lot better than I would have thought as evidence of a well-endowed appendage swells within his cargos, and I force my eyes upwards. A move I wish I could take back.

I realize, a little too late, that maybe admiring his body *was* the safer choice. Because as our eyes meet, my lungs lose their ability to hold air, and I find myself breathless. Almost whimpering, I fight the urge to place a hand on my chest as the full impact of his gaze, filled with an unnamed restrained emotion—one that I'm not yet ready to analyze—wraps around my heart like a vise. But ready or not, that look holds me captive.

His rough voice seems to weave through the very fiber of my being as the weight of his gaze somehow intensifies with the force of his next words as they drip, like the sweetest nectar, from his lips. "This is who I am. And my life is devoted to protecting yours."

The words register, and questions float to the forefront of my mind, but they slip away like water through my fingers. Instead, my confused emotions take over as I stammer, "You're... you're beautiful."

His eyes soften, and he gives me a gentle smile before motioning for us to sit. "There's more I need to tell you," Sawyer says, his voice laced with an unfamiliar tenderness as he guides me to the edge of the sand.

"Sit," he breathes as we lower ourselves onto a grassy bank. Somehow, I slide beneath his arm as if it's the most natural thing in the world.

Sitting in comfortable silence, I watch him from the corner of my eye as we watch the waves play. His expression changes a mile a second, too quick for me to pick up on what his internal battle could be. Just when my curiosity was about to win out, his body shifts subtly as his shoulders drop and his back straightens, his expression determined, if not exactly peaceful. I fight the urge to frown because while it is clear that whatever war had been waging in his head was over, what isn't clear is what the outcome truly was. Even more so, what that outcome would mean. I was a little sick of constant unknowns.

With a deep sigh, he rests his cheek on my head. "I've already broken the cardinal rule; there's no use in withholding the rest."

He pauses briefly, "As I mentioned before, Ravens are a rare commodity allocated to guard certain beings. The supernatural council sent my mother to watch over yours when she began her affair with the vampire King. Part of my training was learning about your heritage and how it came to be."

Shifting, Sawyer wraps his trench coat around my back like a large wing. I twist my head to blink at him, his jet-black hair hanging over us. An exact contrast to mine, but it suits him perfectly.

"Please, don't stop. I need closure, Sawyer. Can you give it to me?"

"First, you should know the consequences of what I did last night. When the council hears I revealed my true self, they will summon me, and there's a huge chance I won't return. I'll tell you whatever you wish to know as my parting gift."

If I thought I was panicking or angry earlier, it's nothing compared to the intense pressure that builds in my chest as I try to remember how to breathe. *Parting gift?* I can count the myriad of ways that my life has been torn apart, Sawyer at least, has been one constant. One familiar form that has helped ease all the tension and pain I have felt throughout the years. Losing him is not something I am prepared for in the least. Did I know he was a shifter? No. Did it matter? Also, no. Ultimately, his absence would carve out whatever was left of my heart. I wasn't ready. Not for the moment, where I will eventually look over my shoulder expecting to see his raven form on my shoulder or close by. Nor for the moment that I would call out for him, expecting him to answer before realizing that there would be no response. After my mom died, I had Sawyer. After Sawyer is called away, who will I have then?

I wince inwardly as the darker voice cackles malevolently, seeming to revel in my confusion, while my wolf stirs and whimpers within me—two opposing forces, one sinister and one loyal. I shove aside the headache brewing in my head, struggling to comprehend how I could be born from such a disparate union of species. Vampires and wolves just didn't mix, and yet here I was, battling two sides of myself that shouldn't have been put together in the first place.

I take a deep breath and steel my spine because regardless of the circumstances, I am here now. And while losing Sawyer would be another heartbreak I'm not ready for, I will get through it. I had to. But not without being armed with the knowledge I would need to ensure my success.

"Tell me everything," I nod, gripping his bicep for strength because I have a feeling that whatever he is going to tell me is going to be an easy story to hear.

Lying on the fur rug, I watch the embers dying in the fireplace. Fragile, flittering flames dancing among the kindling in a bid to stay alive. Sawyer is pressed against my stomach in feathery form, his words still sinking. His mother was a guardian to mine, and she watched the entire affair with the vampire king. Then how after the forbidden affair, my mother returned to the shifter camp, married the Alpha as expected, and tried to pass the baby off as his. I.e., me.

Sawyer's secondhand stories spoke of my real parents as if they were a true match. Bonded by the moon. Two intertwining souls that could have stood the test of time if my mother were brave enough. But that's not how I see it. It takes true bravery to put the needs of your unborn child and species before your own. And that's what's the worst of it. My mother tried hard to protect me from the Alpha when my first turn went horribly wrong. There was no denying what I was then. A monster. An outcast, sent directly to the exile hut before I killed anyone else.

I shudder as a chill trickles through me. One that has nothing to do with the temperature of the cabin. Both inner beasts are unusually calm like they are when I visit the gravestone—giving me time to mourn and heal, if at all possible. Stroking my fingers through the white fur surrounding me, my inner wolf nudges down, pretending we're in a pack snuggle. A sad sight for anyone watching the half-breed drowning in her sorrows and spooning a fucking raven all day. There's no telling what time it is through the shutters, but Jaxon's snoring has rung through the cabin long enough.

Pushing upright, my stomach groans. I hadn't felt it before, but now the hunger grips me with an urgent need I can't fill. Another snore rumbles through the space. Slipping the cushion from beneath Jax's head, I bash him with it and slink into the kitchen as if nothing happened when he pounces. He was in full animal mode on the discarded cushion, tearing his fangs into the cotton before coming to his senses. I meet his eye briefly, concerned if this is what giving into my vampire side would really mean—hunched over a cushion like a feral cat with anger issues.

Shaking my head, I turn my back and search the kitchen cupboards. There are dishes, so there must be some food around here somewhere. I hope. Yet as I slam the last drawer shut, I sigh in time with another stomach rumble and lean my hands on the breakfast bar.

"So," Jaxon surprises me from the other side of the island. Composed and seated on one of the bar stools, resting his forearms on the marbled surface. I pause, uncomfortable with his full attention, so my eyes roam over his tattoos instead.

The dark ink is a direct contrast to the paleness of his skin, with intricate patterns starting from his wrists and curling all the way up his arms. On his huge left bicep, there's a Phoenix in hues of orange and red, stretching its wings all the way around the muscle and face stretching upwards. The other upper arm holds the side profile of a beautiful geisha girl, hiding the lower half of her face with a fan, her hair full of delicate flowers in various shades of blue and purple.

"Aspen," his low tone brings my attention back to this ruggedly handsome face, "tell me about yourself." Piercing blue eyes watch my face shift from confusion to misery when I realize...there's really nothing to say. Moving around the bar, I take the seat next to him.

"I already told you about my gifts," I half-shrug. Jax moves slightly so that his thick thigh is pressing against mine, but I shift so the connection is lost. It's been a long time since I've had any physical contact, and I'm not sure it's something I'm overly comfortable with anymore.

"I didn't ask about your gifts. I'm asking about you." I steal a glance in his direction and instantly wish I hadn't. A prominent vein runs along his throat, from his jaw to the edge of his t-shirt. My stomach tightens.

I've tasted blood before, but not like his. He could easily become an addiction, whether that's how it usually is with a vampire or if Jax's intoxicating taste is all his own. I shouldn't allow myself to return to a frenzied state of hunger again, but with so few options, I'm starting to wonder if I really should have attacked him in his sleep. Sunk my teeth into his neck and drank until my inner beast was sated. The very thought has my mouth salivating, and not only my stomach is clenching now. Pressing my thighs together, I lick and nibble on my lower lip. None of which goes unnoticed.

"Um," Jax clears his throat, growing flustered himself. "Let me try a different angle. How about your childhood?"

"Hard pass," I groan. Talk about a bucket of ice water to my libido. Sliding off the stool, I pace back around to the kitchen. There must be something to eat around here. Wood shavings, maybe some dust. All sound like a safer alternative at this point.

"Aspen?" Jax's frown deepens when he sees my reaction to hearing him say my name. My face contorts with anguish, and a small whine slips out from the wolf within me. "I didn't mean to upset you—" he starts to say but is interrupted.

"There's no use dancing around her feelings," Torsten mutters, appearing to take the stool I recently occupied. "Aspen here doesn't care for pleasantries, so you might as well come out and say it." A second pair of tattooed, muscled forearms lean on the bar. One, I'm not so eager to explore while Torsten's pewter gray eyes glare at me. "What were you doing so close to the borderline, attempting to eat one of your own? And what's with the tiny shack? We could scent you all over it. Hardly the residence for the future ruler of your pack."

My nostrils flare, words failing me. Sawyer hops onto the fireplace, twitching his birdy head as he watches on from afar. Gauging my defeated reaction. Torsten would have been right about me ruling had the fact I'm not Conall's kin revoked the future I'd been primed for. To marry the next chosen Alpha and rule alongside him. As my mother did.

"I turned thirteen on a full moon," I sigh, squeezing my nails into my palms. "Supposed to bring great fortune, there was a huge ceremony at sundown. Except I didn't only shift into a wolf, but some kind of monster. I don't remember much of that night, only the blood when I came to. I was exiled to the hut that night for the pack's safety. The rule of my banishment was to suppress my vampire side, but it just...hurt too bad. Caused me to lash out, so Conall decided to provide me with a human a month to hunt and feed on. A convict, rapist, or the like. It did the job of leveling me out."

"You must have deduced what the other half of you was. Why didn't you come to find us?" Torsten scoffs, his whole demeanor taut with irritation. Any form of chivalry he may have shown last night is long gone. Whether that is for the best or not remains to be seen.

"Are you even listening to me? I was cast out of one species for being a crossbreed. Didn't feel the need to endure it again." Silence falls over us, punctuated by the rumbling of my stomach. This time, a cramp of agony flares within, and I do my best to let it pass without showing a hint of pain. Jaxon exhales loudly, peering up at me with his head hung low.

"So...no one is coming for you?" he asks. I narrow my eyes.

"Is that a problem?" A rush of movement rushes through the living area, blindsiding me through my emotional onslaught. Sawyer catches it, though, squawking and flapping his wings, but by then, it's too late.

"Drink," is all the warning I get before Chase shoves his open wrist against my mouth. Blood spills between my lips, and despite myself, I groan orgasmically at the taste. Danger and energy seep down my throat, igniting a fire within. So unlike Jaxon's blood, which calmed me sensually, Chase is invigorating. Every sense is heightened, almost electrified, filled with Chase's taste, his leathery smell, and the press of his skin on my lips. It's exhilarating, almost painful, as currents of energy pulse through my body, only magnified by the feel of his free hand slipping beneath my tank top to hold my waist.

"Chase," Jaxon snarls low. The wrist is whipped away as quickly as it appeared, leaving me to steady myself on the bar. My chest heaves, my breath erratic. Bursts of gold leak from my eyes as I fight to get a grip, not that Chase allows me such freedom. His hands slam onto the bar on either side of mine, a rumble drawn from his chest as he and Jax enter a stare-off.

Piercing blue eyes narrow from across the breakfast bar, a warning to Jax's snarl causing my own instincts to perk up and listen. Jaxon isn't the kind of boss who needs to shout. Just the thinly veiled threat that he'll fuck you up, and anyone with good sense would obey. That person does not happen to be Chase.

"What?!" He pushes off the counter, raising his arms wide and walking backwards to the keypad by the rear door. "We're just going to have a light sparring session, that's all." Torsten stands, his jaw tight enough to crack.

"Have you lost your damn mind? We're under strict orders to protect her, not attack her." Meanwhile, I'm standing there, trying to push frustration through my giddy lightheadedness from the recent blood intake.

"She's a hybrid, not a hydrangea," Chase drawls. "Besides, she'll need training for –"

"You've made your point. Just... go easy, okay," Jax warns, and I scoff, more determined than ever to prove myself. Perhaps if these vampires see what I'm really capable of, aside from beating them in a race, they won't insist on treating me, as Chase so aptly put it, like a flower.

Punching in the keycode, Chase causes the shutters to rise. The sun must have only just tipped beneath the horizon, the sky a vibrant wash of orange and pink. Jaxon and Torsten shoot from the stools into the only crook of shadow between the staircase and the overhang of the archway. Chase doesn't retreat. Not when a hiss is drawn from his teeth, or his skin reddens and steam rolls from his tattooed arms. No, Chase smiles like a maniac, feeding on the pain.

"Come on, Aspen, time to put those fighting skills to the test."

Releasing the back door, Chase flexes his biceps before stepping out on a strangled roar. I merely watch him go, six-foot three-ish of flowing hair and inked muscle squeezed into a vest and cargos, until Sawyer squawks by my ear. Jolted back to my senses, I steady my breathing. Proving myself starts now.

"Don't you dare interject," I mutter to the bird, dislodging him as I stride through the back door. Sawyer hops onto the railing, strangely silent. Whether he agrees or not, Sawyer knows me better than anyone, and he'll know I need to do this. To follow this path, stretch the beast within I struggle to control. I wasn't finding any answers in shifter exile, and I'm ready to learn now.

The woodlands create a semi-circle around the front of the cabin, a patch of soft dirt separating Chase and I. Leaning against a trunk, a growing shadow from the tree line has started descending. Still, that crazy smile spread across his face is in place, and I match it. Chase is a fine specimen, his brown hair shifting in a light breeze, emerald eyes fully focused on me. But that smile is something else. Razor sharp fangs extend, grazing his lip.

At last, a worthy component, the voice in my head sighs. For once, I'm inclined to agree. Dragging my boots through the dirt, I inhale the pine-infused air. It feels like days since my early morning escape with Sawyer, which turned out to be unexpectedly deep and heavy. I'm ready to feel alive. Rolling my neck, I set my feet and raise my fists. Chase hangs back in the growing shadow, his brow hitching.

"Not quite," he beckons me closer with two fingers. I ignore how hot that 'come hither with his inked digits was. "First, I need to warm you up."

"Wear me out more like," I quip back, not catching the innuendo until Chase chuckles. The air shifts around my ass, but the hit doesn't land as Sawyer swoops in, pecking Chase in the temple. Batting the bird away, the vampire knocks into my back and rushes to right me. One hand splayed across my midsection, the other cupping my breast. A throat is cleared somewhere out of sight, causing Chase to release me, but the heat remains.

"Push-ups, sit-ups, and squats. Show me what you've got," Chase clicks his fingers. I grab those fingers, quickly snapping them back with a harsh crack for daring to click at me like a dog. Muffled laughter touches my ears from an unknown source as I drop to my hands, following Chase's following orders. Every exercise he commands of me, I give without breaking so much as a sweat. Apparently, Chase thinks himself above running drills alongside me is beneath him. Or maybe he's enjoying being in command for a change. Either way, as the midnight blanket of night falls over the sky, the 'warm up' only makes me more restless.

"That's it, I'm done," I jump down from the branch I was using for pull-ups. Sawyer remains close enough should I need assistance, but I'll make damn sure I don't. The moon has risen over the clearing, causing my wolf to stir within, soothing and agitating me at the same time. We're all desperate to burn the ache from my limbs, and this pre-warm up isn't going to cut it. "These drills are child play compared to what I'm going to do to you."

"I don't doubt it," Chase agrees from across the clearing. "I'm surprised you did them for so long. I'd only wanted the moon to rise so I get your wolf at peak strength. Good to know you have a submissive streak in you though."

The night air becomes thicker, almost alive as it fills with tension. Energy thrums through my veins, the power and intensity from his blood still coursing through me; overwhelming in all the right ways. Still, despite the power of his blood, I knew the boost wouldn't last forever, and as I stand in the clearing facing the cabin, my skin itches with the need to move, to fight. To fully work out the ache in my bones, to *destroy.*

Briefly closing my eyes, I fight back the influx of emotions that would betray me in a heartbeat. But by the way Chase casually leans against the cabin wall, his 6 foot plus body encased provocatively in fitted combat pants and a tight black tank top; his tattoos and defined arms on full display in the pale moonlight, he knew exactly what the wait was doing to me. By nature, I could wait hours for the kill, for the rush that comes with the sensation of delicate skin ripping through my claws, but with the high from his blood, it felt almost impossible.

Slowly, he pulls off his tactical belt from his hips, letting it fall to the floor as he pushes away from the wooden panels, his long hair flowing down his back. His body flexes as the moonlight highlights every movement of his pale skin. His green, iridescent eyes shimmer with interest as he knowingly scans over my vibrating body. He felt what I did back in the cabin, there's no doubt. The electric shocks between us, and even though I wouldn't admit it, he is just as curious. Curious about how our bodies would move together, even if it were in the close heat of combat.

After reaching to tie his hair into a tight knot on the top of his head, Chase slowly pulls off his tank, throwing it onto the ground. I almost whimper as heat floods to places it shouldn't, and I fight to keep my gaze focused on any indication of his next movement and not the pure steel that is his perfect fucking body.

I barely resist telling him to hurry the fuck up so we can get this shit started when the slightest flex of his muscles is my only warning as he leaps into the air, moving with a fluidity and elegance that contrast his size. Powerful legs propel him off the ground, launching him towards me with knees bent as fists angled towards my face. Stepping back from his aim, the wind shifts alongside my pivot, allowing my vampire to lead as I land a hit on his side. I go down to one knee, turning and letting my other knee drive into the back of his, causing him to stumble.

Chase's eyes widen in surprise, and he grunts in pain. I smirk, but the wasted moment means I'm still on the ground—a fact he takes full advantage of, landing a roundhouse kick to my face.

"Fuck," I curse as I use the force of the hit to propel myself back, flipping my body to land into a crouch instead of falling onto my back. Annoyed, I spit the blood from my mouth. I should know better than to make a stupid ass mistake like that. The power of his blood prevents my ribs from cracking, but I feel the last vestiges of that strength finally leave my body. I feel my eyes flash with gold, desire giving way to true anger. I hadn't thought Chase would go easy on me, but I hadn't fully expected to be kicked in the face, either. Chase laughs, the deep sound flowing through the air as light as the breeze but with the impact of a freight train.

"Is that all you've got, *Princess*?" Chase goads me. A growl makes its way, unbidden, from my throat. I feel something within me shift, power building, almost choking me with its intensity. A surge of energy, unlike anything I have ever felt, even with the rush of Chase's blood. As if a dam had burst, my claws unsheathe, longer and sharper as I fully surrender to the power that's always laid underneath the surface, my very soul waiting to be fully unleashed.

I open my senses, allowing myself a few seconds to bask in the heady feeling. Drunk on power, my eyes hyper-focus on every slight movement of his muscles. My eyes prick, catching the sound of his blood thrumming through his veins and breaths softly sawing from his lips. Even the gentle shift of his hair moving in the wind. I feel my face melt into a feral smile, my teeth sharpened as my fangs extend from my gums.

"I'm not a princess. I'm a fucking survivor, and you'd do well not to forget that." Chase crouches low, a matching smile playing on his lips briefly. He's downright heart-rending in his magnificence. His mouth moves, but the tones are almost too entrancing to catch, my blood responding to the heat in his voice, laced with a perfect combination of lust and disdain.

"Oh, Aspen, I knew you'd be special." Without pause, Chase unleashes a whirlwind of action, the movement almost silent as his eyes flash red, the smirk undying on his lips. The way he moves - with a speed and ease mesmerizing in its power - would have been impressive if I wasn't focusing on fucking destroying him just to prove I could.

As his body comes into contact with mine, I stay on my feet, absorbing the impact as I reach up, my hands on his shoulders, and pull myself up to flip over his back. My claws pierce into his skin as I flip, my wrists bending as I work my claws deeper into his shoulders before my body turns, landing graciously on my feet facing his back.

Chase roars in pain as I follow the path my claws started, tugging lower. There is no resistance as I tear into his flesh, blood pouring down his back. Chase launches forward before the blood flow stops, and his skin starts to knit together again slowly. I frown at the wounds not fully healing as quickly as expected.

He spins, face filled with fury and a heavy dose of surprise. Slowly, we fall into synced movements, circling one another as I lick the blood off my claws, savoring the taste.

"Interesting," Chase murmurs to himself, knowing I'll hear it anyway. "Not bad for a novice. But you still have a lot to learn, and I'm not one of your weak pack mutts." The depraved voice in my head moans lustfully, the excitement of battle coursing through my veins, the desire for bloodshed insatiable as my instincts take over. Chase may be older, but he admitted to being curious about me. Well, here I am.

My body moves through the clearing, my legs quickly eating the distance between us. Chase grabs my wrist as my claws go for his neck, and twists sharply, causing me to bend forward right before driving his knee into my stomach. Once. Twice. With a roar that shakes the very essence of the trees around us, he grabs me by my throat, lifting me off the ground, his face snarling into mine. A moment intended to be menacing, but as he presses my body against his, our breaths mingling from exertion, I raise my gold-induced eyes to his. Suddenly, time seems to stand still.

Even if his hands weren't around my throat, my ability to breathe would still have been limited as all the air drains from the very top of my head down to my toes; the tension between us charged with a raw, magnetic energy that is impossible to ignore—a solid force, palpable to us both.

Chase's green eyes glint with a mixture of amusement and desire as he licks his dangerously full lips, a deep-seated hunger in his gaze. My body responds in kind, my desire flushing through my nerve endings. Permitting my feet to touch the ground, his hands are still firmly around my throat, only this time, his thumb caresses the pulse in my neck. Pulling me under a spell, we just stand there, neither making a move and unable to look away from each other. Fuck the moon, what I wouldn't let him do to me in this endless moment. Finally, Chase breaks the silence, his voice low and husky.

"Well, Princess, I must say, you've exceeded my expectations." Using the distraction, I dig my claws into his hands, shoving Chase away and shaking away the sensations coursing through my body.

"I told you, I'm not a princess," I reply, my voice just as low. Chase looks at the cuts on his hands, falling into a trance. Again, the skin doesn't immediately heal, and I admit, I'm just as curious. Chase's lips quirk as he moves back into my personal space. I don't resist his hands running down my arms, marking me with two thick lines of his blood. If there's a deeper vampire meaning to that, I wouldn't know, but Chase's features flare with some unreadable expression.

"No." He presses closer, taking a deep breath, his gaze slightly glowing and never leaving mine. "You are something else entirely. Something... mesmerizing."

My heart skips a beat, but the moment is quickly broken as another voice fills the clearing.

"What the fuck is going on here?" Jaxon's gruff tone vibrates with anger as he shoots closer, his body moving with preternatural grace. Mint body wash invades my senses, cleansing me of the fog in my mind. In a fresh change of clothing, Jax folds his arms over a white vest, camo green cargos, and military-style boots. His hair hangs over his shoulder, water dripping from the thick braid. I arch a brow.

"You left me at the mercy of your soldier whilst going to have a shower?" I take a few measured steps away from the pair of them. There are too many smells and strong undercurrents of lust in the air, and I'm not sure how much of it is coming from me. "What if one of us lost control and killed the other?"

Sawyer squawks from an above branch, a mocking raven's laugh that says he'd have never let me fall into physical harm. Jax is also inclined to chuckle.

"Considering the only blood coating you is his," Jax looks me up and down, "I would say you managed to hold your own."

"She did more than that," Torsten appears out of the forest's shadows. Slapping Chase hard on the back, a grunt is drawn from the vampire's lips, his green eyes still not as pissed as they should be. I cut him to ribbons, and it only managed to increase his warped pleasure. All three turn to face me, inquiring gazes hunting for unknown answers. The golden glow is yet to leave my eyes, mainly from the strong scent of blood sinking into my skin. If it weren't for the present company, I'd have resorted to licking myself clean, searching for the same high Chase's blood supplied.

Luckily, Jax clears his throat, interrupting my train of thought, and relaxes his stance.

"I've received word from the king. We have a new set of orders." He steps forward, offering me his hand and waiting for reciprocation. Sawyer lands on my shoulder defensively, but I take it anyway. "Amendments have been put in place at the castle for you, Aspen. It's time to meet your real father."

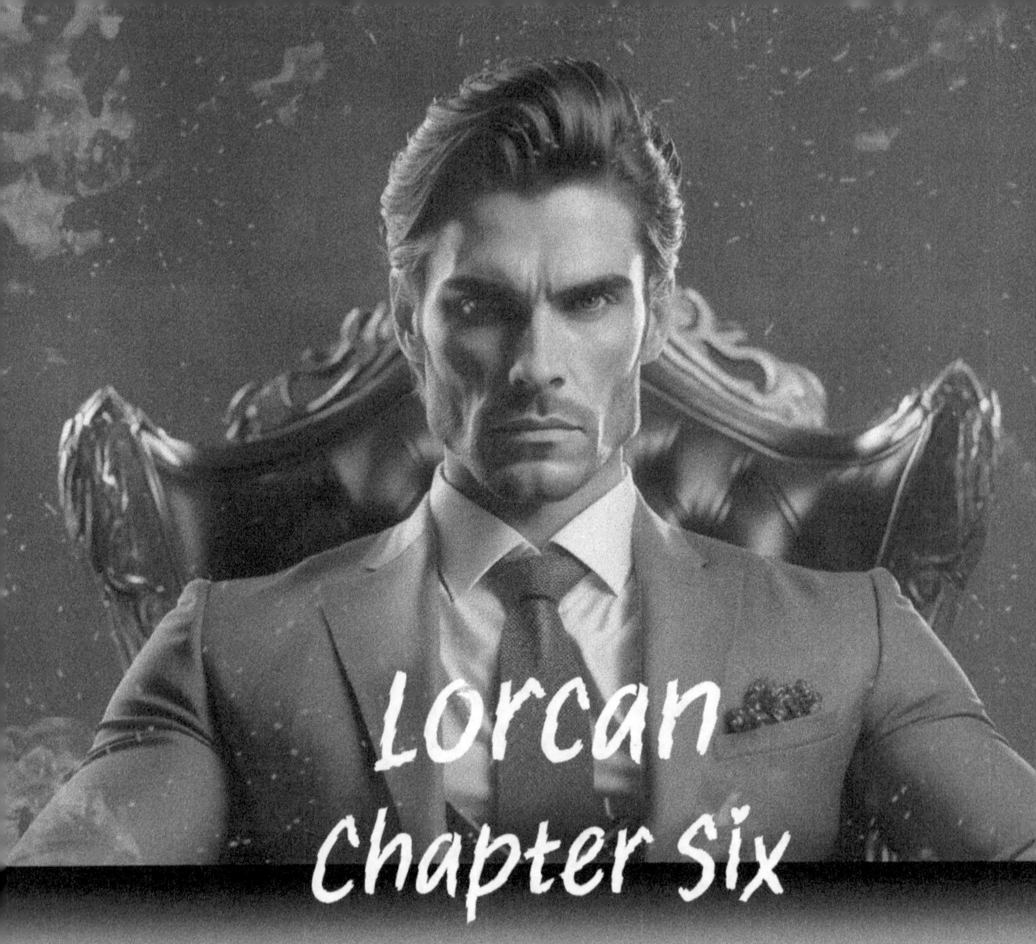

Lorcan
Chapter Six

"King Lorcan, they have arrived," my assistant, Nova, informs, poking her head into my office. Light brown hair hangs from a high ponytail, and she pushes red-framed glasses up her nose with a skinny index finger. The ones she always pairs with red high heels.

I give a single nod, and she retreats just as quickly as she came in, gently closing the door between us. I wasn't in the best mood before receiving the call from Jaxon, and now I'm furious. A daughter of mine - a hybrid of two species - exiled. Outcast and forgotten. Since I learned of Aspen's existence, I've been planning. Bidding my time, but now I wish I hadn't waited. This changes everything.

The constant ache inside my chest tugs uncomfortably, which I uselessly try to rub away. Nothing ever soothes the pain, and nothing ever will. With a sigh, I stand from my leather chair and walk slowly towards the door, dragging my hand along the glass surface of my desk.

My office is my sanctuary, even if it was recently renovated at the insistence of the Techies. They're adamant that we must keep up with human advances or risk falling prey to them once again. I'm a creature of habit, preferring the traditions I've known for centuries. Not the damn screen on my desk that connects me to an outside world I want no part of. Here, I can ignore my personal problems and focus on the issues at hand. Enabling the vamps to thrive, keeping our armies strong and enemies at bay.

Making my way through the stone corridors with long, measured strides, I descend a winding staircase on the far east side of the castle, leading to the indoor botanical gardens. The entire east section is dedicated to the few females amongst us, giving them room to flourish. There's space for all the arts and the freedom to indulge their every whim. From a large hall for instrumental and singing practices, a pottery room complete with kilns, art studios, a gallery to display their creations, and a two-story library with books lining every wall. Everything a wondering mind could ask for while weighing up marriage proposals.

Hesitating outside the glass doors that lead to the gardens, I nervously rake a hand through my slicked-back hair. A shiver courses down my spine, and I take a moment to steady my breathing. If my fellow vamps could see me now, they'd surely laugh at the wreck I've become. I'm not the confident king I once was—I avoid public events and shirk meetings whenever possible. Too much has transpired, leaving me a shadow of my former self.

Straightening my black shirt, I step forward, and the automatic doors slide open. The humidity hits me first, then the scent of blossoms and musical notes of chirping birds. The rounded extension was built with UV-protective glass panels, creating a domed ceiling. Evidently, a mirror image of the gymnasium recently built on the far side of the castle. Shades of lush greenery stretch across the greenhouse, welcoming me into their fold. I don't often visit, as this is the female's sanctuary - but I do like to marvel at their hard work occasionally.

Tropical plants, from large palms to ferns, stretch towards the moon, creating a natural leafy canopy in its honor. On the ground, varieties of colored flowers line twisting walkways leading to a waterfall in the center. A powerful cascade of water rushes from the edge of a vast rock, plunging into a pool of rippling water. The plumbers assured me of a draining system linking to a continual cycle, but I don't honestly care. We all have our roles; plumbing is theirs, ignoring the rising realization that I can't continue much longer is mine. Stopping by the water, I watch the glimmering scales of large Koi fish dancing beneath the surface, their scales glinting in the moonlight.

Rolling up my shirt sleeves to the elbow and opening my top button, I realize I've left my jacket and waistcoat behind. The big show of power I had prepared in my office was meant to impress Aspen, my suit of the finest caliber, but this will have to do. At least with every Vamp, including the females, making the most of their precious time outdoors, we have complete privacy. The rear doors left wide open should prove less intrusive for Aspen's senses, and the foliage mirroring the shifter camp should provide her with a calming oasis. Although, it seems there's much I don't understand about her upbringing.

I stroke the leathery skin of a banana leaf hanging low, waiting to meet my daughter. To be blessed with another child, a female no less, is a miracle, but I know this won't be the happy reunion I may have wished for. My world ended the night Orianna told me she was returning to the shifter pack to marry the Alpha. She told me to leave and never return, to allow her the chance at a happy life. And I did...until a raven brought me the news of Orianna's passing. No, my world ended *that* day, for she was no longer living her happily ever after somewhere with someone. It didn't have to be me as long as it was everything she deserved.

Finding my inner strength, I follow the sound of multiple heartbeats and the winding footpath. But before I round the final corner, I still because sitting on a stone bench under huge umbrella-shaped leaves is a female, so like her mother, I could have fooled myself for a moment. Jaxon senses me before turning on his heel and dropping to kneel briefly. Torsten and Chase do the same, and I'm confident the raven on Aspen's shoulder inclines its head. Aspen, herself ignores me. A lump rises in my throat, threatening to choke me from the inside. The males present quickly dismiss themselves, but their heartbeats don't drift far enough to be out of earshot. Drawing closer, beneath the shadow of the leaves, I see

Aspen's hair is not pebble gray like Orianna's but a stark white to her waist.

"Aspen," I start, but trail off because what else is there to say? Only when she peers up do I see my sole contribution to her existence. Midnight blue eyes that blaze a path of fire into my very soul. Multiple emotions shine from within, but anger is the most prominent. I can't help but crack my first hint of a smile in years. With the clench of her jaw and the rigidness of her small frame, I'm taken back to a place I'd long since forgotten.

Orianna was the epitome of beauty, her petite frame exuding regal grace and formidable strength. Shifters and vampires had always been mortal enemies, but she defied every obstacle and introduced me to the true depths of passion. And then, just as suddenly, she shattered me—leaving behind no remnants of the vampire or king I had once been. For years, I attempted to gather the fragments of my soul and piece them back together, but they never quite fit as they used to. I will forever be broken, but for that brief, exhilarating moment in time, it was utterly worth it.

"I, um," I clear my throat. "I apologize for any inconvenience that may have been caused to you during these past years, I was unaware of your-" Aspen snorts and rolls her eyes, which is a grave insult for a king, but I can forgive her insolence for a while. Taking a deep breath, I move forward and gesture to the empty space on the bench. She doesn't react, so I take a seat. The raven stays, and even without being told about his shape-shifting abilities, I can tell who and what he is. If Aspen has been assigned a guardian like her mother, it's clear that she holds significant importance in the supernatural world, just as I had suspected.

Exhaling, I knot my fingers together. There are no right words, nothing that'll give us back the thirty-odd years I've missed. But the best I can give her now is the truth and hope it's enough.

"She was really something, your mother. I want you to know that my involvement with her wasn't a power move, not on my behalf, at least. It isn't easy for me to admit out loud, but I would have offered your mother the moon if she'd let me retrieve it for her. Orianna made her choice, and I have respected that all these years. But if I'd known about you. If I'd know what you'd been subjected to..." I glance over in time to catch a glimpse just as a tear slides down Aspen's cheek before she turns away, and a pang of pain pierces through my fractured soul, yearning to soothe her anguish. My own flesh and blood, suffering from a life she never should have been forced to lead.

I attempt to clear my throat, "I truly hope Conall wasn't too harsh on either of you when he discovered the truth."

My throat tightens as I nearly choke on Conall's name, bile rising in my throat. My fingers twist and contort until the skin around my knuckles stretches paper thin and bulges with rage. Memories of our last fight haunt me like a ghost, vivid and pulsating with life. We went for each other's throats, and Orianna acted as the rope that pulled us apart, her words a blade that splintered me from the inside out. I chose him, Lorcan. Leave us be. Blinded by heartache, I stumbled away, shattered into a million pieces — never to look back. But here I stand now, wishing I had fought harder to stay.

"Conall was the best father I could have ever hoped for," Aspen's voice is small, vulnerable. "He taught me to love and laugh, to hunt and fight. He would let me ride on his wolf's back under every full moon since I was old enough to sit upright. We used to dance around the campfire and hike mountains to map the stars. He was my teacher and guide, and he loved my mother with a ferocity I've never seen in others." As she intended, a stab of anguish digs deeply into my heart, but I manage to refrain from letting it show. Just. Aspen twists to stare straight into my eyes, hers beginning to glow softly as her temper rises.

"And then it all ended because of you. My wolf was unleashed on my thirteen birthday, along with another beast I refuse to acknowledge. I drained and killed a quarter of the pack before realizing what I was doing. That night, I saw Conall's heartbreak and his love for me vanish instantly. Almost...almost as if I had imagined my entire life before that moment," she laughs bitterly.

"Sometimes I wish it were a dream because then it wouldn't have hurt as much as it did to see that light fade from the eyes of the man who I thought hung the very stars himself. But that night, I was banished to the exile hut, cut off from the others, and completely disowned. I was a scandal he couldn't stand the sight of."

Another tear escapes her eye which she angrily swipes away with the back of her hand. Aspen takes a steadying breath, battling her instincts to lash out. Affection isn't my natural state, yet I yearn to pull Aspen into my arms and protect her from the outside world, even if I'm inadvertently the cause of her suffering. However, my only crime was loving her mother deeply enough to respect her wishes. Does that make a fool or an asshole? I open my mouth the respond, but Aspen cuts me off, her voice spiked with venom.

"I realize that the blame doesn't rest solely with you, but my mother isn't here to defend herself anymore, so you'll receive every ounce of my hatred on her behalf." Her words cut me deeply, but it's her expression which hurts the most—barely contained rage, fangs exposed with a growl emanating from deep within her chest. On a lasting snarl, she shoots away in a blur of speed, leaving me to deal with the information and heaviness she's imparted.

"Well...that could have gone better," Chase comments, stepping into the moonlight. "Ow, the fuck?!" He hisses as Torsten yanks his head back by his hair, and Jaxon punches him in the jaw. I ignore them all, leaning forward to rest my bare forearms on my knees and choosing to stare at the ground beneath my polished black shoes. Thoughts whirl—emotions war. Many revolutions were just unknowingly spoken of.

Eight years ago, a raven transformed in my bedroom, her words carrying like sledgehammers as she spoke of Orianna's sudden illness and the consequences. I heard of a child of both species but was oblivious to Conall's misconception that Aspen was his real daughter. Never taught to accept her vampire side, and she now suffers from it.

What was Orianna thinking? That staying within her betrothed's realm would keep the peace between our species? That he'd be a better father than me? If only she had asked for help - I could have given them sanctuary and treated them like the royalty they were.

"We will get her back," Jaxon kneels before me, determination darkening his blue eyes. I can only nod, my throat too tight to speak, and press down on his shoulder in silent command, go after Aspen and take all these idiots with you.

More blurs race passed, leaving me alone with the gentle crashing from the waterfall. My brain works overtime as old wounds reopen and emotions barrel through me. Grief is the strongest, closely followed by confusion. A shuffle sounds at my side, and I glance across at the small raven, tilting his head towards me. Offering my hand, he hops onto my wrist, closely noting the torment tearing at my features.

"Sawyer, isn't it?" I ask, and he nods. "I met your mother briefly. She told me you would keep Aspen safe, and for that, I thank you. You are welcome at my castle, and none of the vampires will mean you any harm after I give the order. Please just...help her adjust," I plead. An immortal king pleading to a damn bird. Yet this is my life now. Sweeping out my hand, Sawyer spreads his wings to take flight, soaring from the greenhouse toward the hidden cabin—the same one I built to share my life with Orianna.

Branches grab my hair, and shrubs latch onto my combat boots, but there's no stopping. No holding back the blur of rage, flying through the forest like a bullet lost to the wind. Only when my feet hit the beach beyond the cabin do I falter and stumble to stop. The softness of sand gives way beneath my soles, and I crash to my knees, permitting the tears to finally fall.

I hate him. How accepting he was. How he *apologized* for the inconvenience that is my life. I'd wanted him to be an asshole, validating me for cursing him every day since I discovered who and what I was. But now...now I'm left with self-loathing for not reaching out to the vampires sooner. I let my pride and stubbornness in what my mother tried to build get in the way. In conclusion, I've only done myself a disservice.

You should have let me in, the internal voice mocks, and I slap myself around the face. I can't handle any more anger as my eyes burst with gold, and my fangs extend painfully. I want to rip the nearest piece of flesh to shreds, devouring screams and feeding on agony. I would have done it to the king himself if his understanding hadn't blindsided me.

"Conall, please let me see her!" my own scream reverberates around my head. Smoke invades my lungs from the huge fire in the center of camp, the sound of screams filling my ears. Separated or not, the pack loved the alpha's mate. Her nurturing nature is evident in the crowd gathered around her cabin, chanting, and rocking for a miracle. Then there's the firm shoulder, shoving me back a step.

"You need to go," Conall's psycho apprentice growls. Black of hair and soul, his wolf rolls just beneath the surface of two huge arms shoving me back a step. The rules of my banishment were absolute. My mother could visit me, 'at her own risk,' but I was never to enter the pack's camp again.

Even still, knowing that I might not get another chance, I fight and refuse back down.

"Father, please!" I scream again, pushing back with all my might. Only then does the commanding male on a fallen log-carved bench stand. Thick fur capes hang from his shoulders, enhancing his huge size. Dark-cropped hair and blue eyes highlighted by the raging fire in the center of the camp. Turning slowly, an evil and loveless man stands mere feet away, but there might as well be miles between us.

This Conall isn't the same shifter who raised me or the only father I had ever known. His cold eyes barely register me crying and pleading for his attention. If only I'd been the powerful wolf, he'd always dreamt I'd be. The fact that I am that and more doesn't matter; I'm not his and he couldn't stand the sight of me after my first shift into the monster that I am.

"I'm no father of yours. Get her the fuck out of here, Kofu."

Falling back into the sand, I'm slammed into the present, although the searing pain of the past lingers, all too real. Tainting my veins, causing my blood flow to sizzle beneath the surface. The illness passed through her system swiftly. From healthy to lifeless within two days, her body dumped on the steps of the exile hut for me to deal with.

Like that night, a pair of tiny talons drop onto my shoulder. When I held her to me, she was cold and pale, with cracked lips and eyes drained of color. After burying her, I unleashed my wolf, giving her complete control whilst I hid from the world in her furry cocoon. There's no telling how long for, but I do know Sawyer stayed the entire time. When I ran, he soared overhead. When I curled up and whined, he curled into my fur.

"Don't leave me," I whisper into the soft breeze. I can bury my past, concealing my grief. I'm well-practiced. But losing Sawyer now isn't a reality I would survive.

The sound of a steady drum of a heartbeat, soon joined by two more, reaches me. Apparently, the vampires following couldn't hang back any longer. Jax's earthy scent, crisp with an underlying sweetness, rolls over me first. I raise my head from my palms and look straight ahead, thankful that the tears have finally stopped and the numbness has settled back in. He settles into the sand on my left, the other two dropping on my right. Chase outstretches his legs like he's in a spa, all of us content to sit beneath the moon.

Gentle waves roll back and forth under a blanket of midnight blue embedded with glimmering stars. The lunar face shining down at its own reflection in the water soothes us all until the easing beat of my heart falls into rhythm with those nearby, and my thoughts drift away. A hypnotic trance lost to the waves.

"Let's place a wager." Chase's sudden words make me flinch, his deep voice at odds with the serenity of our surroundings. Quirking a brow around Torsten, his green eyes seek out mine. His face is relaxed, the glow from above accentuating the harsh lines of his cheekbones and jaw. Tilting his chin upwards, he purposely gives me a clear view of the fluttering pulse in the side of his neck.

My fangs extend, and my eyes start to glow before I'm able to snap them closed. But it's too late. I've latched onto the sound of blood rushing through his veins and the scent of leather creeping beneath the salty breeze. Crippling hunger tears through me, my nerve endings sparking for another hit of Chase. Too akin to addiction for my liking.

"What kind of wager?" I manage to croak out, facing forward to avoid his probing stare.

"If you catch me before sunrise, you can have the master bedroom." Chase chuckles. My heart stutters. A race? No, not a race – a hunt.

"Ha!" Jaxon pitches in from the other side. "I'm not missing out on this. We can all outrun Aspen until sunrise. Count me in." Another stutter. A shrill of excitement races along my spine.

Sawyer tightens his claws on my shoulder while Torsten grunts, dropping his arms over his knees. "I'll raise you one better. I bet I can evade Aspen in wolf form." At this, my head snaps to him so quickly that my hair whips me around the face. Torsten's eyes are sparkling with mischief. I steel myself, not melting into those gray depths. His white hair, cropped at the sides and left longer on top, tosses about in the wind. My hesitation doesn't go unnoticed, but a quirk of his brow brings me back to the present.

"And if, for some reason, I don't manage to catch you?" I ask, taking shallow breaths. My wolf quivers with excitement, just as she does when anticipating a full shift. A slow smile stretches across Chase's full lips as I lean forward.

"*When* you lose, you have to kiss one of us. A little kiss-*Chase*, if you will." My smile spreads to copy his as Chase's eye glistens, his tongue passing between his parted teeth. He knows what he's doing. Giving me the perfect outlet for my anger, shaking the weight of bone-deep stress. The wind changes behind me as Sawyer shifts, his legs appearing on either side of me in thick, black material. Heavy boots push into the sand, and strong arms wrap around me.

"Think about this," he growls into my ear. "Once you shift, your wolf takes over. She'll act on base instinct, hunt for the kill." A raw chuckle leaves me, the ache to stretch my wolfy legs already taking over.

"I know that, but these vampires reckon they can handle it. Besides," I twist my head to grace lips with Sawyer's. "You can't be jealous if you don't participate." Both beasts inside snicker, in harmony for once. Timidness may have won without their approval, but there's no backing down now. Sawyer's breath fans my face, his black hair sweeping low and tickling us both. On either side of my arms, I can feel the vampires drawing closer, shuffling into the reckless decision I'm about to make.

"Deal." Standing, I stretch my neck and crack my fingers. "You all should take the chance at a head start," I gesture back towards the tree line of the forest with my chin, striding towards the sea. A round of groans sounds, and when I turn, four huge alpha males are standing and facing me. Strong arms crossed over chests; eyes zeroed onto my body.

"Hell no," Jaxon mutters. "We're not missing this for anything." Heat crawls up my neck and into my cheeks. I've never had one male's undivided attention before, let alone four. They're fascinated, thrumming with anticipation, as if I'm all that matters to them at this moment in time.

Kicking off my boots one at a time with the opposite foot, I hook my thumbs into my waistband and push the cargos down to the sand, stepping free. Then, I lift the hem of my vest and pull it over my head, chucking it aside and avoiding all eye contact. I'm comfortable with my naked body, being a shifter, and needing to shed my clothes regularly, but this is different. Under the guise of their stares and the moon, I'm thoroughly exposed for my nakedness and all the other secrets I try to hide.

Pulses quicken. The scent of his arousal penetrates the air. It's a heady combination from multiple sources, filling my senses until a lust of my own overpowers me. Raising my gaze, I focus on Sawyer. He must have seen me like this hundreds of times, yet his fixed expression breaks me—strained, his jaw tight enough to crack a tooth. Onyx eyes with no hint of white consume me, pulling me into their inky depths. I take an unplanned step forward, the rest of the world fading. And then, before I do something stupid, I sharply turn to stare at the moon. Relenting to the lunar pull dragging my wolf to the surface, I start my shift.

My nails sharpen and grow into claws, white fur seeping from my skin. Abruptly, my back cracks, bending me in half. Every bone snaps, extends, and reforms, one after the other. Pain ripples through me as my body contorts at awkward angles. Yet, despite the agony, I barely release a whimper. I'm accustomed to the discomfort of shifting since I've experienced it more than the average shifter would in their entire lifetime.

Reshaped by the new alignment, my nose stretches forward to form a muzzle while a tail bursts free from the base of my spine, sweeping the sandy floor as my teeth stretch and sharpen. I rear forward, four large white paws finding the sand as I shake out my new fluffy exterior.

I've caught my reflection in the river before, and I know I'm not the average wolf. Compared to my mother's gray-speckled fur, mine isn't just white but luminescent. I'm the embodiment of the moon, glowing as currents of power move through me. My fangs are twice as long and twice as deadly, my eyes molten gold as the vampire within me shines through. Along with the additional speed and strength other shifters aren't blessed with, I'm a force to be reckoned with, and I don't know why I've kept myself caged this long.

Strolling in a lazy circle to assess the figures before me, my mind recognizes them individually, but all my wolf can acknowledge are the delicious scents. Fresh pine, leather, and honeydew hit me tenfold, my tongue hanging out desperately for a taste. Jaxon steps in front of the rest, every bit the commander of his army. My wolf bristles and croons at the same time. Jaxon is everything we would hunt for in a mate; strong, fierce, yet understanding and considerate. My inner monster also approves, but we're getting ahead of ourselves thinking of mates. Tonight, we just need a distraction—a reason to feel alive and possibly wanted by another creature.

The vampires are equally as impatient, their fangs bared and snarling at the ready for a long-perceived foe. Through it all, Chase's shit-eating grin is dazzling just before he shoots away, the others right behind, disappearing into the forest beyond. Let the games begin.

Chapter Eight

Chase

By the moon, she's magnificent. Even before she shifted, her lithe body had my pulse racing. Where the vampire females are all six-foot-tall and stick thin, Aspen is shorter and a thousand times sexier—curving in the right places, an expanse of creamy skin from the dip at her waist to the flares of her hips. Her perky breasts are the perfect size to fit in my hands, well-defined abs showing through. Practically drooling, I had to clench my fists to stop myself from grabbing her and driving her into the sand beneath me.

She tilted her face to be bathed in the pale moon's light, appearing like a goddess. An ethereal being put on this earth to cross my path and tempt me with her perfect body and spunky attitude. And then, she shifted.

CHASE

Her wolf is bigger than I expected, at eye level whilst on all four huge paws. A coat of white covers her impressive form, two rows of sharp teeth, including the protruding fangs, glinting in the moonlight, and her eyes...holy shit. Her navy irises are now glowing orbs of gold. She's no ordinary wolf; she is truly a mix of both genetics that created her. And damn if she looks hungry.

I shoot away, leaving the sand far behind to dart between tree trunks. Good thing I fed back at the castle while she was talking to Lorcan, or I'd have been out of this race before it had even started. I'm under no illusion in my mind that, between her wolf and vampire speed, Aspen will catch me eventually. But this game is akin to foreplay, and she'll beg for a kiss by the night's end. True, I'm under strict orders not to fornicate with the princess. That luxury is to be kept for her betrothed, but I can't help if she comes onto me. Hunts me down and lets her animalistic side take over.

Turning sharply, creating a path with my scent, I run one way and another. Diving through thick plants and rounding back on the way, I came in an attempt to throw off Aspen's wolf for a while. The rocky ground beneath me barely moves under the swift speed of my feet. Birds flock from the trees in panic as I crash through bushes, not bothering to mask my sounds. There's no escaping the hybrid, and I really don't want to anyway. Let her get hot and hungry, yearning for me alone.

The glimmer of water up ahead catches my eye, and I head toward it before throwing myself high into the air and landing on the other side of the stream. Landing in a crouch, I stay low behind a bush and wait for the wolf to appear—adrenaline coursing through my body, an unwavering smile pulling at my mouth. I know Aspen could have caught me already, so is she toying with me now or not coming at all? Although I sensed the hunger within her; she wants this just as much as I do. Heavy footfalls from the others pound into the distance, the caw of a raven overhead. Pussy couldn't beat her on foot, so he's soaring through the night.

A flash of white zooms in front of me at a rate I can barely track. Damn, she really is fast. On the opposite side of the stream, the wolf paces along the bank, keeping its golden eyes locked on me. Grinning, I lean down with my hand cupped and quickly splash the cool water into her face. During her flinch and the brief close of her eyes, I vault myself upwards and grab onto a branch, pulling myself up and leaping to an adjacent one.

The wolf below shakes her head, the wiggle making its way all the way down her back and finishing with a wag of her tail. Looking around for a second, her head whips upwards to see me perching on the branch above. With a howl, she leaps over the river and jumps against the thick trunk holding me, leaving deep gashes in the bark. I laugh loudly, the noise echoing around the forest as I stand and hop from branch to branch. Following beneath, I keep the luminescent animal in my peripheral vision as she jumps up, trying to snap at my ankles.

The next branch cracks beneath my weight, and I hurdle toward the forest floor. A pair of solid forearms catch my flailing body midair, Torsten tossing me back on my feet to run side by side. The wolf is hot on our heels, howling to the moon.

"As if I'm going to let you win that easily, if at all," he growls, slapping the back of my head. I can only laugh, preferring to make Aspen work for me anyway. We navigate the forest, covering miles in mere minutes. After a while, it becomes apparent we're no longer being chased and slow to a stop.

"Now, see what you did. She's gone for Jaxon," I sigh. Torsten rolls his gray eyes.

"Jaxon has enough honor not to break the cardinal rule. None of us can claim her yet. We need to prove ourselves worthy in the king's eyes." This time my sigh turns into a full-on groan. Don't get me wrong, following orders is what got me to be the army's second in command. I've been a loyal vamp my entire existence...but there's something about her. Something freeing, raw, and brazenly beautiful. If there ever was a time to throw out tradition and make sure she sees me, this is it.

Resting my boot against a boulder, I straighten the t-shirt I had to don after Aspen scratched the shit out of my back. The scores have finally healed, but the fact that she could harm me so deeply is interesting in itself. Torsten rests against a trunk, assessing me too closely.

"I'd forget what you're thinking if I were you," he warns. Good thing there's only one Chase, then, isn't it? "You know as well as I do that the few females we possess must marry for strength. When the future of our species is at stake, Lorcan can't afford to make foolish decisions." And speaking of mistakes, our king is making many by ignoring whatever is happening to him. Those he permits entry into his office noticed long ago that something is affecting Lorcan. Physically and mentally, but he's 'dealing with it' by hiding away. Pushing off the boulder, I spear Torsten's chest with my finger.

"The funny thing, Torst," I quirk a brow, and he slaps my hand away, "is you thinking we *possess* those women at all. I say let them choose who to moon bond with. It's their lives to live."

"Very insightful, but I'm afraid we don't have the time for such luxury. Mates can be born centuries apart, and without the females baring children – the likelihood those mates are born at all is slimming." A soft scratching from above draws my attention to the raven hidden within the shadows of the autumn leaves. Sneaky fucker.

"I say we drain that bird of blood before roasting him for fun," I grin, and Torsten laughs, suddenly back on the same page as we clamber up the tree.

Chapter Nine

Sawyer

Not happening. Not on my fucking life.

First, we've entered some ridiculous hunting game when Aspen is most vulnerable. Now I catch those two knuckleheads talking of arranged marriages and the future of the vampire species. Something isn't right about the timing and urgency of kidnapping Aspen after all these years of ignoring her existence. And there's no fucking way I'll allow one of them to kiss her tonight.

Flying above the trees, I gain a wide enough view to follow the blur of luminescent white through the forest. I had to learn quickly how to track her when she was at full speed, and the key is height. Swooping low, crisp leaves scratch at my feathers as I tuck my wings into my body. My talons latch onto the scruff at her neck, tugging me along for the ride as I spot her target. A flash of pale muscle, the trial of brown braids. She's hunting Jaxon and rapidly closing the gap.

I can't let that happen. I can't let her catch him or allow the cascade of events that would take place if she does. With her wolf calling the shots and her emotions still raw from meeting her father, she'll either screw or kill him. Possibly both. As her guardian, I must save her from herself at the best times.

The wolf whips her large head aside, snapping for me. I release her fur, spreading my wings wide to lift high into the air. Safely out of biting range. Up ahead, Jaxon diverts left, launches himself onto a trunk, and backflips over Aspen. Landing in a crouch, he flashes a fang and spurts away, with Aspen eagerly following behind. I know what they're doing. Enticing her. Ensuring she gets the thrill of the hunt before relenting and taking advantage. Not on my damn watch.

This time when I swoop towards the wolf, I shift mid-air. My wings spread wider, the trench coat clinging to my arms billowing. Instead of landing on Aspen, I barrel into her. A heavy mass of fur and limbs rolling through the dirt, punctuated by the deep rumble of growling. Round my arm around her neck, I wrestle to subdue the wolf whilst grunting in her ear.

"Shift back, dammit," I toss her into the forest floor. The wolf jumps up, lunging for me. She dives into the underarm of my trench coat, her teeth missing my ribs by mere inches. Shedding the sleeves, I wrap them around her head and land my knee into her gut. "Aspen. Come back to me." Stilling, the wolf pants. Lowering her head, she whines, and I release her from the confines of my coat. Crouching down, I stare into the golden eye assessing me and reach up to stroke behind her ear. "That's it, Pumpkin. It's me."

I exhale heavily, flapping out my coat to encase her naked body when she shifts back. Tonight took a turn I wasn't expecting, but it's done now. The wolf shakes her fur the way she does when preparing to shift back, except she doesn't make it that far. Lashing out suddenly, the wolf's jaw clamps down on my neck, squeezing shut. I freeze in shock, remaining perfectly still. Those golden eyes watch me closely, her teeth sinking into my flesh a millimeter more to gauge my reaction. I don't give her one.

No screaming or reams of panic. No fear for her to feast on. The wetness of her tongue lazily slides across my skin, lapping up any blood I have spilt. A shudder rolls through her spine, her following moan too human-like to have come from the wolf. In the next second, she's gone. Dashing through the trees with a chunk of my throat in her mouth and the last flash of her tail disappearing from sight.

I tumble aside, gripping my neck. Blood gushes between my fingers, the thud of my pulse slowing as my body prepares to heal. Going into a state of hibernation, I can only lie here, lost to the forest's shadows. Had it been any other creature to cause me harm, I'd have healed instantly and continued fighting. But not where hybrid wounds are concerned.

A twig cracks somewhere nearby. I heave onto my back, hoping to see my attacker before they strike. Whoever it is doesn't near, watching my struggle from a distance. A gurgled choke erupts from my mouth, a bubbling trail of blood seeping between my lips as I feel the tendons in my neck begin to stitch back together. It's a painfully slow process. Especially considering that Aspen is nearby in a feral state, and I'm supposed to guard her. Eventually, I'm able to sit upright and inhale large gulps of air, filling my lungs to capacity before exhaling.

Looking around, Aspen is nowhere to be seen. I focus my hearing, but in this form, I can't quite place her fast-paced heartbeat amongst the other animals in the forest. Her unique wolf scent isn't close by either. I've lost her—no doubt to the fanged monsters who have used reverse psychology to trick her into kissing them. The Aspen I know would have run back to the cabin and already be asleep in the bed, refusing to be bated. But her wolf relies on base instinct. Driven by the need to hunt and consume.

Suddenly, a flash of white rushes towards me from the left at an un-trackable speed. I turn to face her head-on as she collides with me, sending us both flying and skidding through the mud. Before I can even think about the pain racing up my spine, her heavy form lands on me, cracking at least two of my ribs.

Aspen presses her front paws down on my shoulders, pushing me further into the dirt. Bared teeth on show, a growl emanating deep within her chest. This is the wolf I've come to recognize, and she is astounding. A lethal beast of such magnificence. A spirited female caged by her cross-breeding.

"You're so fucking beautiful," I breathe. Despite wheezing, while my ribs knit themselves back together, I reach a hand up and stroke the soft fur behind her ear again. She immediately snaps at me, just short of taking off my fingers. I soothe her with soft sounds, allowing her to recognize me as not the enemy. A few minutes pass, a battle for self-control and conflict raging behind her golden eyes.

The crack of a bone shatters the tension between us. Instantly checking myself over, I soon discover it wasn't one of mine. Another crack follows until a symphony of breaking bones returns the Aspen I've longed to see. Firmly pinning down my shoulders, her lips hovering inches above mine. She's panting heavily, which has nothing to do with her shift. Retaining their glow, her eyes become hooded as I trail my hand through her hair. Aspen tries to suppress a groan as I massage her scalp, a fang tearing into her bottom lip in the process. The scent of my blood on her tongue plows into me like a freight train, the most intoxicating aroma of us mingling filling my senses.

I can feel my control slipping away like water from a broken dam. An unstoppable wave of desire takes its place as I am overcome by the need to have her, to keep her, and own her completely. My primal urges demand satisfaction, and I give in with reckless abandon. My hands snake around her waist and lock her against me as my lips crash down on hers.

"I-shit, Aspen," I mutter against her lips. "I'm so sorry-" her lips slam onto mine—a feverish need claiming us both as we fight to get closer to each other. Our kiss quickly turns desperate and passionate, her body undulating over mine with a delicious friction that I can feel through my cargos. My hands move all over her like they have a will of their own, exploring every curve. The craving to have her here and now rises up fast and strong within me, threatening to consume us both.

My lips crash against hers, tasting the sweet nectar of her blood. I'm not one for such a craving but there's something about her that makes me feel like I'll never be able to deny it. The kiss grows more passionate, a frenzy of tongues fighting for dominance. Aspen holds my face with an ironclad grip and drags her nails through my hair, sending shivers down my spine.

Before I can notice what she's doing, her fangs sink into the vein of my neck. She drinks deeply and hungrily, each pull drawing out an animalistic growl from me. My hands slip around her waist to press our bodies together tighter as she drinks in my pleasure.

My eyes roll back in ecstasy; this is entirely new to me, yet so familiar at the same time. This moment between us is chaotic and wild, feral and alluring. It's clear - undeniable now - that Aspen has enthralled me from the first day we met. Anything for her; to protect her, win her, belong to her.

A rumbling stirs my senses, and I force myself awake to see the star-spangled night sky above. The moon is a bright beacon, piercing through the thick clouds like a lighthouse guiding me into danger. Like a bucket of ice-cold water poured over my skin, I suddenly lurch upright, away from Aspen.

"Fuck!" I gasp, half-shoving Aspen off me. Her hurt navy eyes bore into mine as she looks at me incredulously. "Oh no, I didn't mean..."

"Shit, Aspen...I..."My hands hover in midair, my instincts telling me to touch her again—to make amends somehow — but I don't trust myself. I'm afraid if I do, I'll never be able to let go.

A throat clears through the trees, and I spin on my heel to witness a figure cloaked in darkness in a large trench coat, just like mine.

Without warning, pain sears across my cheek as Aspen slaps me. Her navy eyes filled with hurt and loathing. She spins and takes off in the opposite direction. While part of me wants to chase after her to explain everything, as I look towards the figure in the shadows, towards the senior member of the Supernatural Council, I know it's too late - there's no going back now.

With one last fleeting look over my shoulder at Aspen's receding form, the feel of Aspen still lingering on my skin like an unforgettable scent, I turn-- knowing that despite wanting her, refusing the council wasn't an option.

"Where's bird brain?" Chase chuckles, along with Torsten and Jax, leaning against the cabin.

"Get fucked," I groan, stomping through the open front door before sunrise.

It took me most of the night to exhaust my wolf and inner monster of their conflicting desires. Sawyer's kiss and the heady spill of his blood left me high, intoxicated, and craving for more. Transitioning from feeding on one human a month to three supernaturals in the span of just a few days probably wasn't the best idea, but fuck if I don't want more. But then came Sawyer's sudden dismissal, and my wolf's wounded pride was just as formidable to suppress. Now I'm naked, filthy, and about to be locked inside a cabin for the best part of twelve hours with these cocky assholes.

My feet land heavily on each wooden step of the stairs and through the master bedroom to the en-suite. Tossing my white hair over my shoulder, I step into the shower, uncaring of the temperature. All that matters is scrubbing away a night's worth of adrenaline and rejection whilst my fangs throb. I groan, slamming my head against the wet tile.

"Haven't you had enough?!"

This is only the beginning, the voice in my head replies. I drown out its chuckle, clawing shampoo through my hair. Only when I'm thoroughly rinsed clean of dirt, and my body has been washed vigorously with a rough sponge, do I step out of the shower. The mirror above is coated with droplets of condensation, but my reflection stares back perfectly. And I don't like what I see—pointed white teeth that refuse to retract hanging over my bottom lip and my navy eyes a shade brighter than I was used to. My skin appears paler and flawless, blending into my white hair. Even my muscles appear slightly thicker, with a clear line of definition below my biceps. I'm becoming one of them.

You're becoming your true self, that voice pipes up again. I shake it loose. This is all happening too fast. I'm changing quicker than I can track, and I worry that I'll wake up and not know who or what I am. I'll be the monster I've kept caged for so long. Groaning, a fang cuts my lip, and the door flies open.

"What's wrong? I smell blood," Jaxon bursts inside the room in a blur and grips my face in his large hands. He doesn't realize I'm butt naked and damp until it's too late, his labored breathing against my face mixing with the sudden plume of arousal penetrating the air.

"I'm fine," I frown, tearing my head from his grip. Wrapping a towel around my middle, I quickly exit before my body takes control of my actions without my consent. Only to find two exceptionally large, extremely ripped vampires lying across the bed wearing nothing but a pair of boxers and intrigued smirks.

"I'm seriously not in the mood," I sigh. "Just be gentlemen for once and fuck off."

"Nah ah Princess, you didn't win the bet," Chase shakes his head slowly enough for his hazelnut brown locks to shift in steady waves. "You didn't catch any of us, so it's time for your forfeit." Puckering his lips.

I plaster a smile and shrug. "You're right. Deal's a deal." I allow my towel to fall free. Jaxon steps forward of his own accord, his sheer alpha power skating across the skin at my back. Both vampires on the bed drop their mirth-filled expressions, nostrils flaring and pupils dilating. Strolling with an exaggerated sway of my hips, I crawl up the bed to be sandwiched between Chase and Torsten.

Yes, my inner voice hisses. She guides my movements, pushing my chest out to faintly connect with Chase's. His long hair pools over the forearm, holding him up, his tattoos on full display. From war scenes to a language I don't understand, he is covered from neck to waistband and beyond. As are the other two in the room, breathing so heavily, their desperation is palpable. I feed on it, inhaling the sweet scent of eager dominance. But the only one that matters here, is mine.

My arm moves faster than Chase can track as I grab his heavy balls through his boxers and squeeze hard. At the same time, I throw my head backward to connect with Torsten's face, the crunch as orgasmic as kissing them would have been.

Dirty liar, the beast inside groans while my wolf howls with delight. Landing my elbow in Torsten's ribs, I arch my back to shove him back the way he's unknowingly shuffled until I broke his nose. Clamping my hand tighter around Chase's balls, I'm sure I felt a pop as I growl into his shocked face.

"Get the fuck out of my bed so I can get some beauty sleep. You really don't want to test me when I'm sleep deprived." And damn him, Chase cracks the hint of a smile.

"Oh, I really do," he mutters. With a gasp, Chase rips himself from my grip and rolls off the side of the bed, crotch in hand. Torsten doesn't bother trying to fight further, retreating with a blood-smeared face as he and Chase leave the room like a pair of wounded soldiers.

Dropping my head back on the cushions, I sigh before picking up on Jaxon's heartbeat from beside the bathroom door. Piercing blue eyes don't leave mine, his fingers twitching by his side. He takes a step closer, then another until he's leaning over the bed. Just as I open my mouth, ready with another threat, he lifts the covers and gently pulls them over me, tucking the cotton into my sides.

"You'd make a great addition to the vampire army if you weren't royalty," he whispers, and as I lie there, he places a single kiss on my forehead. "Sweet dreams, Aspen."

"If you're ready to move further within the castle, Princess," a sweet woman with hair as black as the raven shifter who's disappeared guides me through the botanical gardens.

"Please, just call me Aspen," I repeat for the hundredth time. She inclines her head and smiles, although I know she won't. The inner doors slide open, presenting the hallway of the east wing, and both me and the entourage at my back pause. Powerful scents tingle my nostrils uncomfortably, but thankfully the migraine doesn't return. Sighing in relief, I step over the threshold and realize I did so alone.

Catching sight of the three behind me, they incline their heads and stride back through the gardens the way we came. Suddenly, I feel exposed. Unprotected. Only the knowledge that at least Jaxon wouldn't have left if I was anything other than safe permits me to continue Morevan's tour.

"I've spoken with Nova, the king's assistant, about you having a patch of the garden to care for yourself, if you would like that?" the female enquires, her tone light and friendly. She's much taller than me, rivaling the height of the males, but where they are all brute strength and muscle,

Morevan is extremely thin. Even her voice sounds fragile, too soft to bounce off the stone castle walls.

"I would love that," I smile. I have yet to see the king again since I basically blamed him for ruining my mother's life, but I'm sure he wouldn't deny me the request of planting some white dead-nettles like the ones climbing my mother's gravestone. In fact, I reckon he'd allow me to create an entire memorial. If the hushed whispers between the vamps at the cabin are anything to go by, Lorcan needs me to move into the castle as soon as possible for some unknown reason, but with that comes a decent amount of leverage.

"This is our library," Morevan pushes a huge, curved door open. I should help, by the way her arms are shaking, but my jaw is too busy dropping to the ground. More books than I could have ever imagined line the curved hall, their floor-to-ceiling bookcases only interrupted by the circular windows up high. Alcoves of cushions have been created beneath each one, providing a true sanctuary for those needing an escape. Either side of the room has a brass, curving staircase leading to a second story of heaven.

"The female vampires take shifts throughout the east wing, but we all have our preferences. Mine is the garden," Morevan's warm brown eyes sparkle at the mere mention. Now, I notice those appearing between the bookshelves, equally as tall and slender as Morevan. I tug on the baggy hoodie I was provided, conscious of my larger breasts, ample curves, and thicker thighs.

"Do you think it possible for me to borrow some books to take back to the cabin? I can get the guys to take a stack each," I force a smile that Morevan doesn't reciprocate.

"Aside from the king, males aren't allowed in the east wing. Especially those in the army." I frown, a protective streak rising within before I can determine where it's coming from. Morevan's eyes widen, her head bowing of it's on accord. "Forgive me, I didn't mean to insult your candidates. What I meant to say was that this is our sanctuary. Away from those who are ruled by their primal urge to breed. It's for our safety." Morevan closes the library door, urging me to follow, but I remain frozen in place.

"What do you mean, candidates?" Morevan peers back, the small smile on her face slipping.

"For the Moon Bound trails," her voice drops, and her eyebrow hitches. "They have told you of the trails, surely?"

"Of course," I fake a smile, flapping my hand between us. "I just didn't realize everyone else knew."

"Oh," Morevan stifles a small laugh. We continue to walk, and this time, I keep up the pace to hang onto her every word. "The trials are an event for be sure, even for the common female like me, but yours - the entire castle has been preparing for years." Dread trickles through me.

"Years?" I search for the right thing to say. Whatever keeps her talking. "Wow, I didn't think it would be so...public."

"Naturally," Morevan inclines her head. "Only the best will do for the future king of our species. You, being the older princess. will put your future mate in line for the throne. It's why the king insisted the entire army must participate to ensure the strongest bloodline. And given that you are half shifter, you shouldn't bear the infertility problem the other vampire females suffer from. Tell me, is it true wolf-kind birth entire litters at once?" My gut twists, and my feet refuse to take another step. To my left, an elongated gallery presents my escape from Morevan's probing stare.

"Would you mind if I..." Words fail me as I try to be polite. Oh, screw it. "I need to be alone," I demand sharply. I hate myself for the vicious tone, but what's worse – Morevan doesn't flinch. She smiles, curtseys, and leaves while shame gnaws away at my insides. I'm not this privileged bitch they expect me to be. With royalty comes an expectation that one can be an outright dick that no one can challenge, but I never want to be that person. I just need a moment to compute everything she's unknowingly told me.

Candidates. Trials. Future king. My mate. *Other princess.*

Ducking through the door left ajar, I head for the bay window at the gallery's rear. The display room is filled with masterpieces, from paintings and sculptures to ceramics which must have been created in the females' art studios. The walls are lined with intricate flourishes of wood, carved from top to bottom between the canvases hanging on them.

Like all others I've seen, the ceiling is impossibly high, making me feel like an ant in a giant's world. This one, in particular, is breathtaking. Gold leaves travel around the edges and towards the center until they meet to form large flowers. Between artfully painted figures depicting the vampires at war, crystal chandeliers highlight the sculptures forming a line down the center.

One sculpture halts me in my tracks for reasons I can't quite pinpoint. Crafted from white marble, it portrays a girl lying on her side, her hair cascading over her face. Though her modesty remains intact, she appears vulnerable. Every detail, from the lifelike contours of her body to the silky texture of her hair, speaks to the artist's extraordinary skill. But it's the emotion emanating from the figure that truly captivates me. She embodies a sense of hopelessness, a feeling of isolation. Even though we share physical traits like her petite stature and curved frame, there's something... more... about her that resonates deeply within my soul.

I've been this girl before-- experienced that crushing hopelessness, the endless void yearning to be filled. As I stand here, gazing at her, long-forgotten emotions seep back into my chest, feelings that haven't haunted me as much lately. They'll never completely vanish, but there's a new sensation now—something light and airy that sends butterflies fluttering in my stomach.

A hand softly grips my shoulder the way Sawyer's claw would. My heart squeezes painfully, so much that I don't even care who is behind me. He shifts, dragging across my fluttering pulse, causing me to shiver. The roughness of those fingertips speaks of years of violence, but the gentleness speaks directly to my inner beast. She rears her ugly head, taking control of my actions. I press my cheek against the back of the hand as it cups my jaw and take a moment to let Torsten's scent wash over me, breathing him in as if he could douse the negative feelings within.

"Forgive me. I shouldn't be here," he whispers into my ear.

"So why are you?" I reply just as quietly. He's breaking rules to be here with me and damn if I can't appreciate how out of character that is for him.

"I don't have an answer to that question, just like you don't have a reason for not pushing me away yet." The word 'yet' lingers in the air. Surprisingly, Torsten guides me towards the expansive bay window over-looking the sea and leads me into a concealed alcove at the back of the room. Nestled between the window and the wall behind him, he wraps his arm around my waist, his cheek brushing against mine.

"From the moment we parted, my soul has been desperate to return to you, to make sure you're okay. But you weren't. I could feel it. Actually, I don't think you've been okay since the race last night."

"Since when has your soul cared about me?" I deflect. A spike of anger rolls through me that must have come from my wolf. How dare Torsten appear like this now, all soft embraces and perfect words, to screw with my already jumbled thoughts.

Perhaps he's been trying to do just that since the beginning, and you've refused to let him in. I tut at myself, preparing to throw Torsten's arms as far away from me as possible.

"Oh, I've cared, Aspen." My name is a sin on his tongue—a beautiful crime against my psyche. My hands grip his, and after a brief struggle with my self-control, I pull him tighter. Enveloping myself in his strong arms and trying not to wonder what he's been up to for his sudden change in attitude. Turning my head into his fresh t-shirt, I inhale but can't scent another female on him – so that rules out one theory.

"Then why wait until now to tell me?"

"I don't think you've been ready to hear it. And I get it. Jaxon is charm-ing, Chase is the loveable asshole. You needed an asshole to take your frus-trations out on, and I was happy to be of service. Whatever it takes to hold your interest just that little bit longer." Staring at the moon hanging from a star-filled midnight sky, we remain quiet. Still, just as it did on the beach, my heart falls into rhythm with his. It should probably freak me out, but it is likely to be a vampire trait over anything else.

But nothing this easy can last. I can't allow myself to fall into the perfect slot between Torsten's arms and pretend the rest of the world doesn't exist. I can't allow myself to be won like a second-hand prize and handed over to the biggest brute. I thought the shifter camp's rules were dated, but the vampires are outright archaic. My only saving grace are the romance novels that my mother would sneak to me from the human world to know any different. Perhaps those false notions of love will be my downfall, but my heart knows I don't want to be a consolation.

"How do I know anything is real? Aren't I just a prize to be won? Maybe it's not even about me, but about becoming king." Torsten merely chuckles, lowering his head so that his lips hover near my collarbone, not quite kissing me but tantalizingly close.

"I suppose the truth is out," he sighs but I catch a glimpse of his smirk as I pull away from his embrace. Turning to face his sheepish gray eyes, Torsten reaches for me, but I cross my arms, creating a barrier between us.

"Believe me, being king is a burden none of us desire. If you'd asked me last week, I would have told you I secretly dreaded the idea of being mated to a hybrid and then having to rule by her side." He lowers his head with a sigh, understanding that whatever was happening between us has reached its end, at least for now. "And now?" I urge. Torsten looks at me from underneath his sweep of white hair.

"Now I want to win, and not for bragging rights. I want to win you." The air rushes from my lungs, all inhibitions washing away with the next stroke of Torsten's knuckles on my arm. He silently asks for my permission, and I don't deny him. My wolf whines, refusing to submit while the inner beast leans forward, presenting herself with a coy hint of a smile on my lips. I try to reign her back, but it's too late. Torsten holds me close, lowering his face to brush his jaw over my cheek. A hand wraps into my hair, tugging my head back to stare into his eyes. Desire radiates from every pore, his full lips parted enough for his fangs to poke through.

Take us, the voice begs. She's stronger than before, more stubborn to being suppressed. Her urges are primal, and she wants Torsten. My tongue darts out to lick my lips, causing his gaze to zero in. Target locked; lips loaded. Lowering his head with painful slowness, my eyes flutter closed as the faintest brush of his mouth graces mine.

"Well, isn't this cozy?" Chase's chuckle echoes around the gallery. The second I'm aware of my senses, I hear his heartbeat and find him slung over the sculpture I resonated with. Pressing my lips together, shame coats my cheeks. My emotions are a mess of hunger, cravings, and the slither of good sense seeping through.

Slamming down a wall between us, I walk away from Torsten, taking deliberate steps and holding my head high. I almost did something foolish, forgetting myself for a moment. But if I acknowledge that I don't truly hate him, I don't know what that means or where it leaves our relationship. Fortunately, Chase appears at my side, sparing me the embarrassment of whatever quip is probably simmering on his tongue.

"Jaxon is restocking our blood bags, and then we're good to go." My eyes narrow, but I manage to keep my composure for the most part.

"Oh, that's right. You three need your strength to ensure the litter I am to carry has a formidable bloodline." His boots fall short, and a curse falls from his lips.

"Ahh, shit."

I leave the gallery, and the two males muttering behind. Even Jaxon will have to wait, although I won't forget how he withheld the truth and led me to believe the vampires were welcoming me with open arms. Storming through the east wing, I brace my hands on the ceiling-high door separating me from the rest of the castle, anticipating the onslaught of senses-override in search of the one I'm truly pissed at. Lorcan doesn't want a daughter – he wants an out. Better yet, heirs. More hybrids to utilize. Sawyer is right, I didn't ask the right questions, and now I'm going to get some answers.

Lorcan
Chapter Eleven

"Excuse me, you can't go in there!"

My brows raise at the commotion beyond my office door before it bursts open. Aspen stands, eyes blazing and radiating fury. Raising a hand, I dismiss Nova before offering Aspen a seat across my desk. She picks it up and throws it into the mirror above the fireplace instead.

"I'm sensing there's something on your mind, Aspen," I stand slowly. There aren't many things in this world a vampire king like myself knows to be cautious with, but a powerful hybrid who blames me for her mother's death is definitely one of them. Watching on, I permit Aspen to trash my office for far longer than necessary. Had I been the ruthless king I once was, she'd have been in the dungeons by now – kin or not. The truth is...I just don't give a fuck anymore. I can't muster a single shit about anything, and that's why I am no longer fit for this role.

When the rest of the room is destroyed, Aspen swivels to face me. Her navy eyes are tinted with gold, her fangs protruding and sharp. White fur ripples along her arms as her shoulders jerk of their own accord. She's fighting against a shift, but I'd be lying if I pretended not to be interested in her wolf form. Would she resemble her mother? Does she bear any more similarities to myself?

Clenching her fists, Aspen growls, low and deep. Holding my hands up, I slowly round the glass desk, knocking the computer monitor and causing it to wobble, an idea presenting itself. I rarely look at the blasted thing anyway. It's all for show. Apparently, I need the latest and greatest human, technical advancements to keep up with this new era. I simply can't adjust to a world that's passing by so quickly when I have no real desire to be in it.

Although every male is trained to fight at a very young age, the skill invaluable should any threats surface, I allow all vamps to choose their own vocations. As I've discovered the hard way, our long existence can become unbearable without having a hobby or skill to focus on.

Upon venturing into the human world, the Techies decided to build themselves a warehouse on the edge of the castle's surrounding town. Soldering irons and the likes line the walls, with worktables in the center covered in screens, gadgets, and a shit-load of wires and circuits. It keeps them entertained, and I trust my vamps when they tell me the humans are becoming more advanced. Our species needs to be prepared should they discover our existence. Again.

Tearing the wires from the flat screen monitor, I offer it to Aspen and then step aside as she punches it through the desk. Glass shatters, and the scent of her blood hits me—the perfect blend of Orianna and I invading my nostrils.

"Are we quite finished?" I manage to ask, my insides restricting. Not again. Not now. I've been regulating myself so well. The door opens once more, and the three I instructed to protect her slip inside with their heads lowered. I'll deal with them later, and not just because they made no rush to aid me in here. Only cowards hang outside the door, and I didn't promote fucking cowards to rule my army.

Righting two armchairs, I place them before the fire currently burning an oil painting portrait of myself. With slow and purposeful movements, my daughter lets me guide her by the shoulders and ease her to sit as I take the other chair.

"Aspen, where is your Raven?"

"He…he's gone," she croaks, throwing her hands over her face. Guilt tugs at my shriveled heart, steering up another bout of anguish. Deep down, she's a scared girl who wants to confide in her father. Had I been that male since birth, this situation would be so much easier.

"Tell me what happened," I carefully demand. I've done my fair share of research on the Supernatural Council and their delegation of Ravens since Orianna's came to me. Once assigned, the guardians are not permitted to leave their charge.

"It was stupid. Chase challenged me to a hunt, Torsten wanted to try and outrun my wolf through the woods. We were just burning some frustration," her navy eyes slide to me briefly. I bite down on the inside of my cheek to prevent my cheek from twitching. Sparing a quick glance back, they've yet to take their eyes off the damaged carpet, and for good reason. Those assholes will be serving time in the dungeons. I trusted them to protect her, not dare her into being reckless.

"Emotions were running high. I couldn't separate my wolf from my… vampire," she snarls the word like a curse. I swallow my own growl at her display of disgust. We're the superior species. To be one of our kind is a gift, never a curse.

"What do you mean, separate?" Jaxon steps forward, hands braced in front of gray sweatpants. Always the soldier. Watching her spike of irritation at Jaxon's voice, I lean back in my seat, resting my crossed fingers over my stomach, although my patience is almost non-existent these days.

"You know how it is," Aspen growls. "Imagine that voice in your head that never shuts the fuck up being at war with a wolf prowling within your skin. They fight and argue; meanwhile, I'm trying to keep us all in check." I catch the worry in Jaxon's icy blue eyes and shake my head slightly. Nothing Aspen said makes any sense, but one problem at a time.

"So, you were racing through the woods," I bring her back to the problem at hand. Apparently, I can't trust my men to have her best interests at the forefront of their duty, I can at least rely on the Raven.

"Right, so, um," Aspen grips the sides of her head. White hair spills over her face, shielding her from view, but I reckon that was the purpose. "I was closing in on Jaxon, I think. My wolf has taken over at this point. I remember Sawyer tackling me, urging me to shift back. His voice drowned out the others in my head, and somehow, he got through. I shifted, but I still wasn't in control. I...I kissed him," Aspen barely whispers, shame lacing her voice. "I fed on him, there was a flash of bright light, and then he left. That's it."

This time, my cheek does twitch. Just below the eye socket. My breathing shallows, my own grip on reality slipping.

"Aspen, I need you to think really carefully," I lean forward and tilt her chin to face me. "Did he drink from you too? Did any of your blood enter his system?" Aspen's navy eyes flick back and forth, replaying the memory before those dilated irises return to me.

"I think my lip might have been bleeding when we kissed. Why?"

"Fuck!" I shoot out of my seat. Three pairs of muscled arms are there in an instant, restraining me, but I'm not king just for appearances. Shoving the three away, I roar at the top of my lungs. Aspen's heartbeat begins to race. I'm scaring her, and I don't give a shit. Our entire plan is fucked. Years of preparation ruined. "Get her out of here!"

Aspen is forcefully removed from my office, much to her displeasure. Her screams can almost be heard over the sound of my foot splintering the wall. Whatever she didn't originally wreck, I make quick work on destroying. The chairs are in pieces, and the rest of the desk is smashed through the stained-glass window. A slither of moonlight peeks through, mocking me.

The swapping of blood between supernaturals under the moon's clear light seals their bond. Not to be done so on a whim, becoming moonbound is sacred, only for the truest of mates who have overcome many obstacles and challenges to be together. For the power of the moon to interlink each other's souls and allow them to share one for the remainder of their lives, never to be without the other - if you don't want your soul to fracture.

A ripple of anguish explodes within my chest. I gasp, drawn to my knees. Glass shards splinter my skin, but nothing compares to the agony inside. Hot as an inferno, I choke against the onslaught. The heartbreak of a broken moon bind often leads to suicide. The pain is indescribable. The link is irreversible. And these absolute fucking idiots allowed our best asset to bond with a creature of another species. The more I think, the angrier I'm becoming.

"Call off the trials," I croak. "There's no use now." Meticulous planning, and they couldn't have waited a few more days.

"The plan still stands. This doesn't change anything."

"This changes everything!" I shout. I genuinely thought Jaxon would be the champion. I've been grooming him to take my mantel since we discovered Aspen's existence. The trials were to be a formality. I *trusted* him to keep her safe. Whether she was raised by me or not, Aspen is my flesh and blood. She's mine to protect, and in not ensuring she has the best possible mate, I've failed her. The same way I failed Orianna.

Something inside my chest splinters. The affliction I keep trying to patch over and hide anyway slams into me with the force of a battering ram. I stagger forward on all fours, dragging myself onto the shaggy rug before the fireplace. A thump against my side lets me know I've collapsed, although, in my mind, the room is still spinning. The pain is a raw ache that robs me of all comprehension and breath.

"Lorcan!" Jaxon dares to call me by my name, attempting to lift my six-foot-four bulk of muscle upright. I refuse to obey, reserving my energy for the next round of crippling fire burning through my being. I thought it would have lessened all these years later. I was wrong. "Try to see sense. The trails can go ahead. Aspen has multiple species within her. For all we know, she may be able to have multiple mates too."

My chest lessens the faintest amount of pain, enough to breathe shallowly. Could it be possible? I had accepted the Raven would remain with her for good, although his disappearance doesn't bode well. All I wanted is to save Aspen, the broken bond I'd suffered with for too long, and when I thought it couldn't get any worse, Orianna's death broke me. My body is decaying from the inside. It won't be long before I beg for a stake to the heart to put me out of my misery. But not until the future of the kingdom I've built is guaranteed.

"This only could have happened if they were true mates," Chase pitches in. "It would have happened eventually." I hadn't realized he was still in the room, but with his presence comes the return of fury. Vaguely noting the male kneeling before me, I swipe my hand to bat him away. Fucking Chase.

"You caused this," I shakily point a finger. "You and your stupid notions set them up perfectly. Moon help me, Chase, if you don't perish in the trials, you'll do so in the dungeons. Leave me."

"Of course, your majesty." I sense a hint of resentment in Chase's tone, but with his exit, I can recoil within. All I feel is agony and death. Internal death. The edges of my vision darken, and I'm half tempted to lie here forever more. Time simultaneously passes and stands still, my thoughts fleeting like leaves on the breeze. I'm cursed by my duty to uphold appearances, but once upon a time, I was prepared to walk away. Love makes you do crazy things, and I was a day away from storming the shifter camp and claiming Orianna in front of her betrothed—one single day.

Hands-on my shoulder rouse me ever so slightly. Through a daze of memories, I can almost imagine it's Orianna herself, coming to save me. But as the fog clears, I find myself cupping the cheek of my assistant, Nova, as she holds a blood bag in her hand. Clearing my throat, I attempt to sit upright, but she refuses to let me, instead, pushing the blood bag tube into my mouth, she patiently waits for me to drink it all, dabbing my mouth of any spills. So weak. So pathetic.

"Stop taking care of me," I grumble when she retracts the tube. Nova masks her concern with a small laugh.

"Even if I wanted to, I'm bound by duty. As are you. So, get up. You have some explaining to do to the Techies and carpenters." Nova peers around the room, her milk chocolate eyes scanning the destruction of wallpaper to curtains. There's nothing like some father/daughter bonding.

"I don't have to explain myself to anyone." After a few long calming breaths and extreme focus, the heaviness in my chest lifts a minuscule amount as I bury the emotions I can't handle. Bury them so deep I can pretend they don't exist for a while longer.

Sitting up straight and gradually blinking to clear my vision, I see Nova next to me on the rug, her red heels tucked beneath her. Her lipstick and hair tie share the same vibrant hue, and her long brunette ponytail drapes over her shoulder. I've always wondered why she chooses to help me when she has the freedom to pursue any interest she desires. As she turns her attention to me, her eyebrow arches quizzically. "Are you going to let me call for the doctor yet?" Nova asks as she does every time.

"No," I growl bluntly. It's enough that my assistant and those in charge of the army have seen me in such a state. I don't need anyone else in my business. What I do need is to step down from my duties and be alone. After the trials, I'm considering moving into the cabin permanently, like a retirement home for those with nothing and no one to live for.

"Lorcan," Nova states. I don't like the familiarity in her tone or how close she's getting to me. I push everyone away for good reason. "How many more times are we going to allow this to happen?

"Leave it the fuck alone." I snap, although she doesn't react in the slightest. "There is no 'we.'" Drawing a deep breath, I let go of any lingering tension in my body. "I assume you heard everything from your desk outside. What am I supposed to do about this unexpected mating?" Nova's casual appearance doesn't falter, her posture ramrod straight without effort, whereas I feel so tense that I might break a rib if I move too suddenly.

"Not all mating's can be planned. Vampires and alike should be open to follow their instincts." I roll my eyes at Nova's assessment. She's never hidden the fact that she hates the Moon Bound Trials and has long since refused to participate. "Aspen doesn't understand our ways. Nor does she know the logistics of how we use the moon's power, especially for events like this."

I grunt and she sighs, "What I'm saying is, you should either explain it to her upfront or give her some exemptions for simply living her life."

I know all about living the life we choose, and it doesn't work. The trials ensure suitable matches are made, not rash ones.

"What strikes me as odd is her naivety. If her soul is fully bound to another by the moon, how has she not picked up on feeling his emotions? She must have noticed a change." I question.

Nova shrugs, a gesture I hate, but rather than snapping, I grind my teeth to the point of cracking. "My guess is that her emotions are constantly raging anyway, she's probably confusing any changes she's feeling with adapting to a new lifestyle."

I sigh. It's pointless to sit here any longer and guess. Jaxon may have a point in Aspen taking multiple mates, which means I must ensure the trails occur immediately before the Raven returns with silly notions of running away together.

Forcing myself to stand on shaky legs, pain shoots across my chest like an internal slap-- a constant reminder of the one-sided bond I will never be free of. I need to be alone. I deserve to be alone.

Making my way towards the door, I dismiss Nova to her regular duties. I'm done with this conversation. I'm done with just about everything. Instead of obeying as she should, she reaches out to grab ahold of my bicep in an effort to stop me from leaving. I growl at her loudly and flash my fangs in a warning that has her retracting her hand. Smart move.

"Lorcan," Nova says softly. As if I'm some kind of wilting flower. Fuck my life. "Aspen is an incredible female; she can handle herself. And if not, she will learn. Give her a chance to make her own choices."

"Look at me," I snap harshly. "We do not have time for such luxuries, Nova. I need to ensure someone is ready to take over when I fall victim to my pain and am unable to rise again. This is about more than just her."

The longing and regret weigh heavily on me as I consider the possibilities for Aspen's future. Moon knows, I wish I could give Aspen what Nova is asking. To help her find her soulmate and for their bond to be unbreakable and everlasting. For her to lead our kind with empathy and understanding, uniting, and safeguarding our species with a strong, formidable mate by her side. That's all I had ever wanted to do with Orianna, but I never got the chance.

There's really no surprise what I did after evading Torsten back at vampire castle. I ran.

Afterall, it's what I'm best at – fleeing my problems and hiding behind my wolf. Huge white paws hit the mud, speeding me in whichever direction she chooses. The moon upon my fur brings the usual euphoric feeling. I sensed multiple vampire presences trailing me since using a warehouse roof to jump the town's protective wall, constant shadows over my shoulder that couldn't keep up. As soon as I shifted, the confusion left my system, and all that was left was bitterness and an unhealthy dose of embarrassment, all of which my wolf only intensified.

I've allowed myself to be fooled into thinking I was special. Desired, even. Torsten says the last thing they want is to be king, but I'm not buying it. Even when being forced to compete in the trials, who wouldn't fight for the key to the kingdom? Especially with the bonus chance of having offspring when your species is struggling to do just that. Forget finding my place amongst the vampires; I was intended to be a breeding mule and nothing more.

I finally stop darting between trees and skid to a halt in front of the exile hut. How did I get back here? I'd been so distracted; I didn't even realize I'd crossed the shifter blood line marking the edge of the territory. The sun makes its first appearance over the horizon, so my fur retracts, and my bones readjust into my usual form. I could pull on the moon's lunar face to stay in wolf form, as it is still visible in the reddish glow of the sky, but it would take more concentration than I'm currently capable of.

At least, I guess it's safe to say the vamps shouldn't be tailing me anymore. Since I'm here, I might as well find some of my old clothes – especially now that I'm naked for the next twelve-ish hours until night falls again. Taking a second to listen around me, I don't pick up any shifter heartbeats within range, so my visit should remain discreet.

Pushing the creaky door of the hut open, I quickly deduce that the small space has been trashed. Typical. The contents of the drawers are spewing over, and thick claw marks are gouged deeply into several parts of the stone walls. However, on closer inspection, I realize my belongings are in boxes to the right of the hut, along with the books my mother used to gift me.

The items scattered across the broken wicker chair and the floor are from a male. A strong scent of cedar wood fills my nostrils. The single bed is a ruffled heap of sheets, and the few pieces of crockery lay dirty in the sink. It seems there is a new resident living here already. Does that mean he's been banished, or did he see an opportunity to escape the pack's constant strokes and snuggles?

Wolves are overly affectionate, which was probably the hardest part of being exiled. I insisted my mother remain at the shifter camp, unaware of what was blossoming inside of me. I was already disgusted with myself for what I did the first time I shifted. The number of people I killed. The members of *my* pack who are no longer around because couldn't control the beast inside of me. I couldn't have lived with myself if I had ever hurt my mother. Those nights as a lone teen were the worst, but at least no one else was around to witness them.

The shifter living here, however, is seemingly alone. A fate worse than death in the eyes of some of our kind. No, not ours – *theirs*, I mentally berate myself. Figuring I don't have long until this new occupant returns, I busy myself dressing in a pair of faded blue jeans and scruffy white sneakers, which match a white V-neck t-shirt. Then, I leave the hut I've spent the majority of my life in. Willingly, this time. Although as my foot hits the first step, I realize I have no idea where to go. Tucking my tail between my legs and returning to the vampires doesn't sound appealing. Nor does showing my face for Conall and the shifters to scorn at. No, the only place I won't be ridiculed is beside my mother's grave.

The sun is shining brightly with the promise of a beautiful day by the time I reach the foot of the hill. I turn my face upwards, basking in the silence within. My turmoil is caused by two creatures of the moon, so in the brief moments I allow myself to enjoy the simple human pleasures of the day, all is quiet. Keeping my senses aware of a possible ambush, I leave the safety of the tree line and stroll up the steep incline.

I think back to life before my first shift. When I lived in the alpha cabin. When my mother would sing to me whilst brushing my hair, hold me through a thunderstorm, and sit on my bed to play card games when the pack went out to hunt. I was always so worried for Conall, eager for the day I could join him. Be a formidable member of the pack and make him proud. Now, all I can hope is that my mother's soul is flying free and not trapped somewhere waiting for me to sort my life out. She'll be waiting forever at this rate.

It's still here—the rounded slab of granite with her name etched into the stone. I'm not sure what I anticipated. Graffiti, maybe. Or the stone being shattered, and the surrounding plants crushed. As I kneel in the earth's indentations that seem to cradle my knees perfectly, my fingertips brush against the white flowers, and I furrow my brow. Someone has been tending to her gravesite.

Tears prick my eyes, and suddenly a barrage of words tumble from my lips. I don't hold back – from being taken to the castle, ending up at the cabin with the vampire trio who kidnapped me, Sawyer's kiss, Lorcan. How can so much have happened in such a short space of time? I barely recognize my own voice, speaking of the species I despised and confusing notions of desire. Of males who challenge and provoke me, intrigue, and charm me.

Afterward, I feel refreshed and mentally cleansed. It always helps to neatly tuck my thoughts into little compartments of my mind. With my mother's stoic help, I've concluded I need to return to the castle or the cabin at least. Not because Lorcan thinks he can control a future I'd previously given up on, but to understand exactly when I'm saying no to. Despite claiming not to want to be king, at least Torsten plans to compete in the trials and win my hand in marriage, and I need to know why.

When the sun has passed overhead, I kiss the stone slab goodbye and venture down an almost vertical pathway near the base of the hill, leading to the sandy beach below. This was my secret escape; a small curve of golden sand enclosed by caves on either side. I remove my shoes and hitch up my jeans, entering the cool water with a sigh. The rolling waves leap forward to greet me and then regretfully retreat, almost as if the crystal blue water is clinging to my ankles, desperate to stay.

Calmness washes over me, all my senses at peace with my surroundings. From the salty smell, the sound of gulls overhead, and the feel of water lapping at my feet. Serenity stretches towards the horizon in a mask of shimmering blue. Prior to last week, this was the closest taste of freedom I'd ever had.

But it can't last. The vampire in me rears her ugly head before long, filling my mind with orders to return to the castle. A lingering darkness within my soul, forcing unwanted urges and pushing against my wolf for control. She bites back in turn, and I'm left as a vessel. I sometimes wonder how I'd be without them, and the truth is depressingly obvious. I'd be a no one, who nobody was interested in. I run my fingers through the sand, allowing the grains to slip through my hands as easily as my grip on control does.

Amongst pondering how many sand exile huts I'd have to make and destroy to finally put my past behind me, the twittering of voices sounds over the crashing waves. A small rock tumbles down the steep pathway. The laughter grows louder, and my time has run out. Using my vampire speed, I shoot into the nearest cave, crouching to hide behind a boulder deep within.

Boycotting the rest of the pathway, rapid thuds of boots hit the sand. Shadows cast across the back wall, intruders trampling through my oasis to dump cooler boxes of beer bottles inside the cave.

"Hey Gabe, get the fire going," a familiar voice commands. I slump down behind the boulder, resting my forehead on the stone. It would only be my terrible luck to be trapped in a cave with the same crowd I grew up with. Attended the shifter's version of school with. A building adjacent to the mess hall, where young alliances were formed. Each generation of the pack tends to band together, and had I been 'normal,' I'd have radiated toward Radley's crew. For once, I have to thank the moon for not being normal and missing the hazing initiation stage. I was just tormented from afar instead.

You're stronger now, the voice in my head pipes up at exactly the wrong time. *You could take them all.* Usually, I can push that beast down and see reason, but this time, my head tilts of its own accord, my psyche stretching against my will. Tingles rack my gums, fangs elongating in time with claws breaking free of my fingers. Gold taints my vision as my eyes begin to glow. She's never done this before, and I can't stop it. I also find I don't want to.

Let's show them you're not a reject. I shudder, her voice feeling like too much of a caress. *Prove you can't be beaten.* More shifters enter the cave, their laughter grating on my last nerve. My head tilts again, irritation spiking through the inner beast. She fills my mind with visions of bloodshed. Torn limbs, silenced screams. Pushing back to my feet, my jaw hangs loose with anticipation as I move to take a step out from behind the boulder. Suddenly, a body appears at my back, and a hand wraps around my mouth.

"Don't," a low, graveled voice murmurs in my ear, and I'm tugged out of sight. "You're better than this."

"Get off me, Sawyer," I mutter low, wrenching my arms from his hold. He releases me too easily, and when I hunt for him in the darkened space behind, all I see are smoke-like wisps resembling his trench coat. No raven shifter to speak of, and my heart clenches. He's not really here. More like an astral projection sent to save me from myself. "Where are you?" My voice wobbles, a slice of agony I don't understand slicing through me. True, I've missed Sawyer's presence, but this is more. As if my soul is reaching out for the wisps that embrace me.

"Return to the castle. The trials begin tonight." With that, he disappears. Sucked into an invisible void which leaves me cold from the loss. He wasn't even here, yet his withdrawal hurts as much as his rejection in the forest.

Are we going to obey the command of a spirit? My head jerks aside, the vampire inside trying to take over again. My golden eyes burn brighter, searing through my skull. Using the boulder to steady myself, I hunt for my wolf. She's whining, confined to the corner of my being. She isn't one to cower, causing indecision to war within. Poking my head out, I catch a glimpse of the younger pack members, now huddled around a campfire where, no doubt, a series of orgies are about to break out.

"Here's to being free of the mutt," Gabe announces. Beer bottles clink in celebration, smiles covering their faces. Drawing my tongue over my fangs, I chuckle to myself.

"Yeah," I whisper to myself. "I'll follow Sawyer's order, but not without having some fun first."

Flexing my fists a few times to get my blood pumping, I step out of my hiding spot, ducking under a low overhanging rock and speeding forward to race around the uninvited guests. Arousal stings my nose, jeering laughter assaulting my ears. Lashing out a hand, I grab Gabe around the neck and throw him into the opposite wall. His beer bottle shatters across the fire, engulfing the cave in a blaze of heat. As I keep running, faster than the shifters can track, I throw my fists into various faces and yank out handfuls of hair. Only when I stop, the image of rage and power, does everyone gasp, realizing who I am.

"It's the reject!" Keeley laughs, clapping her hands like the deranged, dopey dick she is. The shifters jump upright to crowd me, filling my eye line with cocky smirks. "Tut, tut, tut," Keeley continues, oblivious to my claws lengthening with black talons. Much like Sawyer's. "What will Conall say when he finds out you came crawling back? Just like he said you would."

I merely smirk. If Conall thinks I'm so predictable, I'd like to see what he makes of this. Shooting my arms out, I sink my claws into the necks of those closest and tear out their jugulars. Power thrums through my veins. I shiver from it, launching myself into the next shifter awaiting their fate. This time, I use my teeth, tearing through skin like silk, ripping flesh about, and drinking the blood that pours down my throat. It's a massacre of screams as I relent to the monster who's waited so long to be freed.

A male I vaguely recognize as Radley, after growing his hair long and bulking up significantly from the clingy momma's pup I once knew, cages Keeley in his arms as if that will save her from my wrath. Tearing her free by the ankles, I whip her around the cave like a shotput, laughing mechanically when her hair catches fire and I release her. Limb's flailing, she flies towards the beach beyond the entrance and slams into the sand. Then I tear onward towards my next object of prey.

By a stroke of luck, Brendan manages to catch me by the throat as I'm blurring around the cave to kick up a tornado of dirt. Grabbing hold of his wrist and using it to hold my weight, I kick my sneaker into Radley's jaw. Blood spews sideways from the impact, covering Gabe's bare chest in the sticky liquid. The copper flooding my senses have my stomach churning for a taste, but I don't want them. I have four males in the forefront of my mind, and only one of them will suffice. Perhaps more than one until I've taken my fill and shown them the hybrid I really am. Still clutching Brendan's hand at my neck, my head tilts again.

"Say hi to our ancestors for me," I flash my fangs. My voice isn't my own, laced with an echo of threat. Radley's grip falters, and that's all I need. Snapping his fingers back with a loud crack, I land in a crouch and don't hesitate to end this. Kicking out my foot to connect with his shin, the bone splinters, bursting free on impact. As he's tumbling downward, my keen vampire eyesight watches in slow motion for the exact moment I can crunch my elbow into his nose, sending him flying onto his back. Limp. Lifeless.

"That's enough," Gabe growls, holding out a hand. My instincts want to snap it, but I hesitate. As the only shifter left standing, no one can bear witness to the slight incline of his head or how he covers his crotch just as the scent of urine reaches me. Fucking priceless. Maintaining Gabe's eye contact, I sidestep around the edge of the cave towards the entrance.

Leaving one to live and telling Conall how he pissed his pants whilst watching the rest of his friends die will be my parting gift to the shifters. There's no returning after this, and I find I couldn't care less. With a smirk and double middle fingers raised, I shoot away in the castle's direction, chuckling the entire way.

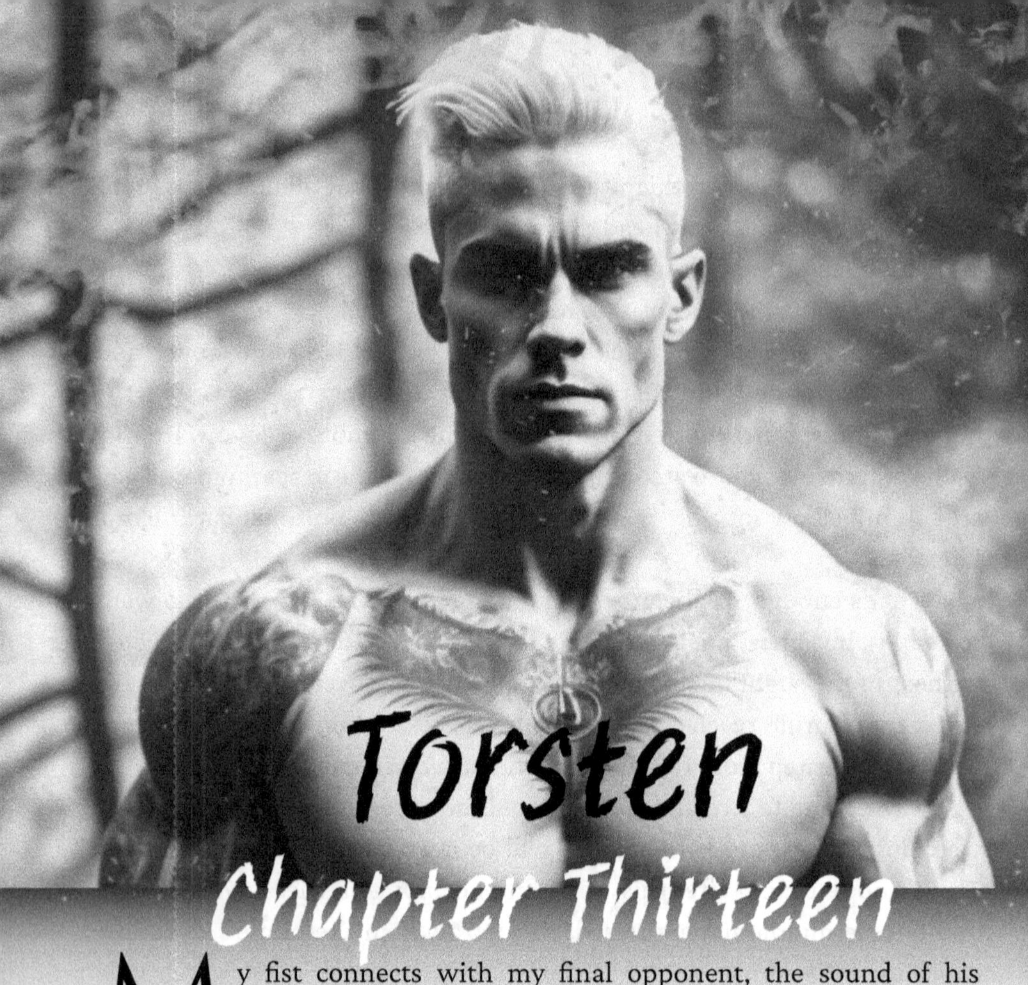

Chapter Thirteen

My fist connects with my final opponent, the sound of his cheekbones shattering ringing in my ears. A fresh spray of blood flying from his mouth splatters my face as he falls to the ground with an endless thud. The roar from the audience overpowers the final claxon, announcing the end of the fight. One hour of pure bloodshed, fury, and adrenaline. One hour of feeling something I've been chasing my entire existence – alive.

The bloodied, bulky weight of my victim lies still at my feet as his body struggles to heal itself. His injuries are substantial, as his limbs contort at all the wrong angles. A feat only a fellow vampire can manage because we're not shady fucks like the shifters who need to rely on claws and teeth. My fangs are reserved for the pleasure of feeding - not to rely on to win a simple fight.

Rolling the tension from my shoulders, I inhale the heady scent of blood that coats my torso like a second skin, all of which isn't mine. I'm not sure at what point my vest was torn off during the fight, but I certainly was wearing one when I walked into the arena. Across the dividing ropes, Jaxon, and Chase grin back at me, having also succeeded in the first trial. In the last quadrant, Carrick paces like a caged animal, glaring and snarling as he struggles to regain composure.

Four elite contenders were chosen based on their brute strength to compete against those deluding themselves into believing they had a chance with Aspen. There was never any doubt about the winners, but if my army hadn't at least made an attempt, I'd have strung them up and drained their blood myself. It's all about maintaining a façade, but Lorcan knows that his future heir needs more than mere strength. The real tests commence now that we've swiftly eliminated the weak. We will be pushed to our limits mentally, physically, and emotionally to prove that we can lead under immense pressure. We won't buckle, even as our current king tries to hide the fact that he's teetering on the edge himself.

A royal guard approaches, his dark eyes laced with boredom. Like myself, Nealon is six-foot-three, stacked with muscle, and commands attention. Given my father's dream for me to become a guard myself, I also had my hair cropped short at the back and sides. If Jaxon hadn't claimed me as his second-in-command, I'd most likely be standing tall in the black and gold uniform on the other side of this imminent interaction. However, if I was, I'd have taken the guard's vow of celibacy and would be forbidden to pursue Aspen. Nealon takes one look at the pathetic excuse of a competitor on the floor, clicking his fingers for a clean-up crew to swoop in before clasping my shoulder.

"No surprise you've won this round. Although, something tells me the next test won't be as straightforward for you," he says with a smirk. "Go shower and feed. The next round starts in six hours. Report to the dungeons by sunrise."

I watch Nealon retreat the way he came, my eyes drifting across the amphitheatre. Male spectators filter out from the stands, eager to visit the blood bank. The females are kept separate in a self-contained balcony flanked by more guards. Lorcan's velvet chair sits central, giving a perfect view of the action if he'd bothered to make an appearance. Instead, his assistant Nova stands alone, unprotected, with a clipboard in hand to take notes. No one would dare make a move on Nova... if they wish to keep their heads, that is.

"The lengths we go to for a night off training," Chase jokes, slapping me hard on the back. His eyeline follows mine, a chuckle leaving his lips. "She's not here, Torst. I've been checking for her scent, but she will be."

"How can you be so sure?" Jaxon steps forward, crossing his arms over his chest. Again, his shirt is a distant memory, rivets of blood running the length of his body.

"She has no idea what she is or what she wants. We can give her those answers; if not, we can at least show her a good time." Chase punches our shoulders playfully, and we repay him with a bundle attack. Chase's ribs crack beneath mine and Jaxon's assault, our bulk pinning him to the ground amongst the river of blood we've previously chased. No amount of beating can break the stupid smile on Chase's face, so we leave him with a few last kicks to the gut. Cheery asshole.

The knot of worry over Aspen hasn't lessened, so I lift my face to the night sky through the arena's open top and gaze upon the clouds, hoping for a glimpse of tonight's moon—anything to soothe the usual hitch to my heartbeat.

The moon controls every species on the planet, whether they acknowledge it or not. The vampires are ruled by the crescent moon, due by the week's end. On that night, we will all be extra horny since it's the only night of the month vampire conceptions could take place – if we were to be so blessed. Pregnancies amongst our species have diminished at such a worrying rate - for all we know, we're the only Vamps left.

In an instant, my thoughts turn sour. A war is taking place between my head and my heart, and I don't have the luxury of indulging it. As with all female pairings, my king has ordered me to participate in the Moon Bound Trials. It's my duty to continue our species, but my desire is to explore my connection to Aspen. Should I lose, I'm destined to watch her mate with another.

I sigh as I stroll toward the modernized locker room. Vines climb the crumbling walls and disappear into every crevice they can as if they alone were holding the building together. Passing beneath a stone archway, I head inside to find a clean set of clothes and a towel folded neatly within my designated locker. I slam the metallic door shut and promptly smash my own head against it. Stupid fucking thoughts, all coiled within my father's voice to prove myself. Be the best or disgrace his reputation. Ultimately, his high title doesn't mean shit when he died at the hands of humans. No one breathes his name now, and he was certain I would be the downfall in our bloodline.

Peeling off my clothes, I step under the searing stream of water and let out a hiss as unexpected pain stings various parts of my body. Fuck, some of this blood coating my body may actually be mine. I'd been so caught up in the excitement of the fight I hadn't felt much else. I stand under the water, watching the red liquid swirling around my feet before disappearing into the drain.

I'm careful not to rub down the silver residue stuck to my skin from the knuckle dusters some pussy opponent opted to wear over his training gloves. I get it – considering the fight was never going to be fair, and a lesser vampire would need to play dirty to be in with a shot at winning, but if even one of my tattoos is marred after this, he'll have hell to pay. Vamps are allergic to silver; it slows our healing process and is the highest cause of death amongst our kind. Thankfully, I can already feel my skin itch, stitching itself back together again.

Pumping the shower gel on the wall, I go about washing myself. Scrubbing my hands through my hair, I stand under the spray with my eyes closed, braced by my fists on the tile. I'd hoped tonight's win would bring me a sense of relief. I'm one step closer to being allowed to court Aspen. But now I've met her, now I've seen home much my best friends want to win too, a dull sense of dread is becoming rooted in my soul. She's incredible and deserves a male who can care for and challenge her daily. But am I prepared to destroy my own brothers to prove I'm the male for the job? I swear, just thinking of us conjures her vanilla and raspberry scent, filling my mind with silly notions until I open my eyes.

"Finish what you started," Aspen states and I startle. Between my tense arms pressed against the tile, there she is. Fully dressed, standing between the spray with her attention rooted on my face. My cock jumps in response, a groan disguised within my throat. The white t-shirt she's wearing dips low into her cleavage, her filthy jeans quickly becoming sodden. But it's her eyes that capture my attention. Fierce, wild, the navy shade appearing so bright, they are practically electric blue.

"Where have you been?" Is all I can ask. Everything about her expression, from the stern set of her jaw to the dare she's presenting me, is out of character from the timid and hungry female we initially captured. Don't get me wrong, Aspen's a force to be reckoned with. But with each passing day in our presence, I see her walls crumbling and glimpses of the scared girl underneath who is desperate to be accepted.

"Unimportant," Aspen guts her chin out. "You were going to kiss me in the gallery. Finish it." Pursing her lips, my gaze is drawn back to the heavy rise and fall of her wet chest. Pert nipples push against the white fabric which has quickly turned see through.

"I, um..." my voice lowers as an arrow of lust shoots directly for my cock. "I don't think that's a good idea."

"I didn't ask your opinion. You said you wanted me. Prove it." Her hand clamps closed around my shaft, and I release the pent-up groan.

"Lorcan would have my head," I mutter, filled with self-loathing. I was stupid in the gallery. So close to throwing away a lifetime of busting my ass to prove myself worthy. I'm thinking more clearly now, but when she's goading me, not even I'm vampire enough to deny her.

"Go ahead Torst," Chase chuckles. The bastard stands a few feet away, blood-soaked and leaning against the tiles. Jaxon also appears, his expression equally as grave as mine. He knows as well as I do that fraternizing with Aspen is a sure-fire way to end my life. But then I look into her demanding navy eyes and wonder if it might be worth it.

"Is that a command, Princess?" I ask, giving myself an out whilst holding Jaxon's eye. His blue gaze darkens. Aspen's hand squeezes tighter, stealing my next breath.

"Don't even fucking think about it," Jaxon warns me. More like he threatens me in a low enough growl that my sensitive ears barely catch it.

"Make me forget my own fucking name," Aspen quickly counteracts, and I'm a goner. Royalty or not, I wouldn't leave such a request from Aspen unanswered. Crashing my lips against hers, I grip Aspen's nape and close the gap between us. Aided by the shower, we slide against each other until I grip her thighs and lift her higher. My naked flesh presses against hers, her sodden clothes rough against my skin as I press her into the tile. She gasps, and I slip my tongue through her lips and groan as I explore Aspen's sweet mouth. Savouring her taste.

There's no softness between us but a raging inferno of ragged breaths and greedy tongues. A struggle for dominance that heats my deadened heart and has nothing to do with the scolding spray pounding down on us. The heavy weight of my thick cock rests at her core, throbbing with need.

Knowing Chase and Jaxon are watching only enhances the sin I'm committing, an urge for them to watch me claim her igniting within. I'm not sure why Aspen chose me, considering she's been nothing but hostile toward me since we met, but I wouldn't question the gift. I admit that approaching her in the gallery must have been conflicting, it was even for me, but I wanted her to hear me for once. See me. Aside from the cat and mouse, back and forth. Her soul was tormented, and I only sought to soothe it.

I'd never imagined we'd get to this without needing me to win the trials, but I still intend to win. More so, now she's filled my senses with her soft moans and the rolls of her hips against my shaft. I must prove a point, showing I don't need Jaxon's charm or Chase's cheek to be enough. These males are like my brothers, but there's only so long I can live in their shadows.

Gripping her thighs, my hold becomes punishing. Desperate. Yet I can't pull back. My tongue scrapes her fangs, the urge to break the skin and let her taste me all-encompassing. And the worst part is, no one tries to stop me. She welcomes me, opening her body, locking her ankles at my back. My hand travels, one finger stroking the pulse in her neck, drifting downwards to where I twist her t-shirt in my fist. A last-ditch attempt to withhold from ripping the damn thing off and leaving bite marks all over her breasts. My dick jumps in agreement with that image, and I tug on the shirt, the seams snapping music to my ears.

"What the hell is going on in here?" A voice cuts through the world of bliss I'd tumbled into. Time had stood still, and Yarik's harsh tone brings me crashing back down to earth. Risking a look over my shoulder, I exhale in relief to see the royal guard is seemingly alone. Tugging down the gold cuffs of his uniform, he diverts his eyes as I set Aspen on her feet. Jaxon immediately grabs her wrist, whipping her behind him. A snarl is torn from me on instinct, and Yarik curses. I have no right to show such possession. I've screwed up, yet her being torn from my protection is a blow I wasn't prepared for.

"It's not what it looks like." I hedge, unable to turn around as my raging erection will give me away. It's exactly what it looks like. Pumping more shower gel from the dispenser on the wall, I proceed to re-wash myself, careful to avoid the areas Aspen's heat pressed against me. "I suppose there's no use asking you not to report this to the king?" I attempt to ask in a nonchalant tone.

"I have a duty to uphold," Yark states coldly, his boots stomping away with more vigor than he arrived with. Fucker snuck up on me. Noting Jaxon is guiding Aspen safety from a rear exit, I punch the tile, busting my knuckles.

"Well, that's not going to help," Chase tuts. I block him out. Ignoring how he wipes my hand clean, switches off the faucet, and wraps a towel around my waist. I can only stand there, wondering when my control became so weak. It doesn't matter either way. I'll be disqualified before the next round. I traded one, albeit incredible, kiss for what could have been a lifetime of happiness.

An onslaught of heartbeats pounds within my ears. Looks like tonight's casualties have finally roused, the locker room filling with a mass of ripped shirts and scowls aimed in our direction. My grimace is hard-set, and my muscles tense for another round of fights to burn off this remaining steam. Instead, with a modicum of restraint, I pull on the sweatpants supplied and storm through the center of them. I've been craving a challenge for centuries. A real purpose. Fuck the trials, I'll win over Aspen instead. Offer myself and allow her to decide my fate. That's the only way I'll know if I ever truly had a shot.

Chase
Chapter Fourteen

"You," I click my fingers as I enter Jaxon's room without knocking. He stands from his bed, takes a step towards me, and I shove him aside. "Not you. You," I point at Aspen – also perched on his bed. I knew Jaxon, the almighty savior, would take the first opportunity he saw to get Aspen into his room. It's nothing to boast about; even the commander has the same basic room as the rest of the army.

When Aspen feels ready to enter the castle permanently, she'll be gifted a suite fit for an unmated princess in the east wing. I've already heard rumors of renovations they've been making to adapt the suite to her needs. It just so happens that her needs are also at the forefront of my intentions. Tossing a clothing bag her way, I pull a blood bag from my pocket and chuck that at her too.

"Get dressed and feed well. We have around five hours until the next trial. Let's try not to let your three top champions kill each other through jealousy when you start sucking on my neck like a leech, yeah?" Aspen's mouth drops open, but there's no time to suck my dick. Whisking Jaxon out of the room, I close the door to give her some privacy. Not from me – but the rest of the fuckers who can scent her in the castle. In the army quarters, of all places.

"Feel like telling me what's going on?" Jaxon folds his arms and tilts his head. Despite being the exact same height and build, it's hilarious that he still tries to square up to me. If I had been Lorcan's favorite, I'd have been commander, and I'd never pull this shit with him.

"Not really, but since you won't let it go," I grip his arm and force him the walk down the corridor. Not far enough for Jaxon's door to be out of view but out of earshot of Aspen. "The princess is horny and looking for a purpose. I'm about to give her one."

"Taking advantage of her in a vulnerable state is a surefire way to get yourself disqualified from the trials too. I suppose I shouldn't argue. Both of your stupidness is going to give me a sure win." Jaxon grunts as Torsten approaches. Rubbing the back of his neck, he shows none of the glowing satisfaction I will have for days when I snag a kiss from Aspen myself. She offered him everything the three of us have wanted since first seeing her, and now I know she's game, I'm turning up the charm. She won't be able to resist me after this. "Such a bunch of assholes," Jaxon huffs. "Don't bitch when you have to watch me love her for eternity."

"I don't think so." I raise my index finger, halting him from walking away. "You said it yourself. She can take multiple mates."

"I said, perhaps she could," Jaxon's blue eyes narrow. I twist my lips.

"Good enough for me. Besides, this is only natural to her," I flick Torsten's temple to bring his attention back to the present. "Pack mentality. She's been sizing the three of us up from the start."

"Vampires are solitary creatures," he grunts in defeat. If his shoulders slump further, I'll stake and seal him into a coffin myself. Jaxon scratches his stubbled jaw, lost in thought which ends with a chuckle.

"You'll never get your theory past Lorcan."

"Aha!" I slap his shoulder, my excitement bubbling just beneath the surface. I'm practically bouncing on my heels. "That's the best part! I don't need to. You're a sure thing for becoming king now, right? Decree number one, allowing your best buddies to mate with your wife." My eyebrows dance as I nudge Torsten. No one looks at me like the fucking genius I am, but they'll see. I've never felt so sure about anything in my existence, and the alternative isn't worth considering. I knew long ago, I wouldn't be the one to watch my brothers die in order to win a female. But that was before I met her.

"Well, nothing's going to happen while we're gossiping in the hallway," I usher away my dark thoughts. "Clothes are waiting for you both in my room. Go change, I'll watch over Aspen." Jaxon slams his hand into my chest, a growl at the ready. I don't react, having anticipated such a response. "I'm not going to interrupt her, I swear it." The twinkle in my green eyes must convince him as the two enter my bed chamber to dress. At almost exactly the same time, the door to Jaxon's room pops open. I rush forward in a blur of speed, blocking Aspen's exit and crowding her back in the room.

"Not so fast, baby," I grin, closing us inside. "I need to approve of my choice first." Aspen's smile is nothing short of mischievous as she steps back to let me look at her. And I look. I fuck her with my eyes.

I've taken credit for Aspen's outfit, but Nova acquired it. The King's assistant handled my request, all the while reminding me that Lorcan is going to kill me for it. I would have been more cautious if Torsten, the bastard, didn't now have a score beside his name. He managed to win over Aspen without trying, and we've moved into 'fair-game' territory. It doesn't matter who wins the trials if the moon doesn't bond us; a connection has to be established, and I'm all in.

Aspen's white hair hangs over a black bralette, twisted into a thick braid. The scrap of material is basically a bra with added floral lace underneath, with black straps crisscrossing over her cleavage. Below a scandalous span of bare skin from her toned abdomen, dark denim shorts hug her ass, and she's opted for her white sneakers rather than the heels provided. I smirk, biting my bottom lip.

"I'm going to tattoo you," I mutter under my breath.

"What?" Aspen asks, but she heard me. Offering my hand, I pull her close, dipping my mouth to her ear.

"Not tonight, but soon. I'm going to see your gorgeous body covered in ink, starting with a wolf here," I trace her hip with my knuckles. She shivers, and I continue. "A dragon, like Jaxon's, across here." I spread my palm over the lower half of her back. Trailing up the length of her spine, Aspen arches into me. So responsive. "A pair of raven wings spanning the length of your shoulders." My touch lingers, skating across her soft skin. Venturing around her neck, I dip two fingers between her cleavage. "Thorned vines holding roses starting in your sternum." Aspen's eyes fleck with gold as she peers up at me, lost to my seduction. Touching her like this breaks every rule I know, and I couldn't give a fuck.

"And that just leaves you," her brows quirk. My smile is full, fangs bared.

"I don't need to mark your body, baby. I'm going to leave my imprint in all the places no one else could reach." Aspen's breath hitches, a heady dose of her lust perfuming the air. Exactly how I want her, held on the edge of yearning. A healthy glow to her skin lets me know she's fully fed. *Perfect.* Tonight is the night she falls for me out of desire, not desperation. Dual heartbeats sound beyond the door, our time alone swiftly coming to an end. "Let's get out here before I change my mind and decide to find out if you taste as good as you smell."

"Wait, Chase," Aspen halts me from reaching for the door. Indecision wars within her brows, enough to make me hesitate too. "I did...things at the shifter camp yesterday. There might be repercussions." I exhale, my smile coming back in full force. Here was me, thinking it would be something serious. If anything, I'm even more turned than before. Cupping Aspen's cheeks, I place a light kiss on her forehead.

"There's nothing you can do that I won't support. I trust you, and I've got your back." "I promise."

THIS PART of the town is a long stretch of road dedicated to bars, fully stocked with blood taken from humans when intoxicated. It's a small high, but the best we can manage without bringing too much attention to ourselves. Lively music tumbles out of various doorways, blending into one another. Vamps are singing and dancing in the street, their senses dulled as they experience being carefree for a short space of time.

Flanked by the two behind, Aspen is on my arm, drenched in the huge coat Jaxon insisted she wore, a small playing at the corner of her mouth. She's not had the chance to see us like this, and it's about time she knew there's more to life here than imprisonment within the stone walls.

As we approach the lone door between the bars, I can't help but grin at the bold red neon sign above it. Next to an animated girl in a bikini provocatively bending back and forth over the hood of a car, the words 'Car Wash' stand out in vibrant red. The pulsating music and murmurs from the select few I trusted to work tonight spill out from the building.

"You have a vampire nightclub, and you're only just showing me this now?!" Aspen gasps and punches my arm. Grabbing her hand, I waste no time dragging her inside. Once past the first round of security, and after her coat has been tossed on the ground where it belongs, I take her hand back, stroking my thumb in light circles over the back as we pass through a slim corridor where neon lights highlight every scrap of white on our bodies. My shirt is luminous, my fangs glowing with promise. Her answering smile is everything as our excitement builds.

Approaching a second set of heavy double doors, my gaze remains on her face, drinking in her expression when they open of their own accord. Assaulted by blaring music, a bass vibrates heavily throughout the room. Aspen's hand slightly tightens on mine while she adjusts, no doubt pulling on her wolf to take the edge off her keen senses.

The entire room is hidden beneath a spongy brown cover, from the walls to the floors, even the bar and DJ booth. I lead my date for tonight, alongside Jaxon and Torsten, over to the bar.

"Four shots of IB," I order from the bartender. A younger vamp by our standards and one of the last born. He's slow to obey, considering we're the only customers for tonight, reaching for a decanter of chilled Intoxicated Blood and pouring our drinks with painful slowness. And to think he put in an application for the army. We'd chew him up and use him as a toothpick to get the rancid taste of insolence from our teeth. Narrowing my eyes, I take the four glasses, handing them out to each of us.

"Bottoms up," I urge, tilting Aspen's glass for her. Once drained, I pluck it free from her fingers and lick the rim clean—a gentle promise for what's to come. The gold flecks in Aspen's irises become more prominent, tracking my tongue as it wipes my lips free of blood. Not to worry; this is just the beginning.

I order another round with a flick of my wrist, holding her gaze the whole time. Once a replacement is placed beside me, I raise her chin with two fingers, dangerously exposing the length of her creamy neck, and raise the glass to her lips. She parts them on command, taking all of the crimson liquid in one sultry swallow. My dick jumps to attention.

A ten-second countdown commences from the DJ booth, alerting all the club's occupants to get to the dancefloor. It is just the four of us tonight, but that doesn't mean the energy levels are low. Swopping up Aspen, I shoot us into the center of the room, planting her down with my hands clasped on her waist. Jaxon and Torsten are there in the next second, refusing to let their doubts keep them from what's about to happen. Never mind the fact that Torsten won't look Aspen in the eye.

As the DJ's countdown reaches zero, I can feel Aspen's body tense up, as if she'd take off running if I weren't holding her so firmly. Suddenly, hidden vents in the ceiling open unleashing a sea of foam. At an inconceivable rate, a thick blanket of bubbles fills the room while music pounds from giant, protected speakers. The DJ booth is shrouded in beaming lights, giving a center point amongst the rising foam. *'We Found Love' by Calvin Harris* rolls across the front in block text. Whatever this human music is, I'm into it.

"Come on, Pumpkin, show me what you've got."

"Pumpkin?" she laughs. I cock a brow, and she nods. "I much prefer it to Princess." Releasing Aspen, even before the room is fully filled, I begin to jump. Fist-pumping the air, my shoulder bumping against Torsten until I force him to join me. The sweet laughter of my companions fills my ears, and finally, they give in. The foam rises, weighing us down as our bodies bump into each other.

"Take a big breath," I tell Aspen just as another wave of bubbles crashes overhead, sealing us inside. All other lights are switched off, allowing the DJ booth to pierce the foam tumbling onto us, highlighting the millions of tiny bubbles blocking Aspen from my line of sight. Running a hand along her arm, I notice the goose bumps that awaken in response to my touch. Pulling her small body into mine, I find her back to my front. Caged in a trap of my creation, lost to anonymity. I could be anyone, but she knows it's me and pushes her ass back into my crotch anyway. Lowering my head into the crook of her neck, we find a rhythm together, our bodies flush against each other and swaying in our cocoon of foam and depravity.

Song after song, the perfect curve of her ass grinds against me deliciously. A male is at her front, and I don't care who it is. All I'm invested in is my cock pushing against her with the evidence of my intention and my fully exposed fangs scraping across the smooth skin of her shoulder in time to the fluttering pulse in her neck. Her groan reverberates through us both, filling my mind with images. Premonitions, because Aspen will be pinned beneath me and writhing before the night is through. I spin her away from my body into the male nudging my arm for a turn. I instantly miss her warmth, but I know my limits. I need to cool off.

Heading to the bar, I take it upon myself to finish the leftover drink Jaxon wouldn't touch, and I watch the lights flicker over the silhouette of three figures. The blood tastes sweeter, knowing it wasn't mine. Our perfect Jaxon can't be seen touching this inebriated shit, not when his reputation is clear of any infractions. Lorcan should see him now, allowing the princess to dance against him while making no move to touch her. Must be agony.

"You know, I knew you were a jackass," the bartender kid says from behind. "But this is the dumbest stunt I think you could have pulled. It's like you don't even want a chance to be her mate." I don't react, keeping my smirk in place as I slowly turn to face him. Dark, trimmed hair and dull brown eyes stare back at me, not a trace of nerves to be seen. Maybe he would be a good fit for the army after all – he's suicidal enough.

"There's no need to be bitter because your ranking is too low to compete. Perhaps by the next trials, you'll have proved yourself enough to run with the big boys."

He rolls his eyes, "not all mates are females, you know, and not everyone is interested in your dick-measuring contest."

I chew on the inside of my cheek, just about holding back from a quick retaliation for the sake of wanting the last laugh. In fact, it's none of my business who this little shit wants to mate with.

"If you truly liked her, you'd withdraw. It's obvious who's going to win, but it's the princess who will end up hurt. All because you forced a connection and conflicted her mind," he says with a shake of his head.

Lifting the decanter, the youngster refills my glass and leaves me to stare into the mirror beyond the bar. My smirk has fallen, a tight pinch residing between my brows. Swirling the liquid in the glass, I watch in the reflection as my two best friends grow closer to the girl I'm unwittingly falling for faster than intended. It's only when presented with the notion that I should let her go that the depths of those feelings truly present themselves.

"Hey, where do you go?" Aspen pops up at my side. I'd seen her approach but made no move to welcome her. "There's enough of me to go around, don't you agree?" her lips tilt, tugging on my arm. I have to laugh and obey, turning to face her with my head hanging low.

"You're going to be the death of me."

"Oh, I'm planning on it," she chuckles. I tease her braid between my fingers. Her cleavage is directly in my eye line, rising and falling heavily. A warm blush coats her skin, one I can't resist shifting to brush the back of my fingers over. Still smiling, Aspen tiptoes up to softly press her lips against mine. I freeze, allowing her to pull back of her own accord.

"Thank you for this. It's exactly what I needed," Aspen murmurs against my mouth. Ahh, fuck it. Holding onto her perfectly dented waist to keep her balance, I give her the full measure of my passion through a responding kiss. She tastes sublime, as I knew she would. A special blend of power and beauty wrapped up in an intoxicating package.

Bringing one hand up to hold her nape, I kiss Aspen hard enough to bruise, slipping my tongue between her willing lips. Our tongues duel, our bodies rolling to the beat, desperate to be free from our clothing. The club fades from existence so that just she and I remain in our passionate embrace. Breaking our kiss, I stare down into Aspen's beautiful face, praising myself for the dark hue of her lips and the scent of arousal surrounding her.

"I will always protect you, Aspen." I brush a smudge of foam from her cheek. Speak directly into her ear, I can't resist curling my tongue along the curve. "Build a connection with Jaxon. If nothing else, he'll be able to secure you a safe future."

"Oh, every girl's fantasy. Security," Aspen smirks, and dammit, I just fell for her a little harder.

"Do you trust me?" I ask. After a beat, Aspen steps back and folds her arms. I brave a look at the wall of foam, noting the two idiots bopping around inside and oblivious to our conversation. I prefer it that way. On Aspen's nod, I sigh. "I need you to do me a favor. Seduce Jaxon."

"You're asking me to seduce your friend?" she pops out her hip. I really wish she wouldn't make me repeat myself.

"I'm telling you, I have a foolproof plan. But if it shouldn't work out, for whatever reason, I need to know you'll be worshipped. I love Jaxon like a brother; he'll give you the life you deserve. For both of us," I grip the back of her head, "for all of our sakes, don't let that chivalrous pussy let you slip away." We share a laugh, our foreheads pressing together. "I'll still be right here. For now, give him the push he needs."

Turning Aspen by the shoulders, she waits for Jaxon and Torsten to approach. Reaching behind, she gives my dick a farewell squeeze that will fuel me for whatever trial is to come. Sauntering towards Jaxon, Aspen pushes a hand against his chest, walking him back into the sea of foam.

"What was that about?" Torsten asks, but I don't answer. There are no words to be spoken, but *there are* plenty of blood-filled decanters to be drained while I watch the show. Aspen isn't just any female; she's an enigma. Power runs through her veins. I want her to thrive, embrace all of her gifts, and be there with her every step of the way. Even if it has to be from afar.

"Where are you taking me?" I ask Jaxon, not complaining when his hand slips into mine. Fresh air filters through the foam on my skin, creating a deep chill that I relish. Anything to soothe the burning of my betraying loins.

I let Chase get into my head and influence my actions. The blood they fed me was tainted, evident by the light-headed spin swirling around my head. Anyone in my position, presented with three interested males and only a few hours to enjoy them, would also walk hand-in-hand while Jax smiles and tugs me to wherever he was taking me.

Reaching the edge of the small town, we trail the edge of the wall towards a series of houses set aside from the rest of the territory—a small suburb fitted with manicured lawns and white picket fences. My heart thumps in my chest, my senses on full alert. Chase and Torsten aren't too far behind, keeping a reasonable distance.

I can only imagine the threats Jaxon promised when I went to the club's bathroom for a moment of peace. Unfortunately, no amount of water splashed on my face or slaps I gave myself helped to unscramble my thoughts. Without Sawyer around to talk me down from the ledge of bad decisions, I'm left at the mercy of two primal beasts within. One of which is currently horny as fuck, and the other is whining to be petted and told she's a good girl.

"Lorcan thought it best that mated couples have a haven away from the pressures of the castle. He may be many things, but your father knows something about nurturing love."

"Yeah, right." I snort. The dirt path we're following suddenly becomes stone, a road diverting in three directions. As if constructed from the front cover of a magazine, the expansive building is clad in white and artfully decorated in the light of the moon. Telltale shutter systems have been implemented over bay windows, the Techies leaving their mark with keypad entry systems.

"No, really, Aspen," Jax pulls me to a stop beside a small gate. "You saw Lorcan the other night. He's suffering, and there's no amount of time or distraction that will heal him. I know we've ambushed you with all of this, but you might want to consider building a relationship with him. While you're still able to."

"So, how many mated couples live here?" I ask, swiftly turning my head and changing the subject.

"Currently, there aren't any. Our females have never been able to survive childbirth." My jaw drops open, eyes whipping back to Jaxon's saddened blue gaze.

"Never? But…" my brow furrows. That means none of these vampires have known what it's like to have a mother. To feel nurtured. and it's still up for debate whether I've actually survived, but I'm thankful for the time I had with her. Yet, no females mean no new generations. "Fuck Jax, how many vampires are left?"

"A hundred or so. Less than our rivals believe. It wasn't noticeable until only males began being born—a dark time for us all. Males were driven crazy by their need to reproduce. Resorted to kidnapping, and rape, things I'm not proud to have witnessed. Lorcan was just a commander back then but saw the need for a change." I peer back to the looming castle on the heightened mound.

"He became king to save the remaining females," I nod. My teeth sink into the inside of my cheek, not wanting to sympathize with him. Refusing to let the blossom of understanding resonate within. I need someone to hate. Someone to blame, and I'm worried that if it isn't him, it will probably be me.

"Come, there's something I need to show you."

"Wait, last question. If females are unable to have children, why were these houses built? Surely couples won't last long enough to enjoy them." A lump rises in my throat.

"Aside from yourself and your sister, Lorcan has forbidden all future pregnancies. What you see now, the vampires you meet…we're all that will ever be. Our species ends with us." Shifting his hand to interlink our fingers, Jax opens the gate and leads me inside. As promised, I leave the subject at the fence. The porch is wide, clad in white wood beneath an overhanging porch. Pushing in the keycode, Jaxon gestures for me to enter the darkened space.

"So, what did you want to show me?" The door slams closed.

"This," his voice breathes beside my ear. Spinning me around, Jaxon pins me against the door. His weight traps me as his sinful mouth begins its attack. Kissing, licking, nibbling, and scraping his fangs along my shoulder, neck, and jawline. I groan, desire quickly overwhelming my surprise.

"I thought this was strictly against the rules," I mutter. A smirk hitches my lips, coming directly from my inner vampire. My wolf shudders, slipping me the last thought of 'Jaxon will suffer for this' before she's suppressed. Jaxon's jean-clad thigh pushes between mine, reminding me of how wet I've been since Torsten's kiss and Chase's lust-filled words.

When his lips finally take mine hostage, I am already panting from the heat radiating from his body. Calloused hands roam my waist and stomach, pushing the bralette higher to brush his palms across my ribs. His exploration of my body continues up my back until he holds my nape firmly, forcing my submission to his desires. This vampire is going to own me in every conceivable way before sunrise, and I'm going to let him.

Bending to throw me over his shoulder, a surprised scream escapes my throat. He chuckles, the rumbling passing through my torso pressed against his back. Carrying me up the stairs and into a bathroom, Jax plants me inside the shower cubicle and turns the water on. There's no hint of protest from me when he steps into the glass chamber, fully clothed, and closes the sliding door behind him.

"You're filthy," he groans, his eyes on the stains running from my shorts, dripping down my thighs. My inner vampire groans in delight as I manage to retain a hint of control.

"Sure," I laugh. "This has nothing to do with Torsten's and Chase's scent being all over me." Jaxon's blue eyes turn glacial, the jealousy swirling in the depths, causing me to bite my lip. He doesn't like that. Pulling my lip free with his thumb, Jax shoves me beneath the spray and stalks directly after.

His collared, black shirt is immediately soaked through, revealing every rippled muscle of his abdomen through the material. My throat is dry, craving him. Desperate to lick a pathway between each ripple in his abdomen towards the deeply engrained V lingering above his waistband. Flicking my eyes lower, his full, impressive length is visibly outlined through dark blue jeans.

"I need you to command me," Jax barely manages to grit out, his voice constricted. Inhaling deeply, the truth of his desperation is thick. He's barely holding back, a sense of duty gripping the last of his reservations. I could toy with him, but fuck if I don't want him just as much.

"Take me." Kicking off his shoes, Jax takes his shirt in both hands and yanks hard. His biceps flex against the short, restricting sleeves as buttons burst around the booth like plastic bullets. I'm too distracted to flinch, unable to stand and watch his perfect body being revealed any longer. Stepping forward, fully under the spray of warm water, I reach up on my tip toes to push the shirt's collar over Jax's corded shoulders.

Once the material drops onto the floor, I kiss over the expanse of tattoos he bears, stopping to pay distinct attention to the dragon head in the center of his chest. A rumbling growl passes beneath, more beast than male. Boldly, despite fumbling, I reach for his leather belt, unbuckling and pulling the length free from the hoops with more finesse than I thought I could manage.

Jax launches forward and grips my hips, pushing me backward against the cool tile wall. My back momentarily arches, causing my breasts to jut outwards. Keeping his head hung low, Jax's lips are teasingly close to my aching nipples as he unbuttons my shorts and hooks his thumbs in the waistband. Slowly, so damn leisurely, he pushes them down to the floor and kneels to remove my shoes. After helping me to step free, Jax's eyes glow with hunger, my bared pussy so close to his mouth. Considering Chase supplied my outfit, it's no surprise I had no underwear on. His breath fans me as I try not to quiver under his scrutiny, water cascading around us like a curtain.

Running his hands up my smooth legs, his mouth worships my thighs, kissing and trailing his fangs across my sensitized skin. Planting a brief kiss against my clit, he stands back to his full height, towering over me. I scowl. While his slanted smile against his harshly handsome face is a sight to behold, the sight of that handsome face between my thighs is one I want branded inside my mind for good.

Yet still, I can't force him to hurry his exploration. Pulling my bralette over my head, Jax fills his palms with shower gel and begins massaging my breasts skillfully. Oh, so slowly, flicking his thumbs over my nipples more times than necessary. The scents of vanilla and coconut envelope me as I relax back against the tiles, giving myself over to his expert touch.

When he presses his lips against mine, Jax spreads the suds over the rest of my body-- now that he's made enough lather between my cleavage to clean a small herd of elephants. Once covered as far as he can reach, except for the one place I'm aching for him to touch, Jax pulls back and unhooks the shower head from the wall, using it to wash me clean. This is the true Jaxon. Caring, calm. A balm to my soul.

Hovering over my breasts, the pressure of the water beats off my unbearably hard nipples, spiking me with a tense pleasure-pain combo. Moving the shower head lower, he hooks my left leg in the crook of his arm and raises it, fully opening me to him. The jet of water is placed over my center. Water beats against my clit, causing my breath to catch and my toes to curl. My body is rigid, the assault intense. And there's not a second Jaxon doesn't drink in, his eyes zeroed in on my pleasure.

Too soon, Jax replaces the shower head in its holder and switches the water flow off. Still holding my leg high, he bends to take one of my nipples in his mouth while his free hand cups me roughly between my legs. I hold onto his large shoulders tightly, my nails embedding into his pale skin. Sucking my nipple mercilessly, his fangs graze and cause my own to lengthen in response. His thumb circles my clit as he moves his mouth to repeat the assault on the other nipple. The room is filled with my moans, echoed by the vampire inside, forcing my head to jerk sideways. She's done waiting.

Thrusting my hand into Jax's braided hair, I use my enhanced strength to push him to his knees. Still in drenched jeans, Jax blinks his blue eyes up at me, droplets on his lashes. My inner vampire sighs contently at his submission. Jaxon may not know of the war I fight on a daily basis, but thankfully he's playing into her desires. I hate to think what she'd have me do if he refused.

Kissing my stomach, my leg is dropped over Jax's shoulder as his hands thrust my hips back into the wall. The rough pad of his tongue runs the length of my pussy. Again, and again. Steady, slow measures that draw a gasp from me every time. No matter how much I push him closer, shamelessly grinding against his face, Jaxon gives me what I need. Not what I want. My body shakes as a tightening builds deep within my core. Replacing his thumb on my clit with his lips, Jax sucks hard, ridding all rational thought. I'm a slave to his touch. At his mercy. Lost to the rhythm he sets, alternating between teasing my clit and dipping his tongue to my soaking cunt. My skin grows taut. Everywhere I can feel is overheated, preparing to break apart at the seams.

I barely register that he's moved until I feel a long digit smooth its way inside me. I moan loudly, tossing my head back. Jax pumps his finger in and out of me, still at an infuriatingly relaxed pace, while his tongue focuses on my clit. Growing frustrated, I claw at his shoulders, silently begging him to finish what he's started. He teases me, keeping me balanced on the edge of this feeling for so long that I think my legs might give out.

Suddenly, two more fingers plummet inside my pussy, and I cry out. An orgasm rips through me, my walls tightening and contracting around his fingers while he continues to stroke me leisurely. His unhurried movements draw my climax on and on, pulling every ounce of pleasure from my body. My back is arched, my glowing eyes squeezed shut, allowing me to ride the waves crashing through me until they cease and Jax finally relents.

Standing with a content smirk, Jax eyes the flush I feel coating my neck. Lifting me into his arms, he slides the door back and carries me to a bedroom with an extra-large, king-size bed. Gently placing me onto the plush covers, I bit my lip as he strips from his wet jeans. His cock jumps free, jutting out eagerly as my brows raise at his size. I knew it would be impressive, but fucking wow. Not just at his length. The sheer girth is wrapped in a thick vein, leading from the base to the plum-colored head, which appears silky smooth. I lick my lips on instinct.

"You know, what I was telling you outside means that I've never...been with a female." Jax hesitates at the foot of the bed. I snort.

"Oh, please. I smelt the amount of sex and heard the moans when I first arrived at the castle." I roll my eyes, but Jax's grave expression only deepens, and I push up on my elbows. "Wait. There are only twelve females to a hundred men. And Lorcan doesn't allow them to mix, so," my brows raise. "You and...Chase? Torsten? Both or others?"

"As I said, we're primal creatures. We have base needs that can't be denied. Does that bother you?"

Bother me? I'm currently envisioning a threesome of white hair and green eyes that leaves me unbelievably wetter.

Beckoning for him, Jax lowers his mouth-watering body over me, his knee nudging my thighs open to settle himself there. His cock presses against my core eagerly. Lust filters through my hooded eyes as I hold the sides of Jax's face and pull his mouth onto mine. I don't care about his past, as I don't expect him to judge me for the pleasure I took from the humans I was given to hunt. Consensually, I should add – I'm a freak, not a nymphomaniac. They weren't aware I'd literally eat them when I'd taken the pleasure I needed. Yeah, we all have pasts, but I can't deny that I want to be a part of Jaxon's future in any capacity.

Jax kisses me slowly and passionately, but something has changed. I feel it in the rigidness of his body, his shallow breathing. Breaking away, I hunt his gaze and discover, it won't meet mine.

"You really don't realize how special you are, do you?" I observe. He pressed his lips together tightly, and I have my answer. Without much effort, I push Jax onto his back and straddle him.

"I'm one of many," he shrugs. "Any vampire could have been sent to fetch you that night, and it would have been him in this position now." I laugh with a heavy dose of shock. Apparently, I'm fickle enough to fall for any vamp who takes the time out of his busy schedule to pay me attention. Pulling his braid over his shoulder, I stroke the coarse brown dreadlocks before hitting his cheek with them.

"Listen to me very carefully, Jaxon," I command, sensing his internal berating. "I wouldn't be naked and straddling any old fuckface just for the fun of it. Now put your reservations on hold and prove to me that I chose you for a reason."

Something in my words has triggered a reaction from Jaxon, one I can't fully read. "You choose me?" Jaxon asks quietly.

It's my turn to shrug. "I'm here, aren't I? Rock my fucking world, and don't let me regret it." After a beat of staring at me in awe, Jaxon jerks upright to crash our lips together and pull my weight down on top of him. His biceps lock a cage around me, his mouth devouring mine. The long hard length of his cock pushes against my core, asking to be granted access. But first, a round of teasing as he forced me to endure in the shower. I let my fingers skim his body, tracing feather-light touches over his torso, testing if he has any weak points. At least on the surface, there are none to speak of, but he enjoys my exploration regardless.

Mimicking me, Jax trails his hand down my body, skimming my breasts and stomach until he reaches the apex of my thighs. Instinctively knowing I'm wet and ready, he guides his dick into my entrance and slides himself in with agonizing slowness. All at once, my wolf howls inside my ears while the vampire in me hisses *yessss*, the thickness of Jaxon's cock making us all lose our damn minds. He's so thick, that vein is doing untold things to my subconsciousness. Every nerve ending comes to life. Stretching me, edging me toward an orgasm I'm not prepared to give him easily. Holding my hips in mid-air, Jax pulls out, repeating the process several times until he's fully seated inside.

"*Fuck.*" Jax's jaw is tense, and his body stiff. "You're *so* damn tight." Smiling at the prospect of affecting me just as much, I grind my hips against his groin—a gentle roll that causes us both to groan audibly. Beneath the sound, a third moan catches my ear, and I chuckle. Arching my back, my ass bounces, the sound of my pussy gripping his cock overwhelming. On my next blink, Jax is cast in a golden hue, my eyes burning bright within my skull.

"So fucking beautiful," Jaxon marvels, but I don't want his praise. I want his submission. Slamming my hands down on his chest, I steady myself to work up a faster rhythm—a harsher one, where each connection causes a slapping sound alongside our ragged pants. Twisting Jax's dreads around my hand, I secure his head in place and flash my fangs.

"I wouldn't goad me right now if I were you," he grits through clenched teeth. Unable to resist his challenge, I tut. Gums tingling, my jaw hangs loose as I relent to the other forces aching for control.

"Promises, promises," I respond, my voice laced with a rough echo. I relish the feeling of him deeper than any other could ever be. If there was a pivotal moment in life where someone who be content dying just after, this would be it for me. This cesspit of heaven enveloped in the scents of our lust, with two different heartbeats lingering nearby. When I refuse to release his hair, Jax releases a warning growl and then moves. A blur of movement which sees me on my back on the mattress. His tattooed fingers close around my neck, and fucking finally, the rest of Jax is presented to me.

His cock slams into me, all the way to the hilt, where he rocks until I cry out. Then again as his hand wraps around my hair, tugging roughly as his cock hits me with the force of a jackhammer. This time, I scream, fingernails scraping the arm holding my hair, and he grins.

"I warned you," he gloats, repeating the process over and over. Each powerful thrust draws my walls closer to tensing around him. I want more, need more. My hands grip his hips, and I aid his pace, tugging him against me until a final scream rips me apart. Waves crash through me like a tsunami, and I happily drown. Lost to the three sides of my being finally syncing into one. We break together, our vague concentration centered on the beautiful vampire thrusting into me at an unperceivable rate. My fingernails tear at his skin, the scent of his blood spurring me on. I'm hurting him, yet the rush of ecstasy pulsing through me only grows stronger. And when he reaches beneath me to place a large hand on the small of my back, tilting me into his oncoming thrust, he seals his own fate.

Every nerve-ending is alive, the brush of his skin on mine like lightning dancing over the surface. Pounding my flesh, ruining me for any other. Owning me, as he has since the moment his baby blues set on me in the forest. In my darkest moment, Jaxon stepped out of the shadows to entice me. Yet it's not until he's giving me the full wrath of his strength and skill that I can fully appreciate how much I've been aching for this. The fire in my core has barely lessened before beginning to stir again, coiling into a formidable feeling I can't contain. I have to climax with him. Break with him, and then we'll piece each other back together again.

My fangs tingle painfully, at their fullest length, against Jax's shoulder while he continues to ram into me repeatedly. I bury my face into his neck, inhaling his delectable scent. Fresh pine rolls over my senses, and the drum of his pulse calls to me on a primal level. *Fuck it.* I spear my fangs into the side of his throat, setting off a chain of reactions from the first hard suck. His blood flows over my tongue. His sweet taste makes me light-headed until he roars his release, not once relenting the violent pounding. We crash together, spiraling into the abyss, never looking back.

Once our breathing eases, his gaze meets mine. Beautiful blue irises flanked with gold, while black lines appear around his eyes. I see the struggle contorting his features, but he can't resist a fleeting look at my neck.

"I will hunt down every mother fucker who has ever made you feel worthless and rip their throats out," Jax growls protectively. Little does he know, I did just that yesterday. I stroke my hands over his back, feeling the evidence of my attack, although Jax visibly relaxes and continues through gritted teeth. "I want you so fucking bad, Aspen. Your mind, your body, your soul, and everything that comes along with it. I knew the moment I met you, my world would be turned upside." His full grin is deadly, full of threats I want to see through to the end.

"Bite me, for fuck's sake." I avoid his sentiment, offering him my neck. His dick is still nestled into me, rock-hard and ready to go again. "Unless Chase and Torst have something to say about it." Across the room, a pair of shadows step free from the corner beside a looming wardrobe. Torsten's white hair hangs forward in shame of watching, but Chase has no such qualms.

"No arguments here, as long as I get a turn," Chase smirks mischievously. A turn at my neck or my pussy, I'm not sure to which he was referring, and honestly, I don't fucking care.

Chapter Sixteen

I'm starving. Not in the, *damn, I could really use a blood bag,* kind of way. But in the actual, *I'm going to starve to death, and all of this will have been for nothing,* sense.

Upon arriving in the dungeons, we were shown to our individual cells and locked inside. That was around four days ago if I'm keeping count correctly. It's hard to tell with the lack of windows or guests in our underground prison. Unlike the modernized version of a dungeon, with all hi-tech locks and glass doors, we've been abandoned in the archaic part of the underground tunnels. These cells haven't had captives in decades, but I can still pick up on the shifter blood that once coated the stone walls.

I've always considered myself a patient male, able to endure the urges others barely control. But this is different. The gut-wrenching hunger tearing me apart makes it impossible to hold onto thoughts of my night with Aspen. The ones which may have seen me through if my stomach wasn't trying so hard to cave in on itself.

Still, the flashes of her legs straddling my waist and her white hair tumbling over her shoulder, stroking my abdomen while those navy eyes, like the midnight sky speckled with golden stars, consumed me, were keeping me sane. If only, just.

She could be my mate, my entire universe if I prove myself worthy. I'm not like Chase, not even Torsten. Convincing myself that I'm enough is nothing but a hollow promise until I win the trials. Aspen deserves a champion, and that's exactly what I'll be for her.

Instead, I'm stuck here. In a world of reverse psychology, fighting for the very woman I could die thinking of. Not knowing where she is now, if she's safe, and what's happening in the world above our heads. That's the worst part. I can't protect her down here. None of us can.

Sitting on the uneven, rocky floor in the dark, like rats waiting for scraps. Nothing in my centuries of life has ever felt so degrading as this. The most elite of us left to suffer. I have considered that Lorcan found out after our escapades with Aspen and has decided to end the trial permanently, although that wouldn't explain Carrick's presence.

"Tor-" I croak through a throat as dry as the desert. Up to this point, groans from the adjacent cells have kept me company, but it's their silence that has become unnerving. "Ch...Chase?" Nothing. No replies. I curse mentally, drawing my eyelids closed.

Four. Fucking. Days. Lorcan's most trained and ferocious warriors, locked up and starved deep under the castle. If anyone decides to attack the castle now, his strongest defenses are rotting away in cells, and it would take weeks for us to recover, if we ever do.

Most Vamps would be fully decomposed by now. These cells are built with thick silver bars, meaning we can't touch them without melting the skin from our hands within seconds. Despite being able to see in the dark, the bleakness of our surroundings weighs too heavily. Occasionally a drip of rainwater leaks through the cracks in the ceiling, echoing painfully through my over-sensitized ears.

The inside of my throat is so raw that I struggle to draw breath, and swallowing is a fleeting memory. I know, without checking, that my cheeks have become hollow, my skin a pale shade of gray, and my eyes most likely have lost all of their coloring by now. Bones protrude in the areas where my skin has begun to shrink in on itself. Soon enough, there will be no coming back. In a day or so, I won't be much more than a skeleton, incapable of movement or speaking. If only I had drunk from Aspen as she requested.

That thought sends another sharp wave of agony through my body. I can't live in regret, not when I wrung Aspen of all the pleasure her body could offer. But drinking for her vein was a gift I couldn't take. She may not understand our ways, and I'm not the asshole who's going to use that against her.

As I lay back and rest my arms beneath my head, my deteriorating mind wonders. Drifting back and forth like tumbleweed, considering how the vampires have arrived at this precipice. How we've been driven to hiding in the mountains and risking our lives for the chance of finding a mate. Whether it be our fated mate or not, all many of us want to feel is love.

Some of our kind believe we shouldn't hide any longer; venture into the human world to impregnate humans. I can't say the thought hasn't crossed my mind. Genetically we're the strongest beings on the planet, yet we've isolated ourselves and live in the shadows like parasites. And now I've felt what it's like to have a female touch, worship, and pine for you, I can't deny I want that for the rest of the species too.

It's not like it hasn't been done before. We have our very own human experiment living right here in the castle we've claimed. It's possible for daywalkers to be born, yet Lorcan refuses to admit it as a viable option. My mind shifts then, to dreams of being able to shed my UV affliction, for just one day. Beyond the stone wall surrounding the castle and its town, our land is so serene. Stunning in the moonlight, but I bet it's nothing short of glorious in the sun's rays. From the rugged mountain peaks and long sandy beaches to sparkling lakes and rivers, we truly do have the perfect place to keep to ourselves.

A muffled sound pulls me back from my thoughts, somewhere between a strangled cry and a grunt. With an embarrassing amount of effort, I shift onto my side and sigh. How much longer are we going to be stuck here? Footsteps echo from the staircase leading down into the dungeons, but I can't move again to look. My muscles have seized into the fetal position, a rogue curse stuck in my throat. Inside my mind, I'm screaming, yet on the outside, I'm frozen in place. Keys jingle in the lock, the bars squeaking in protest as the door is yanked open. Thank fuck! But no one enters.

I vaguely hear each door opening and fight to part my lips, enough for noise to leak through. My jaw cramps, sweat beading my brow from pure concentration. Each time I try to desperately hold on to a coherent thought, it eludes me, and I'm mentally stretching my arms to grab it and pull it back.

Suddenly, something smacks me in the face. It falls against my cheek, soft and cold. Bit late for a cushion now, I think wryly, especially one that small. I don't bother to open my eyes as the footsteps retreat, leaving me here to waste away. But then again... what's that smell?

I force a long inhale, dragging in the coppery scent until it hits the back of my throat. Holy shit, it's blood. Not just any blood, the rarest type we stock - AB negative. I manage to crack an eyelid ever so slightly despite the slice of pain I didn't think an eyelid could feel. There's a full blood bag right beneath my nose, begging me to empty it. If only the guard who dropped it could have kindly uncapped the tube and fed me the way I damn deserve after all of this.

I attempt and fail to move my arms. As if I'm in a mental straitjacket, they refuse to respond. My little finger twitches but the rest of my hand is too depleted to move. I close my one open eye and push all my focus into moving something, anything. The strain I'm putting on my weak bones threatens to snap them, but that smell is sending me into a frenzy. I desperately try to wet my cracked lips with my tongue, but there's no moisture to be found.

Eventually, after far too fucking long, I manage to shift half an inch forward and push my face down onto the blood bag. With pure determination and a shit load of pain, I curl back my top lip just enough to extend a fang and sink it into the outer sleeve barring me from the life-saving nectar inside. After a few tense seconds, the bag bursts and my cheek falls heavily onto the hard floor, shattering it on impact. Fucking *ouch*.

The scent overwhelms me as the blood covers half of my face, and I manage to draw some of the delicious liquid into my mouth. After I manage the first painful swallow, I start to come to life gradually until I'm sucking the blood from the grooves in the rock like a goddamn leech. This is beyond humiliating, but I can't bring myself to give a shit right this second.

Ignoring the mouthfuls of grime and grit, I'm forced to swallow down; I begin to feel a bit more myself. Still lying on the floor, I stretch my limbs until my organs are fully functional again, the way they should be. Wriggling my toes, rolling my ankles, and twisting my body around the cell until I feel well enough to sit up. I've already sucked the floor harder than a cheap hooker; I'm not going to put falling on my ass to today's list of things to do.

At least another hour must pass while I, not so, patiently wait for my calf muscles to strengthen before I attempt to stand. With the cell door left wide open and no guard in sight, I can't risk stumbling into the silver bars and adding third-degree burns to my recovering body. I'll need to feed many more times before recovering enough to function as it is.

Pushing myself upright, I shuffle towards the exit, careful not to move too quickly, though desperation is clawing at me to be free of here. Every cell door in the row is wide open, but I can't see or hear any movements inside. I stop, glancing at the staircase. Aspen will be up there, within reach. The woman I've been starved and tortured over. Love is a gift only twelve of our males will have the chance to claim, but my feet won't move. Instead, they take me further into the dungeon to peer at the two males I care for lying deathly still on the stone floor with a full bag of blood next to each of them. Carrick is in the last cell at the end, the one I completely ignore.

A lesser vamp would walk away. A shittier one would take the blood bags with them. But my father raised me with dignity. *'Empathy makes you strong, and sympathy makes you noble,'* he would say. He believed our greatest asset was compassion and then would beat me senseless for not being the greatest. I still had to be the best of the best but also give a shit about those I shat on as if that's not confusing for a young vamp seeking his father's approval.

At first, I attend to Torsten, tipping the bag of blood into his parted mouth. His skin had begun peeling, his muscles worryingly thin, but his condition doesn't come close to Chase's. In the next cell, colorless eyes stare at a spot on the far wall, blood smeared across his chin from slicing open and sucking on his bottom lip. His hands are almost pure bone, his body a fifth of the vamp I know.

Gently, I roll Chase onto his back and lift his skull-like head in time with dripping shots of blood into his mouth. Despite barely having strength myself, I have to manually make him swallow by rocking his head against my shoulder. Once the blood bag is drained, I quickly toss the bag aside and drag him into the cradle of my weak arms.

"Come back to me, you jokey little prick," I mutter. "Wake up, so I can beat you for scaring me." When the male in the adjacent cell stirs, I lift Chase and shuffle into it. Placing him beside Torsten, I stroke Chase's bald head. He's going to be pissed about losing his long, brunette locks if he can transition back to the male I previously knew. For all our sakes, I hope he does. There's nothing to be done but wait for the blood to work around their systems and get more help.

Anger churns in my gut, pushing me on, even though my own body is failing me too. Despite my reservations, I stop by Carrick's cell, push the blood bag tube between his lips, and walk away. That's as far as my duty goes towards one of my own, even if Carrick's motives in these trials are warped. He hasn't been quiet about wanting to be king, and at no point has he mentioned the desire to take a mate. His morals, or lack thereof, define his character, and his character was shit.

I stumble numerous times, my knees slicing open and not healing, but still, I press on until I make it back to the staircase, leaning against the wall for support. Shuffling up the steps, I'm practically crawling by the time I reach the top.

A royal guard meets me at the top of the stairs, making a show of announcing me as the winner to the waiting crowd. Fists pump in the air and bang on firm chests, our motto being chanted on repeat.

'For our King and our Kind.'

I fight a scoff, allowing the guard to help me through the mob. To risk our strongest soldiers by leaving them in a state of slow, lingering malnutrition. Only now is the true weight of agony settling on me. Give me a good, clean fight any day, and I'll take the win within five minutes. But this is insanity. Reaching the back of the males, turning down the hallways towards the blood bank, the females are waiting there. Royal guards try to keep Aspen at bay, but she ducks pasts, her face filled with elation as she runs for me. Unfortunately, she doesn't rely on her vampire speed, giving the redhead who blurs past, screaming my name to fly into my arms first.

For once, my inner vampire and I are in complete agreement. *Who the fuck is that?*

All these days, I've been pacing around the East Wing, distracting myself in the botanical gardens, I haven't been interested in meeting the other females. Now I'm berating myself for thinking these three males I've been fretting over wouldn't have another woman in the exact same position. We won't even think about where Sawyer might be or with whom, but Jaxon? Of all the males I thought wouldn't have any skeletons in his closet, he was the one I trusted the most. Now, I'm not so sure who I've been envisioning, who I've been fantasying about having sex with over and over again.

My footsteps halt, embarrassment clawing up my throat. The redhead has her arms locked around Jaxon's neck, and he's making no move to push her off. Backtracking, I ignore meeting anyone's eye contact and retreat to the suite I've been assigned. Shooting through the lower level of the East Wing, I come to the winding staircase before hearing footsteps above. A female vampire I don't recognize turns the corner, a royal guard at her back.

Bright green eyes narrow as she halts, taking me in with a long, bitchy, all-the-way-down-and-back-up-again look. Even from a step below, I can tell we're of a similar height, her figure plumper than other vampires I've seen, and she knows it. Her breasts are pushed together in a floor-length gown fit for a ball. Clinging to her curves and showing a hint of leg through the thigh-high slit, she's every bit the regal princess a castle would expect.

I knew exactly who she was merely from the scent we share with Lorcan. My half-sister. The sibling I wish I had during all those lonely days. The princess who should be preparing to become queen, instead of me fumbling through a lasting panic attack. With a flick of her bouncy brown curls and a raise of her chin, she strides past, shoulder barging me on the way.

"The fuck," I growl, but her guard gives me a grave look. His blue eyes are too alike Jax's, despite the shot of blonde hair on his head. Following his charge, I forget the pair of them, not stopping again until I'm slamming the door to the royal suite closed behind me.

Chest heaving, I slump against the door, facing the huge open-plan room splayed before me. A wide glass dining table and four leather chairs sit to the right beside a newly built kitchenette with gray marbled worktops over black cupboard doors. State-of-the-art equipment has been installed for my benefit, all-electric and shining chrome.

Pushing upright, I walk over the plush, beige carpet towards the charcoal corner sofa. On the opposite wall, a pebble-gray backdrop showcases a large flatscreen TV that I have yet to learn how to use. This is much like the cell phone Nova gave me, which sits on the coffee table between the sofa and the cabinet, all resting on a plush plum-colored shaggy rug. Even the accents of gold on the light fitting above my head are just as modern and luxurious as the rest of the suite I've been gifted.

My mother could have had this lifestyle, but instead, decided to throw it away. Until her dying day, she was empathic and caring, her duty to her people always coming first. We only spoke about my real father once, soon after we'd first been exiled, and a scared thirteen-year-old wanted to understand why. Why was I so different, why was it a problem, and why hadn't she ever warned me? Although the conversation was brief and the answers to my questions were evasive, the pain held within her eyes was enough for me never to bring it up again.

I always thought of her as a goddess in her linen and leather attire, holding a thick wooden shield and iron-headed spear, never shying away from fight until it came to Conall's rule. Her soul was beautiful, every fiber of her being focused on helping anyone or thing around her. So, I decided at my adolescent age that I wouldn't berate her for the one time in her life she had done something purely for herself. She deserved happiness, whatever form it came in.

I lie, waiting for my inner vampire to take over. This is a routine I'm becoming accustomed to. Battle against an onslaught of unexpected emotion, then allow her to squash it with harsh words spoken into my ears. Usually filled with revenge and bitterness, but after that, a dulled sense of numbness seeps in, and I'm able to breathe easier once more. Such an event has happened many times over the past few days when the worry grew too much. I just didn't think I'd have to face it again so soon. I also didn't plan on returning to the suite alone but turns out the male I was counting on has another to attend to his wounds.

There's a desk behind the sofa, complete with a black leather swivel chair like the one in Lorcan's office. Well, before I trashed it. I've left the window above wide open, fooling myself into thinking Sawyer might suddenly appear. It's clear he's gone for good, and the thought causes my heart to squeeze and not in the figurative sense. My chest cramps as I hiss through my teeth, gasping for relief from the misery. Fisting my hands in my long hair, I spin, unsure of what to do with myself.

Heading to the kitchenette, I load some chips and dips onto a tray before venturing to the sofa. I haven't been told to stay here, but I haven't been given permission to explore the castle at my leisure either. Now I know Jax is alive, and knowing he wouldn't have left Torsten and Chase behind had they not been okay, I can hide away. Tucked out of sight from the judgment I received today.

And that suits me just fine. If this suite is to be my prison, I will gladly remain. Each evening at sundown, a food basket is left on the doorstep, and as long as I keep the metal shutter open, I can't be bothered during daylight hours. It took me ten whole seconds of arriving to spot a cabinet in the living area beneath the mounted TV, fully stocked with books. The smell of aged pages was undeniable, and that's where I'll have to seek happiness from here on out.

Moments later, I am curled up on the sofa, fully invested in a romance novel between mutants and a ghost, when a loud knock bangs on the front door. I flinch and then scowl as I'm pulled out of my literary page stupor, right as I'm in the moment where the female lead was about to choose between her head and her heart. My frantic turning of the pages must have blocked the sounds of someone coming up the hallway.

Well, fuck them, I mentally roll my neck, book boyfriends wait for no one. Burying my face deeper in the book, I hope whoever it is will take the hint and disappear. But the knock comes again, even louder this time before the doors burst open anyway. If it had been anyone else, I'd have turned my back and ignored them, but upon seeing a version of Torsten and Chase that makes my eye bulge, I rush to meet them.

"Oh, my shit," I breathe, my hands hovering over Chase's unconscious form. Torsten stumbles, unable to carry his friend anymore, and drops him into my arms. "What the fuck are you doing here? Isn't there an infirmary or somewhere you can take him?!" Torsten leans his weight on my shoulder also, and if he hadn't been a fraction of the size I last saw him last, I would have crumpled. Awkwardly kicking the door shut, I maneuver the pair towards the bedroom by staggering through an open, rounded archway to ease Chase onto the spongey mattress.

"He needs you," Torsten croaks, laying himself down by his friend. My hands hang at my sides, panic rooting me in place. Torsten's pale skin is flakey, as if he's taken a cheese grater to his limbs. His white hair is still in place, although the grayness of his eyes is paler. Unlike Chase's, whose once emerald green eyes are now bleached white, his head free of hair and body a pewter gray. Lacking all muscle, I wouldn't even know it was him if Torsten hadn't carried him in with the last burst of strength he could manage.

"I don't know what you think I can do," I say, a quiver in my voice. Torsten reaches out for me, shuffling back to leave enough room for me in the middle. I do not comply. I'm having a hard enough time trying to remember the males from the cabin, who charmed and challenged me into feeling for them. Never mind climbing into bed to play a rousing game of 'Who's the bonier spoon.' There's not enough shower gel in the world to rid me of the ick I get just from the thought. Yet, they did this for me. In some twisted sense, this proves the depth of their sacrifice. The lengths they're willing to go to. I shake my head.

"You all need to stop. I'm not worth this," I gesture to them both. "I...I can't watch you suffer. Just have me if that's what you want. I'm right here, I'll mate with either one of you. Just...stop." My stomach churns as tears spill down my cheeks.

I have seen a man I considered my father reject me in a blink of an eye. I lost my mother, never being able to say goodbye. I have been thrown into exile, outcasted from the only home I knew, ridiculed, and hated. But never have I experienced such strong feelings for not just one but four individuals so quickly and profoundly, only to witness them unravel right before my eyes, all due to a warped sense of duty and honor. I understood that our worlds were vastly different, supernatural's had to follow a distinct set of rules than humans, but duty and honor should never amount to *this*. To hollowed-out, tortured shells of men who just days ago were formidable, strong, and charming.

I force myself to look away, fighting back the wracking sobs stealing my ability to breathe. Because even armed with the knowledge of my history and the battle scars of my torrid past, *nothing* prepared me for how my soul is tearing itself apart just by looking at the two figures in my bed, starved, pale, and *broken*.

I turn as the bed shifts slightly, and this time when Torsten moves, almost as if in slow motion, I realize why I didn't hear him beyond the door. His body is weak and depleted, his movements clunky and robotic, as though his life force was slipping away with each step he took. His heart-beat was faint but discernible, with infrequent thumps echoing through the air.

"Shifter blood, and those of other species, hold potent markers vampires can't produce. He'll heal far quicker by your vein than with the human blood bags." A thin hand touches my shoulder, and I steel myself. *Don't flinch. Don't gag.* "Please, Aspen. Do this, and I'll withdraw." Turning to look into Torsten's pale eyes, my lip wobbles.

"I..." I can't say that. Can't tell him I don't want him to withdraw because then comes the knowledge that we will never be together. I under-stand only one can win, but until that day, I can live within a pretty fantasy where nothing has to change. Jaxon can return to his past lover while I lustfully hate him from a distance, while Torst, Chase, and I remain in limbo. But that's not rational. Not even logical.

Without another word, I crawl up the bed, angling my body towards Chase. He's so still. At the very least, I know I need to do this to repay this debt. I never wanted any of them to suffer, but they did in my honor, and now the guilt is tearing me apart. I'd do next to anything to put the easy smirk back on his face. Cupping his face, Torsten helps as much as he is able, maneuvering Chase towards my exposed neck. It takes a painstaking amount of time to rouse him enough, but upon feeling the flutter of my pulse against his lips, primal instincts take over.

Holy shit.

Chase's fangs spear my neck, a rough growl drawn from him at the taste of my blood. Given his weakened state, I wasn't prepared for him to latch on so hard. He sucks with coarse desperation, greedily gulping down mouthfuls of blood. It takes too much effort not to let myself reveal how good it feels, especially when my nipples are rubbing against the cotton of my t-shirt. Becoming aroused by a decayed vampire wasn't on today's agenda, but it's not just some underfed beast. It's Chase.

He takes long drags, consuming the very life from my body. Torsten becomes agitated at some point, his grumbles lost to the haze claiming me. I can't focus, my entire being centered on the assault on my neck. Each pull on my vein makes a beeline to my G-spot, and I'm losing myself, adrift in a tide of ecstasy.

"Enough, asshole," Torst argues, and my eyes snap open. He's right, Chase is taking too much. And I need to save some to aid them both. Pushing back on Chase, his strength increases with each drop he consumes. My wolf whines inside my ears, hiking up a sense of anxiety. Losing control isn't a position we are comfortable in, regardless of the reason.

Shoving at Chase more forcefully this time, he falls back, tearing a chunk of flesh from my neck. A burst of glimmering green eyes zero on the mess he's made, his lip pulled back on a snarl. When he lunges for me again, I punch him in the face and shoot away in a blur of speed. Grabbing Torsten's wrist on the way passed, I rush us into the bathroom and flick the lock as Chase collides on the other side. Banging, roaring like a monster possessed.

"Well, this is fun," I roll my eyes. Lowering Torsten into the bathroom, I straddle him and hang the dripping wound over his mouth before it heals. It's safe to say that I need to tread carefully until these males have their full senses back. Torsten is much calmer, though, laying patiently while drops of crimson patter over his mouth, chin, and chest.

Oh, just sit on his face already, the voice in my head tuts. I shove her aside. Horny bitch. Instead, I watch Torsten's features restoring at a rapid rate. Pewter gray eyes blink up at me, his jaw appearing sharper. The muscles beneath me expand like a balloon, filling his chest and biceps. Hips thicken beneath me, as does the cock, which is immediately erect and pushing against my center. The wound on my neck heals, ending the spell we'd become captured in, drowning in each other's eyes.

On the other side of the door, the noise has ceased. Much to my vampire's disgust, I peel myself from Torsten, leaving him to finish healing. When I don't hear any movement on the other side, I poke my head into the bedroom. Chase has crashed on the bed, his face smeared with blood against the pillow. A snore leaks from his gaping mouth, his body taking longer to repair than Torsten's did. Stubby, thick brown hair now coats his head, his limbs twitching every so often. A shudder runs through my own spine, preceding a pair of arms wrapping around my middle. Torsten holds me tightly, his chin on my shoulder.

"You're angry."

"Yeah, I'm pissed as all hell." I agree. Testing if he can handle my weight, I lean back into his chest, chewing on the inside of my cheek. "What's the point in winning me if you're all dead, and apparently, you don't even need to be unmated to participate." I throw my arms up in the air. Torsten's hold doesn't ease, his comforting presence washing over me like a balm to my soul.

"Let's leave him to rest. I have an idea that may relax you." My inner vampire perks up her ears, and somehow, I think she'll eventually get her way.

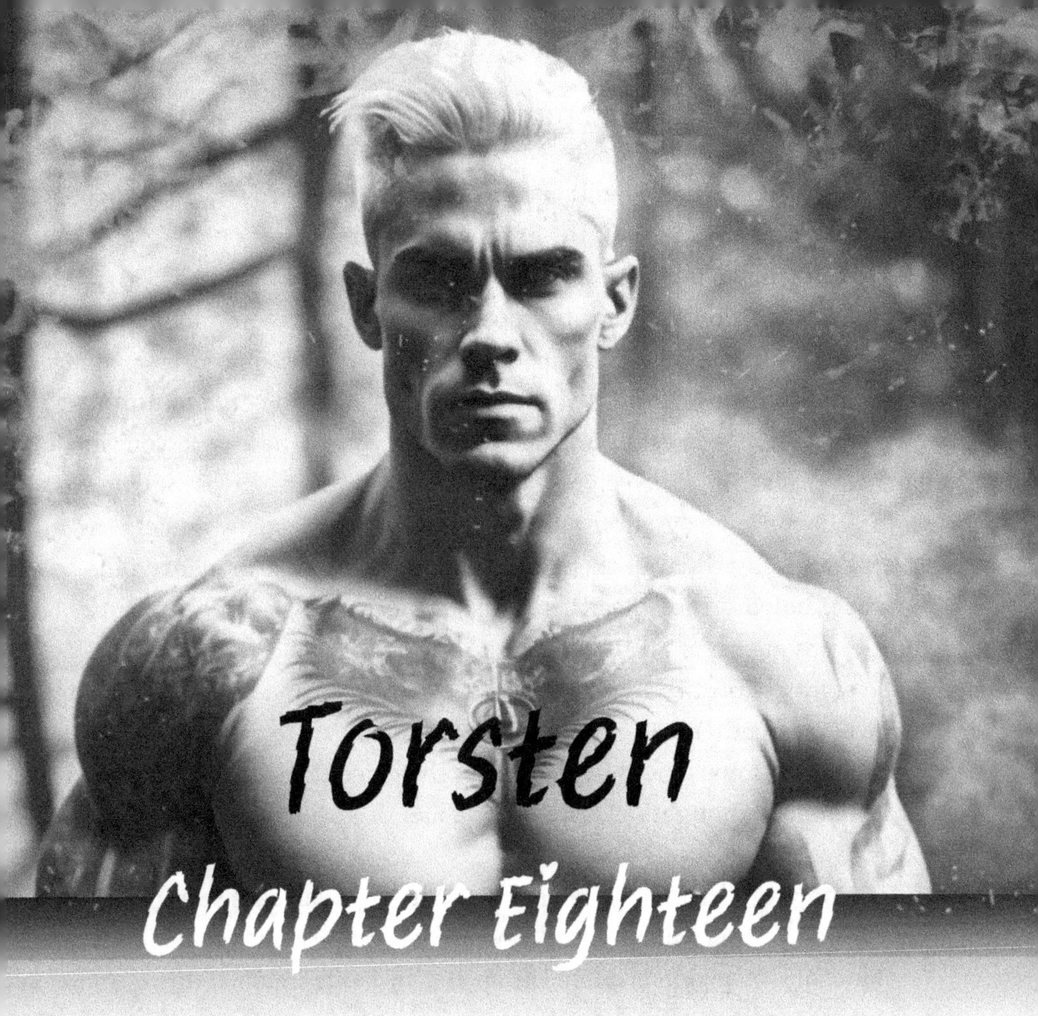

W e are walking down one of the long, stone corridors towards the castle's west wing, hand in hand. This will be the first time Aspen meets other members of the army, and I want them to know she is spoken for immediately. We found suitable workout gear in her wardrobe, and both knew the female's version of a gym wouldn't be enough for her needs. Now we just need to get to the main gymnasium because I can't stop peering back at her plump ass swaying in purple leggings or how her vest hangs loosely over a black sports bra.

We turn the corner and pass through the open double doors into the gym. An ambush of chatter and sweat hits us tenfold, her clench on my hand tightening. Checking she's okay, Aspen juts out her chin and continues inside. Upon smelling her delectable scent, every male inside stops dead and stares at us in the doorway. No turning back now.

"I'd like to introduce you all to Princess Aspen." I wince at her glare in my peripheral vision, but to introduce her simply by her first name would be considered offensive. Turning to look into Aspen's doe eyes, I smile reassuringly. "Aspen, this is most of our army. They'll serve and protect you to the ends of the earth. You can trust everyone in here with your life." She half smiles, looking slightly uncomfortable, and waves out at the Vamps subconsciously shuffling towards her. Clicking my fingers on a growl, reminding them of their manners, everyone in attendance falls to one knee, bowing their heads in unison and causing Aspen to flinch. I chuckle, waving a hand through the air.

"Everyone return to what you were doing. Aspen and I will be working out in here together." The Vamps stand and return to their equipment, although I don't miss the shifty side-eyes they give each other. I can practically hear their thoughts. 'Lorcan won't like this,' but does Lorcan really like anything these days?

"Seeing you all authoritative is kind of hot," Aspen says softly, leaning into my side. Lifting a hand to my chest, I gasp in mock offense.

"Kind of?" A giggle is pulled from her luscious lips, capturing more than a bit of attention from the Vamps pretending to work out around us. Moonlight illuminates the space from above the glass roof. I lead Aspen to the other side of the gymnasium, pointing out modernized exercise machines to the left. On the other, the dumbbells and weight benches live, with multiple pull-up bars in the surrounding area. In the space before open electronic doors leading to a running track, Vamps are sparring on large foam mats, and I see her interest fully piqued.

I had intended to take her outside, away from the crowds, until Aspen abruptly stops and pulls back on my hand. Entranced by the fight currently taking place, her eyes track the sprays of blood, teasing her thumb over her fingertips. There's no protection here, our quick healing allowing us to beat the shit out of one another and still walk out of the room laughing.

"Would you like to join us, Princess?" A cocky Finnian asks, noticing Aspen's intrigued gaze. Fucking Finnian. The other Vamps drop their raised fists and turn to face us, brows quirked. On instinct, I put my arm around Aspen's shoulders and drag her into me.

"No fucking way," I say at the same time she yells, "Hell yes!" Spinning her and blocking out the muttering vampires by crowding her.

"I don't think this is a good idea. Despite being complete cocks, these are some of my most elite soldiers. You will get hurt."

"And then you can kiss me all better." Aspen tiptoes and briefly presses her lips on mine before slipping out of my hold and waking over to the group, confidence swinging with every step. I run a hand over my face. Jaxon is going to dismember me and spread my bones individually so they can never be found.

Finnian's eyes stay on me as Aspen passes him, his tongue sticking into his cheek with his grin wide and flashing both middle fingers in my direction. I lean against the wall behind me, crossing my arms to stop myself from racing over and dragging Aspen back to the safety of her room. This was a fucking terrible idea, but I remind myself that she is a force to be reckoned with. More than that, she needs a chance to be free to make her own decisions without the weight of constant expectations or possible disappointment.

Finnian, seemingly the ringleader of this little shit show, places his hand on the top of her back, causing a deep growl to escape me.

"I'm Finnian, your highness. And this is Keary, Niall, Magnus, and Cade," he points out the others to her. Aspen shrugs his hand from her back, soothing the storm within me. *Slightly.* "We'll be kicking your royal ass today."

"It's lovely to meet you all, but please call me Aspen. It'll be much easier to pronounce after I've finished wiping the floor with all of you." Her tone is sarcastically sweet as she flutters her eyelashes at the squaddies around her, causing them all to smirk. I rub the center of my chest in an effort to keep calm.

Fanning out into a circle of predators around her, arms are stretched, and jokes are cracked. Aspen's eyes seek out mine amongst it all, bright with excitement. I just hope she's still smiling in five minutes. Despite the invite, no one wants to make the first move against the princess, everyone standing around, seemingly unsure, until Niall dives towards her from the side. In a blur of movement, Aspen swiftly moves out of the way and grabs Niall's overstretched fist, promptly shoving it backwards into his own face. Bending low, she sweeps her leg out to take out Niall's, causing him to collapse on the floor and the rest of the Vamps to burst out laughing.

"Who's next?" Aspen bobs on the balls of her feet and asks boldly. I'll give her that one, but I'm worried Aspen can't rely on the element of surprise again. I've personally trained these vamps to anticipate anything —even the distraction of pretty eyes and innocent smiles.

The commotion is starting to draw a crowd, so I move closer toward the group to keep my hybrid in my sights. Niall stands, laughing while holding his broken nose, and taps Keary on the shoulder, making him the next to face off with Aspen. She zeros in on him and smirks, outstretching her hand and flicking her fingers upwards, mouthing, 'Bring it.'

With a chuckle, Keary moves forward with a swag to his step, blocking Aspen from my view. Quickly bringing up his knee, Keary catches Aspen in the side, and I hear a soft 'oof' leave her. My blood boils, and red curtains my vision, rage suddenly consuming me at the thought of her in pain. I prepare to intervene when a choked sound fills the air, echoing around the domed roof. Keary's body crumbles to the ground at my feet, holding his swollen throat as he tries to draw in his next breath.

"Tap me," Cade says, his hand stretched by Keary's face, who clumsily slaps it. Cade runs at high speed around Aspen, and just when my heart is about to jump into my throat, she surprises us all by closing her damn eyes.

"What is she doing?" Torin asks by my side, peering around the heads of those in front for a better view. I grab the fucker in front of me by the scruff of his neck and toss him aside instead of responding. The blurred figure of Cade advances on Aspen from the left when she rapidly squats down and shoves her weight sideways into his legs, causing him to fall head over ass on the opposite side of her.

As she stands to her full height with a smirk, Magnus takes the opportunity to throw a punch at Aspen's pretty face. She tries to dodge at the last second, but his fist catches her jaw regardless. Blood sprays from her mouth and lands on the floor beside her with a splat.

Every male in the room stiffens. The aroma of her blood filters around us quickly, pulling groans from half of the crowd at its sweet yet powerful scent. Then, all eyes present begin the glow with flecks of oranges and golds, Aspen's included.

I'm about to get her the fuck out of here when her elbow connects with Magnus' ribs, a crack preceding his grunt of pain. The sole of her sneaker connects with his femur next while she grabs his wavy, brown hair and throws her forehead into the center of his face. Magnus' nose explodes on impact, covering Aspen in his blood.

Throwing his body to the floor like a rag doll, Aspen sets her sights on Finnian, who's been hanging back and enjoying the fight before him. He looks turned on, the fucker. Finnian is stacked, almost as big as me, his bulging biceps covered in tribal tattoos. His vest clings tightly to his frame, and his thighs fill out the standard black cargos.

He and Aspen begin to circle each other slowly, the grin on his face showing he's relishing this. It was apparent the fucker let the others go first to give himself the chance to size her up, and he likes what he's seen this far. Aspen makes the first move this time, throwing a punch toward his stomach, which he blocks easily. Attempting again, Aspen lunges toward the male, throwing jabs at him. Grabbing her wrists, Fin tosses Aspen to the floor with a snigger. Jumping back up, Aspen uppercuts Finian's ribs and throws her fist into his cheek when he bends low enough.

His face flies to the side, but when he turns back, his eyes are gold, and his fangs are on full show. With a hiss, Finian dives forward, knocking Aspen to the ground and landing on top of her. She fights to push his bulk off her, but his size alone is enough to disable her. I hover on the circle's edge, unsure if I should step in or let her handle the situation alone. Pushing on his shoulders to create space between them, Aspen slams her knee into Finnian's balls, causing him to howl and roll off her. A collective wince passes through the spectators, most of whom grab a hold of their own junk in sympathy.

Finnian is back on his feet soon enough, throwing punches at Aspen's face. Her eyes glint as she keeps focused, and even without training, she dodges expertly. Diverting her attention with his fist, Fin throws his shoe into Aspen's stomach, sending her skidding backward and landing in a crouch.

Her face lingers on the floor for a beat. Long enough for me to consider the possibility that she's had enough. But a second later, with a flexing of her shoulders, Aspen's muscles ripple as a cloak of black shrouds her. Frowning, I move to step forward but stop because, although invisible to those not looking for it, a hint of black smoke now rolls from Aspen.

Standing slowly, her nails lengthen into black talons, the smoke billowing from her too much like the outline of a trench coat for my liking. Whatever is happening here, I have the distinct feeling it's nothing to do with her hybrid nature.

With a growl, Aspen launches herself high into the moon-lit air, flying towards Finnian. Mid-leap, rapid cracks sound all at once as Aspen's clothes tear from her body. Landing on an unsuspecting Finnian, a six-foot white wolf snarls down at him, grabbing his throat between her teeth. Panic floods into his rounded eyes and he taps the floor beside him repeatedly.

"I'm out, I'm out!" He gets out. But she doesn't relent. Her paws still hold the blackened claws, pushing them into Fin's flesh too easily. His cry is nothing short of agony, causing the rest of the vamps to panic. With one jerk of Aspen's teeth, we'll lose a soldier we can't afford to be without. The elites are rare and take decades to train. Rushing over to her wolf, I stroke the soft patch behind her ears.

"Aspen, it's Torsten. Look at me," I try to hold the attention of her golden eye. Continuing to stroke her, black smoke intertwines with my fingers, and I curse to myself. Whatever Sawyer is doing to her, I'll kick his feathery ass for it next time he dares show his face. Rivets of Finnian's blood spill from between the wolf's sharp teeth, dripping onto the mats.

"Hey, the fight is over, you've won," I try again. "Let's go for a run outside." Conflict passes through the wolf's features, her nose twitching as she leans into me, not yet ready to release its prey. With a stern look, I will Finnian not to fucking move.

Our kind hasn't dealt with a wolf attack since the shifter wars. We lost too many numbers in those dark days, and to add further insult, Lorcan demanded we retreat. Forfeit and return home, filled with contempt. But had we continued to fight, Aspen may not exist.

Stroking the length of the wolf's snout, I slowly cup her lower jaw with my other hand and pull her mouth open enough for Finnian to slide out from beneath. She remains still for me, seeming not to want to cause me any harm. One wrong movement and I could easily lose my fingers. Not having the good sense to fuck off, Finnian crouches nearby, blood oozing from his chest and throat, releasing a low whistle.

"She's fucking amazing," he says appreciatively. I release Aspen's mouth and continue to stroke the back of her fluffy head until the black smoke fades away. I notice to sudden shift as Aspen's wolf regains control, her body slumping the entirety of her weight onto my shoulder. Finnian reaches out to feel the fur by her leg, but Aspen's wolf snaps, latching onto his hand. After a deep rumble and a shake of her snout for good measure, she releases him and turns back to nuzzle into my neck.

Finnian simply laughs while the rest of the crowd shift closer to get a better look at her. None of them would have seen a wolf up close who wasn't trying to kill us. Pride swells in my chest, their admiration feeding my ego. This incredible being is the only one like her, yet here she is, nudging her head in the crook of my neck.

"Having fun?" Jaxon's voice sounds and the crowd parts on instinct. Heads lower as he strides through the center, back to full health with a solid glare in my direction. I can't bring myself to care, but Aspen's wolf jerks to attention. Pulling her lip back to reveal her teeth, she growls, much to my surprise. Standing, I try to approach but the wolf bars me from moving. Her tail curls around my back, her huge size making the dome feel smaller. I continue to stroke her behind the ears, whispering reassurances into her ear. For whatever reason, the wolf seems fond of me, and as I begin to walk toward the moonlight shining beyond the open doors, she keeps pace, trotting by my side.

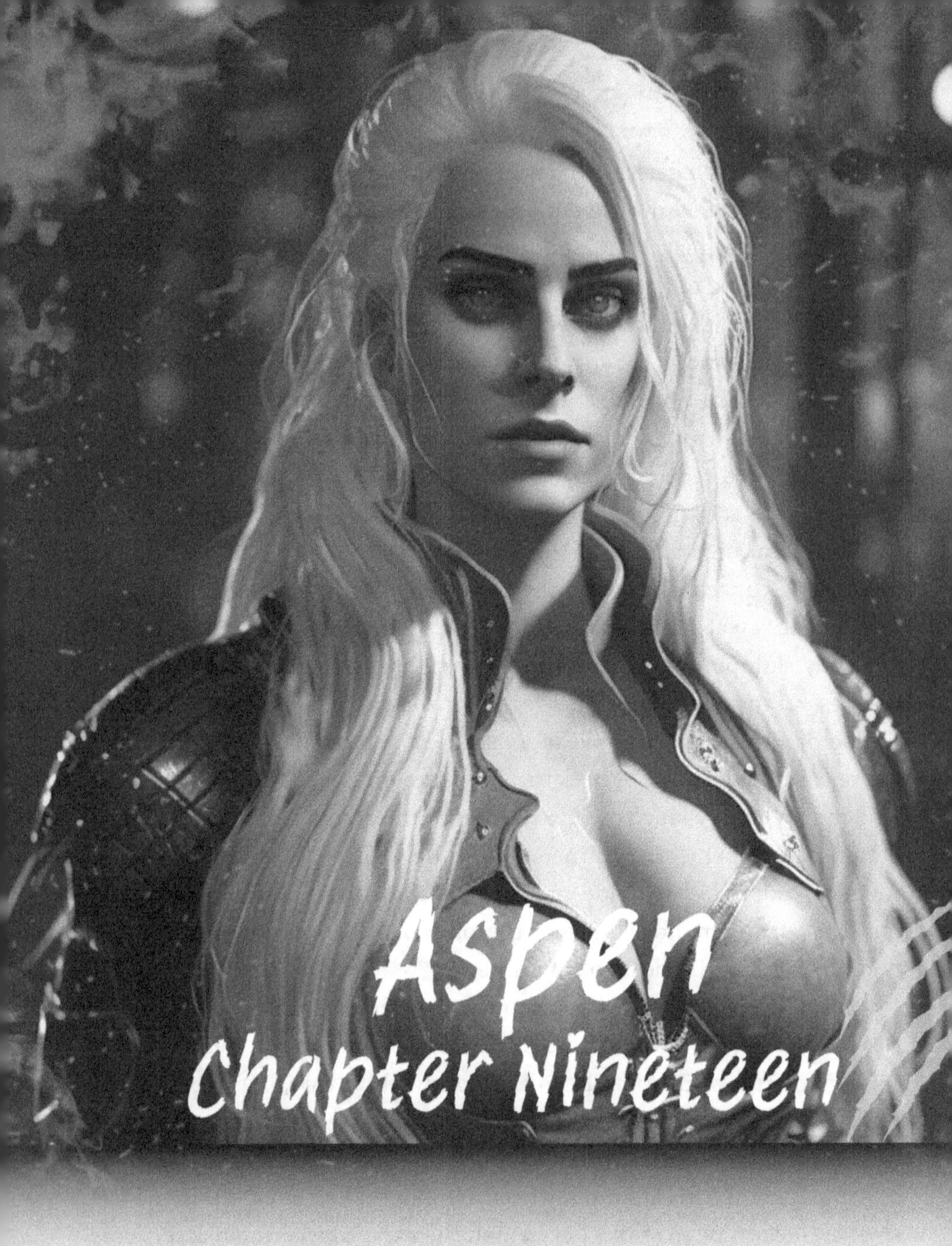

My wolf stays close to Torsten's leg as she pads across the synthetic rubber of the outdoor running track. There's a group of vampires racing around it, tripping over each other at the sight of a white wolf crossing their path. More males use outdoor gym equipment, from high jump bars to metal power-towers, the faint beat from their headphones reaching my sensitive wolf ears as they run drills alone. Moving onwards, my wolf looks up at the rock-climbing wall looming above us. The moon is hidden from this angle which causing the wolf to whine as she dashes forward back into the light.

Glancing back, every male inside the gymnasium's doorway stares on in fascination. I duck my large head, brushing against Torsten for comfort. I may have overstepped, crossing a line I knew better than to pass, but I can't describe what came over me. My actions weren't my own, controlled by the desire of another. I only hope I don't find myself cast out for that infraction, because I truly have nowhere else to go.

Reaching the tree line adjacent to the castle, my wolf snaps at Torsten's ankle playfully and bolts into the woodlands beyond. Enjoying the chance to stretch her legs, she speeds deeper into the dense forest, diverting from the path built into the dirt. Pouncing over a fallen trunk and maneuvering through the thick shrubs, narrowly avoiding thorns and holly bushes, she thunders onwards.

Adrenaline rushes through our veins, the fast pace of our joint heartbeat echoing loudly around her large rib cage. Woodland creatures scatter ahead, rushing to move out of the way from the snowy tornado flying towards them. Four paws assault the earth heavily, reverberating around the trunks like a stampede. Further ahead, my wolf latches onto the repetitive sound of water crashing noisily and sets the flowing waterfall in her sights.

Skidding to a stop at the lake's edge to watch as an aqua avalanche pounds viciously into the water, my wolf waits as Torsten speeds to a stop by my side, his hand finding a smooth patch by my wolf's ear to stroke. A shiver runs through the beast on the exterior, a shot of passion zipping through me on the inside. She leans into his caress, rubbing her head against his shoulder. My wolf is completely smitten, him being the first male to tame and understand her.

After running the thick pad of her tongue across his face, she wades into the water and sinks into the murky depths. Once far beneath the surface, I drag her inside begrudgingly and put her back in the cage of my being. Breaching the water in my human form, I bob in the cool waves and smile slyly, only to find it's no longer Torsten awaiting me at the edge of the bank. Instead, Jax stands tall, formidable, and curious. With my wolf no longer tainting my thoughts, the wash of anger I so recently felt toward him lessens, but it doesn't disappear.

"Will you let me explain?" he asks, his voice low. The icy water makes me all too aware I'm completely naked, and none of that contributes to my resulting shiver.

"No." I sink beneath the water once more. The moon's light reflects against the surface while I hide in the darkness, hoping Jax takes the hint. I can't look at his icy blue eyes without appreciating their inverse effect on me. One that ignites a fire within that refuses to be doused. I want to prove a point, to live out a bitchy tantrum I didn't get the chance to experience as a teen. Jaxon withheld a truth I should have been aware of *again*. A lesson needs to be learned.

A whole minute goes by, and my lungs begin to protest. I imagine Jax has stalked away, preferring to relent than let me drown myself. Swimming up to the surface, I take my first breath as a huge splash erupts at one side, then the other. Hands grab my thighs, dragging me back under. Lips seize mine from an unknown source, and I guess that's the point. To prove my body will react regardless. Bitterness doesn't exist in these inky depths as those sinful lips slide over mine. Heat burns at my core, the stolen kiss igniting a spark of fire within that I enjoy all too much. Hands grip my waist, spinning me swiftly and with ease. Another mouth claims mine. The fire begins to rage, consuming me until our united flame stokes a bond that remains unbroken.

Breaching the surface, I inhale through my nose as my mouth is held captive. Held flush against one solid body, the other is quick to cage me in. Hands roam everywhere. Sliding across my skin, aided by the water. One clamps over my eyes, barring the view from whoever seals a hand over my neck, tilting my chin aside and opening me up to him. My mouth parts, permitting full access. The lake steals the ability to use my senses, deciphering who is who, and since I've come this far, I relent in trying to.

Keeping me afloat, I pour everything through our physical connection, pushing my tongue into his mouth to battle against his. Whoever this is. The solid erection jutting into my thigh throbs, and my pussy is equally eager. With my legs wrapped around my assailant, I'm forced to grind myself against him shamelessly to relieve some friction. A second mouth places tender kisses along my shoulder, preventing me from looking at the dynamic I've found myself in.

Dragging me to the edge of the water bank, I'm lifted and sat on a rock. The hand over my eyes is forced to withdraw and slowly, I blink my eyes open. No surprise, Jaxon is floating between my open legs, my bared pussy exposed to the fan of his breath.

"Before you say anything, she's my sister," he rushes to say. My mouth had opened with an argument, and promptly clamps shut. "Twin, in fact. Sorcha was pulled from my mother's lifeless body after I was delivered. The break of my parent's moon bond destroyed my father, so Scorch and I were raised in the east wing by the other females. It's why I'm given so many special privileges, and why I was trusted to be your protector. Lorcan trusts me to control myself."

"Well..." I breathe, utterly lost for words. A part of me wants to curl up in embarrassment but Jaxon's intense stare and my pride won't allow me to. "You fucked that up." A handsome smile breaks across his face as Torsten hangs back, chuckling—four words that summarize the entire situation perfectly.

"I sure did," Jax agrees, his hands skimming my inner thighs. "Permit me to make it up to you?"

"I command it." My chin pushes out. Jax's responding look is nothing short of blissful satisfaction. Noting the serenity in his blue gaze, I don't know how I could have doubted him—loyal, steadfast Jaxon. A flutter beats within my chest, butterflies growing in my stomach. More than just desire is at play here; I'm falling—free diving into a chasm of pale blue and pine leaves. I should feel scared, vulnerable. But instead, I know I'll be safe, that Jax's strong muscled arms will break my fall and hold me close, protecting me from the outside world.

His hands shift higher, nearing my pussy as it throbs with need. A moan filters through the night air, and I still - vaguely aware through my mental fog that the noise didn't come from any of us. Jax looks back to Torsten, who shrugs, sharing the same thought. Another loud, lustful moan rings out from behind the waterfall beside us. I focus my hearing and only now pick up on the two heartbeats concealed within the depths, the sound of flesh pounding against flesh and scent of arousal thick enough to penetrate the cascade of water.

Looking into Jax's wide eyes, we burst into laughter as I slide back into the water and us him to stay afloat.

"Come on, let's head back," he says, still chuckling. "I have some groveling to do."

"Some?" I snort. Leaving the couple to their hidden fuck-sesh, we emerge from the water, collecting the males' discarded clothing. They dress as I allow my wolf to take back control and shift so I can re-enter the castle with my dignity covered.

Now at ease with Jax again, although I notice the way she lingers a millimeter closer to Torsten, we reenter the castle and pass through the gymnasium. Playfully snapping at Finnian when he tries to stroke my wolf again, I can tell he's going to be an asshole most of the time, but I think I like him. In fact, I'm surprised by all the Vamps who offer me admiring smiles as my wolf strides past. This is me in my truest form and being accepted as such - there are not even words to describe how that feels.

We navigate the hallways towards the east wing, the moon beating through every open window to allow me to retain this form. Upon approaching my suite, a group of females enter the hallway, taking one look at the three of us, and flee in the opposite direction. I shift back to human form and shrug, pushing the door open and stopping in m tracks.

What the fuck am I looking at right now?

Chase is standing by the dining table, in a suit jacket and tie – no shirt, holding a red folder and a long, plastic ruler. I eye him suspiciously before stepping inside so we can close the door. Completely naked, I find myself surrounded by three males who so recently returned from the dead, an air of need transferring between them all. Chase briefly pauses in front of me as he glides by, green eyes flicking from mine to my lips before continuing past.

"Take a seat, *Aspen*," he drawls my name seductively and rounds the dining room table.

"Should I put some clothes on?" I ask. It's shifter nature to be comfortable in my own skin, but three-vs-one puts me in a vulnerable position I wasn't anticipating. Yet.

"That would be wholly beside the point," Chase smirks. His hair has reached shoulder length now, where it seems to have stopped. The brown locks are glossy, the scent of shampoo emanating from his recent shower. On the surface, it would be easy to presume he's back to his usual, playful self. But I'm not naive enough to believe that. Behind his smile, a shadow of guilt twitches at the corner of his lips. Chase needs to feel forgiven, not that I needed another reason to let this scene play out.

Placing down his folder, Chase removes the blazer and places it over the back of the chair Jax has dropped into. All three have taken the opposite side of the table as I sit, folding my arms over my breasts. I roll my eyes internally as all three try to intimidate me with intense stares in varying colors, hunting for a weakness I refuse to show. I wouldn't have survived this long if I were so easily broken.

Rolling my tongue over my teeth, I break the silence first, taking a wild guess. "You planning on whipping me into mate material? Is that what's happening here?" All three fail in holding back a groan, fangs sinking into their bottom lips. I smile; it's almost too easy to reverse the roles. Whilst regaining their composure, I reach forward, poking finger into the red cover of the folder and take a sneak peek. "This is full of blank paper?" I query, when the plastic ruler snaps down on the back of my hand in a flash. "Ow!" I whine, soothing my hand and frowning at Chase.

"Behave, or next time, it's your ass," he slaps the ruler against his own palm, the sound bouncing off the walls and sending an internal vibration straight between my legs. *Yes, please*, my vampire injects. I lift my brow expectantly and gesture for him to continue.

"I've concluded you're too unruly," Chase states. I release a bitter laugh.

"And you're dressed like that because..." I roll my hand. A wicked grin pulls at Chase's mouth.

"Because I can." His eyes are gleaming with excitement, so I'll play along for now. How's *that* for not being unruly? "We need to set some ground rules while you're in the castle. Basic etiquette, so I don't have to beat a royal guard into telling me where you are the next time I wake alone in your bed."

"You did what?" Jax asks and receives a flick of the ruler on his cheek.

"Shh." Chase paces back and forth, wearing a line into the carpet, tapping the ruler on his chin. "We can start with leaving a note. Better yet, you could wake me to ensure your entourage always consists of three."

"You did try to rip my jugular out and drain me of blood," I point out, leaning back in my chair. Jax shoots to his feet.

"You did fucking *what*?!" This time, when Chase attempts to hit his abdomen, Jax rips the ruler from his grip and snaps it in half. The pair begin to squabble whilst Torsten is left to pick up where Chase left off.

"Ignore him, he's coming down from a mess of feelings he doesn't understand. It is worth saying, though, that being accompanied would be best, even after your display in the gymnasium. Rumors will already be circulating about your strength, and to some, that may present a new challenge." Reading my cocky expression, Torsten leans across to take my hand. "I know you can hold your own, but it's not the vamps who are desperate for a mate you should worry about. There are some who don't believe in mixing species or having a queen who doesn't know our ways."

"I would agree with them on that point," I sigh, pulling my hand away. "I don't want to be your queen. I just want..." My voice falters. For most of my life, I'd clung to the idea that I just wanted to be alone. But that's no longer the case. I just don't know in what capacity I dare envision a future, because none of the versions in my head are likely to come true.

Becoming aggravated with my own dark thoughts, I huff. Physical exertion is needed before I sink into a pit of despair that will see me pushing away everyone in this room. Standing, I throw the chair aside.

Chase and Jax put their fighting on hold to watch me place a hand on my hip and raise a brow.

"Look, I was under the impression you guys were here to fuck me. If that's not what's happening, please show yourselves out and I'll take care of it myself." I've never seen vampires move so fast. One moment they are across the table, the next they're surrounding me, chests bump my arms and a firm hand cups my nape.

"Don't be gentle," is my last request as my body is bent in half, my top half hitting the cool glass. The hold on my nape remains tensed, at odds with a hand stroking the rounded hump of my ass. One of them massages my cheek appreciatively, whilst another brings down a sharp slap on the other side. I cry out, jerking against the glass. All three bodies behind me freeze, a sense of uncertainty palpable. Still bound by duty, it would seem.

"Do. It. Again." I order and feel them relax. The hand soothing me moves onto the affected cheek, rubbing away any lingering soreness as the spank lands on the other side. I groan, wetness pooling between my legs. My eyes are tightly scrunched while I fight with the emotions within, desire blossoming in my core. My nipples are painful pebbles squashed against the icy tabletop.

"I think you like that, don't you, Pumpkin?" Chase's silky, deep voice purrs. I whimper in response. Two hands grip my cheeks tightly, parting me. Whoever is holding my nape falters, all of them taking a moment to appreciate the sight of my glistening pussy awaiting more. Fingers find my slit, sliding through the wetness before seeking my clit.

"Oh, she definitely liked that," Torsten agrees. "She's so wet for us," he bends over to speak into my ear, "and we haven't even started with you yet." A slight tremor races down my spine at his warm breath, fanning across my ear, his words thick with a promise of what's to come. One long digit plunges inside me, and a thumb presses firmly down on my clit. Pinned beneath Torsten's bulk, I can't move. Instead, I simply lie there and take the assault of pleasure. The finger slides in and out leisurely while I squirm against his body.

"Don't move." He commands. But it's so good, I can't help to rock my hips in time with my assailant. Torsten growls in warning, the vibration from his chest seeping into my back as the hand is removed from between my thighs. I release a dog-like whine at the loss of contact, and as Torsten withdraws, a hand sharply slaps my ass again.

"It seems like you need some help with keeping still," Jax says, delicately tracing fingers up and down my spine. My wrists are captured and held together behind my back in one large hand as the material of Chase's tie slips beneath them. After securing a tight knot, a hand comes back down over the tie, knowing I could easily rip the restraints if I were so inclined. It just happens that I'm not in any rush to finish what has been started. Ruffling catches my ears before the blunt head of a thick cock pushes against my entrance.

"I wonder if you could tell us apart by our cocks," Chase muses out loud. The delicate stroking of my spine has started up again, and I groan at the idea.

"I think it's an experiment worth trying." Pack orgies are nothing new to my kind, although I never thought my experience with them would be with so-called solitary monsters of the night. No complaints here.

My hip is gripped tightly as a cock slides into my cunt, aided by my wetness to slam home instantly. *Oh, my fuck.* Intense pleasure crashes through my entire body, causing me to squirm for relief. His girth is so wide there's no escape. Only the guttural noise that leaves my throat as I'm forced to wait for his next move. Two hands close over my shoulders, the cock pulling almost fully out, leaving just tip inside, before ramming back in fiercely. I cry out, and by the third time the action is repeated, I'm screaming all three of their names. Whoever it is, they work me into a shift frenzy, only relenting when my walls explode around him. Waves upon waves of pleasure crash through me, keeping his cock tightly squeezed within.

I shudder in the aftermath, coming down from my climax with weepy moans. Even after he retracts, I feel him everywhere. Etched into my core.

"Fucking Chase," I groan breathlessly, and a deep chuckle confirms my suspicions.

"She's good, I'll give her that." Hooking my leg up onto the table, I feel the brush of cool air against my center as I'm left wide and completely at their mercy. I struggle against the bind on my wrists, my shoulders starting to ache. Gentler, this time, a cock pushes into me. Unhurried, measured strokes that build the same intensity within. *Torsten.*

His dick hits my sweet spot every damn time, his balls slapping at my clit with each thrust. My back is coated with sweat, but the glass tabletop keeps my front cool. I can already feel the build-up of my next orgasm stirring, the delicious feeling I'm becoming quickly addicted to. Every stroke inside me, every bounce of my butt against his groin, is halfway between a tease and a promise of impending bliss.

I marvel in the pleasure he gives me so easily, pushing back to meet his thrusts eagerly. His grip on my waist turns bruisingly tight, and his steady rhythm picks up, becoming frantic. His groin slams against me, my ass rippling and my back arching from the onslaught of his cock. Maintaining the increasingly rapid speed, my inner walls start to flutter, and I give him what he's looking for. A tsunami hurtles through me, causing stars to burst before my glowing eyes. A hand tightly grips my hair as a gravelly roar fills the room, my orgasm spurring on Torsten's, and he joins my symphony of moans. We break together within the need to delay the inevitable. Not when our bodies are craving to be joined as one.

"I can't handle how fucking tight you are," Torsten mutters. I smile, savoring the knowledge that I can bring a known warrior to his knees just by lying here. Imagine what I can get him to do when I actually put in the effort. Lowering over me, Torst kisses my cheek, the heat of him radiating through me until I don't know where he stops, and I begin.

I prepare myself for round three, steeling myself for the veiny width I know as Jax. Yet it doesn't come. The tie at my wrists is released, and I gasp, rolling my shoulders and stretching my fingers to regain blood circulation. Rolling me onto my back, Jax smiles before sliding his arms beneath my body. Lifting me from the table, I'm cradled to his chest and carried through the bedroom, the evidence of his erection kept locked within his cargo trousers.

Once he's placed me into the shower, Jax turns on the faucet and steps back. I reach out for his hand, a frown between my brows.

"I'm groveling, remember? I won't take you again until I deserve you," his head inclines. My frown deepens.

"Then get in here and start earning it," I tut, dragging him back inside and pushing a bottle of shower gel into his hands. Chuckling, Jaxon obeys. He obeys me for hours, massaging the length of my body, fondling my breasts, and kissing me passionately until I deem him fully forgiven.

Cracking my neck side to side, I stretch and bounce on my sneakers. The four of us are standing in front of the rear gymnasium doors, trying not to fidget. The entire population of the castle has squeezed into the training space this morning, going against our usual sleep pattern to attend.

Dressed in baggy gym wear, I share looks with my brothers and Carrick, the buttmunch at the far end of the starting line. He ignores us, a brute of cropped dark hair, bulging muscles, and ignoble intentions. He doesn't stand a chance of winning this final round. The fact that the king has allowed myself, Torsten, and Jaxon, to participate shows Carrick can't be trusted to take over the kingdom. His presence is merely a checkbox exercise, but the moon knows one of us three will be walking away victorious.

Lorcan decided to be present for this final event in his twisted trials. I reckon that has more to do with the fact we were escorted from Aspen's suite, and she's been given top-of-the-range security for the past week to keep us away. It's funny how the tables have turned, from her only being trusted under our protection to now stealing glances at the audience just to see her. But I understand – we took more than should have been on offer. The critical thing to remember, and what I argued with Lorcan until he slammed the door in my face, is that it was 'on offer.' Aspen may hide behind her attitude, but she's fallen for each of us, and I won't hear any different.

Vampires grumble at our backs, uncomfortable with the sun sitting above the UV-protected dome. Their eyes are not used to the brightness like the soldiers. State-of-the-art gym equipment has been moved into a different part of the castle to allow room for the extra bodies, considering none of us are exactly small. Even the females have been huddled in the corner, barely separated by a red rope. Mirrors span the opposite wall, reflecting the light I've become accustomed to. We train in here every day prior to sunset, more so within the past week. Exercise is my go-to. It's the only time I don't feel so contained, like an animal stuck in a cage.

Only now, that's exactly how I feel. Especially with a fully suited Lorcan on his fucking velvet throne, which he insisted on having carried in, just to take up extra precious space for the others to squeeze around. A pretentious move from a male we all know is slipping. Murmurs pass between those standing behind him, impatiently waiting for the game to begin. They're not the only ones.

"A reminder of the rules," Nealon unravels a scroll as if he couldn't have memorized them beforehand. "In preparation for today's event, a flag has been hidden deep within the forest inside the protective wall. One single rose has been placed alongside as a favor to the princess. Both must be retrieved and returned in order to be named the victor," Nealon nods, wrapping the scroll neatly. "And all is to be completed during daylight hours."

I groan, edging a step back from the double doors barring me from burning to death. A large digital clock placed at the top of the rock-climbing wall shows we have less than a minute left to prepare. Deep breaths Chase, you've got this. All I have to do is run at my absolute top speed, literally smell the roses, retrieve the flag and get back before all of my skin has melted from my bones. Simple.

The clock ticks down to zero, and a claxon vibrates through the entire vampire territory. One side of the automatic doors opens remotely from a control panel at the back of the gym, the warmth of outside slamming into me like a boulder. I wouldn't have heard the collective intake of breath over the ringing in my ears if it hadn't been made by every single being in the room, quickly followed by the shuffle of feet trying to get as far from the door as possible. This is it. One mini step forward, and I'd be surrendering myself to my execution.

"Wait, don't do this!" Aspen suddenly cries through the murmuring crowd. The following grunts sound like a struggle, but I can't let myself hang around to see. Aspen's a tough girl, she can take care of herself. The others hesitate, but I'm not waiting a second longer for the line of sunlight on the floor to get any closer to my sneakers, my skin already beginning to sizzle just from the heat.

Shooting forward first, I am completely unprepared for the pain which instantly assaults me. It's like nothing I've ever felt before, the sun directly overhead, leaving me with nowhere to hide. The full, unhindered brightness blinds me as I squint against the assault searing its way through my retinas. Covering my eyes with my hand, I push my legs at top speed, jumping a hurdle I know is there from memory and racing for the cover of the forest ahead.

I'm under the lush green canopy within seconds, although it provides little relief. The sun's rays pierce through the gaps in the branches, turning the forest into a laser field rather than the serene woodland I was expecting. I don't waste time trying to dodge the spears of light, my skin bubbling and blistering already.

I keep moving, blurring around trunks, concentrating on my senses as best I can. The smell of burning flesh is overpowering, and a blister pop next to my right ear. Wetness trickling down my shoulder in a thick river of pus gives little reassurance that I'm going to survive this.

Without slowing, I rely on my instincts to guide me through the forest, my sight beginning to fail me. I crash into a trunk, agony slicing through my torso as hysteria sets in. My mind drifts from my pointless existence to marveling at the blurred colors of a fox I shoot past. Skidding to a stop, I'm stunned by the vibrance of its fur coat. Never have I seen anything quite like it, even if my vision is fuzzy. A twig snapping nearby causes him to scatter away, my competitor closing in.

There are no friendships out here. I'm suffering and dying, all in name of taking Aspen as a mate. I thought I could give this win to Jaxon, relying on him to repay the favor, but some things changed. As a point of pride, I want her to look upon me as her champion after a week of pining from a distance.

Slapping myself across the face, I inhale deeply and will myself to focus. That's the pain talking. My body has officially entered fight or flight mode, to the point that I can't remember what I'm even looking for. I lean briefly against a large oak tree, soaking in the shade as I take a few deep breaths. After a few gulps of air that I curse for not being some sort of balm to my skin, the faintest, sweetest scent reaches me. Much like...a rose! My feet start to move before my mind can catch up. Sharply turning left, I narrowly avoid another thick trunk as the scent grows more potent. Small stones along the dirt path barely react to the swift movements of my feet. A rumbling waterfall calls to me, my body begging to feel the soothing liquid, but there's no time.

All I can do is keep moving.

My skin is taunt, becoming an irritating combination of itchy and don't-you-dare-touch-me. I fly to a stop at the water's edge, almost falling in as confusion rakes through me. The scent here is strong yet fleeting until I turn my attention to the waterfall across the pool of glistening water. If I dive in, I know in my heart I won't resurface. I'll take the easy out, hiding within the icy cold water until sunset. And if I do that, I might as well move to shifter camp and declare myself a pack whore.

Rounding the water bank, I dive through the waterfall, hoping there isn't a solid wall of rock to greet me on the other side. The relief of cold water dousing my skin and the darkness of the cave behind it makes me whimper, like a dog who's finally had his cone removed and can lick its mangled manhood.

Beneath my sneakers, a bed of colored rose petals, ranging from the deepest red to the palest pinks, is just barely visible as my eyes begin to adapt to the darkness I'm accustomed to. At the back of the cave, a blood-red flag is hanging from a groove within the rock.

Clever little spot they've found here, using the powerful speed of cascading water outside to cover most of the flowery scent while giving us a small amount of time to recover.

Rolling my wrists, I refrain from looking at the damage lining my body, already knowing it's not a sight I'll be able to forget. My thoughts turn to my brothers, wondering where they are and what state they're in. I had the sixth sense that someone else was close, surely, they'd have arrived by now. Treading carefully over the petals, an idea sparks to life. I'll wait here, giving the three of us a chance to feed on each other, recover and return, all holding the flag. Three victors. Three mates, as if our hybrid princess deserves any less.

A body crashes through the water, rolling across the cave floor. The pervasive scent of crimson-streaked, raw, boiling flesh and bursting boils causes me to cringe. Covering my nose with the back of my hand, I brave a second look at the aggravated cysts spreading across his face, using his tattoos to identify him. I kneel, careful not to touch the Vamp before me.

"Carrick, are you"- a fist connects with my jaw so fast, I didn't anticipate it. His pale brown eyes begin to glow as he snarls at me, throwing his shoulder into mine with a roar of anguish and lunging for the flag. Recovering quickly, I catch his ankle, digging my nails into his bubbled skin and yanking him backward. Carrick crashes into the floor, yelling in pain as I shoot up and pick the flag from the stone holding it. Stuffing the material into my pants, I boot him in the ribs and leave him on the floor, wheezing. He'll be fine, he has enough shade to wait out the day whilst healing.

I, however, will not be waiting around for him to keep trying to steal this stupid piece of fabric from me all day. Scooping up two handfuls of rose petals, I fill my shorts pockets and, with a quick bounce of my heels to gear myself up for another round out in the open, I jump through the waterfall.

Maybe this time...nope, it's not any easier the second time around. I take the shortest route back to the castle, jumping over fallen branches and boulders as I go. The pain is unbearable, my teeth gritting as a tear escapes the corner of my eye. Sizzling as the salty liquid slides down my cheek, a hint of steam temporarily fogs my vision. I bet that scars permanently, damn it.

Pumping my arms faster and legs harder, I'm almost at the forest's edge when a groan catches my ear. I don't slow as I turn my head to the side and see a body slumped against a large, mossy tree trunk. His features aren't visible beneath the oozing yellow of his flesh. A rancid scent of burning flesh assaults my nostrils a second later. I don't even think about what I'm doing as my legs turn towards him, and I bend low, heaving Torsten over my protesting shoulder, and keep moving. He's a heavy fucker like the rest of us, and my back is screaming in protest. But leaving him behind was never an option.

"Come on, big guy. Let's get you back home," I mumble incoherently. Far, *far* in the future, I'm going to make it my mission to remind Torst how I saved his ass like a saucy fireman every time I see him. I just need him to hold on for a few more seconds while I get us across the last leg of this death trap and back into the safety of the shadows.

With one last exhale, I leave the tree's protection and wince as the sun's full heat rages down on me once more. Torsten's body hangs across me limply as he's either passed out or died on me. My calves struggle to keep moving as I fly over the painted white lines of the racetrack, my skin growing too tight around the muscles. I'm sure I'm about to seize up and fall on my face in a giant cocoon of my very own skin.

Black spots are starting to obscure my vision as one of my feet doesn't move fast enough, and I stumble a few steps before colliding with the floor. My nose crunches beneath me and I instantly feel thick liquid spilling from my face as a final fog overtakes my brain. Torst falls from my grip and skids a few feet away from me, his glassy gray eyes the last thing I see as my own drift closed and give in to the symphony of pain my body can no longer shut out.

"CHASE!"

I can't feel any part of my body, yet it's all screaming at me. My internal organs, movements, and even thoughts are suffocated by the rigidness of my limbs. Blistering heat surrounds me, making it impossible to draw a breath as if I'm drowning in a vat of acid.

"Chase! Where is-" Words are lost to the roaring in my ears. For a while, I'm pretty sure I am dead. The pain had ebbed away to nothing, and I was strangely at peace, calm even. Nothing existed but the emptiness that has been present inside me longer than I care to admit.

A dream filters into my mind of a white-haired girl pulling on my arm and begging me to take her. To fill her, own, and claim her. Navy eyes branded inside my mind blink long, sultry lashes. A gentle smile that hides her insecurities. But I see her. All of her. For despite all the injustices dealt in her favor, she's stronger than any of us ever could be...filled with an attitude that I take pleasure in toying with but never want to break. The push and pull, the games we play, all add to her allure, but I crave something deeper. I'd willingly offer my soul to her for even a fragment of hers in return. Not just because she's a rare, viable female but because she has become my everything. Because she's all I have.

I groan, my throat raw as the pain rises once more as I begin to stir, the relaxed fog slipping instantly. I desperately try to grab at the image, eager to watch the scene play out. From the hammering in my head to the cramping right down in my toes, my body starts to pulse as the regeneration process kicks in. Screams explode inside my skull, a fire stoking in the pit of my stomach, threatening to burn me alive from the inside. Yet I can tell externally, I'm completely still.

"Listen to me, baby," a sweet voice whispers into my ear and spears me directly in the heart. "I need you. Please answer me." More agony tears through me limb by limb, as does the anger directed squarely at myself and the wasteful, useless life I've led. I have no mate to mourn for me, no achievements I will be remembered for. If this is my last day of existence, there's nothing to suggest I ever mattered. So, the real question is, do I accept that fact and give in, or do I fight to change it? A growl sounds then, one which isn't my own, before my head is thrown backward for another blossom of pain to flare.

"Wake up, asshole. That's a command." Her voice cracks, splintering my being in half. Gritting my teeth until my jaw cramps, I push all my energy into my hands. As the burning increases, a roar fills my mind, but I keep pushing until my little finger twitches. Internally, I collapse, a rush of relief rushing through me like a tsunami. But it's not enough.

Wetness is pushed against my lips, spilling into my mouth, and leaking down my throat—the sweetest, rarest taste that can only come from one source. Activating my organs, I gasp and fly upright, blinking my vision clear. And there she is. Beneath the gym's dome, reflecting around her like a halo. She is as beautiful as ever, even though her eyes are large, and her cheeks are tear-stricken.

"Chase, did you get it? The flag?" she asks, worry affecting her voice. Internally, I'm smiling because soon it'll be announced that I'm her new mate. I did it for us. "Chase, please, give me something. Jaxon is still out there, and they won't end the trial until it's complete. Where is the flag?!" Aspen grips my face, and I groan. The brief moment of bliss has died a sudden death. I fight to open my mouth, but my body still does not correspond with my brain.

"Pa...pa..." I try to croak out, but the fire has crept its way into my throat, and talking feels like I've swallowed a handful of razor blades. Instead, I force my eyes to lower to my crotch, and Aspen groans. Muttering I'm an asshole again, her hand dives into my pants, knocking my dick around roughly to retrieve the material. Whipping it out harshly, I flinch and groan again.

"It's here!" Aspen shoots upright, waving the red flag, but no one moves. Nealon stands just inside the doorway, his arms folded and scowl deep.

"I'm sorry, Princess. That's the decoy." My heart stills.

What the fuck did he just say?

I struggle to follow the following movements as my brain descends into a hazy state once more. With the loss of Aspen's blood and not nearly having enough of it, each breath rains down more pain, reigniting the flames licking my skin. I topple over, my temple crashing on the gymnasium floor.

Torsten is there, being attended to by a round of royal guards. Between us and the open doorway, the sunlight creeping inside emphasizes a long smear of blood from being dragged inside. I fight to shuffle back, wanting to be as far away as possible, until I see a curvy silhouette dart past Nealon and disappear into the light.

Chapter Twenty-One

I'm no stranger to running beneath the midday sun. Whether from an ambush of shifters or my own feelings, running is in my nature. But now, as my arms pump and thighs burn, as my heart pounds and breathing shallows, I wish I could have been saved this run. If these archaic, outdated trials didn't exist, there would be no need for the men who are chipping away at my hardened heart to prove themselves any further. I don't want a male who will die for me, I need one who will live for me. Stay with me.

Tearing through the forest, I hunt for Jaxon's scent. My inner beasts shy away from daylight, but I surge them to the forefront of my being with vigor. A heavy dose of honeydew hints at me, the scent I recognize as Torsten as I pass a patch of flattened grass beneath a tree trunk. Evidence of his burns have stuck to the bark, leaving behind gloopy pus trails and skin patches. I shudder, forcing the image of him lying still on the gymnasium floor from my mind. How much more do they have to suffer in my name?

The forest blurs by in a rush of browns and greens, a distinct lack of woodland animals present as I listen out for heartbeats. The further I run, the more my throat clogs with emotion. Why do males have to be so damn stupid?! Chivalrous, sure, but also narcissistic, egotistical assholes. Was I supposed to find their rotting corpses appealing? No. I find their muscles and tattooed bodies far more alluring, especially when they are naked and grinding, fill me to the-

A groan flutters to me on the wind my speed creates. Skidding to a stop, I search for it. The waterfall thunders to my left, and although I consider the males may have needed to cool off, Chase's scent is all over the water bank. He wouldn't have left Jaxon had they been together. I shoot in the opposite direction, arriving at the stone wall surrounding the territory before mentally retracing my steps.

Time ticks by as I backtrack, keeping to the wall's edge to shoot from one side of the forest to the other. The noise doesn't sound again, nor do any others. The woods are unnaturally still, and the longer Jax is out here, the less chance he has of surviving. Tensions are rising, as well as the heat, forcing me to stop and take stock of what I'm even doing.

He was looking for a flag. The point of the trial is to push competitors to their limits. So, the guards wouldn't have hidden it somewhere dark and shaded. It would be out in the open, where the sun would shine with the full force of UV. I look across the forest, between the speckled illuminations penetrating the canopy, and tilt my head upwards. You've got to be kidding me.

Hanging directly above a patch of grass I've crossed multiple times, Jaxon's arms swing freely from a mesh netting. Strung upside down in the trap, he's fallen into a shaded patch against the tree trunk, except for one beam of light. Spearing the trees, it penetrates his chest, his t-shirt melted into the burns underneath. As soon as I see it, I smell the rancid bubbling of flesh, which causes me to gag. Spitting the taste from my mouth, I lunge for the tree trunk, starting to ascend when a hand grips my ankle.

Dragging me towards, I kick out, my free foot connecting with the foot of my attacker. My back hits the forest floor beneath Jax, my vision barely catching up before a large stone is swinging toward my face. Rolling at the last moment, I jump to my feet and grab the back of Carrick's short hair. It comes loose in my hand, his scalp a softened mess of oozing skin. As he rears his elbow back, I'm too busy scraping his remnants from my palm to dodge to solid blow.

He's strong, considering his current state. I see why he was chosen for the trials, but there was never going to be a version of the future where I was his mate. My heart is spoken for, and this fucker's eyes rage with the desire to kill me. Hardly the type of foreplay I've grown accustomed to.

The next time he swings the stone in my direction, I shift position and bring my elbow down on the crook of his arm. Bones shatter on impact, echoed by my foot slamming through his ribs. I relieve him of his stone and blinded by the desperation to save the male hanging above, pummel Carrick's face. Nothing matters but easing Jaxon's suffering. Saving him from his own sense of duty.

Bringing the stone down one last time, Carrick's forehead splits, and he flops back, no longing trying to clasp his hands around my throat. Realization dawns of what I've just done. Nudging him with my boot, Carrick doesn't move. *Fuck.* Jaxon stifles a groan, pulling at my heartstrings, but I didn't come out here to save one vamp by killing another. Grabbing Carrick's wrists, I heave him towards the wall, tucking his body into an alcove of missing stone where the sun shouldn't be able to touch. If he's as strong as he presents, he should be able to survive until the guards return for him at nightfall. Then, without wasting another second, I'm by Jaxon's side in a flash.

"Fuck," Jaxon grunts, his brows twitching but unable to tense, "off." His face isn't too severely burned, but my concern is more focused on his chest. The cavern within his sternum was now hollow, dripping with melted flesh. Using my fangs, I chew through the rope holding him up by his feet. "Must win," Jaxon groans. "For Aspen." The rope gives way, and we sail toward the ground. There's nothing I can do to prevent Jax from slamming into the forest floor, a spray of blood shooting from his mouth on impact. I land in a crouch at his side, instantly trying to lift him.

"News flash, buddy, Aspen doesn't give a shit about some flag." Putting Jax's arm over my shoulder, I grit my teeth and use every ounce of strength I have to raise him a few inches from the floor. A grunt is torn from me as I get him upright, his head knocking against mine.

"No!" Jax suddenly growls, his nails dragging across my arm as I hug him to me. Fuck. Not him as well. "Win...Aspen." His words are slurred, delirious. I glance upwards to the blue flag at the highest point, sticking out between a mass of leaves. Oh, for the love of the moon. Frustration claws at me, but the more Jaxon fights, the more I realize he won't leave without that damn scrap of material.

Shoving him against the trunk with more force than I should, my hands and feet are scrambling upwards. Launching from one branch to the next, I sail to the top of the canopy, tugging the flag free of the crevice it has been stuffed into. A red rose lies on the branch just below, to which I shove the stem behind my ear, uncaring of the thorns. Jumping, I free-fall and land hard beside Jaxon just before he topples over.

"Here, okay. You got the flag, congratulations. What a big," I heave him upright, "strong," I drag him across my back, "warrior you are." My inner vampire chuckles. With a snarl, I clasp Jaxon's hands around my neck and run back to the gymnasium, his feet dragging behind me. My legs buckle just before I skid through the doors, my shins slamming into the tile.

A moment of shock passes through those watching. Willing my legs to heal, I shift Jaxon against my side, his arms still around my neck, and push upright. Jax is a proud male; he would want to finish this bullshit on his feet.

"Did he retrieve the flag?" Lorcan stands from his central throne, a trace of delight hidden deep within his eyes. The air whooshes out of me, the truth staring me in the face.

I'd asked myself how much these males would have to suffer, and now I have my answer. Until Lorcan could undeniably prove, in front of the entire population of vampires, Jaxon is the winner. There really was no chance for anyone else when the king was playing favorites. Chase and Torsten were decent backups should his plan not work out, probably why neither was disqualified for kissing me.

Except there's one variable Lorcan couldn't have accounted for. *Me.*

"I retrieved the flag," I raise the blue material high for everyone present to witness. "I gifted myself the rose. I'm your trials champion, and I-" Jax's weight buckles in an attempt to silence me. Not a chance. Seating him against Chase, who also has Torsten's head on his lap, I straighten at glare directly at the king. "I will choose my own mates. Plural."

A soft grey tweed blazer adorned with a checked pattern hangs over a crisp white shirt and a black tie on my wardrobe door. Along-side the three-piece suit, a canvas bag holds a pair of polished black dress shoes. Just the thought of wearing this ensemble on my tender skin makes me squirm uncomfortably. Grumbling, I dress swiftly, knowing the more time that slips by, the more my stomach tightens into an uneasy knot. Sensing I'm ready or listening on the other side of the door for my satisfied grunt, Sorcha bursts into my room with a wide smile.

"Well, look at you. Going up in the world," she mocks, knowing it'll irritate me. She looks stunning in a black satin gown with elbow-high gloves to match. I eye the low cleavage and missing back section with only thin spaghetti straps holding the piece together. Shoving out of the jacket in a blur of movement, I immediately throw it over her slender shoulders with a scoff.

"You're not going to be seen like that." My voice is strangled, and it has nothing to do with the discomfort of using my enhanced speed.

"Oh, stop it," Scorch slaps my hands away and tosses the jacket onto the floor. "Half the castle has already seen me on the way here, and I think I'll be mated before the next crescent moon. That solider, Finnian, seems rather wild, don't you think?" Finnian?! A vein bursts in my temple, my fists already clenched when I see the twinkle in her blue eyes.

"You're teasing me," I state. Her giggles cause me to roll my eyes and retrieve my jacket as Aviana enters my room. She passes my sister a black fur shawl and joins her fits of laughter at my expense. I'm still going to claw Finnian's eyes out so he can't ever look in my sister's direction. By Vampire law, if Scorch wants to mate, it will fall to me to prepare the trials to determine a suitable partner for her. But we discussed long ago that she can choose for herself – within reason.

Striding ahead of the females, I lead the way toward the ballroom. Lanterns flicker between oil paintings through the hallways, the following of high heels echoing against the stone floor. Winding through the maze of corridors, I only stop once I've reached the central staircase. Carpeted in a deep purple with a chandelier hanging high above, this area of the castle was one of the last to be recently renovated.

Scorch slides her arm through mine, fur shawl firmly in place, and descends with me as expected. Vamps milling around the bottom level stop to stare, many eyes fixed on her, and I growl in warning. She giggles but doesn't stop me because we both know she's not ready to be courted yet. Approaching the ballroom doors, a suited and booted Chase and Torsten rush to greet me, concern in their gazes.

"We've been summoned to Lorcan's office," Torst relays. Several royal guards hover at their backs, grave looks upon their faces. I release Scorch, telling her to go with Avianna. Her brows furrow, but she obeys for once. The moment she's out of earshot, I stride in the opposite direction, back towards the staircase.

"What is it? Has there been news of Carrick?" I ask. No one can answer me. Carrick hasn't been seen since the final trial. His body was never recovered, almost as if he had vanished. But bastards like him aren't so easy to squash, and it's killed me that I haven't been up to joining the search parties out each night looking for him. He will suffer for his crime of treason against Aspen, I'll make sure of it.

I've spent the past fortnight hibernating in my bedroom while my extensive injuries take longer to heal than usual. Despite being comfortable, the only times I enjoyed my solitude are when Aspen came to visit. I've never been so happy to have such a small, single mattress because she had to snuggle closer to stay in my arms. Even better, Torst and Chase waited outside, guarding my door whilst listening in. Every time Aspen complimented me, a growl sounded beyond the wood. But then it came time for her to leave, and I was reminded that she was spending most of her time in their company instead.

After much insistence, the only other visitor I permitted entry was Sorcha, who attended to the remaining blisters on my chest. Our dynamic is very push and pull, between my desire to protect the spunky redhead without realizing the tables turned and she began mothering me.

Lorcan is waiting in his office, pacing behind the desk as we enter unannounced.

"What's the problem?" I blurt out, forgetting I'm the commander. These days, my heart is in firm control, my actions guided by intuition rather than centuries of discipline.

"You are," Lorcan growls, stopping to drop into his seat. "Remember your place and only speak once spoken to." His nostrils flare, and I force my head to incline. When Chase and Torsten don't do the same, I nudge them until we form a line of submission. Clasping my hands behind my back, I stand at full attention. The suit stretched across my body rubs irritably, as I knew it would. The dress shoes feel clunky on my feet as I tap my heel impatiently. The door behind me opens and closes, Aspen wriggling her way between Torsten and me.

"It's about time," Lorcan criticizes. His navy-blue eyes are so dark, they're practically black. It's true that we have been waiting in a stare-off for the past thirty minutes, but I was happy to prolong this conversation. And now she is here, her vanilla and raspberry scent sweeping over me, and my stance visibly relaxes.

"Oh yeah, sorry about that," Aspen replies. "I didn't want to come." Chase chuckles at the end of the line until Lorcan slams a fist on his desk. Wooden this time, as per the redecoration of his office. No more tech and no more glass furniture – including the boarded-up windows. Pushing to stand, Lorcan's eye twitches as he tries to refrain from the impending outburst.

"Be that as it may, we have a serious problem here." He points between the four of us.

"Have you run out of fresh tie and sock combos?" Aspen asks so innocently, as if I didn't know her better. Chase can't contain himself this time, earning a glare from me—time and place, asshole.

"The naming ceremony is about to take place, and I still have no idea what to do with the bunch of you. Never have I had to deal with such insolence-" Aspen snorts, causing Lorcan to glare daggers. I fight the urge to step in front of her, needing to remind myself that Lorcan isn't a threat. He's a father and a king trying to ensure his kingdom remains in good hands. This time, I share a sympathetic look with Aspen, willing her to give him a break.

"I wasn't raised to conform to vampire law," Aspen raises her hands. "I raised myself, which means I must rely on my instincts to see me through each day. You say I'm being insolent; you treat me as a child because I'm not centuries old. And maybe you're right. But I know myself. I know who I am and what I want." Breaking away, Aspen puts herself halfway between Lorcan at his desk and the three of us watching intently. Her gaze glints while I drink in her appearance for the first time, completely stunned.

White hair falls over one shoulder in loose curls, the other side braided back from her beautiful face. Light makeup has been applied in true Nova fashion, highlighting Aspen's navy eyes with a silver shimmer. Her full lips are a pale, icy blue to match the most exquisite gown hugging her body. Glimmering jewels embedded in the lace, from her chest to the lengthy train, sparkle around hints of pale blue and white. Ice-like spokes create a flourish across her breasts, leaving her shoulders bare. White gloves stretch to her elbows, her hands planted on the flare of her hips. When she moves, I see a hint of her standard white sneakers poking out from beneath.

"I don't mean to be disrespectful," Aspen breathes, addressing Lorcan. "The rules you've had to put in place have ensured the survival of your… our species. Your role is built around making tough decisions; one of those was to seek me out. To trust me to rule alongside a mate. There's much I don't know, but I know my own heart. I want to be loved, worshipped, and protected. So, if you're asking me to choose, to pick one to be content with for eternity, you're not going to like your answer."

The air thickens as a swell of pride puffs out my chest. Had it been any other female, she would have bent to Lorcan's will. Compared myself against my brother's and made the logical decision for her future. But since the day I met her, Aspen has ruled with her heart. Never allowing the pressure to adapt affect her feelings towards us. In this moment, regardless of Lorcan's response, we've all won. Ture equals, only invested in her complete happiness.

"Walk with me," Lorcan commands, leaving no room for disagreement. He walks ahead, and Aspen just after, her head held high as they pass and exit the room. I share a look with Torsten and Chase before rushing to follow. We're led to Lorcan's personal bed-chamber, the scent of Rowena's mother all over his bedsheets. My nose wriggles, and a harsh exhale leaves me.

We're back to this bullshit of self-destruction. Bronwyn is tough to tolerate at the best of times, but when she thinks she has Lorcan wrapped around her little finger, it's insufferable. No matter how many times he picks her up and drops her like a cheap whore, in an attempt to forget how his soul is splintering briefly, she's convinced she'll be queen one day. Only Lorcan won't be around long enough to see it happen.

Opening the double doors leading out to his balcony, Lorcan allows Aspen to pass before holding a hand up to the rest of us. He wants to be alone with her, and if we weren't personally invested in the outcome of their conversation, we would have respected his decision. Instead, as the doors are drawn closed, we rush to the other side and hide within the curtains to listen in. Chase bends low, his head knocking against my dick and putting me in a precarious position.

"You're a stubborn mule Lorcan," Aspen starts, and I slam my face into my palm. "So, you must forgive me for bearing the same trait."

"I do, to a degree," the king sighs. Through a crack in the curtain, I watch him approach Aspen by the rounded stone wall lining the balcony and stop at her side. A full moon beams down from above, coating the pair in a white glow. Two lost shadows against the night, hunting for a way to build the connection they should have never been denied.

"Orianna once told me everlasting love requires an equal amount of compromise and sacrifice. I gave her both. In fact, I gave her everything I had, losing the grasp on my responsibilities in the process. Some of us aren't meant for the life we choose." Lorcan's head lowers, his hands gripping the short wall.

"Was she your true mate?"

"Without a doubt." Lorcan nods, not a breath of hesitation. Angling her body towards him, Aspen raises her hand to touch his shoulder and then thinks better of it.

"I'm thankful that for whatever brief period of time, my mother knew what it meant to be loved. To the point where I'm regretful, I was her biggest sacrifice." Lorcan begins to speak, but Aspen talks over him. "But I must believe her choice was to give me the best chance at a free life. Not one bound by these walls and ancient rules meant to restrict me. I'm a wolf, Lorcan; I don't do well behind stone walls."

"Is this your way of telling me, should I deny your request, you will leave?" My own heart jackhammers in my chest. She's serious about this. Across the glass planes, Torsten's chest rumbles behind the opposite curtain, his eyes beginning to glow with golden flecks. His muscles ripple with the desire to smash something, but a swift whistle brings his attention to my raised hand. If nothing else, I'm still his commander, and it's engrained in him to obey me. The next time Aspen speaks, I note out of the corner of my eye that she's turned to sit on the wall, directly facing the double doors.

"Half of my soul requires freedom, and she finds it in Chase's laugh. In the way Torsten's tough exterior comes crumbling down whenever we're nearby. In Jaxon's soothing presence. They are my freedom. That's the compromise I'm offering, should you be determined, I must stay."

"What of Sawyer?" Lorcan hits back. A long pause follows, Aspen's face falling to shadow.

"What of him? He told me he was my guardian, promised to keep me safe, and left after one kiss." An uneasy feeling churns in my gut. I see what's happening here, the king has seen a last-ditch attempt to change Aspen's mind. Whether his intention is for Aspen to stay with one of us or leave with him, it won't work. I'm more loyal to Lorcan than anyone in this castle, but I'll follow Aspen to the ends of the earth. Wherever she is, that's where my home will be.

"Do you remember the night you told me about that kiss? How I reacted?" Lorcan presses on. Aspen nods. "There's much I need to tell you." I can merely stand here, gripping Chase's shoulder to hold him in place, and listen to Lorcan relay the meaning behind a moon bond, how Sawyer has been chosen for her by a higher power, supposedly rendering her emotionally unavailable to any other. A crack jerks beneath my grip, Chase's collarbone snaps at the extent of my rage, but he doesn't so much as whimper. The fury radiating from him rivals my own.

"I can understand you feel guilty choosing one male," Lorcan continues, "but there is a shifter out there who already has your heart. This is a decision for your head. We need a ruler, and as much as I love Rowena, she isn't up to the job. You're strong, Aspen, you have what it takes to be a powerful ruler. I've indulged your fantasy thus far, but this is merely a blip in time compared to your long existence."

A blip? Did my own king just refer to the depths of my feelings for his daughter a blip? Chase stands now, and despite all of his bravado, his hand slips into mine as his head lowers onto my shoulder. Ragged breaths expand his back, a battle for control taking place. Torsten shoots to my shoulder, patting Chase's head whilst muttering.

"She's going to choose us." I nod, willing myself to believe him. The past few weeks have revealed many things, most of all the lengths the four of us are willing to go to make Aspen's harem work. Her happiness is our only purpose. If I thought either of my brothers felt even a fraction less of the love for her than I do, I'd have taken the tough role of weeding them out. But it's simply not true.

"If Sawyer is my moon bond mate, then where is he?" Aspen asks, and collectively, the three of us tense.

"His soul is bound to yours. You tell me," Lorcan dares her. Golden eyes lift to meet ours through the glass, indecision evident in her brows. I shake my head, barely registering her muttered words in time.

"I'm sorry. I have to know." My heart leaps into my throat, barely having time to react as Aspen throws herself over the back of the stone wall. We don't waste time on the door handle. Smashing through the glass, the three of us rush to the railing, spotting no trace of Aspen in the grass mound or town below.

"What have you done?!" I shout, bumping chests with Lorcan. My hands form fists at my sides, my eyes wild with anger.

"Careful," Lorcan growls, snapping his fingers. A line of royal guards appear on the balcony, rushing to aid the king's command. "I can easily leave you all in the dungeon to rot for real this time. I need an heir, and some false sense of love won't stand in my way."

Aspen
Chapter Twenty-Three

Everything aches. My chest feels tight, my limbs are heavy. I've felt like this many times in my life, yet I still don't know how to overcome it. Usually, I just have to wait for a little time to pass until the heaviness has lifted ever so slightly so that I can resume my business as usual and bury the rest. But it never actually leaves.

After a short while, the gnawing misery subsides slightly, opening the floodgates for another, stronger emotion. Anger. I look down at my sneakers, scuffing up dirt in my haste. The lace dress wiping around my ankle was supposed to be akin to a wedding gown, as I was adamant I'd be walking out of the champion's ceremony with three males surrounding me. Now I'm racing across the mountain ranges beyond vampire territory with no destination in mind. All I need is to put enough distance between myself and the vampires, no doubt, on my tail, so I can stop and give myself a moment.

I couldn't wait around for them to convince me to stay. Lorcan told the truth. I felt it in my soul as soon as the words were spoken. Sawyer has been mated to me by the moon. All this time, I've been bitterly thinking he left. Or maybe that was the easier pill to swallow than to consider he's in trouble. I curse at myself for being so selfish. If anything has happened to him, I will never be able to forgive myself. There's still a lingering hope he's safe, choosing to live a life apart from his duty –and then I'll have my answer. I'll be able to squash my guilt and know my mate simply didn't want me.

Everything in my gut tells me that's not the case, and my feet continue to speed onward, stretching the distance between myself and anyone who may be following. I have no doubt those I considered mine will come for me, but they will be limited to nights. A cunning plan, although I don't feel any better about it. Just when I thought everything was finally clicking into place, I should have known my life will never have a simple happily ever like the books I prefer to lose myself in. There's no use in wallowing in my regret. I just need to keep moving forward and leave everything else behind, knowing I stayed true to myself. Knowing I couldn't accept a fate I had no choice in.

My heart tugs painfully, and I finally let the tears fall, streaming from my eyes to my ears as the harsh winds pummel my face at a fierce speed. Once I'm far enough away from the castle and the life I've come to know, even briefly, I slow by a stream. The rippling water reflects the fullness of the moon. Kneeling low, I wash my face and cup my hands to drink my fill of the refreshing water. Everything will be okay; it has to be. I'm a survivor at heart, I'll be fine in the end.

Removing my dress, I leave it strewn across a boulder with one last lingering touch. Running from the guys was simple, all it took was a burst of adrenaline. No hard goodbyes, no begging or fake promises. They wouldn't have joined my quest to find my moon-bound mate, nor would they have understood my need to find him. Our dynamic was fine when it was the three of them, but they hated Sawyer from the beginning. Which is why, as I stroke the dress, it seems harder to leave behind. The lace is a visual representation of who I nearly became.

Standing under the moon's pale ray, I pull my wolf to the surface. The snapping of my bones barely registers through the void consuming my being. Her unfolding presence soothes my emotions. My body resets in its new skeleton as fur sprouts, covering my form in a familiar white coat.

As my wolf's paws fly across the bark and soil covering the ground with barely a trace, I finally feel at ease. Jumping from boulders, winding through tree trunks, and snarling at the odd squirrel, I let my wolf have complete control. She can have the reins tonight and do as she pleases while I remain buried in a furry cocoon, away from the monsters of this world—those who entice me with pretty words and charming notions. I could have stayed. I would have been happy. But Sawyer guarded me during my darkest times, he fell for me at my worst. I owe him the same chance.

A sharp sting draws my attention to my left hind leg, as I rouse enough to wonder what my wolf ran through. Nettles wouldn't affect her, but a thorn bush could do some damage. On wobbly legs, I take stock of my surroundings as we enter a woodland area. She slams into a tree trunk, the vibration rattling around my skull. What the fuck? I bring my full consciousness back to the surface and, as the forest sways unnaturally, the trunks warping and bending, the full moon blurring above, I wish I hadn't. Although the sting has lessened, my limbs feel heavy, starting to drag behind. I slump onto the muddy ground, a haze flooding my thoughts.

As the edges of my vision blur, a silhouette steps into the light before me. I can't make out any features, my body lying uselessly, and my head too heavy to lift. Maybe Jaxon has found me, coming to rescue me from my own foolishness. A calloused hand grips my snout painfully, tugging my head upwards in a sharp motion. I whine, confusion claiming me. Through the fog, I just about recognize pale brown irises snarling down at me seconds before my world turns dark.

Chapter Twenty-Four

ad I known the sentence I was permitting, I would never have answered the summons. Had I not been my mother's son, I would have relied on my instincts over my sense of duty. Our birthright is a rarity, our submission to the council's will is a gift. Something they seem to have forgotten upon throwing me in this dank, dark dungeon.

If this area is part of the guardian training camp where I was raised, I haven't had the misfortune of seeing it before my imprisonment. I'd only just learned to walk when my mother was assigned to Aspen's, my care transferred to Bran, my handler, and then the training began. Becoming a guardian isn't only a physical commitment but a mental one.

The hatch in the base of the metal bars slides open, and two trays of inedible food slide inside. I don't open my eyes, keeping my back to the cell. Hands resting on my knees, I exhale slowly from my position on the floor, diving back into my connection with Aspen. The ability to find her during meditating has been my lifeline these past few weeks. I've watched through her eyes, calculating the days by her sleep cycle. Her emotions have become my own, from confusion to contentment.

Her arousal has been the hardest to feel, given the males she's been spending time with. I can't pass judgment, not when I've seen the lengths they've gone to be with her. I sense how her heart flutters when they are nearby and how her confidence intensifies. Aspen is her truest self in their company, and it's difficult to know where her affections end, and my own respect for their sacrifices begins. I wake some nights to the instant thought of having four mates before shaking my head clear.

I hunt for her now, but she's too deep to reach. She must be within her wolf, burying herself from the outside world. With extra effort, I can almost connect with the wolf, sensing the pounding of paws against the earth and wild whipping through her fur. Knowing she's safe, I withdraw and turn to face my cellmate. He's a pathological liar in the form of a falcon shifter and currently finishing both trays of food. Rolling my eyes, I lean back against the damp wall.

Without a window and our only light source being from a torch beyond the bars, I'd hazard a guess that we're underground. Not on Earth, though. The Supernatural Council exists in another pane, only accessible by portal. Even if Aspen had the notion to look for me, she never would be able to, and I'm glad she hasn't. I want my mate to live her life, and I shall live through her.

A clinking echoes from the corridor, a figure coming to a standstill before our cell. Pushing a key into the door and swinging it open, I'm swiftly brought to attention by a sharp whistle.

"On your feet, Sawyer," a familiar voice demanded. Obeying, I search the shadows for the pair of deep brown eyes I didn't expect to see here. Bran whistles again, knocking his bootheels together, and strides away. I follow on an invisible thread, unable to break years of training to refuse his command. I'm simply happy to see someone I know. Passing through the door, a guard quickly swoops in and locks it shut.

"Good luck," my cellmate shouts loudly, followed by a psychotic cackle. Rousing those in the cells adjacent, hands wind around the bars, curious eyes peering out. I've been placed with those of my kind, although to have a raven in their presence is a sight many thought they'd never see. Owls, hawks, and a lone griffin in his own cellblock suite at the end of the corridor all glare as I leave them behind in the darkness. A weight lifts from my chest, a thankful smile pulling at my cracked lips. I should have known Bran would come for me.

Stepping free of the pit I'd been left in, I inhale my first clear breath as cuffs are dropped over my wrists. Frowning, a pair of huge eyes dare me to argue.

"I told you, restraints aren't necessary. He'll obey my command," Bran argues, but it's useless. My ankles are shackled next, an adjoining chain linking them to my wrists. A purple twinge of magic circulates the metal, robbing me of my ability to shift.

"We can't take that risk," the beast replies, returning to his ten-foot height. Tusks protrude from his bottom lip, his skin a sickly shade of green. No, I'm definitely not back at the guardian training camp.

The metal tug hinders my every step, and my boots can only stretch as far as the chain permits. My wrists are bound in iron, matching the thick cuffs at my ankles. I struggle within my trench coat, the stiff material crumpled awkwardly across my shoulders. A little overkill, considering I've been left in that dungeon amongst murderers and rapists—those who used their link to coerce and manipulate. My only crime is falling in love.

"Don't say a word, we'll sort this out," Bran orders, falling back a step. Shoved onward by the guard, I pass beneath a pointed archway. Following the glint of gold amongst the black marble flooring, a grand room comes into view, much like a cathedral without a ceiling. Stars linger within a midnight blue sky, bleeding into elongated windows. Figures within the stained glass represent each type of supernatural being, from the well-known blood-sucking monsters of the night and wolves howling at a full moon to those who rely on magic and mystery to survive under the radar.

Crossing a small bridge, my gaze is briefly distracted by a pool of water spanning the length of the circular room. Grecian pillars bearing hanging torches appear sporadically around one-half, the light punctuated by candles scattered across the floor. On the other side, darkness reigns, casting a shadow over a set of steps leading down to the marble flooring. The orc prods me onwards, forcing me to descend to the lowest point. Bran stands back, his expression grave and arms folded.

"You've broken the sacred vow."

An echoed voice reverberates from above as a series of blurred cloaks plummet toward the marble-like fallen angels—eight in total, all hidden within their lowered hoods. Taking distinct levels of steps of their own accord, I can only imagine I'm witnessing the ranks of hierarchy as the council crowds me. The slither of a tentacle slips from beneath a cloak on the second level, the purple appendage seeking out the pool of water behind.

Three beings have opted for the darker side of the cathedral, four others standing towards the light. Given time, I reckon I could uncover which species each belongs to, but it's the largest figure on the highest step who should have my full attention. He stands central, not favoring a particular environment.

"Sawyer, son of Gideon," he continues. I fight a shudder at the name of the raven who left me a bastard. I would have been expected to do the same to many of my own offspring, mating the few raven females until they can no longer reproduce. I've fucked that option, and hence why the figure above booms his words with a thick undertone of irritation. "You've been brought before us for ___."

"The moon bound our souls-" I begin before a host of growls and screeches erupt around me. Tossing a look back, Bran shakes his head in disapproval. This agitates me more than anything else; I've given Bran my complete compliance since I was a child. I'm a product of his training, and this is my first infraction, if I can call it that.

"You revealed your truest self," the highest being continues. "Had you remained in raven form, this would not have been possible. You are not a mate to this immortal. The moon confused your guardian's binding with that of a mate's bond." My fists clench in the cuffs. I've had the same thought, but no matter how many times I've replayed that night in the forest from my and Aspen's memory, I can't agree. I felt her affection, and I know my own is sincere.

"You've taken advantage of your charge and your position," a female voice from my left scowls. A round of hissing punctuates her voice, her hood shifting of its own accord. Clenching my teeth together, I refrain from responding. I don't need anyone's judgment. I know the truth. The figure on the highest point, the one I presume is the leader, stands tall, commanding my focus.

"Your mentor has spoken on your behalf. He has described you as a keen warrior and loyal protector, but what you have done," the central figure lowers his head, "the crimes you have committed are too severe." My heart clenches. Finally confronted with the reason I've been brought here, I can no longer hide within my meditations. Seeing Bran had given me false hope, but I can no longer deny that the chances of walking free of here are non-existent.

"Perhaps he could relocate to another charge," a gentle female speaks up. My head shoots in her direction. She stands closest to the light, a curious shimmer glinting beneath her hood. "Ravens are a valued commodity we can't afford to waste. There are many in need of protection, and the Fates-" The leader growls with the echo of a large beast, his hand shooting palm up to silence her—a glimmer of green scales across his fingers.

"Take him to the holding area while we discuss his sentence. *Again.*" At the leader's demand, the guard grabs my shoulder and rips me away from the cathedral. I fight to look back, giving my savior a brief nod before I'm thrown into a room and locked inside. Bran argues with the guard beyond the door while I pace and fist my hair.

The same pointed arches frame the stain-glass windows, and a beige sofa with gold accents is placed before a wall of bookshelves. Throwing myself back on the cushions and covering my eyes with my arm, I hunt for a calmer place. It takes a few minutes to connect with Aspen, but as soon as I latch on, I slip into her body as if it were my own.

No longer in wolf form, Aspen's eyes blink in and out of sleep. She's jostling, her body braced in a pair of strong arms. I ought to turn away, leaving her in peace, but I need something to hold onto at this moment. It may be the final time I'm able to connect with her and at least I can feel her heart flutter and sweet laughter once more.

Blinking upwards, a strong jaw clenches above us, his head inclined as his pale brown eyes glare back with a heavy dose of contempt.

I frown, my head jerking involuntarily. I don't know this male.

"C-" Aspen tries to speak. Her throat is raw, and her limbs limp. With the rousing of her consciousness comes the assault of sudden pain. A heavy contraption cages her face. The binds at my wrists and ankles are weighted by the same on hers, and as her heart picks up a panicked rhythm, mine's about to cease up.

"Car...rick..." Aspen manages to grunt. The smile on his face makes my stomach roll. A sharp sting pierces her neck, although he made no move to sink his exposed fangs into her. Within seconds, my connection with Aspen is broken, and I gasp, staring at the midnight sky above. A fork of lightning flashes, mirroring the burst of fear I struggle to breathe through.

Movement shifts in the corner of my eye. I jerk upright, swinging my bound hands widely. A hooded figure stills a few moments away, the hood tilting slightly until I drop my arms onto my thighs. Then, despite all of my training and the present company, a tear falls from my eye. My head hangs in defeat. There's nothing I can do, and as my judgment approaches, I wonder if I can plead to have a new protector assigned to Aspen. My dying wish for my fated mate.

"The moon's power flows through your veins," the soft feminine voice sounds. Moving forward, she kneels and pushes back her hood. Shimmering skin and the biggest pair of blue eyes peer up at me. Her pointed eyes poke through blonde braids, a delicate gold crown hanging low over her brows. Confusion rakes my brain, but as she pushes up my trench coat sleeve, my gaze snags on the markings lining my arm. Once black, the branches embedded into my skin glow silver, shining with an ever-moving flow of power. Holy shit. Those blue eyes blink upwards, the hint of worry pulling at the corners of her mouth.

"Save her. It's imperative." With those softly spoken words, the sofa beneath me gives way. I fall into space, the restraints vanishing and allowing my limbs to spread wide. Flailing, I drop through the midnight sky, passing endless stars before appearing on the other side. Boosted by the moon's light, I shift into my raven, ducking my wings and diving towards the Earth. It takes too long before I'm able to recognize the mountain ranges of vampire territory, my wings thrusting wide to circle the land I've previously committed to memory. The glow of daybreak threatens, the asshole vampire who has Aspen soon to be driven into hiding.

Without any notion of where he'd take her, I trail the stream, knowing her wolf would have sought out water had she been in control. Soaring, I take in the panoramic view all at once. Twinkling catches my keen eye, drawing me downwards on a quick spiral. A dress of icy blue lace and diamond has been carefully placed against a boulder, the tracks of paw prints leading into the forest beyond. A caw escapes my beak, a question held within. I know in my body that Aspen can't respond and the longer my talons tap against the boulder beside her dress, the heavier the dread settles within my feathery chest.

There's only one thing for it.

Flapping as quickly as I can, I gain distance on the castle. Powerful beats of my wings see me speeding past the iron gate, over the surrounding town, and directly toward the king's suite. It's the only room I know, and as I approach, I find the rear doors facing the balcony smashed through. A mass of bulky vampires sit within, but there's no time for pleasantries. Swooping directly inside, I shift and land in the center of the suite, seemingly interrupting a tense conversation between Lorcan and the three vamps crowded by guards. A situation I'm all too familiar with and not exactly comfortable in.

"That was quick," Chase tuts, rolling his eyes. His shoulders are slumped inward, his green eyes bleak. Arms crossed and standing by his sides, Torsten and Jaxon glare at me.

"Come to gloat?" Torsten growls. Narrowing my eyes, I turn and address Lorcan instead, not wasting precious time.

"Aspen has been taken. Some vampire called Carrick? She's in trouble," I blurt, despair leaking from my voice. But my dread is nothing compared to the expression which passes across Lorcan's face or the roars of anguish which erupt from behind.

S inged fur. That's what I can smell. It's close but...I can't feel any burning.

Everything is dim in here. Not even my enhanced eyesight can penetrate the darkness ahead. A shadow looms over my shoulder. I turn swiftly in *shock, but it's gone. I spin, becoming lightheaded in an effort to locate it again. But there isn't anyone stuck here except myself.*

A black mass suddenly lunges at me from the front, pinning my arms by my side and leaning into my face. I scream but no sound comes out. Amongst the shifting outline of the shadow, two pale brown eyes come into focus, staring directly into mine as they begin to glow like coals of fire.

Screaming, I'm finally able to wake from the nightmare I've been stuck in behind my closed eyelids. That's when the onslaught of pain hits. Every part of me is numb yet on fire at the same time. Burnt chunks of white fur lay on the stony ground all around me, the edges curled and blackened. In human form, the cold, uneven ground bleeds into my raw skin.

I blink away the confusion, taking stock of my body. There's a muzzle strapped tightly around my head, seemingly made of silver by the blistering covering my cheeks and jaw. Similar scorching sensations circle my bound wrists behind my back and ankles. My silver affliction isn't as strong as a full vampire's, but constant contact does slowly burn my flesh.

The space surrounding me is hollow, a round ceiling hanging above covered in spiked stone, like a concrete jaw about to clamp down. The hard floor is damp, but it's the jagged roughness that affects me the most. A sharp point protruding from the ground is cutting into my cheek, blood pooling into my ear and hair. I try to wiggle onto my back but the fatigue I've cleared from my mind still has a solid hold on my limbs.

How the hell did I end up here? My memories are foggy, and the pain is too distracting now I'm fully awake. Closing my eyes, I focus on my other senses to try to figure out where I am. The air is thinner, as if I'm tucked far, far away from the fresh, oxygenated surface of outside. A continuous drip, drip, drip of water sounds from deeper within the tunnel, droplets echoing around the rocky walls, followed by the faintest sound of ripples. Rainwater, judging by the vague sulfur smell. That, and the almost-suffocating dampness clogging my throat, tells me there's a large body of water nearby, and I conclude I'm probably underground.

If the circumstances had been different, I would have loved to have stumbled upon this hidden treasure cove and explored its depths at my leisure. Cocooned in a forgotten pocket of the earth like this, I would have normally felt at peace in the cool darkness. But that tranquil state is too distant now. Physical feeling begins to settle back into my body, allowing me to flex my fingers – stretching them outwards and then balling the digits back into tight fists behind me, hissing at the burn circling my wrists.

"Ahh, you're awake," a gravelly voice reaches me from behind, causing me to freeze. I'd been so focused on the sounds in front of me with my one available ear, I haven't noticed my apparent captor creeping up from behind. The heel of a boot jabs into my shoulder and roughly forces me the rest of the way onto my back. With my hands trapped beneath me and the weight of the silver muzzle pressing down on my lower face, I helplessly whine like a battered puppy. A humorless laugh forces me to open my eyes and glare at the piece of shit who's done this to me. *Carrick.*

The vampire stands comfortably upright, arms crossed, and neck only bent to glare down at me. His light brown eyes don't give away emotion, and his passive face appears bored. But his stance speaks volumes. Bunched shoulders, rigid posture - he's pissed.

I try to ask what the fuck he's looking at, why I'm here, and what he wants, but nothing comes out. The silver burns have stretched from my jaw to my lips, making them tight and unmovable.

"I have to say, little princess, I'm disappointed. I had hoped you'd prove a bit more of a challenge. Breaking someone's spirit is one of the greatest pleasures in life," Carrick sighs with an evil sneer. My ears twitch. I've heard a similar statement previously from Conall.

Ignoring the insult, I can at least revel in not giving him something he would have enjoyed – although it isn't in my nature to admit defeat. His gaze rakes down the length of my body, making me suddenly aware of how very naked and vulnerable I am. I squirm, desperately trying to twist back onto my side and cover myself from his invasive leer but fail miserably.

"I've had my eye on you for quite some time. Long before our formal introduction in the forest," Carrick bends down, stroking one finger from my chin, between my cleavage, and over my stomach. I jerk my bound legs upwards quickly, a half-assed attempt to knee him in the face and stop his finger from reaching any lower. He chuckles at me, pushing my legs back down forcefully and leaving his hand on my thigh. Bile rises in my throat at his touch, threatening to choke me, but at least he's not attempting anything else... for now.

"You looked quite different the first time I saw you, though. Innocent, young. I preferred your natural hair coloring," Carrick tugs on my white locks. I try to pull back from his grip, but his hand latches on tight, and I only succeed in causing more pain to my own scalp.

Wait... I stop fighting and stare up at him, rendered silent. What does he mean, my natural hair color? The color of their wolf defines a shifter's hair and is only determined upon the first shift at thirteen. Carrick couldn't have possibly known me any earlier than that...right? Lying still, I wait to hear the rest of the story he's clearly eager to tell. That's typically what psychopaths do before they kill their captives.

"Vampires are solitary creatures; we live to play a role and prefer our solace the rest of the time. It was almost too easy for Lorcan to keep his affair going for so long. In fact, he was so in tune with your mother, he didn't even realize I was following him," Carrick smirks, drawing a figure of eight on my eight.

"Even I can admit she was beautiful, but shifters are the enemy. The one foe we've spent our entire existence fighting. I could foresee him planning to bring her to the castle, but she broke his heart before I had to intervene. Destroyed him so much that he never looked back. But I did. I watched her belly swell, I watched you fool the alpha, and then your first shift. It was mighty impressive."

I struggle against my binds, not wanting to hear anymore. Knowing Carrick has been present during my entire life makes my skin crawl. How seriously did he take his detail operation, and just...how thorough was his self-imposed mission? I feel sick, twisting my head away from his penetrating gaze.

"That's right, princess, I was always there. I saw you for the threat you were. It was only a matter of time before Lorcan's discovered the truth, and I'd be damned if some pathetic little half-breed was going to sit on the vampire throne. I had to do something. Little did I know, you were even more pathetic than I realized, and your mother paid the ultimate price."

My breathing slows, barely functioning as my brain hunts for an answer between Carrick's words. My mom died of an illness. There was nothing I could have done, nothing to prevent it from claiming her body...right?

~

"You need to eat, sweetie." Mom shifts the long curls I've let fall over my face, hiding my shame behind the white sheet of hair. The mattress dips as she lays on my single bed, spooning my body from behind. I know I shouldn't waste her precious visits, but I can't bring myself to perk up. If anyone should be allowed to see the real me, it's her. Cradled in her warmth, I release the sobs I've been trying to suppress. I shouldn't be so weak; I should be used to the taunts of other adolescent shifters by now.

"It's okay. Everything will be okay." Mom soothes, whilst stroking my arm. But how can she promise that? They'll never stop because I'm a freak of nature. A reject they won't leave alone.

I'd been swimming in the sea earlier this afternoon, relishing in the burn of my muscles with every stroke I took. The cool water soothes my stress, the underwater world taking me to a different dimension in my mind. Gliding beneath the surface, I can pretend I'm not abnormal or odd. Just myself lost in my own thoughts amongst the fishes.

A sudden explosion of bubbles to my right makes me screech underwater, needing to surface to cough out the water I'd ingested. Another large mass collides with the water next to me, followed by many more. Looking up, I see a whole group of shifters around my age on the cliff's edge, laughing down at me.

A hand grabs my ankle, dragging me under. More hands push down on the top of my head, to keep me struggling in the blue depths, my lungs burning with the need to take my next breath. My free foot connects with the face of whoever is holding my other ankle, and I throw a fist into the nearest groin. I manage to free myself from their grasp long enough to breach the surface and fill my lungs before four young males lurch up and tug me back under.

My struggles are pointless, and I'm not able to catch them off guard a second time. A pair of hands hold each of my wrists and ankles, pulling me further and further down, the light above dimming. The edges of my vision darken. Bubbles escape my lips, and my body's protests cease. Next thing I know, I'm receiving mouth-to-mouth from my mom on the sandy shore in the setting sunlight.

After a while, long after the sobs had stopped and the tears have dried on my cheeks, Mom releases a long sigh and rises from the bed. "Well, I'm not going to waste this meal I've prepared," she says while busying herself behind me, plating up and pulling the wicker chair over to a makeshift crate table to eat alone. Staring at the wooden panel alongside the bed and listening to her soft movements, I soon drift off into a restless sleep filled with aqua ripples and fading light.

The next morning, I received the news of her illness. Flustered, desperate to get to her, I didn't see the words etched into the stone of my hut until I returned, broken and alone. 'Trust the ravens.' I didn't care to heed her advice, not when she hadn't taken that last opportunity to tell me she loved me. Curled upon the floor of the exile hut, I wept once more until every ounce of warmth inside of me withered and died along with her.

CARRICK'S LAUGHTER brings me back to the present. Relentless tears slide down my face, slipping under the muzzle. The saltiness stings the burns on my cheeks, and I can't bring myself to care. Realization must be shining through my leaking eyes as Carrick nods in answer.

"While she was so distracted consoling her pitiful juvenile, I slipped poison into the food intended for you. Your mother paid the price for your weakness. Although I must admit," he teases my hair with morbid fascination. "I was going to wait until our wedding night to reveal my hand once I was named king. If only you hadn't been foolish enough to think those three idiots could be your mates. The only mate you've been gifted is a fucking raven, and not even he could stand staying with you." Carrick stands, laughing louder as he walks away. "I won't fail in killing you this time, Aspen. And I'm going to enjoy every second of it."

Chase
Chapter Twenty-Six

ouncing on my heels at the castle's main entrance, I impatiently wait for the sun to finally set after a painstakingly long day. I don't bode well with the feeling of helplessness, and I was dangerously close to braving another battle with the sun if it will bring me closer to her. Only the thought of not being alive to find her stopped me.

Aside from Jaxon and Torsten at my sides, an entire vampire army is waiting behind me, eager to find our missing princess. The fact that one of our own has taken her, possibly harmed her is too much for any of us to bear. Guilt racks through me for the times I isolated myself from the soldiers behind me, not taking my job as second-in-command seriously. But if nothing else, this treacherous time has shown me that each and every one of the vampires in this castle are my family – and we will bring our rightful heir back home safety.

She will take the throne and lead us all with the compassion and strength I've been honored to have been shown by her personally. At this point, I don't even care if she wants a life with me. Knowing she is safe is enough and I will forever love her from afar.

The royal guards on either side of the giant entrance step forward and lift the heavy plank across the center, pushing the doors open to show the pale orange afterglow of the sunset. A shadow swirling in the sky swoops vertically, shifting mid-air to land on heavy boots. Sawyer stands, jet black hair sweeping low over the taut veins around his eyes.

"I have a lead," he states loudly, although his gaze is on mine. "But you're not going to like it."

"Do I look like I give a shit either way? Where is she?" I clench my fists.

"She's on shifter territory, that's as much of a read as I can get. Kofu, the alpha's protégé, has agreed to meet with you. He'll be at the exile hut in an hour." Whipping his trench coat in a flourish, Sawyer shifts back into raven form and takes to the sky. I don't waste another second, leading the mass of bodies through the town on swift feet. Pouring out of the raised iron gate, we descend on the woodlands before us before splitting up into pre-arranged groups.

"Do you trust him?" Torsten asks no one in particular. He, Jaxon, and I stay together, a small quadrant at our backs.

"The protégé or the raven?" I grunt, pumping my arms harder.

"Both." The bird speeds ahead, strong flaps of his enhanced wings putting us on his constant shadow. I swear on the moon, if he's leading us astray, I'll pluck and roast him for the sheer satisfaction of it.

"Seems foolish for Carrick to hide Aspen in rival territory," Jaxon interjects, taking a small lead. I catch up to his side.

"Maybe that was the point. To throw us off."

"Or maybe it's a fucking lie." Jaxon's frown is engraved deeply, no more words being spoken. We've already discussed everything that needs to be said. No one has slept, instead using the daylight hours to talk strategy and stare at maps. We even passed around Aspen's clothes from her backpack, allowing every solider to memorize her scent – during which I had to leave the room. I couldn't bear that every male in the castle was intimately learning her fragrance. Such a privilege belongs to those Aspen deems fit, and up to yesterday, I thought that was the three of us.

"Torin, take over command," I order. Signaling to those behind, they venture to the west, set on searching the mountain ranges. Every rock will be overturned, every crevice checked, as planned. Upon reaching the base of the first mountain, each Vamp will disperse in different directions. There are many hidden grottos within range, and searching them thoroughly is a top priority. Trusting the soldiers to act on our behalf, the three of us veer left and fly at top speed toward shifter territory, my heart sinking more with every step.

The raven turns back his head, releasing a squawk. I give him the middle finger. It's none of Sawyer's concern how I chose the handle this mission, and since Jaxon has taken to talking as little as possible, I've had to step up. Something about this meeting doesn't feel right and if the shifters try to stall us, I'd rather my troops were still looking everywhere else.

Within thirty minutes, having pushed ourselves to absolute top speed, we're standing outside the exile hut. A shadow is pacing within, his silhouette bouncing from wall to wall by the candlelight. He seems agitated, clawing his hands into his hair and pulling at his t-shirt irritably. The longer we're forced to wait on his small patch of land, the more he makes guttural sounds and attacks the walls or breaks furniture on occasion. Using my enhanced hearing, I listened closely but his was the only heartbeat present inside. Definitely psychotic, but not our kidnapper.

Another approaches from our right, stepping free of the tree line surrounding the small structure. Kofu, I presume. A couple inches shorter, built like a ton of bricks and covered in ink. Wearing dark jeans and a leather jacket which fits snuggly, his wide chest is bare underneath. Halting a few steps from us with a mocking smile, I steel myself to this spot. It goes against my nature to be this close to a wolf and not try to kill him. At that moment, Sawyer swoops down and shifts, landing between the standoff taking place.

"You told me you have news of Aspen's location," he leads strongly, not a hint of our collective desperation present. Kofu nods slowly. "And what do you want for her safe return?" This takes the wolf by surprise. Pulling his hands free of his jacket pockets, Kofu releases the fists held there. He was expecting a fight. Perhaps that all he wanted.

Taking a step towards Sawyer, I watch the wolf carefully, his head tilting to speak into the raven's ear. "Take her far away, and don't ever let her come back." His words are low grunts which take us all by surprise. I cock my head at his strange request.

"Does the alpha know you're aiding us?" I ask. I take the flash of warning in Kofu's brown eyes as a solid no. Even curiouser, but there's only time for him to humor me once more. "Who is that?" I ask him, jerking my chin in the direction of the exile hut. Kofu wears a scowl, the deep V between his eyebrows suggesting it's a permanent fixture of his sullen face. His dark hair flicks forward into his dead eyes, which sit above unnaturally sharp cheekbones.

"Oh, that? That's none of your fucking business." He sneers. "Come on then, do you want your precious half-breed back or not?" Turning and casually walking away, without the slightest hint of urgency in his steps.

Growling, I follow and intentionally ram my shoulder into his. His animalistic snarl penetrates the forest.

"Enough," Jaxon snaps at me. I argue that this fucker is wasting time, but Jaxon won't hear it. Gold flecks glint in his blue eyes, his teeth exposed with ragged breaths. He's struggling to control himself, so I step down and back in line with him and Torst.

"Can we get a fucking move on? I can sense she needs help," Sawyer storms ahead, rubbing at the back of his neck. He's beyond agitated, and as much as I should sympathize, I just hate him all the more for throwing his moon bond in my face. I grind my teeth. I'll be seriously pissed if this is all some time-wasting joke to hold me back from finding my love. Damn, I love her. Kofu breathes out a laugh, which just angers me more.

"She'll be fine," he responds calmly, tapping his sternum beneath his jacket with two fingers. I raise my brows, but he doesn't elaborate.

"You know that how?" I stride to Kofu's side, gesturing to the place on his chest he touched. His mouth slants into a sideways smirk. Talking to this little shit was already infuriating, before he opens his jacket lapel to reveal a wolf's head on his right pec. One half of its face is black, a honey brown staring out from the shading. The other side is purely white, a deep blue eye which can't be any other than Aspen. My heart sinks.

"Oh, you didn't know? Aspen was supposed to be my betrothed before the truth of her heritage was revealed." I stop dead in my tracks. Tensions are already running high, but the thought of Aspen wedding this asshole just about pushes me over the edge. No. There's no way Aspen's wolf would be drawn to this cocky fucker with his dead eyes and shitty over-grown hair.

"You're nowhere near good enough for her," I spit onto the ground, my fangs lengthening. Kofu's cocky smile slips as he turns back, the scowl returning in full force.

"And you are?! You only had her for a few weeks and you fucking lost her!"

Yeah, okay, I'm not worthy of her either. I don't think anyone truly is. Whomever Aspen chooses will be the luckiest being in the world after I've rescued her.

"And what did you do to aid the hellish life she was leading?" I shout. Kofu squares up to me and I shove at his chest.

"You have no fucking idea," he throws a fist, which Jaxon catches. The commander shudders with a lack of restraint, the veins corded so tightly in his neck, he looks prepared to snap.

"I swear, if you two don't quiet the fuck down, I will raze this entire land, killing everyone I come across until I find..." he exhales harshly, "My. Fucking. Woman." Meeting Kofu's eye, I run my teeth over the length of my fangs and incline my head. Accepting my compliance, Kofu continues leading as I trail ten feet behind. Far enough to see an ambush, should it arise. Silence weighs heavily as five males from three species press on, hunting for the female who has no right to entice us all yet managed to without trying.

"For the record," Kofu breaks the silence, "I would never cause Aspen harm. Even after her true nature was revealed, I always intended to wed her. To challenge Conall, become alpha and bring her back to the pack. I grew up believing Aspen was meant to be mine." I fail in trying to mask my responding groan. Torsten smacks the back of my head.

"You speak in past tense. What changed?" Jaxon asks calmly, maintaining pace with Kofu. The wolf peers over his shoulder, snarling at Sawyer.

"The raven nearly pecked my eyes out every time I came to check upon her. Turns out I'm not the only one who was pining for what he could never have," Kofu's hair hangs over his eyes so I can't gauge his true emotion, but mine happens to have lifted. Smirking, I open my mouth to gloat that Sawyer did in fact get her, but Torsten hits me again. We breach the edge of the forest at the base of a hill and divert to a steep path to a beach below. My combat boots hit the sand, my body shaking with tension but Kofu refuses to up his pace. Following the beach around the outside of the steep cliff, a cave entrance comes into view, hidden away from prying eyes. Carrick couldn't have found this place by accident; he'd have to of known of its existence before bringing Aspen here.

"What's going on here?!" a figure lands in the sand blocking our entrance. I peer up at the cliff's lip, noting the distance he just jumped. Standing to full height, a beast of a male glowers at us. The thick hide of a bear hangs over thick shoulders, his outfit made from a mixture of leather and linen. In one hand, he holds a spear, a metal and wooden shield in the other. It's good to know the shifters haven't advanced in the past few decades, and I recognize Conall from the thick scar covering his left eye. Similar to a wolf I faced off against during the shifter wars.

The promise of violence is held in Conall's eyes, all of which aimed at his protégé. Kofu doesn't budge. Nor does he speak. Instead, Sawyer takes the reigns, holding a note of respect in his voice none of us would have been able to manage.

"If I may," Sawyer inclines his head, his black hair falling forward. "We believe someone of importance to us has been brought to these caves and left to die. It's a matter of urgency we inspect them, and after which, we will be gone."

"Who?"

"Aspen," Kofu grunts at least. He's mastered the nonchalant bullshit, acting as if he couldn't care less. If that were true, he wouldn't have led us this far, and now that I see a ripple of anger pass through the alpha, I'm more inclined to believe Kofu's credibility. I have to get into those caves. Suddenly, Conall lowers his shield and spear and smiles. The creepiest fucking smile that would haunt anyone's nightmares.

"So, it is a truce you're after? Well, all you needed to do is ask. Hunt the cave systems to your heart's content, and once you have received your *treasure*," he grins even wider. "Tell Lorcan I will be in contact." Knuckles crack in unison; Jaxon, Torsten and I tensing. We don't want to be in the shifter's debt, but this wasn't our choice. Lorcan forced Aspen to run. He let his irritation for her lack of obedience cloud what was important. No matter who Aspen mates, she's a vampire. She belongs with us, even if I must watch her shack up with Sawyer in one of the mating homes.

"Glady," I force a smirk. Conall's delight is palpable.

"Excellent," he nods and stands aside, permitting our entry. I don't have time to indulge Jaxon's pissed-off expression, we're wasting precious minutes standing here, worrying about politics.

Inside the cave is pitch black, which is fine for our vampire eyesight. Kofu and Conall watch me intently, fresh smirks upon their faces. I don't have time for games. If Aspen is in there, we will find her. Stepping into the dingy space first, the craggy walls are covered in moss and the overpowering scent of damp tingles my nose. The cave narrows slightly before opening into a large cavern, displaying two tunnels branching off in opposite directions further beneath the cliff. Focusing my hearing, only picking up on the multiple, strong heartbeats nearby and dripping of leaking water all around.

"Which way?" I ask the shifters, mainly the one with his hands in his pockets and a bored expression upon his face. Kofu shrugs at me, suddenly tight-lipped now that his alpha is around. They hang back by the mouth of the cave, standing shoulder to shoulder as Conall folds his thick arms. The perfect set-up for an ambush if I ever saw one. I guess we're on our own from now on.

"Let's split into pairs," Jaxon states, immediately stepping closer to

Torsten. I glare at him, finding myself saddled with the fucking raven, but we don't make it that far.

A faint whimper echoes through the tunnel on the right. Snapping my head around, I pause, listening closer. After a beat, a low howl sounds and I have all I need to speed into the shaft, bouncing against the other in a rush to get to her first. Feathers smack me in the face, the raven shifting to flutter through the cave system with more ease and grace than we can manage. Motherfucker.

The deeper we venture, the more pronounced the coppery scent of Aspen's blood becomes. Hope and panic flare to life inside my chest. She's here. We've found her. Whizzing through the network of underground tunnels, I remain latched onto her scent, not slowing for a single second.

I'm so close. Maybe only seconds away from saving my beautiful hybrid and bringing her back to the castle, where she belongs. Once she's fully recovered, I'm going to spend every moment for the rest of our existences showing her what true love is – with or without Lorcan's approval. That's the level of emotion she's awakened within me—the group jester, the one who couldn't take anything seriously. Well, I've never been more serious where Aspen is concerned. She's buried herself so deep within my being, she consumes my every waking thought and blissful dreams.

No one has ever come close to breaching my defenses before, and Aspen barreled straight through them with ease. She sets a fire in my veins and sparks electricity through my bloodstream. I don't want any other. I don't want the throne or the riches, just her. And the second she's back in my arms, I'm going to tell her exactly that.

Aspen
Chapter Twenty-Seven

I rouse to the gentle strokes along my side, trailing from my shoulder to my hip and back again. A smile pulls at my mouth before I've even opened my eyes; the scent of fresh pine surrounding me. Caged between the warmth of bodies, the covers hide us from an outside world. I'm at peace. Jax makes me feel *adored, Torsten gazes upon me like I'm the most beautiful creature he's ever seen. Sawyer is my loyal protector and then there's Chase. Chase allows me to feel alive. There are no words for the antics we could get up to, making love over and over again until we collapse in a heap on the bed. Every day could be like this.*

Blissful. Lost to pleasure, drowning in love. As long as there's a delicious ache between my legs and the contentedness of my men, we could stay here. Drinking from each other, creating a life no one else could interfere in. I'm exposed, my soul vulnerable. Kissing my neck, Jax's fangs scrape against the vein pulsing there, a silent plea. I crane my head to the side giving him full access and an open invitation. Sighing as his fangs penetrate my flesh, lips swallow my gasp, a tongue worships my nipples, and hands push my thighs wide open. This is what life should be, how it could have been if I'd relented to the notion of these four incredible beings owning each and every part of me.

The singe of a burn forces my eyelids to shoot open. Tears leak from my eyes, reacting with the silver of the muzzle. By now, the imprint will have been scarred into my face, a wash of shame trying to pull me back into the dream I'd created for myself. A safe space where we could all just...be. It's not reality, but the more I rouse to a bleak, damp cave, the harder I hold onto the pretty fantasy.

I gave up trying to move, desperate to cover my nudity from the lurking shadows, long ago. Surely Carrick will return soon, and I didn't want to still be here when he does. Between the awkward angle of my shoulders keeping my hands trapped beneath me and whatever lingering drug is still filtering through my system, my limbs just aren't cooperating.

But to do nothing isn't in my nature. No matter how pitiful the situation has seemed, I've yet to truly surrender. In fact, the version of myself I've discovered since being taken to vampire territory would scoff at the very thought. My wolf is cowering from the muzzle, so I call forth the other beast. The same one that I've spent so much time repressing that she now seems unwilling to help me now. I curse her out internally.

Reserving my energy, I try to wiggle further into the tunnel. Away from the direction Carrick left, whilst being fully aware that he was most likely guarding the exit. I'm hardly in a position to escape, but hiding – that's something I can live with. I'm in survival mode, no matter the cost.

Water trickling in the distance calls to me, an invitation too tempting to ignore. My throat is parched, my skin burning from the inside out. Using my feet, I start to slither along the rough ground like an upside-down snake, bending my legs at the knee and shuffling my shoulders backwards, then repeating.

The cave floor is uneven and jagged, and as rocks slice into my back, pain sears deeper than I thought possible, but I keep moving. If I can reach the water source, I can soothe my injuries. In particular, the scabbing burns on my face which are expanding to cover my nose and slowly creeping up towards my eyelids. If I were to simply lie here and wait for the valiant rescue which isn't coming, I'd be dead anyway.

This was a suicide mission. A foolish, split-second decision to leave the vampire's protection in search for a guardian who might not even want me. Hindsight is a beautiful thing, but not when that bitch is laughing in your face whilst writing your elegy. Water droplets from afar beckon me closer, each drip sounding more impatient and eager to greet me. Retreating into my own mind, I try to distract myself from the intense pain spanning my entire back, knowing if I survive this – whatever tattoo artist was chosen for that wolf tattoo Chase spoke of won't have much of a smooth canvas to work with.

The ceiling above is lowering. At first, I thought it was a trick of my mind, but I soon found myself wiggling through a tight cylinder with stone spikes merely inches from my face. The journey is taking longer than I expected, and my body is beginning to feel sluggish and limp – no doubt from the blood loss of my slashed back. I can't go on anymore, I'm only torturing myself before Carrick can.

And here I was thinking you'd grown your own backbone, the voice in my head chuckles at her pun.

By the moon - I hate you, I mentally groan back. Despite the sentiment, relief floods my body. I didn't realize how truly alone I felt until she was ignoring me, but a slither of hope flares. My vampire side is the strong one. She will see me through.

After all this time, you still haven't learnt, she retorts. I stop struggling, laying back beneath a sharp spoke jutting from the ceiling. I could envision it snapping free, impaling me in this tiny passageway and no one would ever know. But still I lay here, waiting for her to elaborate.

You're always at war with yourself, splitting your personality into three. Did it ever occur to you to accept yourself as you are? I'm not a monster; I'm an extension of you. Embrace it. Embrace me. Embrace who you truly are.

A violent shudder rolls through my shoulders, causing a pained groan to halt at my sealed lips. Burns this intense are like acid, seeping into every orifice. Torturing me. Suffocating me. There is no escape, not without help.

I won't save you. I am you. My shortened breath stills. Could it really be that simple? To embrace the beast that I push away? The truth hits me with the impact of a freight train. She. Is. Me. Instead of embracing the gifts I hold, I've been using them as an excuse. Distancing myself, placing the blame on a figment of my imagination and pretending I don't have control. When in reality, I hold all the cards. I am a freaking vampire. It's about time I started acting like it.

Pulling my legs as close as the cramped space allows, I place the worn soles of my feet flat on the ground, ready to propel myself backward. With a final burst of effort, I shove back, and the ground beneath me suddenly gives way. I plummet, bound by restraints and powerless to prevent the impact against a solid wall—a pained scream lodges in my throat, trapped by my sealed lips.

The world whirls past in a dizzying blur as I tumble and roll down a rough slope, finally collapsing in a crumpled heap at the bottom. The ringing in my ears signals that my head took a heavy blow, accompanied by a throbbing pulse at my temple and warm fluid seeping into my eye. Gazing through the haze of crimson, I take in my new surroundings.The cavern is vast and empty, circled by thin, rocky columns like a granite rib cage. Sprinkles of liquid rain down from many of the tiny fissures across the ceiling. The hollow space houses a large pool of shimmering water in the center, causing my parched throat to ache even more at the sight. Lifting my head to continue my visual exploration, a light catches my attention. A perfect circle of moonlight shines through a hole in the cavern's rooftop. A lump rises in my throat, and more tears leak at the sight. If this is to be my death chamber, I couldn't have asked for a more beautiful scene.

Forgetting my pain and thirst, I clamber and slither desperately to reach the lunar light, craving the glow upon my skin. After too much effort and without any grace, I reach the illuminated patch on the ground and collapse onto it.

My wolf nudges her head against my chest then, begging me to let her take over. It's almost too easy. Too simple. I call to her a few times before my body responds, my weakness hindering my ability to shift. The first bone to snap is in one of my wrists, followed by all the bones in my hand, allowing me to slip out of the silver cuff circling it. I sigh in relief and anguish as my arm flops down to the ground, my shoulder finally at ease in its natural position. The next hand repeats the process, my renewed inner hope and strength aiding the transition.

I've never shifted so slowly, but soon I've managed to free myself from the binds holding me and re-adjust my bones into their new skeletal positions. The burns on my face ease as I desperately try to remove the silver contraption from my face, but my hands turn to paws before I get the chance. White fur sprouts from my body to mark the end of the transformation, although the muzzle is still firmly in place – having plenty of room to accommodate my now longer snout.

Sighing, I collapse, intent on flexing my lips to tear them apart. I should be healing, but the puddle of red growing beside my face and the scent of copper surrounding me is not a healthy sign. Staggering over to the clear water, I look at my reflection and notice the pure white fur covering me is turning a deep scarlet, as if a bottle of cabernet is being poured across my wolf's coat. I sway uncontrollably and crash into the shallow edge of the pool. Swallowing a few mouthfuls of water through the muzzle, I gently shift my body side to side, trying to wash some of the blood and dirt from my sticky coat.

But it's no use. I'm too weak, too far past the point of return. I won't recover from this. Not without a fresh blood supply in my immediate future. I slowly drag my lethargic body back to the moon's glow, pulling on its power to comfort me. Even if my body would allow me to, there's no point in trying to escape or run – I have nowhere to go, and no one to run to.

I curl up in the luminescence, soaking in the glorious rays. I want to stay alive so badly. I want to see if I can fix things with my vampires. Above all, I need to know is Sawyer is okay. The vamps will heal, but it's the unknown I can't handle. I thought we might have had more time. Time to cool off, time for me to satisfy my worries and return. But I won't spend my remaining few moments living with regrets. I can feel the life draining from me along with the blood from my open wounds.

I imagine Jax sitting beside me, leaning on my wolf, and stroking my soft coat with his masterful fingers. My spine tingles, my tail wagging gently from side to side, happy to have him here with me in my mind. Torsten caresses the patch between my ears, causing my wolf to purr. Chase's arms circle me in a comforting hug, his face nuzzling in my neck. I even trick myself into believing the shadow of a raven soars gently over-head. Always watching, always caring. In my vision, without the muzzle hindering me, I turn my large head to shower all of them with long leisurely strokes of my tongue. Responding chuckles are music to my sensitive ears.

Water dripping on my face breaks the illusion, snapping me back to the reality of this cold, empty cavity in the earth. Rain falls from the skylight above, although I can only feel it on my face since my body is already soaked through and shivering.

How did it come to this? My wolf releases a series of whines and cries for a life she wishes we could have had. One filled with family and happiness, laughter, and passion. But I quickly calm her with soothing words in our mind. I refuse to go out in a ball of misery or anger.

I choose to be thankful. Thankful that for one millisecond of my life, I felt true love. No matter how brief, I had a team in my corner. That's more than many others can claim to have accomplished and more than I ever dared to imagine. Preparing myself for the inevitable, I'm going to do it with love in my heart.

I love my men. I will live on through each of them. Jaxon, Torsten, Chase, and Sawyer. My pack. I lift my head to the opening above me and howl longingly. My wolf and I howl together with all the love and passion for the beings who changed my world, giving me everything I needed to be fulfilled. With that final thought, as I trick myself again into seeing Sawyer's fluttering shadow pass overhead, I expel the rest of the air from my lungs and lower my head, drifting into the darkness, waiting for me to give in.

Chapter Twenty-Eight

A pool of red. A smear of crimson.

Circling on open wings, I orbit the cave. Evidence of empty blood bags and a discarded duffle bag sit hidden behind a large rock. Someone camped out here, someone who needed a mass amount of blood to heal, and my gut tells me Aspen wasn't provided such pleasantries. No, Carrick must have sat. Gorging. Watching. The only solace I take is that he wasn't feeding on her.

Following the path of blood, I slip through cracks within the stone, focused on nearing sound of dripping water. That's where she would have gone, if given the choice. I may not have the heightened senses to follow her tracks, but I know Aspen. I understand how her mind and wolf works.

Flapping my wings, I soar towards a smaller tunnel. Barely large enough for the expanse of my wings, spokes protruding from the ceiling. Entering on a fast swoop, a glow at the far end allows me to hold onto the hope I've refused to relinquish. I haven't waited this long, fought this hard, for my life with Aspen to be over before it had a chance to truly begin.

The cave suddenly judders violently, punctuated by a guttural roar. Spikes fall free from the ceiling, hurtling down and forcing me to swerve and spin sideways. Damn vampires and their brute strength – although I understand their desperation. There's no time to be gentle.

Breaking free of the enclosed space, I hurtle into an enormous cavern just as the tunnel behind me collapses. Rocks crash to the ground as the structure threatens to crumble. I soar high, taking stock of the cavern before zeroing in on a glossy crimson shape glowing from the moon's faint light through a gap above. My heart stills as I forget how to breathe. Swooping hard and fast, I shift mid-air, skidding on my boots to her side, kicking up a cloud of dust.

"Fuck Aspen," I growl, taking the large wolf's head in my hands. "What did they do to you?!" A heavy muzzle of pure silver weighs her down, and my blood boils to a self-destructive degree. With trembling hands, I unclasp the muzzle, throwing it far away. "Aspen, come on, baby. Come back to me." She's warm yet limp. Placing her head down and shifting my hands to her neck as I try to locate her pulse. The longer I can't find one, the more my gut-wrenching panic increases. No fluttering in her neck, no beating in her chest, and no breath leaving her nose. *No.* I can't be too late. I gently shake the wolf's body, placing kisses along her snout.

"Aspen, please. You can shift back now, I've got you. We'll take care of you." Crimson coats her fur, tainting the luscious white coat, but I can't pinpoint the source of the injury. I suspect they're hidden on the female within as her wolf fights to protect her.

Glancing up at the beam of moonlight, a tear leaks from my eye. Crashing continues to round the foundations of the cavern, the rumblings becoming duller as my mind detaches itself from reality.

Aspen has been the focal point of my life for eight years. Time which flew by without me ever really grasping it. She was never just an obligation. From the day I was assigned to her detail, I knew Aspen would come to mean more to me. Without her knowledge, I gave her my vow—the promise that I would always keep her safe. And I've failed.

Life wouldn't be this cruel to take her from me this abruptly. Our time together has barely started. We still have so much to share, so much to do. I shake her body more forcefully this time, refusing to accept what my eyes are showing me. I need her. Her laughter, her sarcasm, her lips, and her feisty attitude.

I decide to try calling directly to her wolf instead, shoving my nose into her damp neck and nestling into her. Her sweet scent is fading, but it's still the best aroma I'll ever know. I can't live in a world where this smell no longer exists. But the motionless animal beneath my cheek becomes colder with each passing second. An empty vessel of the most extraordinary being that's ever lived. The one who was mine for a single, glorious moment.

Shuffling my knees forward, I lay the wolf's head on my lap. Stroking her ear, caressing her nose. It's only a matter of time before the tie that binds us snaps, and I also draw my last breath. It can't come soon enough.

Tears seep from my eyes, smattering one of the last remaining patches of white in black dots. I smooth them away, not wanting anything to taint her beautiful wolf—especially the love I spent too long holding back. Nothing will hold me back now. I cry with every ounce of my anger and despair. My limbs grow heavy, not as heavy as my heart. Everything else is numb.

The wall at my back explodes, rocks slamming against my back. I don't even wince. Three males rush to her side, three accusing stares landing on me.

"What the fuck?!" Chase growls, making a move toward me, but Jaxon's arm bars his approach. I look down to Aspen's prone form, absent-mindedly stroking her snout. They need someone to blame, and Carrick isn't here, so it's left to me to voice the obvious and destroy my own soul along with it.

"It's too late. She's gone."

Chapter Twenty-Nine

A throat is cleared in the distance, but I don't raise my head to acknowledge it. The tears ran out a while ago, but I still won't move. Snuggled between her neck and shoulder blade is exactly where I should be. I stroke the back of my hand down the soft length of her nose repeatedly.

"The sun will be rising soon," Kofu interrupts again. No one pays him any mind. I'm consumed by grief, fully aware we're all lying directly under the skylight with our wolf. Our Aspen.

"We know," I reply hollowly, mostly so he'll go the fuck away. Leave us to mourn. Leave us to die. There's a pause before a responding sigh.

"Very well. I'll wait outside to carry you out and see your bodies are returned to vampire territory." Damn, I don't want to respect him. I don't want to *feel* anything. His boots scuffle away, leaving us in the peaceful quiet with Aspen once again. I imagine her voice filtering through the air. The attitude she would give me for using her as a pillow. Her attempt to overpower Jaxon and Chase, to shove them off her back. The giggles and mini celebration dance she'd do when we let her win.

Cradling her head, a sob is torn from Sawyer, and I have to admit, he's the one who will suffer the most. He doesn't get an easy out, and out of us all, he's the one with a legit moon bond that will snap, destroying him from the inside. He'll be left alone to endure the agony, and the black tears leaking from his all-encompassing eyes show he knows it.

I barely notice the first ray of light filling the chamber until my skin begins to overheat. The temptation to shoot away and hide in the shadows is strong, but I stay exactly where I am. I won't leave her, neither will those devoted to her memory. We didn't get the chance to complete our mating ceremony, but that doesn't lessen our commitment. We'll follow her anywhere, even to the afterlife.

My skin begins to bubble and blister. My core temperature rising rapidly, and the sun isn't anywhere near directly overhead yet. But the pain of my death won't even compare to the pain of a life without Aspen.

With the loss of the moon, the fur beneath my face begins to retract back to reveal smooth skin. Raising my head, a bone snaps in Aspen's chest cavity, followed by another and another, until the whole cavern echoes with the continuous cracking. Each one pierces my head like a gunshot, felt in the depths of my soul. Soon, our beautiful mate is revealed, her skin too pale and delicate features too slack. Her hair has taken on a silvery dullness that's as devoid of life as she is. I wait on bated breath, a slither of hope snaking through my chest as I wait to see my silent pleading to the moon has been answered, but as the seconds tick by and the burns on my body increase, there are still no signs of life.

Still holding her face, Sawyer presses a wobbly kiss to her lips and eases her head into the crook of Chase's elbow.

"I'm sorry we couldn't have our forever," he whispers. Shifting to stand, Sawyer takes a few steps back. Not moving too far but giving us the space we need. He can mourn long after we've gone, and his understanding of our sacrifice is a lasting gift I'm immensely grateful for.

Moving Aspen, ignoring the agony slicing through me, the three of us bundle around her body on the ground. A tangle of large muscles, all desperate to get closer to the lithe body in the center. Lowering my head on her stomach, I weep silent tears, soaking in the full sunlight from above. Blisters burst over my exposed skin, pulling an involuntary groan from my lips. I hug Aspen tighter, praying I'll be with my angel soon.

"I was meant to be yours," I mutter, stoking her soft skin with a calloused hand.

"We were meant to be one," Jaxon adds. No truer words have been spoken. My best friends, my brothers. The males I grew up alongside, trusting with my life. It was only fitting to trust them to cherish my mate in the same way. Fate isn't a concept I believed in until Aspen. Living by her desires and dying by her will is my destiny. I just wish it didn't have to come to fruition so soon.

A light thump flutters against my hand. I sigh, eager for my heart to stop mimicking what I wish to be true. Burying my face into her abdomen, another soft thump beats. Followed by another. Focusing my hearing over the sound of blood rushing through my ears, desperately trying to keep my body functioning against the onslaught of burning, I latch onto it—the faint rhythm of a heartbeat that doesn't match any of the males in the cavern.

"She's alive!" Elation floods my system, but my body refuses to move. I struggle against the tightness of my charred skin, forcing myself upright and unable to contain my roars of torment. "Sawyer! Get her out of here," I grunt. He's quick to flock to my side, but it's not Aspen he aids. Pushing his arms beneath Jaxon's bulk, he drags my lifeless comrade toward the pool and tosses him inside before repeating the process with Chase. Holding Aspen as carefully as I can, I struggle to shuffle backward out of the direct beam of sunlight. Shedding his trench coat, Sawyer dives into the water, resurfacing with a spluttering pair of scorched soldiers.

Pushing myself beyond the pain, I grip Aspen beneath the shoulders and knees and stagger to my feet. I stumble unsteadily out of the UV rays in the direction I heard Kofu exit. Noticing an opening in the wall ahead, I use my last shred of energy to shoot forward into the safety of the shadows, crashing to my knees and shattering my kneecaps in the process. But I manage to keep Aspen from harm, and that's all that matters.

Placing her down, I notice her wounds still haven't begun to heal. I instinctively tear my burnt wrist open with my fangs and hold the sliced vein above her lips. Using my other hand to open her mouth, I watch my blood drip onto her tongue, urging her to wake enough to swallow. She doesn't stir. Pushing my wrist against her lips, I squeeze the wound to drain as much of my life force into her as possible before the wound closes. *Come on, baby, come back to me.*

Suddenly, Aspen's hand shoots up and clings onto my arm desperately as her fangs bite into my flesh hard, dragging a pained groan from me. She sucks on my wrist with such force, and despite the severity of the situation, my dick can't help but notice. I fall heavily onto my side, wincing at the contact against the scabs lining my body. Once satisfied, Aspen slumps back with a deep sigh. Her eyes flutter open, and she turns her head to face me. Gold specks within the navy depths captivate me—a shocked look of understanding dawning.

"You came for me," she croaks. I can't help my responding smile, even with the anguish my body is drowning in. My injuries are only external. Aspen, is everything internal. My heart flutters, like a young boy gazing into the eyes of his first crush. But that's what she is to me. My first crush, my first love, my first everything.

"I go where you go, Aspen. Even if that means into the afterlife. I'm never going to leave you. I love you with every fiber of my soul, and as soon as I'm healed, I'll prove it to you." Aspen stares into my eyes, hers glistening with unshed tears. Cupping her cheek, I relish the feel of warmth coating her skin. Something I thought I'd lost for good. "I can't live a life you're not a part of." Still, there's no response. Doubt starts to tug at me that she'll say it's too late, so I lean to the side, pulling her closer to press our foreheads together. "Please, say something," I breathe against her mouth. She giggles, and my heart flutters with joy.

"I love you, Torsten." She replies instantly, soothing the war within my soul. Relief washes away all traces of doubt, peace finding me in the forgotten catacombs beneath shifter territory. A moment I had never imagined for myself, but I'd venture to the ends of the earth for her. A tear slips from her eye, rolling down to the shell of her bloodstained ear. "You've beyond proven yourself. My fear is if I'm really worth it."

I caress her cheek and place the faintest of kisses on her lips. "We have an eternity for me to show you exactly how much you're worth and then some." Aspen's joyous expression slips when she notices the blisters slowly healing all over my skin, the ones on my face itching as the scabs begin to peel off. Her brow pulls down in confusion, but I smooth them back out with the pad of my thumb. "Where's-"

"They're okay. Give them a minute, and our moment of solace will be over." Relief washes over her beautiful face. As I watch the scars lining her cheeks from the muzzle begin to heal, the angry red marks softening into her smooth skin, I vow never to let her come to harm again. Not even so much as a paper cut. Aspen's beauty is to be preserved, adored, and worshipped. I smile through my own afflictions.

"What?" she asks softly. I slowly shake my head, warmth flooding my chest.

"I've just realized why you need so many mates," I chuckle. "Loving you is too big of a job for only one male." Aspen fakes a gasp, shooting to straddle my hips. I groan at the added weight to my fragile body, causing her to tut.

"Maybe it's you assholes who need a certain type of woman to keep you all in line." Her head tilts, and her silvery white hair tickles my shoulders, the perfect version of my mate back in full force. Despite the ensuing pain, I can't contain the full-bodied laugh that rakes through me. Only Aspen would rise from the dead to tell me I need to be kept in line. My laughter turns into a dry cough, my brows pinching. Aspen lowers, opening her neck to me in an invitation I can't deny myself.

"I'm so sorry for everything," she breathes once I've had my fill. Sitting upright, I feel myself strengthen and harden beneath her. She truly is insatiable in any situation. "I didn't think you'd understand why I had to leave. I already had everything I needed, and it was incredibly selfish, but I had to find Sawyer." Aspen lowers her tear-stricken lashes. "I needed to know."

"It just so happens, he's the one who found you," I lift Aspen's chin and tilt her head to the male approaching the tunnel. Lacking his trench coat, his arms shimmer with tattoos like I've never seen. A network of branches, from short sleeves to where they fade at his wrist, pulsing with silvery waves. Aspen's chest stills as she rises from my arms, and I can't blame her. Leaning forward, I whisper in her ear, giving her the permission, she needs. "I am also sorry you felt alone in your search. We wouldn't have liked it, but we would have aided you, Aspen. Whatever it takes to fill your heart with the love you crave, consider it done."

Helping her to stand, Aspen tentatively makes her way to Sawyer. I follow, taking the trench coat from his hand to slide her arms into the sleeves, covering her modesty. I move to leave, but Aspen reaches out to grab my hand, holding me prisoner to their conversation.

"There's something you need to know," Sawyer drops his head. We wait for him to find the words, my own grip tightening on Aspen's hand. All-encompassing eyes lift, one single black eye leaking from the corner. "When a guardian takes the vow, their lives are bound to their charge. When I told you, my mother died..." Sawyer looks aside.

"She died because mine did," Aspen whispers in understanding. Stepping forward, she places a single hand on the raven's chest. He immediately covers it with his own. "Tell me, Sawyer."

"It's your wolf, Aspen. She sacrificed herself for you. I felt a part of myself die too, and it hasn't returned."

"No," Aspen shakes her head and withdraws from Sawyer to step back into me. Hurt contorts his face, and I can't fucking blame him. Their bond hasn't even been explored, and he's had to deliver her this terrible news. Moments pass as Aspen stares at her hands, trying to force a shift. It doesn't come. "No, no, no!"

Wrapping my arm around her chest, I grab Sawyer and drag him into her front. He balks, causing me to growl.

"She needs all of us."

"Damn right she does," Jaxon appears in a flash. The darkened cavern does nothing to hide his burns or the thick welt on Chase's face when he emerges a moment later. Blood smears his chin from a recent feed, but it's not potent enough to have started his healing. No more words are spoken as Aspen collapses, taking the four of us with her. Cocooned on the cave floor, we all cry. We mourn the creature who made the ultimate sacrifice. To give my Aspen back to me, and for that, I will be eternally grateful.

Chapter Thirty

I listen to the crying. Drown in it. Even when I cover my ears, I can't unhear the wrecked screams filling the caves. Five united beings, shattered by their grief. And the worst part – I know they'll survive it. That they have each other to heal the broken fracture and fill the void of Aspen's wolf.

Crouching against a cave wall, halfway between the watery cavern and the entrance, I find a small black beetle to play with. It's hard shell moves awkwardly as it crawls back and forth across my tattooed knuckles while long, sharp pincers try to attack the flesh beneath. Even though I give no reaction, the insect continues to strike me, over and over, until thick wings snap up from the bug's tough exterior, and it flies away. He could have left when I picked him up, but he chose to stay and fight. I'm tenacious too. It's what's brought me this far.

Although, as I take stock of my position, I wonder how I've fallen so far. I'm more of a glorified lap dog than a protégé these days. As a child, I was a source of entertainment to the Alpha - a spirit to break and tame. He said he enjoyed my wild nature but then forced me to bend to his will. To be controlled by him. I became his personal project, given vigorous routines and punishing jobs to carry out from an early age.

However, there had been a small bright side to my grueling training days in preparation for becoming the next alpha. The small, blonde girl who skipped around camp, her giggle filling the air and lifting the weight from my young shoulders. Aspen would sneak out to bring me cookies when I was on night patrol before I even reached double digits and creep into the woods while I was supposed to be running drills to play tag.

The hope of seeing her was the only thing that kept me going most days. And then I was told she was to be my mate. I was promised the constant ray of sunshine would remain at my side forever. I'd never truly be alone or an outcast again, and even if I never achieved anything else in life, I would always have a companion at my side.

When her vampire side emerged, no one was more devastated by her banishment than me. I lost everything that day and blamed her for all of it. Conall was right; compassion is weakness. I turned to the dark place within myself and stayed there, hating the world around me for continuing to move on when my life was nothing but bleakness and anger. I didn't need anyone. I needed to keep strong, stay angry and become the most ruthless shifter who had ever walked this miserable planet.

So why couldn't I stop watching the exile hut? Before the raven's presence, *I* was Aspen's loyal protector. I ensured the shifters were kept in line as much as an apprentice could. My title scared most, but not all. When Conall discovered I'd been stalking her instead of doing my duties, he'd beat me senseless – publicly. Yet I couldn't stop, couldn't allow her to suffer beyond the grief her biology caused. Aspen has never been truly alone. She just never knew it.

But what I've seen and heard down here tonight has affected me in ways I can't understand. I was already confused by the weird stirrings in my chest, feelings I'd been taught not to indulge. That was before I heard of Aspen's wolf. Now, the tiny rift within me that held something genuinely good cracks and shatters into millions of pieces. I'd collapse under the weight of it, if I weren't practically dead inside myself.

Forcing myself to regain composure, I stand. I should have left with Conall. Should have stopped myself from allowing my curiosity. I can't unhear the screams or unsee the band of males laying down their lives for the one they love. I'll never be able to understand, nor do I have a right to feel the slither of grief churning in my gut. I was a fraud to think I had any small claim on Aspen or the pain I'd been left to deal with. The males cradling her are the ones who have genuinely loved and lost something precious here tonight.

During the entire walk back towards Conall's cabin, my feet drag. Dark hair swaying over my eyes, my jaw too tight. I've been privy to something fascinating tonight, something I will never know. But I have learned something.

Compassion isn't a weakness. From everything I've just seen and heard, compassion is strength. Love is power. But I won't be gifted with these traits by allowing my soul to connect with another's. No, I'll use force and intimidation to gain respect among my pack. I'll rule with the same brutality as Conall has and hope it brings me the same sense of fulfillment.

Permitting myself entry to Conall's cabin, I lounge on his plush sofa as the sun streams through large bay windows facing west. This is by far the biggest and most luxurious cabin in our camp. For my first few years here, I resided in the shed out back, which had been converted into a miniature bedroom for me. Of course, the best part of the run-down shack was when I would fall asleep listening to sweet lullabies Orianna would sing to Aspen every night as they drifted down to me on the wind through loose, rattling windows.

Shuffling on the stairs behind me draws my attention to the half-dressed, plump female shifter trotting down the final few steps and out of the front door without glancing at me. Conall strides down not long after, only wearing a pair of dark jeans, the fly and button wide open as dull blue eyes settle on me with a smile.

"Do you mind?" I ask, gesturing to his pubic area with a wave of my hand. Glancing down, Conall chuckles and sits in the matching armchair opposite me, making no move to cover the abundance of hair on full show.

"Why so glum, Kofu? I hope you're bringing me good news. Did everything go as planned?" Conall throws his large arms over the edge of the armchair, his tongue sucking on his teeth. I must say, he played his role well, but not as efficiently as I did. Although I won't receive any of the credit when he gets the revenge he's been seeking. I sit forward in the seat and press my elbows into my knees, maintaining his gaze.

"Well, Aspen died," I state, keen to see his initial reaction. His smirk falls slowly and Conall glances into the top corner of the room, but in no way does he look affected by the news.

"That does complicate things, I guess. We will have to find another way to gain access to the castle, maybe during her funeral." Conall looks back to me and shrugs nonchalantly.

"That won't be necessary. She came back to life, but her wolf has gone. Now, only the vampire remains," I sigh. To lose a wolf in any capacity is a travesty. So, the fact Conall looks relieved, bothers the shit out of me.

"Ahh well, we're back on track then. Just one loose end left to tie up." Conall clasps his hands together. Kicking my ankles, he urges me to get up and follow him to the locked door beneath the staircase. Begrudgingly stomping down the basement steps, the single bulb swings, shifting the light around the large room in a circular motion. Shelving units line each wall, a range of weapons on display like a museum. All of them silver.

"I'm presuming everything went well?" Carrick steps forward from a crate he was perched on as if he wasn't privy to our conversation upstairs. Conall puffs out his chest, clasping Carrick's hand.

"It went perfectly," Conall replies. Carrick is no stranger to our shifter pack after a group of scouts found him on our land years ago. I thought Carrick would kill him there and then, but the alpha is nothing if not calculated. Playing a long game is his specialty. He's told me time and time again that Aspen, *the wretched little reject*, would be of use one day. The first lesson he taught me was that acting rashly only ruins potential opportunities. And what an opportunity Aspen has been for him.

A thirteenth birthday that falls on a full moon often leads to our most powerful shifters and their wolf awakening within the same night of a first shift is a great honor. It's how Conall's and my own were called, pinning us at potential alphas, and as such, we immediately become the strongest within the pack. Conall took his power and claimed whatever he liked, including Orianna, the timid, kind woman he only truly wanted upon discovering her affair. If there's one thing Conall can't resist, it's a free spirit to be tamed. Yeah, he knew all along. That's just how devious he can be.

"I upheld my side of the bargain, don't forget to come through on yours. I left her exactly where you told me to, the vamps would have found her instantly," Carrick folds his arms.

"She moved," I drawl, bored with his presence.

"Of course she did," Carrick smiles. I wasn't surprised when he came groveling after his own plan to take the throne was fucked. I could have saved him the time because Aspen would never have gone for a male so like Conall in terms of power-hungry intent, but where's the fun in that?

"You have my word," Conall widens his stance, ignoring our bickering. "You've got me an in with Lorcan, and I didn't have to lift a finger. I'll ensure you get everything you deserve." Smug with himself, Carrick returns to his crate while I pace the room behind me, unable to stand still. "Everything you deserve," Conall repeats with the slightest nod. On cue, I thrust forward, bursting Carrick's beating heart through his chest cavity. His body drops lifelessly onto my arm, protruding from his sternum. His blood splatters Conall's face and body, the warm liquid dripping from his chest like war paint. Retracting my arm, the graying body hits the floor like a sack of shit, and I exhale harshly, juggling the heart from hand to hand.

"Never gets old," I groan, a slither of delight rolling down my spine. Ascending to the main cabin floor, my heart beats in time with the one in my palm. When the sweet retribution of death is all that evokes any feeling within my being, I can't deny myself the base need. After all, I'm a carbon copy of Conall, molded into his image. One more cheating vampire is dead, opening the pathway for more.

Chuckling, I toss the pulsing organ into the fireplace. Roaring flames attack the new kindling, causing it to combust and send sparks of light shooting in all directions. The rapidly decomposing organ's rancid smell fills the air—my favorite scent. A hand slaps me hard on the back, the clearest form of praise Conall will ever give.

"You did well today, kid. Carrick served his purpose, but I wasn't about to put that nutcase on our rival's throne. We're not killing Lorcan just to replace him."

"Who will take the vampire crown?" I ask absentmindedly. My mind turns to Aspen's mates. None of them will go down easily, and the thought of destroying them doesn't sit well with me or fill me with as much satisfaction as it should. As it did before I met them.

"Why, you, of course," Conall laughs.

Patting me a few more times, the only father I've known leaves me to my thoughts, and a moment later, the shower on the level above roars to life. I look at my own hand coated in blood. Whatever quick thrill I felt is gone. Back comes the numbness, detaching me from the world. I drop back onto the sofa and remain there until nightfall. Wasting time, waiting for whatever will return the rush of adrenaline. Conall may have big plans to join the vampire and shifters by any means necessary and breed a mass of hybrids. To create an empire on which he comfortably sits at the top. I just hope that somewhere along the way, I find the fucks to care.

The gentle sound of woodwind instruments fills the air as the double doors of our ballroom glide open in perfect unison. The guards on either side fall to one knee at the same time every other vampire in attendance copies—all except myself, Torsten, Chase, and Sawyer, who stand at the altar's top. We're not missing this moment for anything.

The past few weeks have been chaos, decorating the ballroom for tonight's ceremony. Nothing was too much, no amount of preparation sufficing. Ivory silk has been draped from each chandelier to meet the edges of the ceiling. The speckled marble floor waxed, and the doorknobs polished. Standing vases hold bouquets of lilies from the botanical gardens, filling the space with a strong, perfumed scent. The crescent moon shines from floor-to-ceiling windows, bathing the room in blue and yellow hues.

A floral archway has been erected before the podium, vines twisting around the invisible frame to hold flowers of every color. Beside Lorcan's throne, a newly made one stands proud, complete with mauve velvet cushioning. Exquisite detailing has been chiseled into the wood, creating an image of a forest within the back piece. An abundance of wooden flowers fills the bottom of the space before tree trunks burst out of the foliage and stretch upwards to the rounded moon, which protrudes from the top. Peeking out from the most central trunk is the head of a wolf.

Movement from the open doorway captures my full attention, and my jaw drops to the floor. Aspen steps into view, her shoulders pushed back with confidence. She's magnificent—the true making of a real queen. A floor-length, figure-hugging dress hangs from her gorgeous curves. The material is black lace, circling her slender neck and covering her entire front, with hints of open panels at her waist. I would bet anything that the garment is backless and hangs deliciously low.

As she moves, the dress sways and sparkles in the moonlight. Silver waves across one shoulder sway with each step, her make-up glowing and flawless with a matt black lipstick. Her own blend of punk royalty.

"So beautiful," Torsten breathes.

"So unique," I agree.

"So mine," Chase adds, and Sawyer shifts and punches his arm.

"Ours," he growls, quickly returning his attention to Aspen gliding down the aisle in shining combat boots. Halting to admire the recent redecoration, gasps of awe fill the space as vampires peek up at the princess from their positions on the floor. Lorcan stands and moves over to me, clasping a hand on my shoulder. Everyone else takes his lead and stands, waiting for tonight's immense ceremony to begin. It's been centuries since we've had a wedding, and never has there been one quite like this.

I stride towards Aspen first, my arm outstretched with a smile. She places her hand in the crook of my elbow and walks with me the rest of the way. No jealousy appears in the faces of those awaiting her, an equal truce binding us. Aspen's happiness is paramount. In the dark days after the loss of her wolf, we quickly found our dynamic with Sawyer added into the fold. It doesn't matter who puts a smile upon her face, who draws the laughter from her throat, who brings her body to ruin. Her joy is our pleasure to receive, and power struggles have no place in our pack.

Vampires shuffle to fill the aisle once we've passed, everyone eager to have a decent view. Torsten and Chase quickly place a kiss on Aspen's forehead, Sawyer reaching out to brush their traces from her lips with his thumb. Aspen laughs, finding herself amongst the four of us beneath the archway. Lorcan moves to the center of the podium above, signaling for the female orchestra to quieten as he begins to speak.

"Welcome all to a glorious evening of celebration." Lorcan smiles kindly at Sawyer before turning his attention to Aspen, looking much more himself than he has in a long time. In terms of groveling, I don't think there's a trick Lorcan hasn't pulled to relay his sympathy for the loss of Aspen's wolf. The king holds himself personally responsible, especially as our soldiers have yet to find Carrick. They search nightly, but the more time passes, the slimmer our chances seem. He could be anywhere by now. Although Lorcan has a long way to go, I see a possible relationship between him and his daughter. Eventually.

"Tonight, we not only bond these souls in line with tradition but also accept a new queen to the throne. One who will serve you all with understanding, compassion, and clarity. Above all, tonight, we welcome Aspen as one of our own. This is truly where you belong," Lorcan holds her navy gaze. Pride swells within his chest, sincerity reinforcing his tone. Dressed in one of his usual three-piece suits with his hair slicked back, I see a glimpse of the king that hasn't surfaced for longer than many realize.

Addressing the crowd, Lorcan delivers a speech about acceptance and recognizing new opportunities. Aspen focuses on her father, but I can't take mine from her. It's fine, I heard him practicing this part of his speech through his office door when I walked past every day for the last week.

She is stunning. I hadn't dared dream of the perfect female for me, considering the odds were I wouldn't ever have one, but Aspen is everything I could have hoped for and then some. Sporting a small smile, her chin is raised and her spine straight—the true vision of a queen worth having.

"Aspen, do you solemnly swear to abide by, uphold, and follow the laws of the castle, to respect and comprehend the desires of all our resident vampires? To protect and fortify our kind, ensuring unity and prosperity at all costs?" Lorcan intones the royal oath he took more than a century ago. Aspen's smile remains unwavering, not faltering for even a moment.

"I do," she says seriously, bowing her head briefly. A low rumble of pride emanates from those surrounding her. Nova steps forward, producing a sparkling crown on a velvet cushion. Lorcan lifts the jeweled crown and places it onto Aspen's head. The solid platinum piece is adorned with jewels ranging from diamonds to sapphires and rounded pieces of opal to form a semi-circle pattern around its base.

"Aspen, you have been crowned our new Queen. May your reign be long and joyous." Lorcan smiles down at her, stretching out his hand to gently pull her onto the podium beside him. Turning Aspen around to face the crowd, he loudly relays, "For our Queen and our Kind," to which everyone echoes before bursting into cheers and pumping fists into the air.

"Now, I believe you already have a matter of business to attend to," Lorcan smiles, stepping aside. Aspen commands everyone's attention, her posture strong, relaxed, and confident. Licking her lips, her fangs catch the glint of the chandelier.

"I'm aware my time at the castle has been brief and somewhat traumatic," she passes us a quick glance filled with mirth. "I commend the regulations already in place for your females. Your respect and understanding towards giving them space to thrive is humbling. But I'm approaching you all today with new reasoning." Looking back for Lorcan's approval, the king nods, and Aspen continues, angling herself to the cordoned area of females peering on.

"There's more to a mating than reproducing. There's love, passion, and happiness to be had. Why survive for the sake of existing when you could genuinely enjoy the gift of life? Your lives? My first decree as queen is to permit open marriages and multiple matings without the need for the Moon Bound Trails. I wish you to follow your hearts, build connections and thrive."

Aside from the hungry, lustful groans seeping through the males, a sudden eruption of excitement bursts from the females. Squealing, hugging each other, I catch Sorcha's eye. Large blue eyes beam, and it's only then that I realize the withdrawn lives the females have been forced to lead. Opulent, yes, but filling their time with arts and simple pleasures won't fill the void only a loving mate could. My chest swells, not only for Aspen's ruling but the happiness she's spread within moments of becoming queen.

"By doing so, I declare myself free to mate the four males before me," Aspen continues over the commotion. We don't care that no one is no longer listening; this moment is for us. Not for show or some duty to lead by example. Moving down a step to our eye level, Aspen reaches out, and four hands respond, clinging to both of hers.

"Do you all vow to love me with every fiber of your beings? To rule by my side with honesty and compassion? To protect and nurture not only me but each other for the rest of our existence?" Aspen adlibs, using the oath of her coronation as a base. Our answer is instant.

"I do," we all say in unison, staring deeply into her glistening eyes. Her expression of love, of unadulterated adoration, is my undoing. I rush to kiss her first, a forceful connection with her lips to seal our future. I could kiss her like this forever, surrounded by the celebrating vamps behind, if an elbow didn't barge into my ribs. Chuckling, I release her neck, not realizing I'd pinned her in place before me, and relent her to Chase's eagerness.

One at a time, Aspen seals her bond with those at my side, ending with

Sawyer. Grabbing the lapels of the damn trench coat, he refused to not pair with his suit, her mouth lands on his as a few whispers catch my ears. It will take time for all to adjust to having a third species in our mix, but I know it's not Sawyer's presence that is unnerving. It's the prospect that there are other foes out there that we may not be aware of.

Releasing Sawyer, Aspen beckons us all to join her on the podium, finding her rightful place in the middle. Two males on either side, Aspen looks across at all of us, beaming widely with a sentiment I don't need her to express in words. We're equals in love and duty. Her navy eyes are flecked heavily with gold, her fangs are on full show. Smiling down at my bride, I'm once again floored by her beauty, mind, and the purity of her soul. A scandal brought her to us, but fate sealed our bonds.

Confetti is thrown all around the room, an entire species reveling in anticipation of their new future—the one only Aspen could have provided.

Aspen
Chapter Thirty-Two

A crescent moon hangs above the clear dome, peeking through large banana leaves to light the stone path. Strolling through the botanical gardens, my hand is in Jaxon's while the rest linger close behind. I can sense their nerves rolling off their suited bodies in waves. Considering I just professed my love in front of the entire castle, I don't know what they have to be nervous about. Jax leads me towards the patch of the gardens I have been gifted – a circle twelve feet in diameter. It's not much, but the dead-white nettles I planted have taken nicely.

"Sit with me," Jax asks, and who am I to decline my husband's offer? He sits first, pulling me into his lap to prevent my black lace gown from touching the floor. Torsten lowers by his side, lifting my calves to rest across his legs.

"Guys, seriously. What's going on?" I ask, removing the crown from my head. With them, I'm simply Aspen.

"We have a wedding gift for you," Sawyer answers. I smile up at him. It was never going to be easy for him to adapt to living in the residential mating home with the rest of us, but he's done well. As long as he focuses on me, everything else seems to fade. When the others were already so close, Sawyer tends to distance himself, patiently awaiting my attention from afar. There's also the fact that he keeps being summoned by the Supernatural Council, and one day soon, we will have to face them. But we will do so together. All four of us are a unit now, and we will tackle our issues as such.

"Okay…" I weigh in on the silence when Chase shifts this weight from foot to foot. Jax and Torsten seem to find his squirming amusing and make no move to rush him. Exhaling sharply, Chase pushes his hand into his jacket pocket, pulling out a gift box. Black with a red bow, much like the suit he's opted for. A crimson tie is nestled high against Chase's shirt collar, despite the number of times I've seen him tug at it uncomfortably. He holds out the box, but I beckon him closer instead. As he crouches in front of us, I reach out and pop Chase's top button, dragging the tie looser.

"Ah, thank the moon for that," he groans. I smile, accepting his gift and untying the ribbon. Removing the lid, I gasp. An intricate wooden carving of a white wolf lays on the cushion inside, her head upturned on a silent howl.

"We wanted to honor your wolf and the sacrifice she made to bring you back to us," Torsten says, stroking my leg beneath the dress. Lifting the carving, Chase gently eases it from my hold to place it between the nests of flowers as Sawyer kneels by my shoulder.

"This is from Lorcan," he also produces a similar box. Opening it for me, a plaque sits inside. Gold calligraphy across the black slate reads, '*For Orianna, the purest of us all.*' Tears prick the back of my eyes. Placing the plaque beside the wolf, we all remain on the ground, lost to our thoughts. I'd been avoiding the need to hold a memorial for my wolf, preferring to leave the grief which poured from me in the underground caves. But masking heartache doesn't eradicate it.

This is perfect—a quiet moment to remember. A simple show of devotion nuzzled within the nest of colors and delicate smells my planted flowers provide. I pray that my beautiful white wolf is on the other side somewhere, frolicking through the lushest of forests and swimming in the purest of lakes with my mother.

When Jax finally lifts me back to my feet, I inhale the soothing fresh air drifting from the open doors deep into my lungs. My soul is washed free of regret. A part of me will always be missing, but she traded herself so I could be with the four males surrounding me. So that I can live a full, eternal life. Even Sawyer will remain by my side, as his life is linked to mine in multiple ways.

"The ballroom should be ready. Come, your majesty, you have an after-party to attend." Chase bends low on a dramatic bow. I roll my eyes, dragging him upright by a handful of his long, brown hair.

"I much prefer when you call me Pumpkin," I smirk. Chase's responding smile is full of fang and the promise of fun, his shoulder ramming me off my feet. Laughter echoes around the dome as I punch his back, ordering him to put me down.

"Sorry, I don't abide by your commands anymore," he jerks me about. Dropping me heavily to my feet, his hand instantly finds my nape. "I have free reign to do what I want when I want," he growls. Desire pools within his eyes, and the air suddenly becomes thinner. My own arousal reaches the others, drawing out pained grunts.

"Nope," Sawyer's voice is strained. "Not now, not here." Tugging me from Chase's grip, I'm thrown into the cradle of his arms and carried away.

Peering over his shoulder, I spot the plaque and wolf embedded within the soil. As if this moment wasn't already perfect enough, I feel as if my loved ones are all here with us, surrounding me with their blessing, and I know my life will never feel incomplete again.

"Aww, you're no fun, Raven!" Chase jests before the males start making crude gestures, acting out a boning scene on each other while Torsten licks his lips, and Chase smacks Jaxon's ass. Okay, maybe I'm hoping my mother's spirit isn't present for that part.

THE AFTER-PARTY of my coronation is a celebration as I've never known before. Tables surround the dancefloor, the white clothes matching artfully dressed chairs with pale pink sashes tied into large bows. The vases of lilies have been converted into centerpieces, surrounded by champagne chutes of blood for all. Upon the podium where I recently stood, the Techies have erected a DJ booth, complete with a speaker system and strobe lighting I recognize from the Car Wash nightclub.

Despite being dressed in their finest attire, all vampires present are jumping to the beat of the music and expressing their macho bullshit in the mosh-pit that's formed by the large windows. Finnian started it, which was no surprise. Lorcan slipped out of the room after the ceremonies, leaving us to our festivities. The females dance and giggle together safely behind a wall of guards, protecting them from the males who linger nearby.

I understand my decree is an exciting prospect, but make no mistake, the female's safety is my main priority. By banishing the Moon Bound Trials, my men and I will need to discuss healthy ways to permit meetings between the genders before there's a free for all. Lorcan told me of the horrors that took place before his harsh rulings, and I have no desire to resort to acting like savages.

However, I'm going to take this one last night for myself. To enjoy my husbands before the weight of responsibility hits us tomorrow. That's why I've been swaying in their arms for hours, dancing in tune with their heartbeats, memorizing every fleck of color in their eyes. Every part of them speaks to a different part of my soul, from the scratch of a stubbled chin to the caress of tender fingers. If I were so inclined, I could tell them apart by smell and taste, but why deny myself staring into their beautiful eyes? Icy blue, emerald green, pewter gray, and even Sawyer's eyes that shine black from corner to corner. They all look at me as if I hold the key to unlocking their souls, and I suppose I do. There's just one thing missing.

"Walk with me?" I ask Torsten, my arms currently around his neck. Inclining his head, I nuzzle the side of his white hair as he would to my wolf. We cut a path through the crowd of males, many of the soldiers stopping to congratulate me before resuming their dancing. I collect a clean glass from a nearby table while Torsten is busy signaling Jax, Chase, and Sawyer from a makeshift bar at the back of the ballroom. They meet us at a set of rear doors, stepping onto the balcony. Nealon stands guard inside, closing the curtains to give us all a moment of privacy beneath the moon's light.

"We all good?" Jaxon asks, worry marring his brows. Smoothing away the worried lines with my thumb, I place a quick kiss on his lips. A satisfied sigh escapes him, perfectly echoing my own emotions.

"Of course, I just had something I needed to do." Walking towards the stone wall surrounding the balcony, all three vamps rush to block me from getting too close. Parting Chase and Torsten, I gently lower myself onto the edge. At some point, they're going to have to trust that I won't bolt again. I'm here for good.

"Tell us what you need, Pumpkin," Chase winds his arm around my back. I lean into his side.

"I want you all to moon bond with me." Sawyer is the only one who doesn't freeze, statue still with widened eyes. He knows me better than the rest. He most likely foresaw this when accompanying me to the East Wing library. There isn't much on moon bonds, but I devoured whatever little information there was.

"We don't even know if that would work," Jax's frown is back in full force.

"And we won't until someone tries." I counteract. "The circumstances are all present. A loving bond, a crescent moon."

"We all need to ingest your blood at the same time you drink ours," Torsten starts, and I wave the empty champagne flute at him. One step ahead of mostly anything they can throw my way, I only have one variable left up to chance. Turning my attention to Sawyer, his blackened eyes are already fixed upon mine.

"I'm going to need your help." He doesn't hesitate, striding forward to pluck the flute from my fingers delicately. Without the need to ask, fangs are torn through wrists, and in unison, the vampires drip their blood into the glass. Torsten shifts, allowing Sawyer to straddle the wall and lie me back across the stone, my head in his lap. My chest rises and falls heavily against the lace of my dress. Tremors roll through my entire body, the anticipation too much to bear. Peering up into Sawyer's eyes, the trace of a smile crosses his lips.

"Should we have a countdown or something?" Chase asks, but I can't wait that long.

"Go," is my swift instruction, and they don't hesitate to obey. Within a flash, the piercing of fangs sink into both of my wrists and one in my neck, quickly followed by the heady sucks that make me groan. My nipples pebble, my thighs clenching as my back arches up from the stone. Tilting my head upwards, Sawyer holds the flute over my parted lips and tips the contents inside.

A combination of all three slides down my throat, a final swallow sealing the deal. A bright light glows as the wash of the moon graces all four of us. It shines brighter than I thought possible, forcing my eyes to close. When I'd been in this position with Sawyer, I hadn't been able to notice the change within. It was erratic, but I loved him. That was all the moon needed at the time, but now, it feels like we're connecting all over again.

The bond takes instantly, filling me with blissful intent, just before a tidal wave of emotions barrels through my being. The groan from all other sources on the balcony shows they feel it too, but I didn't need to hear them to know that. I can *feel* them. Love and happiness expand within me until I feel close to self-combusting. With another drag from all source points, I feel my soul winding through theirs, expanding through their psyche.

The glow withdraws, as do the fangs, but we remain in place. Panting. Feeling. Sensations fill me, and no corner of my soul is left untouched. Sawyer's hands sweep into my hair, gently massaging as I rub at the heavenly sensation filling the inside of my chest. I'd never expected to find love, never considered myself a person worth loving. But how could I have anticipated these men who appeared in my life during my darkest moments? Each one, in their own right, is an enigma who has brought light and purpose to my life.

And now that I've been shown the true purpose of existing, I will never have enough.

My kings. My everything. We will rule side by side as they become my advisors, teachers, lovers, best friends, whatever I need, and vice versa.

Finally ready to return to reality, I open my eyes, stilling as I peer up at Sawyer. Angling his head, his black hair falls forward to conceal from the others what has caused my heart to race. His eyes, covered from corner to corner, are shimmering silver.

My back hits the luxurious mattress in Aspen's suite before the lithe minx climbs over me as much as her gown allows. Pushing my trench coat over my shoulders, Aspen's fangs are prominent. Her breath heated and heavy, her eyes hooded. She doesn't waste a moment, jerking my head aside and sinking her teeth into my neck. The spike of pain instantly fades as she takes what she needs, feeding on the vitality of life I've always wanted for her. Sliding my arms around her back, I hold her to me, my cock hardening with each drawn-out suck.

Her hunger for my blood had been overwhelming her since we moved into the residential home, but she also needed time to heal. Time to mourn without tainting her emotions with passion. For this reason, the vampires and I decided to hold back from intimacy. Nevertheless, tonight it would merely be us two—a chance to explore the depths of our passion without interference.

Aspen's full lips find mine, their softness a direct contrast to the firmness of her kisses. Holding the back of her head, I press my tongue into her mouth, caressing with powerful strokes. I can't help the soft moans which escape me between kisses, relishing her touch. Her vanilla and raspberry smell, her very essence. I stroke every inch of Aspen's skin, the open back of her ballgown permitting me to do so. My fingers locate a zip at the precipice of her ass, hidden within the lace. Slowly revealing the lack of underwear beneath, Aspen unhooks the material at her nape and sits upright. The dress falls free, her beautiful body baring itself to me.

I take a moment to drink her in. This isn't like the other times I'd seen her naked prior to a shift or fighting for her life. Not even like the nights I've enjoyed brief moments with her in the dark between the shifters who also have a claim on her heart. This is a moment of exquisite beauty and eternal lust, and it is just for me. Trailing my knuckles across her nipples, Aspen responds eagerly. Dipping lower, I caress the dip of her waist and the flare of her hips before I settle my palms on her thighs.

"Tease me, and you'll regret it," Aspen squirms for further contact, yet nothing will rush me. Tonight, is about righting wrongs and starting our future again. I stole her moon bond our first time without her fully understanding what it entailed, but tonight she took initiative. She accepted all four of us into her soul and asked me to help her do it.

Easing my fingers through Aspen's hair, I pull her down to kiss me again, turning us in the same movement. The hard press of my body against hers in heaven, even through the insipid suit I've been forced to wear. I was wholly prepared to complete the union in my cargos and t-shirt, but apparently, that wasn't acceptable. Aspen wouldn't have cared, though. Dipping my head, I trail kisses along her jaw and neck and take her nipple into my mouth. Her back arches, pushing into me greedily. Unhurried flicks of my tongue while my fingers tease the other. I will worship Aspen, bathe her in love for every moment I'm permitted to remain with her.

There's only so long that I can ignore the summons. The Supernatural Council will lash out if I continue to deny their call, but now's not the time to worry about it. Now is the time to feel alive and be thankful. To revel in a fulfilled life, to love and be loved. Things not even my dreams dared to imagine but have come true, nonetheless.

"I'm warning you, Sawyer. Don't make me wait," Aspen begs. I grin, dragging my fingers down the center of her body. Nearing her clit, Aspen's breath hitches as I briefly pass over the sensitive bud and grip her thigh instead. "That's it."

Locking her ankles behind my back, Aspen flips us both over and pushes down hard on my shoulders. The shock in my expression is mirrored in hers, this newfound strength taking us both by surprise. Aspen has always been strong in more ways than one, but now she has four beings boosting her system, flooding her veins with passion and power.

Bending forward and gripping the collar at my neck, Aspen tears my shirt down the middle. Whipping the tie free, she stills to trace her fingers over the silvery patterns lining my skin. I gained by first when I vowed to protect her, cementing the first branch. The more time I spent as her guardian, the faster the branches grew, covering my body with the evidence of our connection – long before I had a moon bond to be proud of.

"I warned you," Aspen smirks, making quick work of my belt. Opening my top bottom, my cock springs free, as keen as she is.

Jerking Aspen aside, we wriggle out of our remaining clothes before a struggle for dominance ensues, landing us both in a naked heap on the floor beside the bed, panting with arousal. Quickly diving under me, she tucks her legs between us, and using the soles of her feet on my abdomen, I'm propelled into the air. Landing across the room on my back once more, Aspen appears in a flash of movement, straddling my hips. Grabbing hold of my solid cock, she strokes me deliciously.

"Fight me, and I stop," Aspen challenges. When I make no move to interrupt, her hand continues to move my hand up and down my shaft leisurely. A cunning smile pulls at Aspen's lips, her authority causing my hands to fist at my sides. I waited years for her, this is not a test of restraint I will fail easily. Shifting, Aspen places kisses on my lips and neck, my shoulders, and down the rocky path of my abdomen. Pausing with her lips just above my throbbing cock, enjoying herself far too much, Aspen suddenly scrapes her nails across my inner thighs and over my balls. I hiss, ignoring her sly smile by gripping the back of her hair. If she wants it rough, I'll show her rough.

Maintaining eye contact, I lower her head to cover my shaft with her full, pink lips. The lipstick she wore is a distinct memory, and all the vampires will have to remember her by while I'm taking her behind this locked door. Allowing Aspen to take her time, slowly sinking and lifting her head, taking me all the way into her throat, and pausing before sucking her way back up. It's torture, and I only work to spur her on.

My answering growls are music to her ears, evident by her little chuckles around my girth. She's loving this. A hand fists tightly into my newly silver hair, but she makes no move to rush me. Sucking free a bead of pre-cum produced too eagerly, Aspen works my tip with her tongue like her favorite ice cream flavor. She can't seem to take her eyes off mine, which I catch in the reflection of the mirrored wardrobe—purely silver and shimmering like the markings across my body. I radiate the moon's energy, the purity of our bond pulsing from me like a living entity.

I don't look away as I push her head back down and make her take every hard inch into her willing mouth, the scrape of her fangs heightening my pleasure.

"Enough," I growl, pulling Aspen's body upright and spearing her straight onto my cock. Her slick walls accept me greedily in one fluid motion, filling her entirely. Holding her firmly at the waist, I keep Aspen cemented in place whilst tilting and slighting, turning her to feel just how deep I am. Her gasps fill the room, the space between her eyebrows tight. To give her a moment of release, I lift her a few inches to hover over me before slamming her down onto my hips again.

I try to be gentle at first, to go slow enough to drag this out, but neither of us can deny or contain this passion. Pounding into her from below, Aspen is a fool to think she can withhold the orgasm that tears through her, closing her walls around me even tighter. My name is a scream on her lips as she viciously rakes her painted nails down my chest. I shift to roll us over, but Aspen isn't playing this game anymore. Shoving me back down by the shoulders, she growls in my face with a show of her fangs. Releasing her hips, I hold my hands in view as if to say, *okay, baby, your turn.*

Pinning my thighs down with her feet, Aspen rivals the pace I had set. A sheen of sweat covers our bodies, creating a slip-and-slide effect when Aspen rears forward to take my hair in her tight grip. Resting her elbows on my shoulders, she rides me into oblivion. The flutters of her next climax were already building, quickly pulling me over the edge with her. The fire in my core threatens to burn me alive, but I would willingly walk into the flames, allowing me to consume her. Gripping her ass tightly, I support her with fierce thrusts, coming apart at the seams just as my mate screams her own release.

Stars burst behind my eyes, and her roar is drowned out by one of my own, her walls exploding around me, hot and urgent. Taking her mouth, I swallow her groans and relish the jerks of my cock as I fill her entirely with my seed and love. Panting heavily, enjoying the aftershocks and jolts of our slickened bodies, Aspen falls forward into the enclosure of my arms, lightly kissing my shoulder.

"I think…" Aspen pants, allowing me to drag her into a sitting position against the bedframe. "I think the others may have felt that." The heel of her palm rubs at the flush across her chest, and I can't withhold the primal grin taking ownership of my mouth. Aspen gently slaps my arm, although she can't help to giggle too.

Moonlight seeps through the open window, illuminating her. Navy eyes speckled with gold gleam at me, striking me with the radiant beauty of her perfect face all over again. I could lose myself in the pools of blue within her eyes, but I'm not scared anymore because I know that Aspen will always be here as we continue building our new lives together. I also know that when the Supernatural Council can no longer be ignored, she'll be by my side. And if their decision doesn't work in our favor, I know she won't stop proving her love for me. No one can deny Aspen's tenacity. Of that, I'm certain.

Chapter Thirty-Four

Rowena

It should have been me.

Remaining back in the shadows of the dance floor, I watch Aspen return hand-in-hand with her raven shifter. The three vampires relaxing in decorated chairs shoot upright upon sensing her, meeting her halfway on the dancefloor. Their reunion is a little overkill, considering she wasn't gone for an hour. Jaxon lifts Aspen high into the air, swirling her bed hair around for all to see... as if their smiles and overwhelming scents of lust weren't enough to have the rest of us pining with jealousy.

In this scenario, it's impossible for me not to be seen as the 'envious brat' others have called me behind my back for years. I've spent my entire life preparing for the day I would be crowned queen. And today, I watched my father bestow that honor on a sister I didn't know I had until a few months ago.

I should speak with her. Formally introduce myself and show my support. A hybrid myself, of a different nature, I know what it's like not to fit in. But somehow, where I am kept distanced, Aspen was welcomed with open arms, her differences celebrated. As if conjured by my thoughts, Aspen's head turns as she's placed back down, her eyes seeking me out through the crowds. I inhale sharply, pressing myself back against the wall. I should want to share in her happiness, but as she offers me a small smile, I find rather quickly that I would prefer to hide in the shadows.

I bend low in a quick curtsey before fleeing the room, not wanting the new queen, my sister, to witness the weakness of me groveling at her feet. Pushing against the heavy wooden door, I slip out of the ballroom-turned-nightclub and into the cold, stoned corridor. Briefly, I lean the open back panel of my lavender chiffon dress against the cool walls to soothe my racing heart.

The door reopens a moment later, and my guard steps out in search of me. A trick of my mind fools me into seeing an expression of concern, but once his eyes land on me, his impassive blank stare is firmly in place.

Yarik has been following my every move since I learned to walk. An escort, tutor, and keeper all rolled into one. I would go as far as to say 'friend,' but I know the feeling isn't reciprocated. Yarik doesn't show emotion, give praise, or have fun. I'm just a two-decade-long job to him. Whereas he's been everything to me.

I push off from the wall and walk away, desperate for the solitude of my room. Even though he'll follow a few steps behind and stand beyond my door while I cry into the comfort of my pillow. I don't care what anyone else thinks, but Yarik has seen me at my best and worst. I refuse to let him see me at my lowest.

I keep my posture rigidly straight and my strides elegantly long. As required by the princess. Passing the main entrance, I spot Nova at the large, open doors, speaking with two strange-looking males. Heavy fur cloaks hang from their shoulders, stopping short of their muscled leather-clad legs, and black smears of face paint are lined across their cheeks and down their corded necks. Their eyes scan the inside of the castle, briefly falling on me as I continue to walk by.

Reaching the East Wing, I suddenly shoot forward in a blur. Free now that I'm far enough away from all others and can drop the 'prim and proper' act. Hiking up the long skirts constricting my legs, I race up the winding staircase to the residential floor. My suite at the end of the hall is in sight, so achingly close.

No one believes the pretty, spoilt princess can feel sadness. They only see the fake version who floats around the castle, carefree and content. To the Vamps and my father especially, it's a profound notion that I might actually feel isolated, desperate to break free of their judgmental stares and unrealistic expectations. Who could possibly understand the loneliness I battle or how profoundly the constraints upon my life weigh me down? The beautiful tiara I wear upon my head claims me as a royal possession, its heaviness like a concrete collar.

I reach for the handle of my sanctuary, bursting inside in one smooth motion. The first deep inhale of relaxation instantly relaxes me until I hear the door slam and turn to see Yarik standing there.

He's not allowed inside with the door closed. In fact, he's never closed himself into a confined space with me before, always keeping his honor intact. I'm too shocked to say anything, so I stand frozen and wide-eyed.

"Tell me what's wrong." He demands roughly. His blonde hair has fallen loose of his pushed-back style, his icy blue eyes boring into mine. His muscles are tense beneath the black royal uniform he wears with pride, his duty always coming first like a barricade between us. Except for right now. "I can't listen to you cry alone in here any longer, and I can't help if you won't tell me what's the problem," his low baritone fills the space.

I blink once. Twice. Yarik is my guard. The stoic presence who stands beyond my door and silently follows my footsteps. Unlike the other females, I'm not permitted to roam the East Wing at my leisure. I have a tight schedule filled with classes, simple duties, and one nightly walk. The only person I am ever in the presence of, beyond pleasantries, is Yarik. Sure, I talk to him about almost everything because I don't have the luxury of friends. Never did I think he *cared*. Or perhaps it's not worry that causes him to ambush me this way, but irritation. My weeping must really have annoyed him if he is breaking his silence.

Just how long has he been questioning my life choices?

"There's nothing to talk about," I dismiss him. "You know everything about me." Expecting Yarik to leave, I approach my vanity, removing the diamonds in my ears. Next, I unhook the heavy necklace, its teardrop pendant hanging low into my cleavage. At least my mother allowed me simple pleasures, such as the occasional dress that didn't cover me from throat to foot. In the mirror's reflection, I notice Yarik is still staring. His blue eyes track my every moment like a hawk. "What do you want from me, Yarik?! You know what my life is like, you're the one who oversees my imprisonment. Step outside like a good guard dog and leave me to wish my life away in peace.

Crossing his arms, widening his stance, Yarik doesn't leave. He plants himself in my bedroom, crossing a forbidden boundary, and I decide to see how far he will really go to prove his point. Unzipping the back of my dress, the lavender material pools at my feet. A corset cinches my waist and accentuates my breasts, the thong dipping underneath my personal guilty pleasure. No matter what boring meetings I must attend or what my father insists I wear or say, I know under it all, the delicious rub of my thong would drive any vampire crazy if they knew. And now, Yarik knows. Kicking the dress aside, I step up to him.

"I thought you wanted to talk," I cock my head. "Or perhaps that's the last thing you wanted to do. Maybe, now that the royal mantel has been removed from my shoulders, you're hoping to see what I'm capable of." I stroke a finger over Yarik's forearm.

He grunts and bucks me away. "Don't be ridiculous."

Shame washes over me, a burning poker of embarrassment spearing my gut. A flush quickly coats my neck and chest as my temperature rises and my heartbeat accelerates. Of all the emotions I expected to feel today, the harsh sting of rejection was not one of them. I could shout, stomp my feet, and pout my bottom lip like a princess probably would. But I'm done conforming to a society that doesn't want me.

Instead, I opt to shove at his rock-hard chest. Yarik merely stares down at me, appearing bored and making no attempt to move. Very well. That's when I decide my only option is to lose my utter shit. Hitting his biceps with closed fists, I screech like a banshee, releasing the full force of rage I've been suppressing. A burning hatred for the constricted life I must lead, while Aspen is free to take multiple mates and wander wherever she pleases. From the day she arrived, she was given freedoms I've never even had the chance to earn.

I continue throwing punch after punch, trying to extract any sort of reaction from Yarik. I add a kick to the shin for good measure, growling with the full length of my fangs on show. As I lunge for his neck, Yaris suddenly grabs my wrists and spins me around. My back slams against the door, and my mouth opens in shock. No one has dared to touch me so roughly before.

My breath hitches at the golden glow illuminating within his blue eyes, a primal hunger rising to the surface. My wrists are bound by large palms above my head, the heaving of my chest shifting between us. Unable to anticipate his next move, I begin to speak when Yarik shakes his head. A trickle of laughter sounds through the door from the other end of the hallway. Far away enough to move on, none the wiser, but the instant realization of our precarious position triggers something within me.

Wetness pools at my core, the delicious tightness of the thong instantly coming into play. Yarik inhales deeply, the tick in his jaw beating in time with my heart. Keeping me still and completely at his mercy, his head dips.

"Do. It." I whisper, so low only his ears would hear it, and his lips crash against mine. My thighs clench, wholly unprepared for him responding to my goading. My head spins with confusion and a wave of déjà vu since I've dreamt about this scenario hundreds of times before. His mouth claims mine like a male possessed by his inner beast. A hard, heated press. A smooth, sultry assault. Everything I could have imagined, it's that and more. After a beat, I relent to the passion that roars to life inside me and return his kiss with equal vigor – uncaring of the consequences.

Authors Note

Hey there, Maddison here!

Thank you for picking up a copy of Moon Bound. This story is a special one for me, as it was originally my first-ever release. The more I grew as a writer, the more I began to shun my early work, believing it was destined to be shoved into a corner. Until this year, I decided to revisit Aspen's story with all of the knowledge and skills I've learned along the way. Reimagining the vampire castle and the supernatural council has been such a reinvigorating process, and I sincerely hope you've enjoyed it as much as I have!

Next in this series of interlinking standalone, is Rowena's story! Should this series take off as much as I hope it will, I hope to write a standalone for the other twelve females in a vampire castle. Your support in this is imperative, so please recommend, share, and devour!

Acknowledgments

Gosh – where do I begin? There are so many people who boost me on a daily basis. Especially with this whirlwind of a novel that took even me on a wild ride, I've replied on those close to me for their constant strength and love to keep me sane.

To my Keyboard Whores – Every single one of you is a beautiful, inspirational and incredibly hardworking woman I have the pleasure to write with and talk to on a daily basis. From valuable insights to smut-filled conversations, each day brings me so much joy! I'm forever grateful for the friendships we have formed.

Peas in a Taco – For all of your boosting, comforting, brainstorming and friendship, I will always be grateful for the book community bringing us together.

Kayla, Joy, and my Street Moles – For proofreading and content sharing, you guys are my lifeline. The support is unreal and I'm so grateful to have you all in my corner.

To Mr. Cole and the kiddie Cole's – Pursuing a career as an author was never going to be smooth sailing, and isn't one that brings instant gratification. I cannot thank you all enough for the support I receive at home, for the cups of tea after pulling an all-nighter, for the evenings of family games I've missed to make a deadline. You're all my motivation and my solace when the dark, imposter-ish thoughts creep in, and I could have never achieved any of this without you.

To my incredible readers – It's plain and simple; I'm nothing without the readers that support me! Thank you all for devouring my books, and also becoming my friends. I love getting to know you, seeing your gorgeous book shelves and building connections with so many talented and wonderful people!

MADDISON COLE

If you're a new reader to Maddison – welcome to the Mole's Burrow!!

Maddison is a married mum of two, and a serial daydreamer. As a huge fan of all romance tropes, mostly the dark and deprived ones with more d!cks than h0les, she finally decided to put pen to paper (finger to keyboard doesn't sound as poetic) and write her own.
As a child, Maddison was a jet setter and has lived all over the world, only to return to the south east of England, where she is now happily settled. With a double award in applied arts and art history, Maddison is just a creative chick with a dark passion for feisty females and spicy stories.

Facebook – **Author Maddison Cole**
www.facebook.com/Maddison.cole.314
Facebook readers group - **Cole's Reading Moles**
www.facebook.com/groups/colesreadingmoles
Instagram and TikTok - **@authormaddisoncole**

READ MORE BY MADDISON COLE

Fated Mates Shifter Romance

Moon Bound

Soul Bound (TBC)

Mate Bound (TBC)

Vices and Hedonism

A Deadly Sins Standalone

A Night of Pleasure and Wrath

I Love Candy

Dark Humor RH - Completed

Findin' Candy (novella)

Crushin' Candy

Smashin' Candy

Friggin' Candy

All My Pretty Psychos

Queen of Crazy

Kings of Madness

Hoax: The Untold Story (novella)

Reign of Chaos

A Wonderlust Adventure

A deranged duet retelling.

Discreet version:

Descend into Madness

Embrace the Mayhem (pre-order)

<u>Graphic version:</u>

My Tweedle Boys

Our Malice (pre-order)

The War at Waversea

<u>Basketball College MFM Menage - Completed</u>

Perfectly Powerless

Handsomely Heartless

Beautifully Boundless

<u>Exiled Heirs Duet</u>

<u>Interlinking Shifter Sister Standalones</u>

Moon Bound

Mate Bound (pre-order)

Co Writes

Life Lessons with Emma Luna

PRE-ORDER

Playing Games with a Billionaire – Billionaire **Badboys** Book One

Our Malice – Wonderlust Adventure Duet Book Two

Deranged – Mafia Ties Book One

www.ingramcontent.com/pod-product-compliance
Lightning Source LLC
Chambersburg PA
CBHW070602170726
48291CB00003B/665